image COMICS PRESENTS

INVINCIBLE ™

WHO'S THE BOSS

D1244767

CREATED BY
ROBERT KIRKMAN
& CORY WALKER

image®

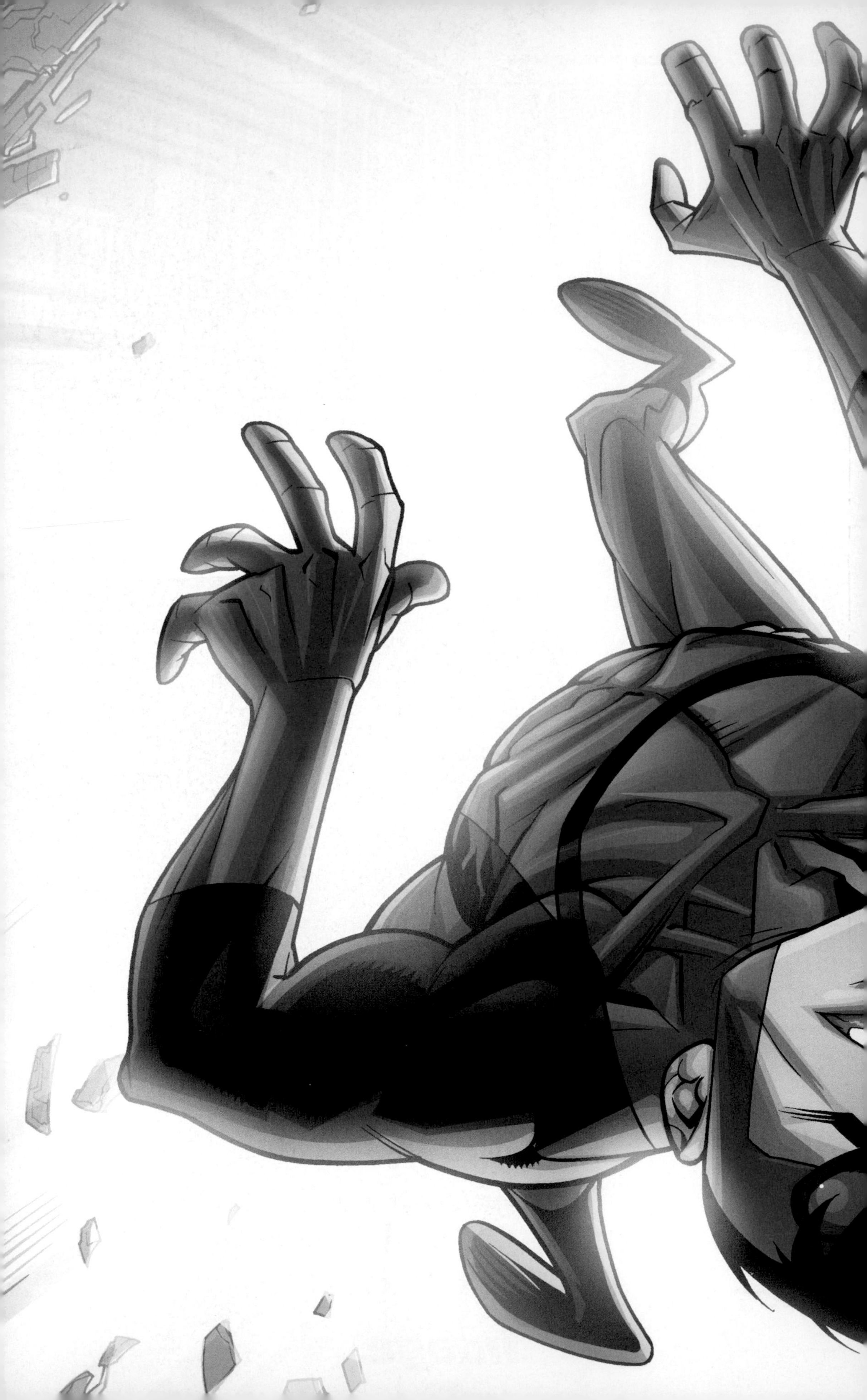

writer
ROBERT KIRKMAN

penciler, inker
RYAN OTTLEY

inker
(chapters 5-6)
CLIFF RATHBURN

colorist
(chapters 1-3)
BILL CRABTREE

colorist
(chapters 4-6)
FCO PLASCENCIA

letterer
RUS WOOTON

cover
RYAN OTTLEY & FCO PLASCENCIA

INVINCIBLE, VOL. 10: WHO'S THE BOSS? First Printing. Published by Image Comics, Inc. Office of publication: 2134 Allston Way, 2nd Floor, Berkeley, California 94704. Image and its logos are ® and © 2009 Image Comics Inc. All rights reserved. Originally published in single magazine form as INVINCIBLE #48-53. INVINCIBLE and all character likenesses are ™ and © 2009, Robert Kirkman and Cory Walker. All rights reserved. All names, characters, events and locales in this publication are entirely fictional. Any resemblance to actual persons (living or dead), events or places, without satiric intent, is coincidental. No part of this publication may be reproduced or transmitted, in any form or by any means (except for short excerpts for review purposes) without the express written permission of the copyright holder. PRINTED IN CANADA

ISBN: 978-1-60706-013-0

www.imagecomics.com

IMAGE COMICS, INC.

Robert Kirkman - Chief Operating Officer
Erik Larsen - Chief Financial Officer
Todd McFarlane - President
Marc Silvestri - CEO
Jim Valentino - Vice-President

ericstephenson - Publisher
Joe Keatinge - PR & Marketing Coordinator
Branwyn Bigglestone - Accounts Manager
Tyler Shainline - Administrative Assistant
Traci Hui - Traffic Manager
Allen Hui - Production Manager
Drew Gill - Production Artist
Jonathan Chan - Production Artist
Monica Garcia - Production Artist

International Rights Representative: Christine Jensen (christine@gfloystudio.com)

image

®

image

CHAPTER ONE

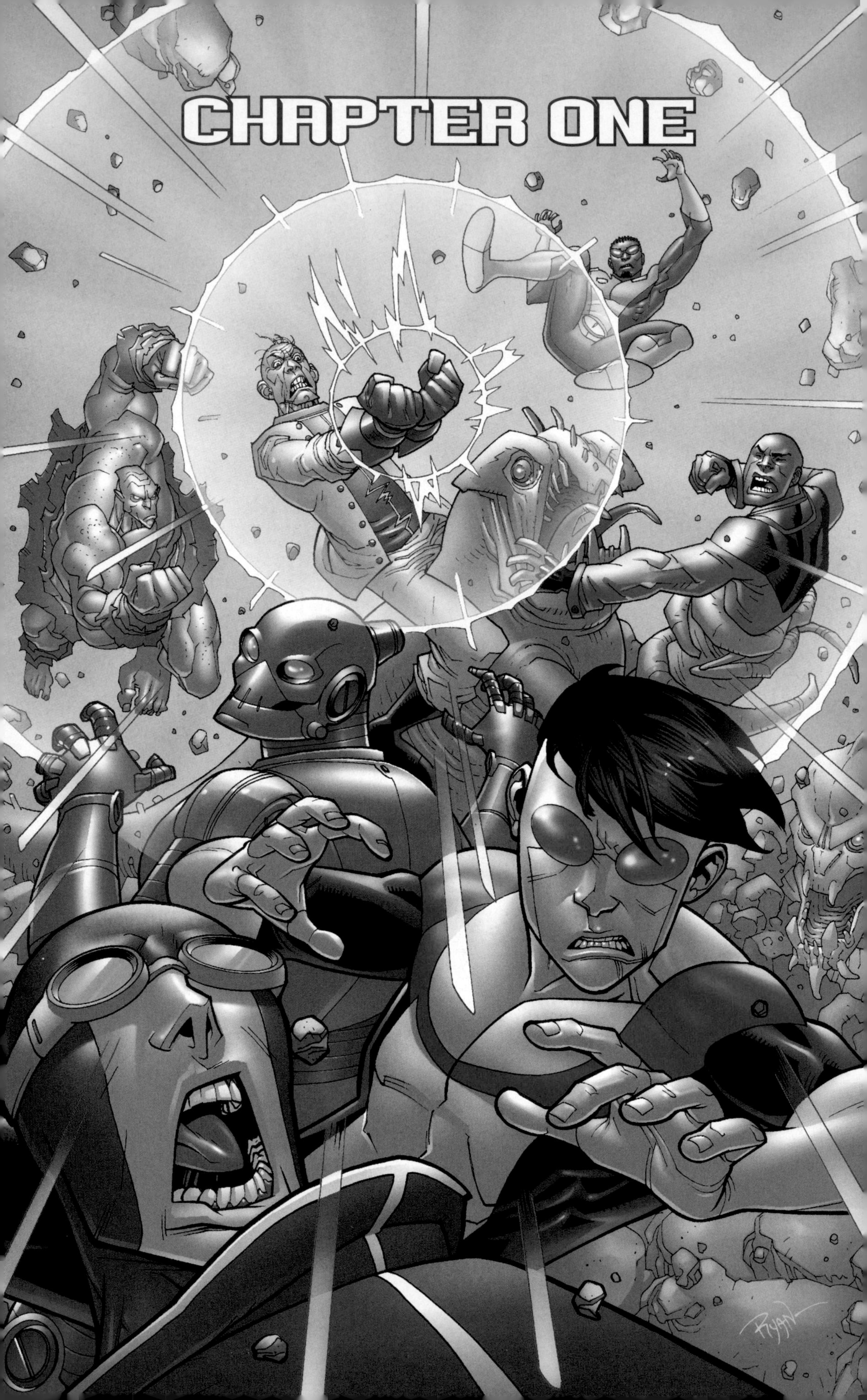

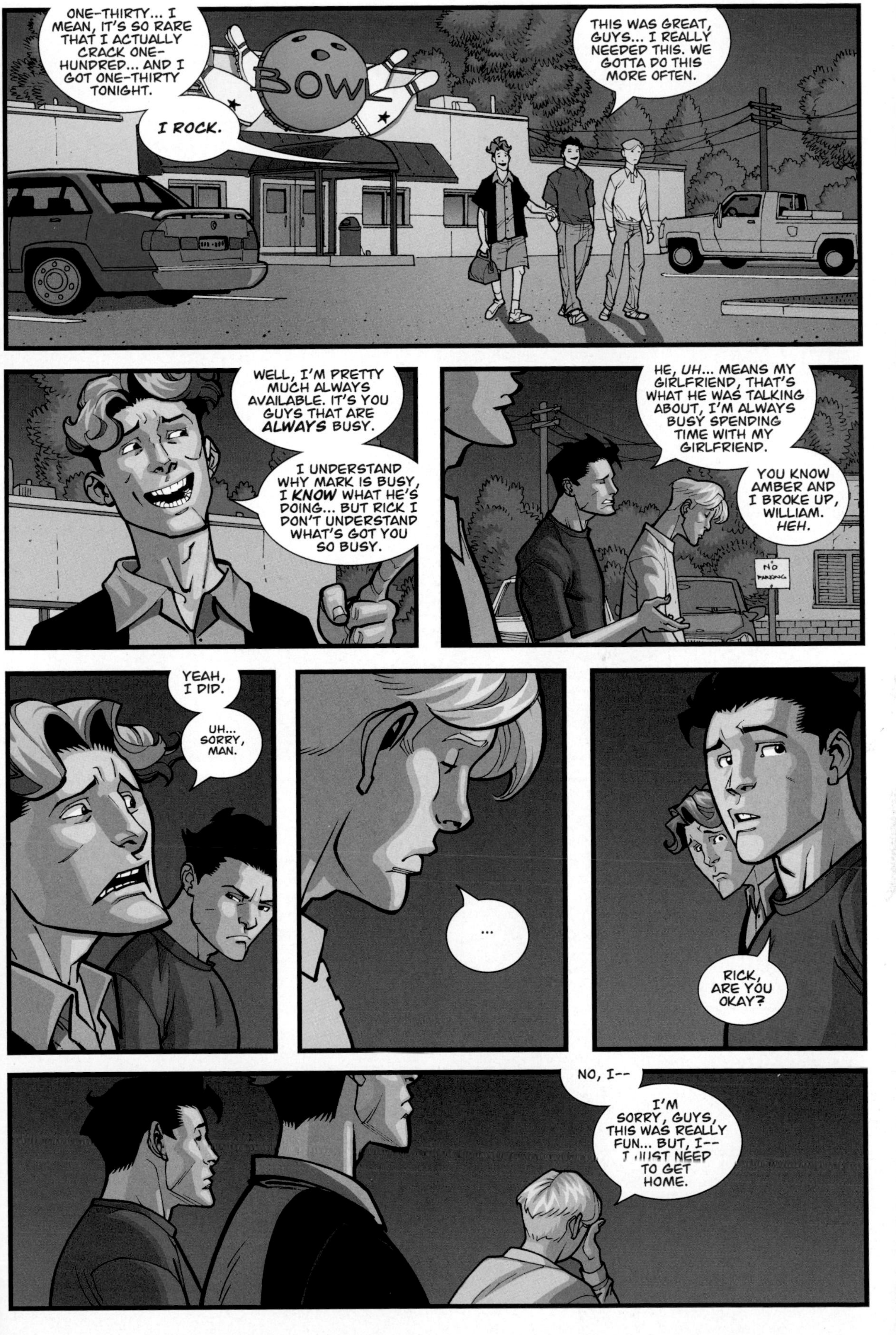
ONE-THIRTY... I MEAN, IT'S SO RARE THAT I ACTUALLY CRACK ONE-HUNDRED... AND I GOT ONE-THIRTY TONIGHT.
I ROCK.
BOWL
THIS WAS GREAT, GUYS... I REALLY NEEDED THIS. WE GOTTA DO THIS MORE OFTEN.
WELL, I'M PRETTY MUCH ALWAYS AVAILABLE. IT'S YOU GUYS THAT ARE ALWAYS BUSY.
I UNDERSTAND WHY MARK IS BUSY, I KNOW WHAT HE'S DOING... BUT RICK I DON'T UNDERSTAND WHAT'S GOT YOU SO BUSY.
HE, UH... MEANS MY GIRLFRIEND, THAT'S WHAT HE WAS TALKING ABOUT, I'M ALWAYS BUSY SPENDING TIME WITH MY GIRLFRIEND.
YOU KNOW AMBER AND I BROKE UP, WILLIAM. HEH.
NO PARKING
YEAH, I DID.
UH... SORRY, MAN.
...
RICK, ARE YOU OKAY?
NO, I--
I'M SORRY, GUYS, THIS WAS REALLY FUN... BUT, I-- I JUST NEED TO GET HOME.

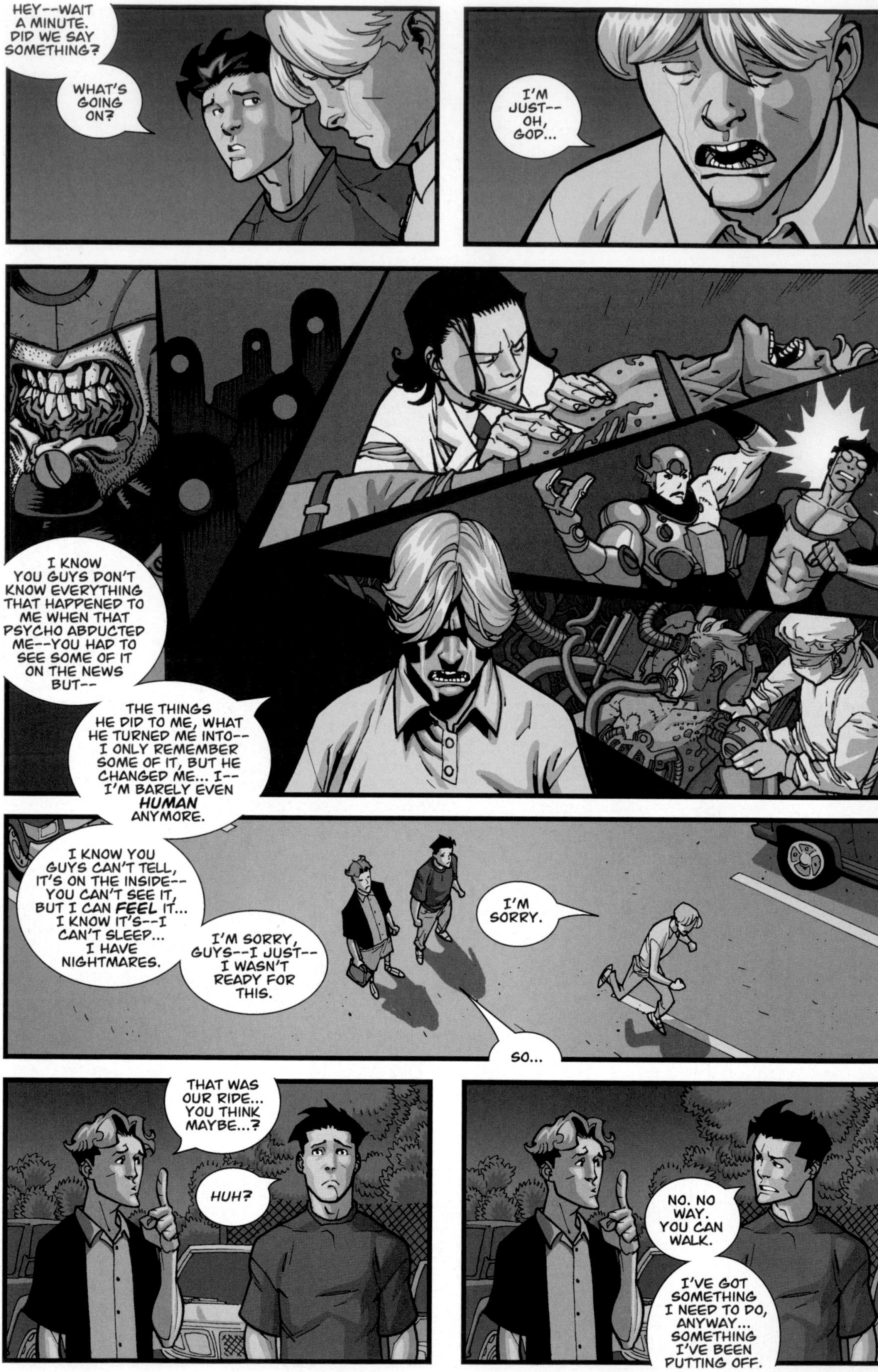
HEY--WAIT A MINUTE. DID WE SAY SOMETHING?
WHAT'S GOING ON?
I'M JUST-- OH, GOD...
I KNOW YOU GUYS DON'T KNOW EVERYTHING THAT HAPPENED TO ME WHEN THAT PSYCHO ABDUCTED ME--YOU HAD TO SEE SOME OF IT ON THE NEWS BUT--
THE THINGS HE DID TO ME, WHAT HE TURNED ME INTO-- I ONLY REMEMBER SOME OF IT, BUT HE CHANGED ME... I-- I'M BARELY EVEN HUMAN ANYMORE.
I KNOW YOU GUYS CAN'T TELL, IT'S ON THE INSIDE-- YOU CAN'T SEE IT, BUT I CAN FEEL IT... I KNOW IT'S--I CAN'T SLEEP... I HAVE NIGHTMARES.
I'M SORRY, GUYS--I JUST-- I WASN'T READY FOR THIS.
I'M SORRY.
SO...
THAT WAS OUR RIDE... YOU THINK MAYBE...?
HUH?
NO. NO WAY. YOU CAN WALK.
I'VE GOT SOMETHING I NEED TO DO, ANYWAY... SOMETHING I'VE BEEN PUTTING OFF.

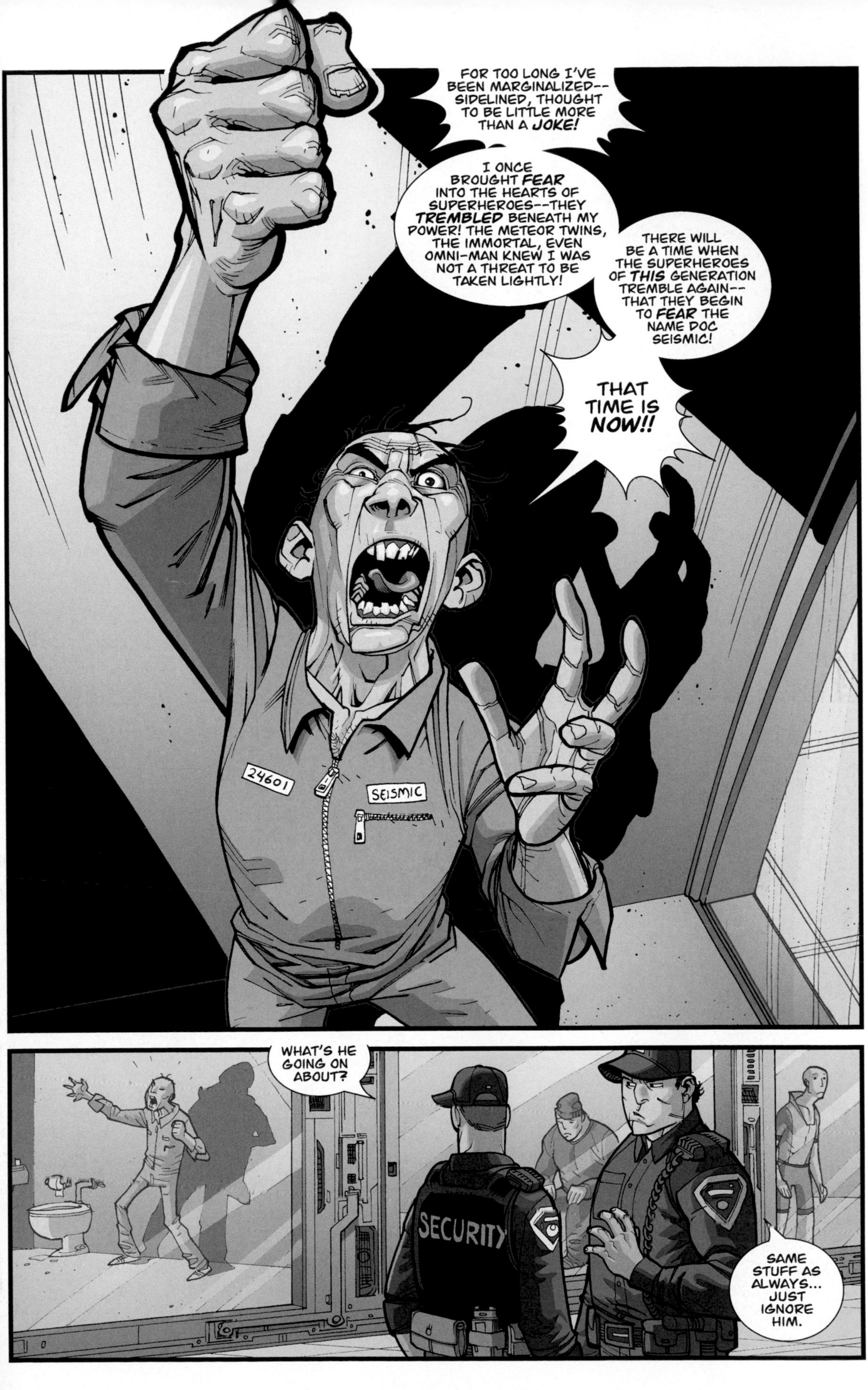
FOR TOO LONG I'VE BEEN MARGINALIZED--SIDELINED, THOUGHT TO BE LITTLE MORE THAN A JOKE!
I ONCE BROUGHT FEAR INTO THE HEARTS OF SUPERHEROES--THEY TREMBLED BENEATH MY POWER! THE METEOR TWINS, THE IMMORTAL, EVEN OMNI-MAN KNEW I WAS NOT A THREAT TO BE TAKEN LIGHTLY!
THERE WILL BE A TIME WHEN THE SUPERHEROES OF THIS GENERATION TREMBLE AGAIN--THAT THEY BEGIN TO FEAR THE NAME DOC SEISMIC!
THAT TIME IS NOW!!
24601
SEISMIC
WHAT'S HE GOING ON ABOUT?
SECURITY
SAME STUFF AS ALWAYS... JUST IGNORE HIM.

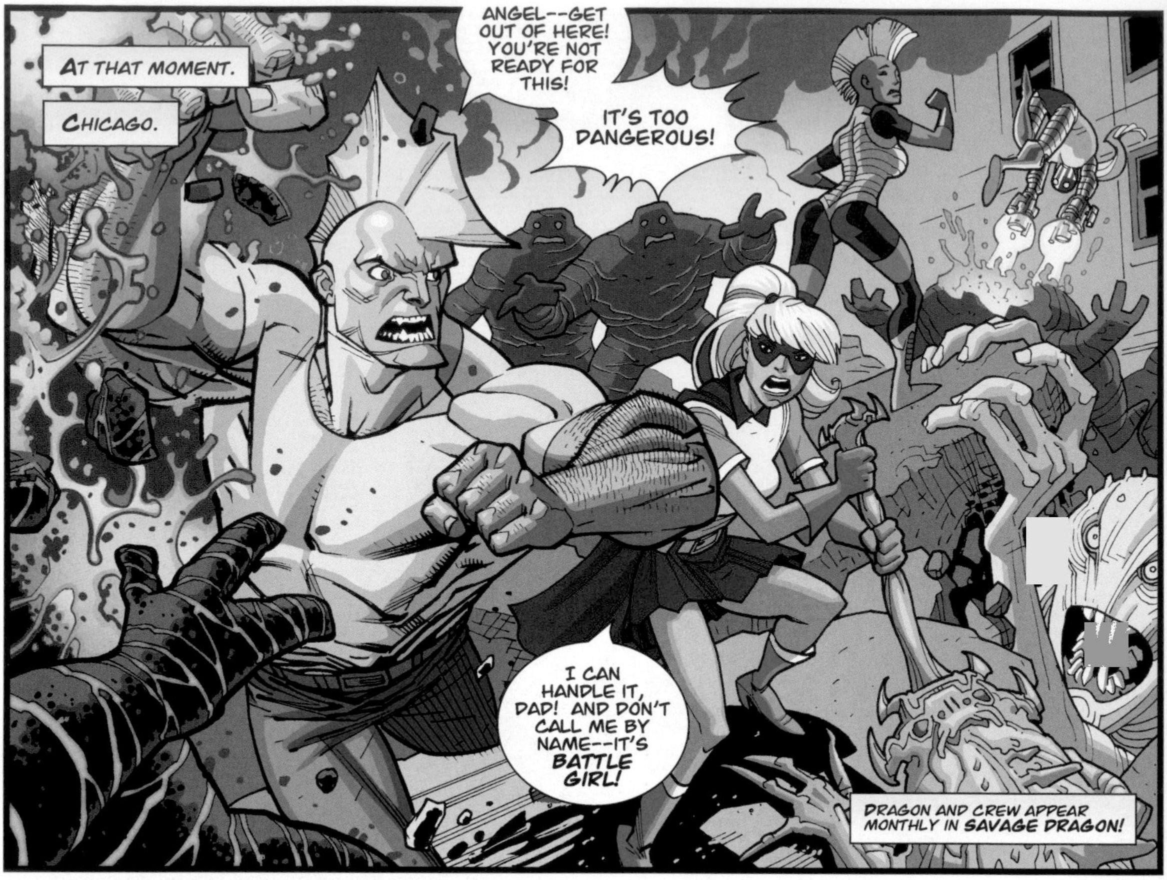
AT THAT MOMENT.
CHICAGO.
ANGEL--GET OUT OF HERE! YOU'RE NOT READY FOR THIS!
IT'S TOO DANGEROUS!
I CAN HANDLE IT, DAD! AND DON'T CALL ME BY NAME--IT'S BATTLE GIRL!
DRAGON AND CREW APPEAR MONTHLY IN SAVAGE DRAGON!

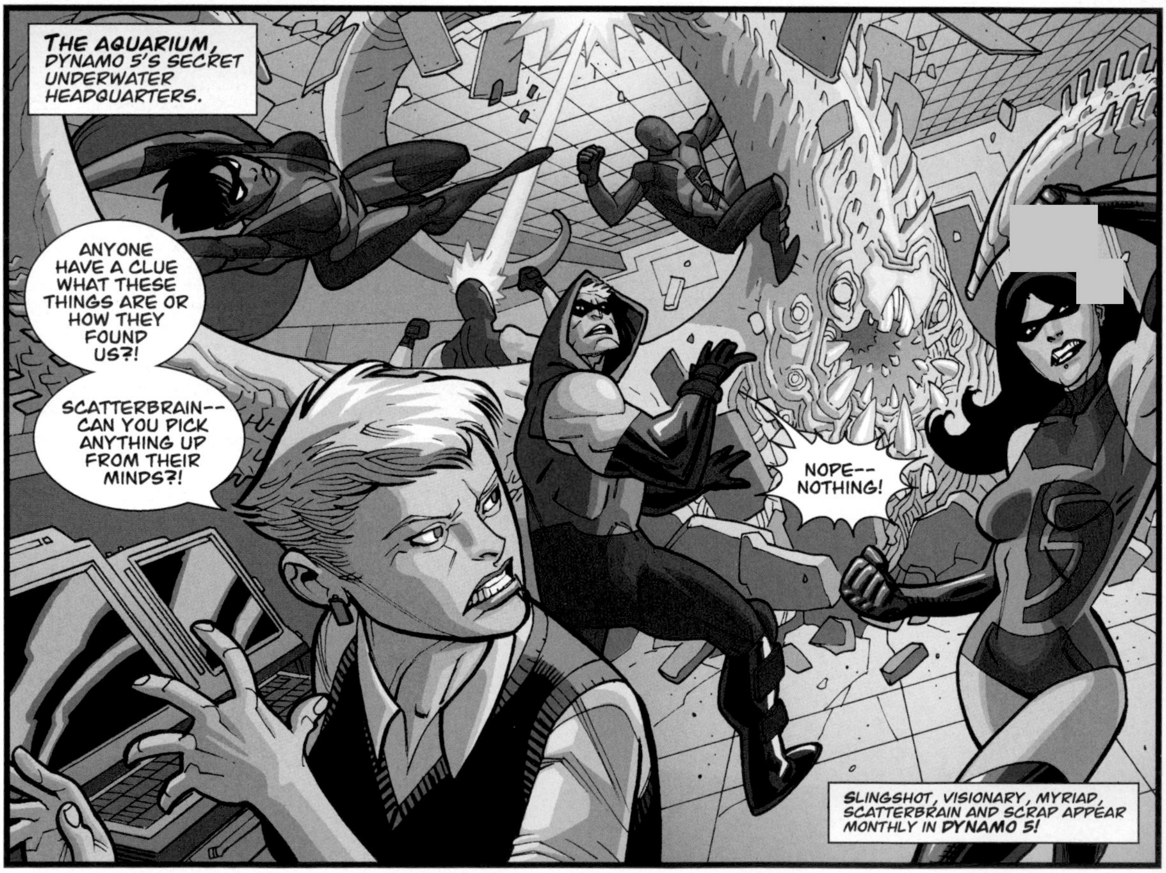
THE AQUARIUM, DYNAMO 5'S SECRET UNDERWATER HEADQUARTERS.
ANYONE HAVE A CLUE WHAT THESE THINGS ARE OR HOW THEY FOUND US?!
SCATTERBRAIN-- CAN YOU PICK ANYTHING UP FROM THEIR MINDS?!
NOPE-- NOTHING!
SLINGSHOT, VISIONARY, MYRIAD, SCATTERBRAIN AND SCRAP APPEAR MONTHLY IN DYNAMO 5!

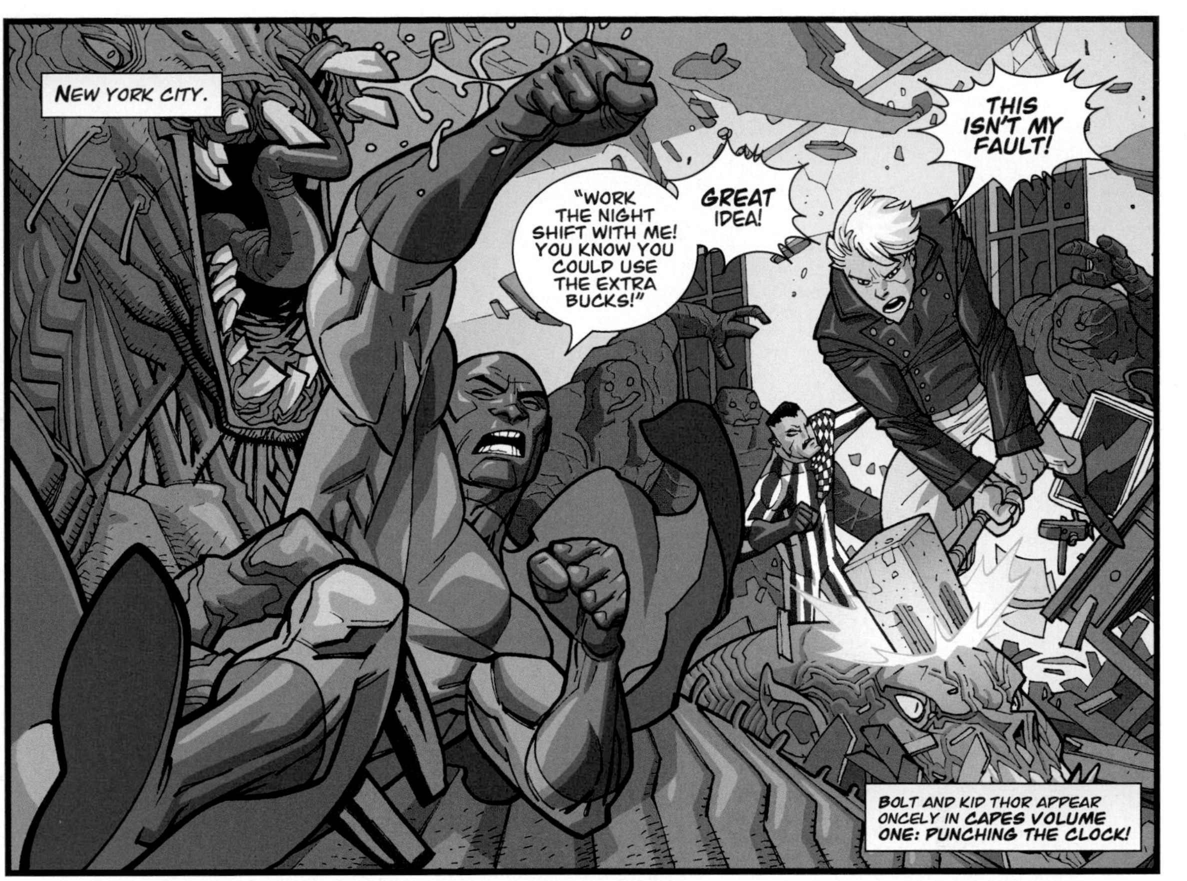
NEW YORK CITY.
"WORK THE NIGHT SHIFT WITH ME! YOU KNOW YOU COULD USE THE EXTRA BUCKS!"
GREAT IDEA!
THIS ISN'T MY FAULT!
BOLT AND KID THOR APPEAR ONCELY IN CAPES VOLUME ONE: PUNCHING THE CLOCK!

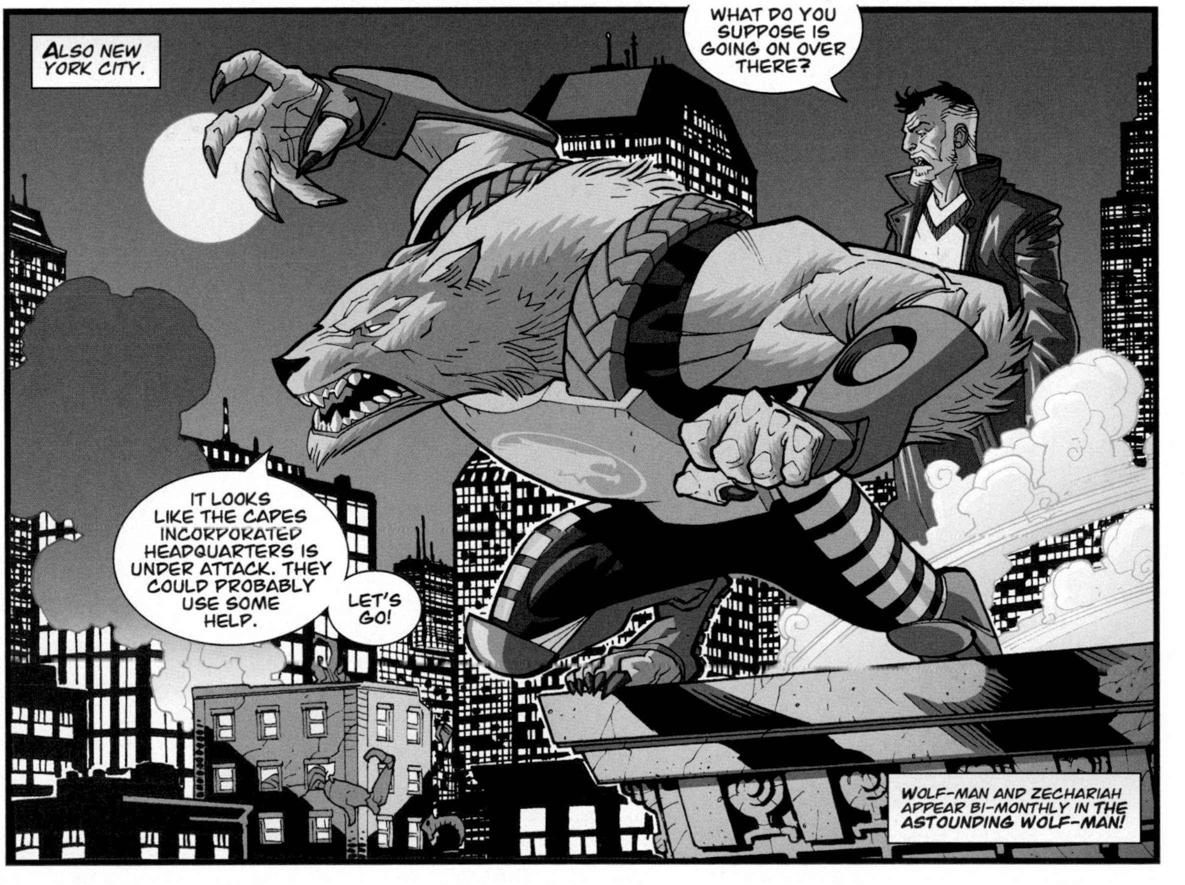
ALSO NEW YORK CITY.
WHAT DO YOU SUPPOSE IS GOING ON OVER THERE?
IT LOOKS LIKE THE CAPES INCORPORATED HEADQUARTERS IS UNDER ATTACK. THEY COULD PROBABLY USE SOME HELP.
LET'S GO!
WOLF-MAN AND ZECHARIAH APPEAR BI-MONTHLY IN THE ASTOUNDING WOLF-MAN!

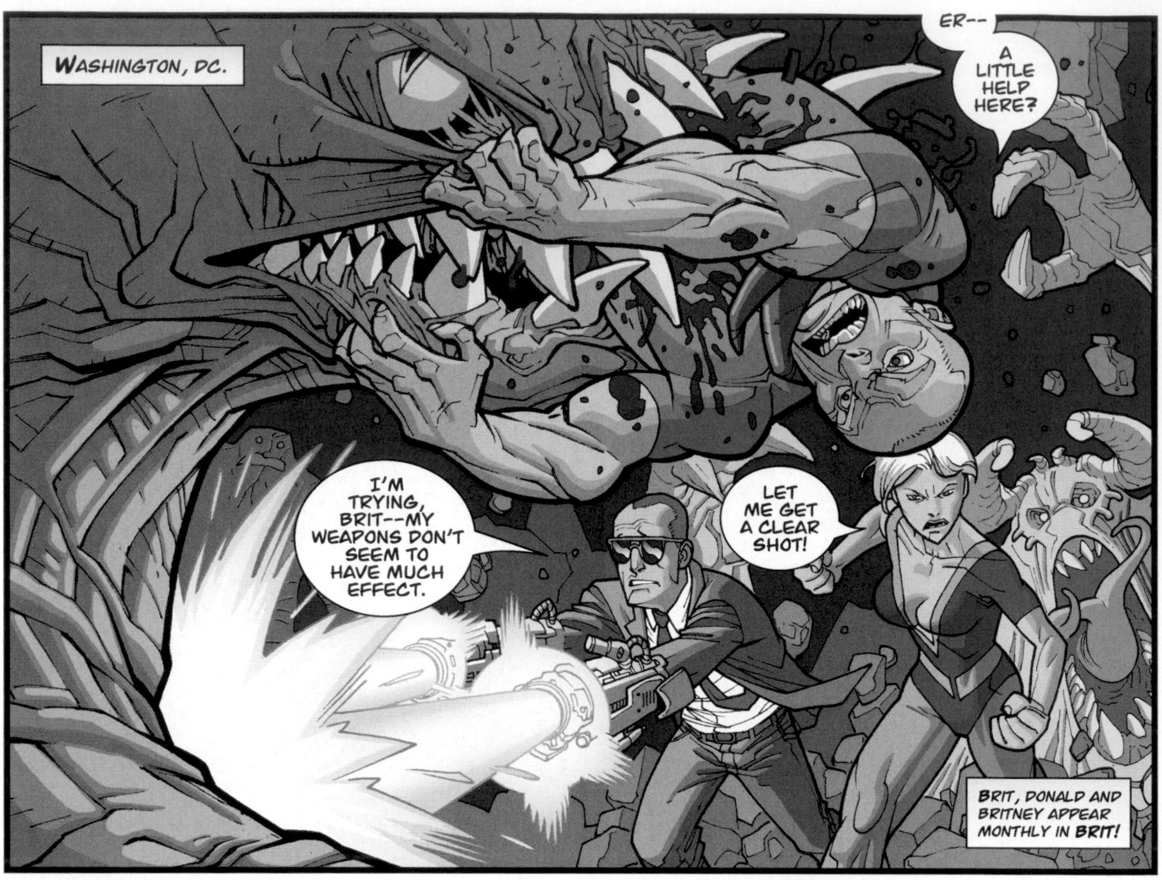
WASHINGTON, DC.
ER--
A LITTLE HELP HERE?
I'M TRYING, BRIT--MY WEAPONS DON'T SEEM TO HAVE MUCH EFFECT.
LET ME GET A CLEAR SHOT!
BRIT, DONALD AND BRITNEY APPEAR MONTHLY IN BRIT!

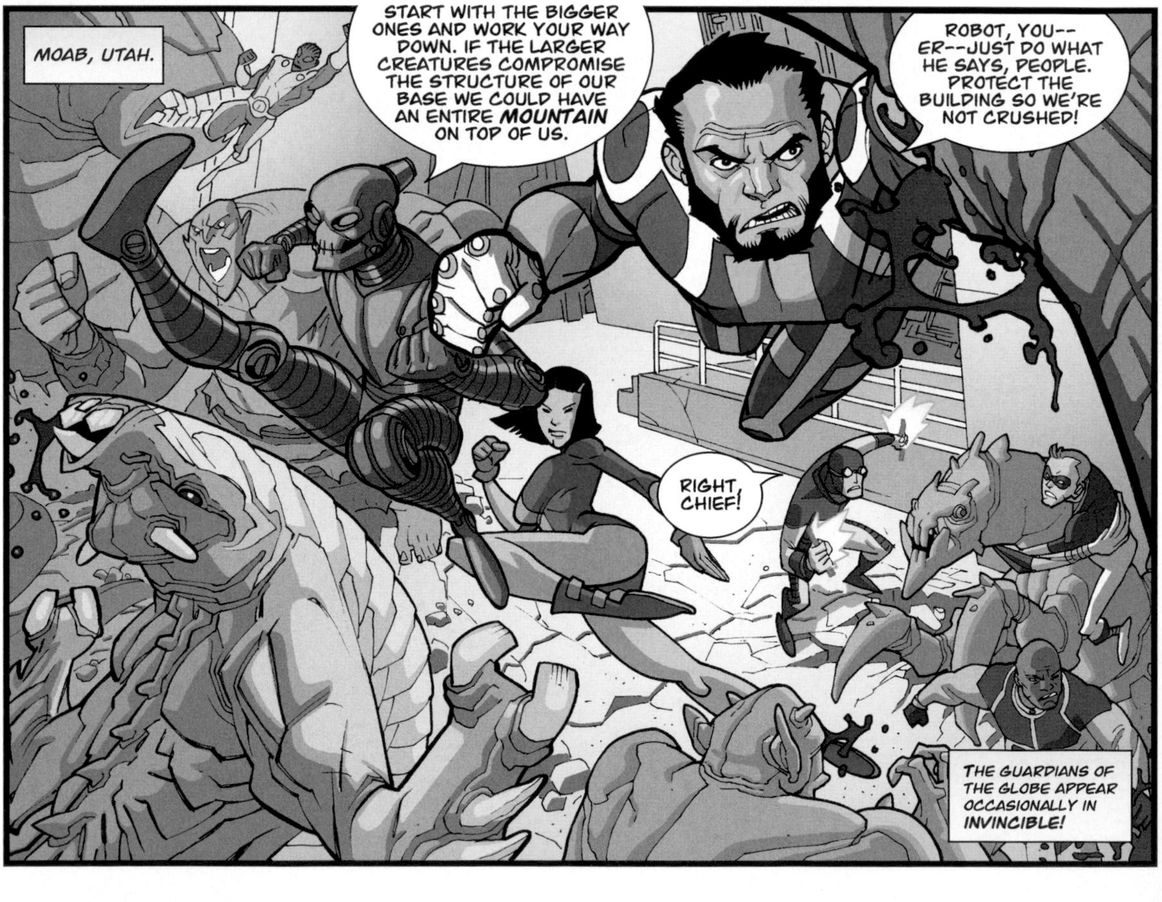
MOAB, UTAH.
START WITH THE BIGGER ONES AND WORK YOUR WAY DOWN. IF THE LARGER CREATURES COMPROMISE THE STRUCTURE OF OUR BASE WE COULD HAVE AN ENTIRE MOUNTAIN ON TOP OF US.
ROBOT, YOU-- ER--JUST DO WHAT HE SAYS, PEOPLE. PROTECT THE BUILDING SO WE'RE NOT CRUSHED!
RIGHT, CHIEF!
THE GUARDIANS OF THE GLOBE APPEAR OCCASIONALLY IN INVINCIBLE!

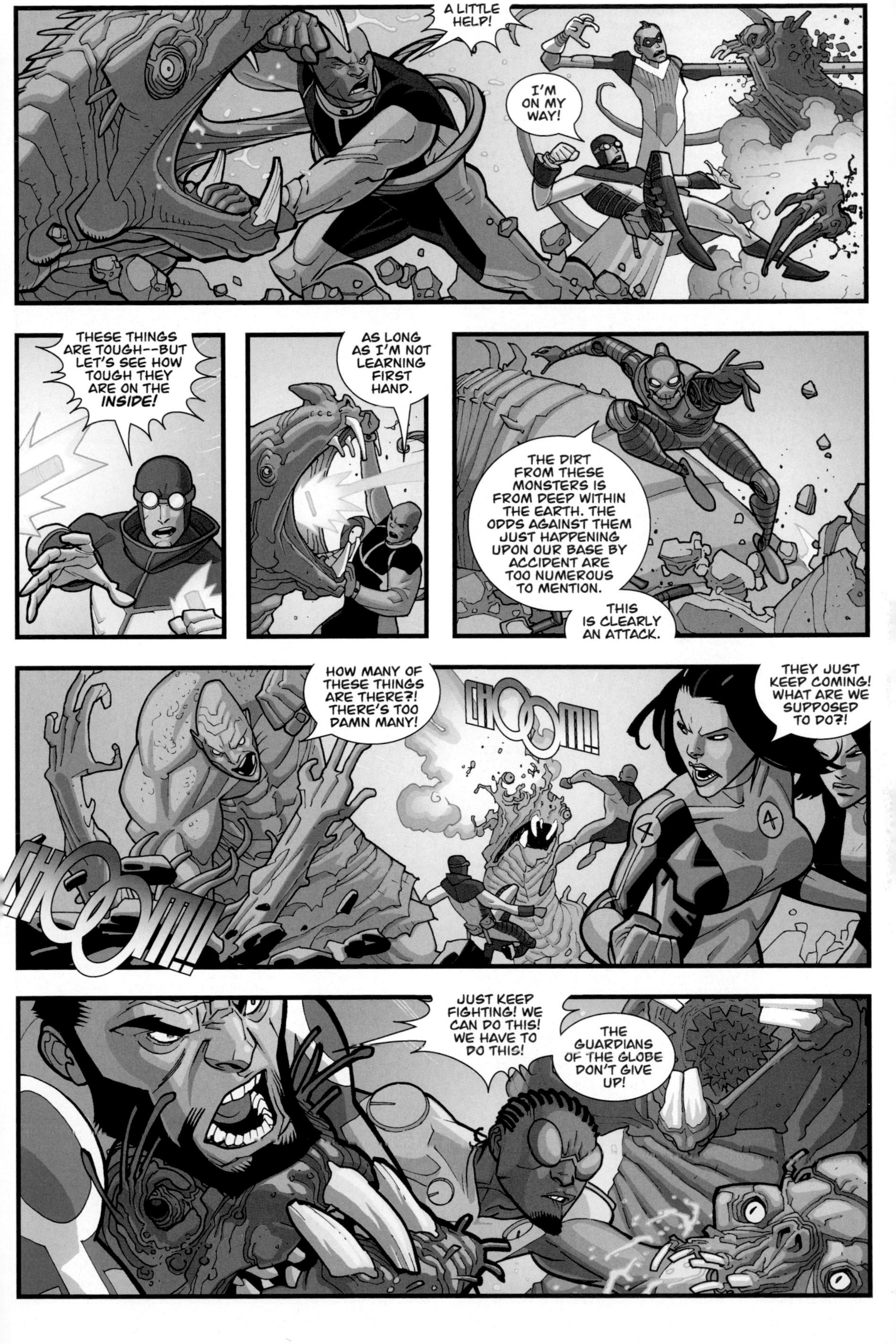

A LITTLE HELP!
I'M ON MY WAY!
THESE THINGS ARE TOUGH--BUT LET'S SEE HOW TOUGH THEY ARE ON THE *INSIDE!*
AS LONG AS I'M NOT LEARNING FIRST HAND.
THE DIRT FROM THESE MONSTERS IS FROM DEEP WITHIN THE EARTH. THE ODDS AGAINST THEM JUST HAPPENING UPON OUR BASE BY ACCIDENT ARE TOO NUMEROUS TO MENTION.
THIS IS CLEARLY AN ATTACK.
HOW MANY OF THESE THINGS ARE THERE?! THERE'S TOO DAMN MANY!
CHOOM!!
THEY JUST KEEP COMING! WHAT ARE WE SUPPOSED TO DO?!
CHOOM!!
JUST KEEP FIGHTING! WE CAN DO THIS! WE HAVE TO DO THIS!
THE GUARDIANS OF THE GLOBE DON'T GIVE UP!

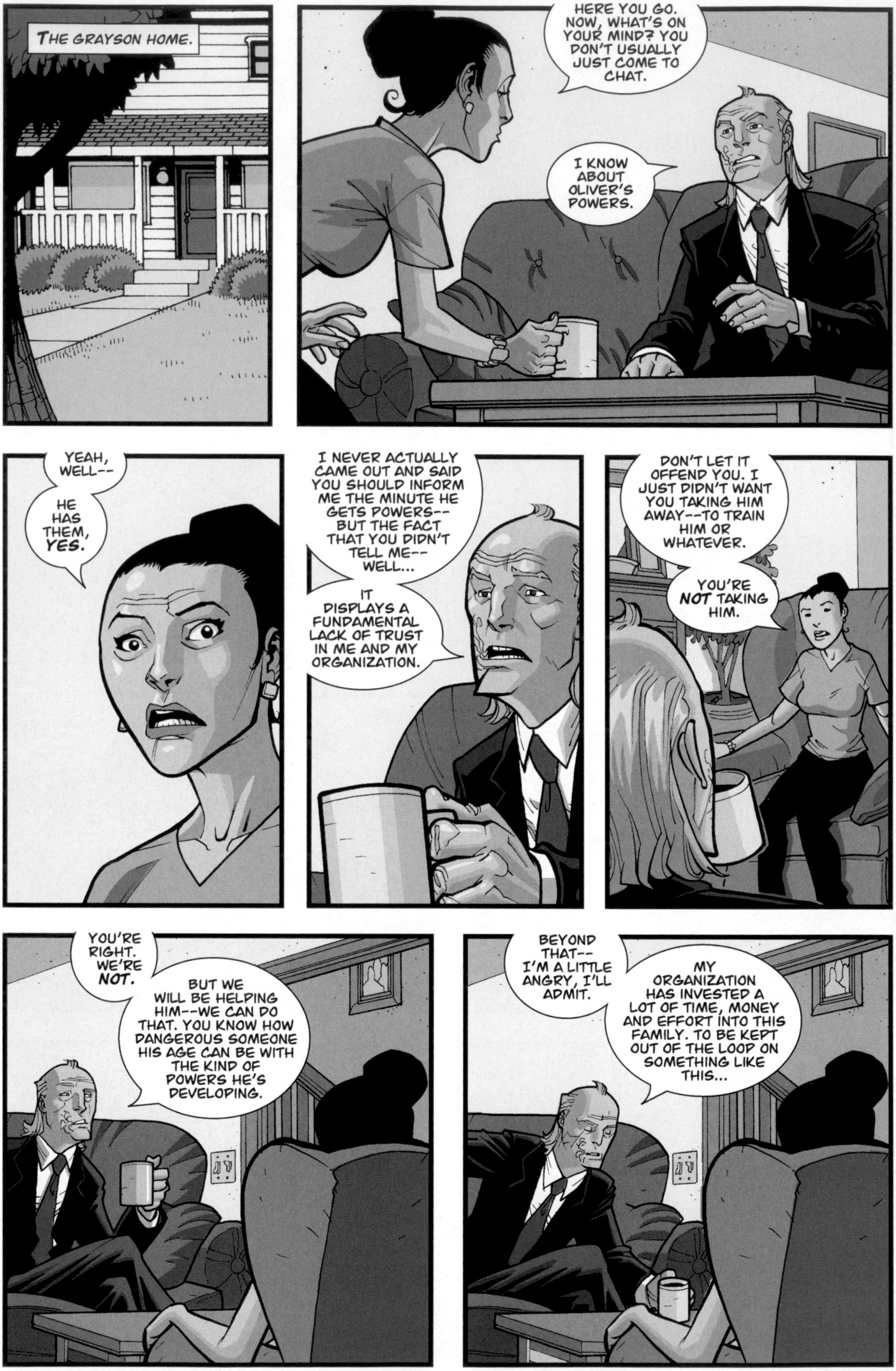
THE GRAYSON HOME.
HERE YOU GO. NOW, WHAT'S ON YOUR MIND? YOU DON'T USUALLY JUST COME TO CHAT.
I KNOW ABOUT OLIVER'S POWERS.
YEAH, WELL--
HE HAS THEM, *YES.*
I NEVER ACTUALLY CAME OUT AND SAID YOU SHOULD INFORM ME THE MINUTE HE GETS POWERS-- BUT THE FACT THAT YOU DIDN'T TELL ME-- WELL...
IT DISPLAYS A FUNDAMENTAL LACK OF TRUST IN ME AND MY ORGANIZATION.
DON'T LET IT OFFEND YOU. I JUST DIDN'T WANT YOU TAKING HIM AWAY--TO TRAIN HIM OR WHATEVER.
YOU'RE *NOT* TAKING HIM.
YOU'RE RIGHT. WE'RE *NOT.*
BUT WE WILL BE HELPING HIM--WE CAN DO THAT. YOU KNOW HOW DANGEROUS SOMEONE HIS AGE CAN BE WITH THE KIND OF POWERS HE'S DEVELOPING.
BEYOND THAT-- I'M A LITTLE ANGRY, I'LL ADMIT.
MY ORGANIZATION HAS INVESTED A LOT OF TIME, MONEY AND EFFORT INTO THIS FAMILY. TO BE KEPT OUT OF THE LOOP ON SOMETHING LIKE THIS...

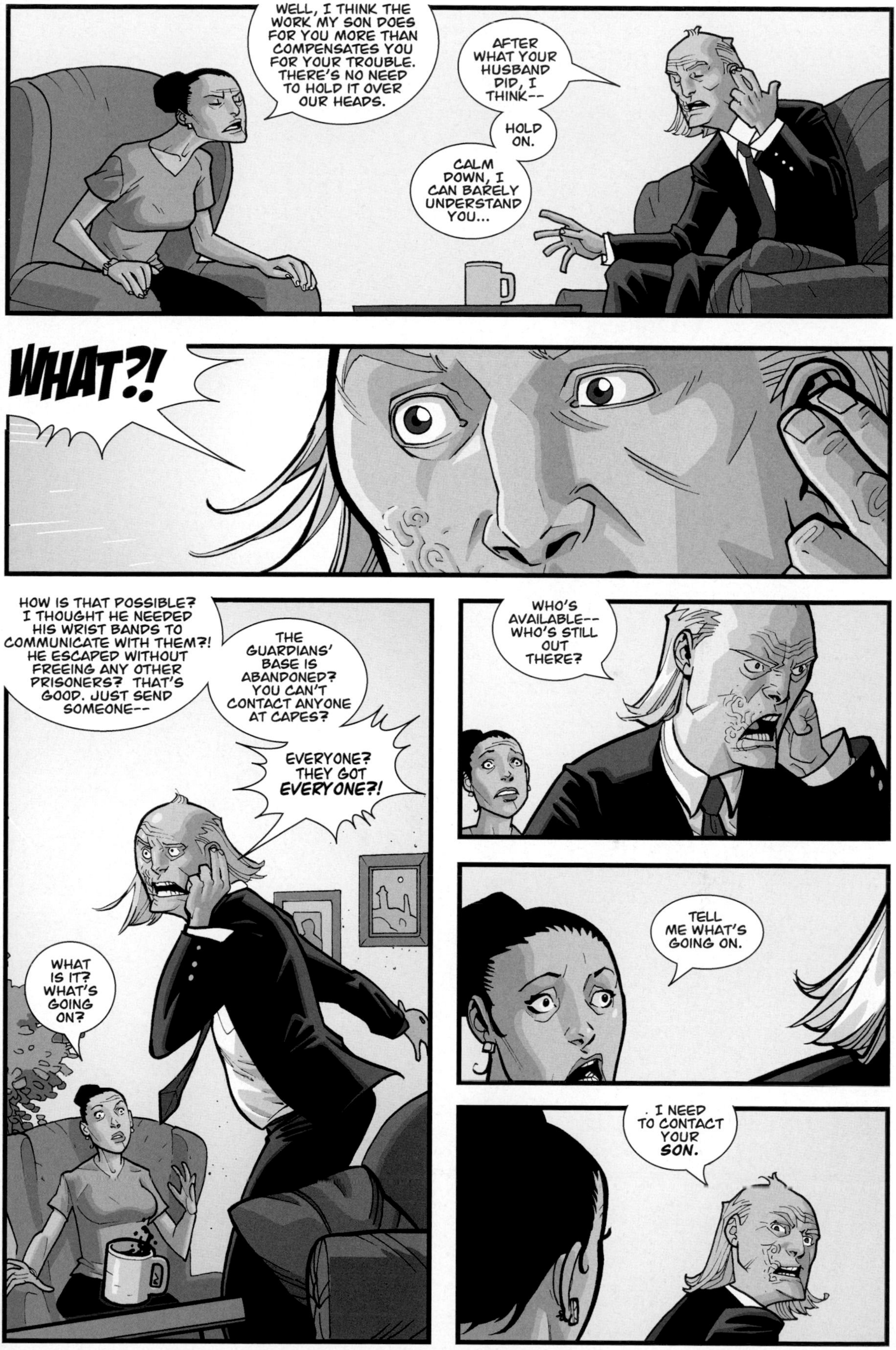
WELL, I THINK THE WORK MY SON DOES FOR YOU MORE THAN COMPENSATES YOU FOR YOUR TROUBLE. THERE'S NO NEED TO HOLD IT OVER OUR HEADS.
AFTER WHAT YOUR HUSBAND DID, I THINK--
HOLD ON.
CALM DOWN, I CAN BARELY UNDERSTAND YOU...
WHAT?!
HOW IS THAT POSSIBLE? I THOUGHT HE NEEDED HIS WRIST BANDS TO COMMUNICATE WITH THEM?! HE ESCAPED WITHOUT FREEING ANY OTHER PRISONERS? THAT'S GOOD. JUST SEND SOMEONE--
THE GUARDIANS' BASE IS ABANDONED? YOU CAN'T CONTACT ANYONE AT CAPES?
EVERYONE? THEY GOT **EVERYONE?!**
WHAT IS IT? WHAT'S GOING ON?
WHO'S AVAILABLE-- WHO'S STILL OUT THERE?
TELL ME WHAT'S GOING ON.
. I NEED TO CONTACT YOUR **SON.**

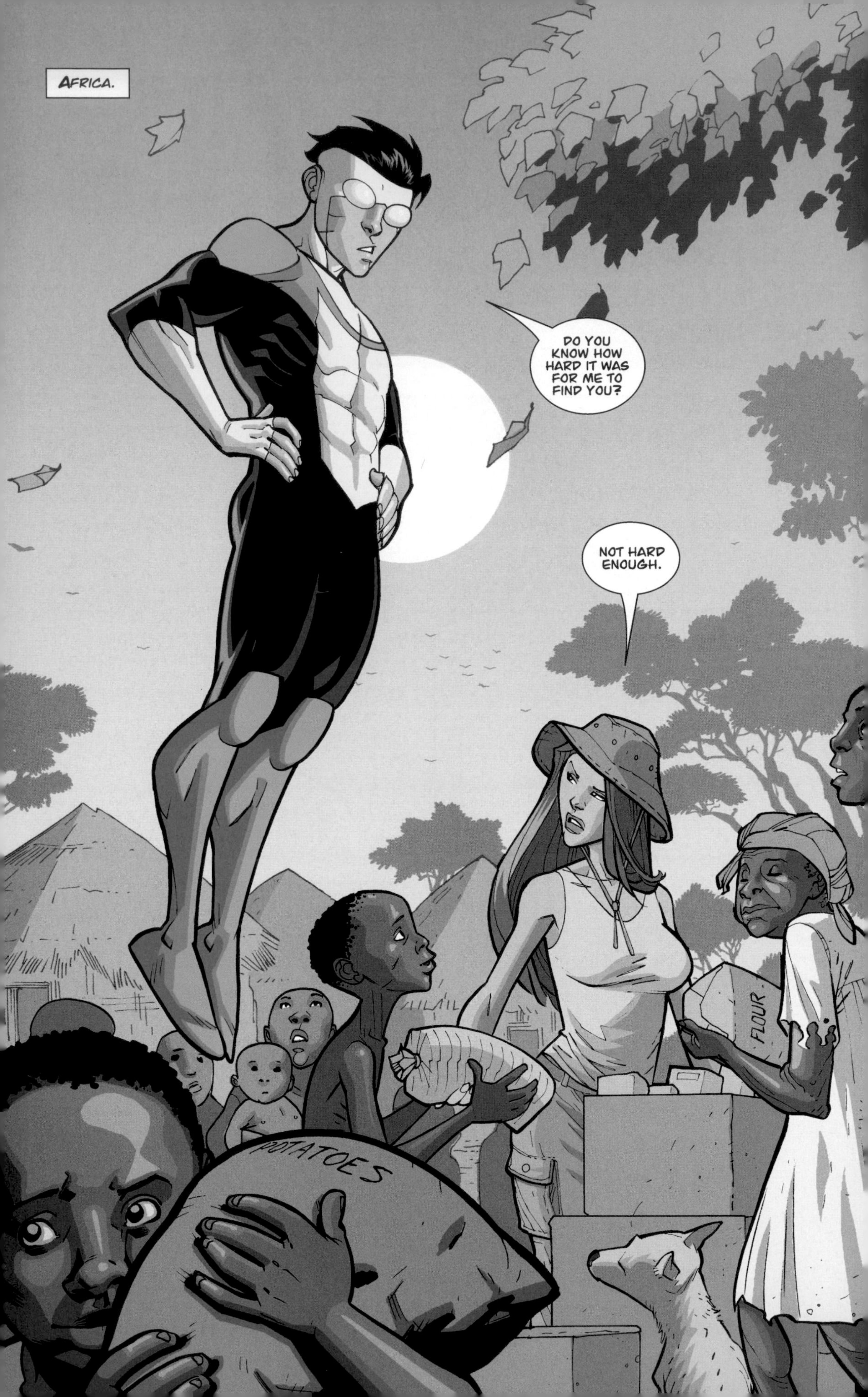
AFRICA.
DO YOU KNOW HOW HARD IT WAS FOR ME TO FIND YOU?
NOT HARD ENOUGH.
POTATOES
FLOUR

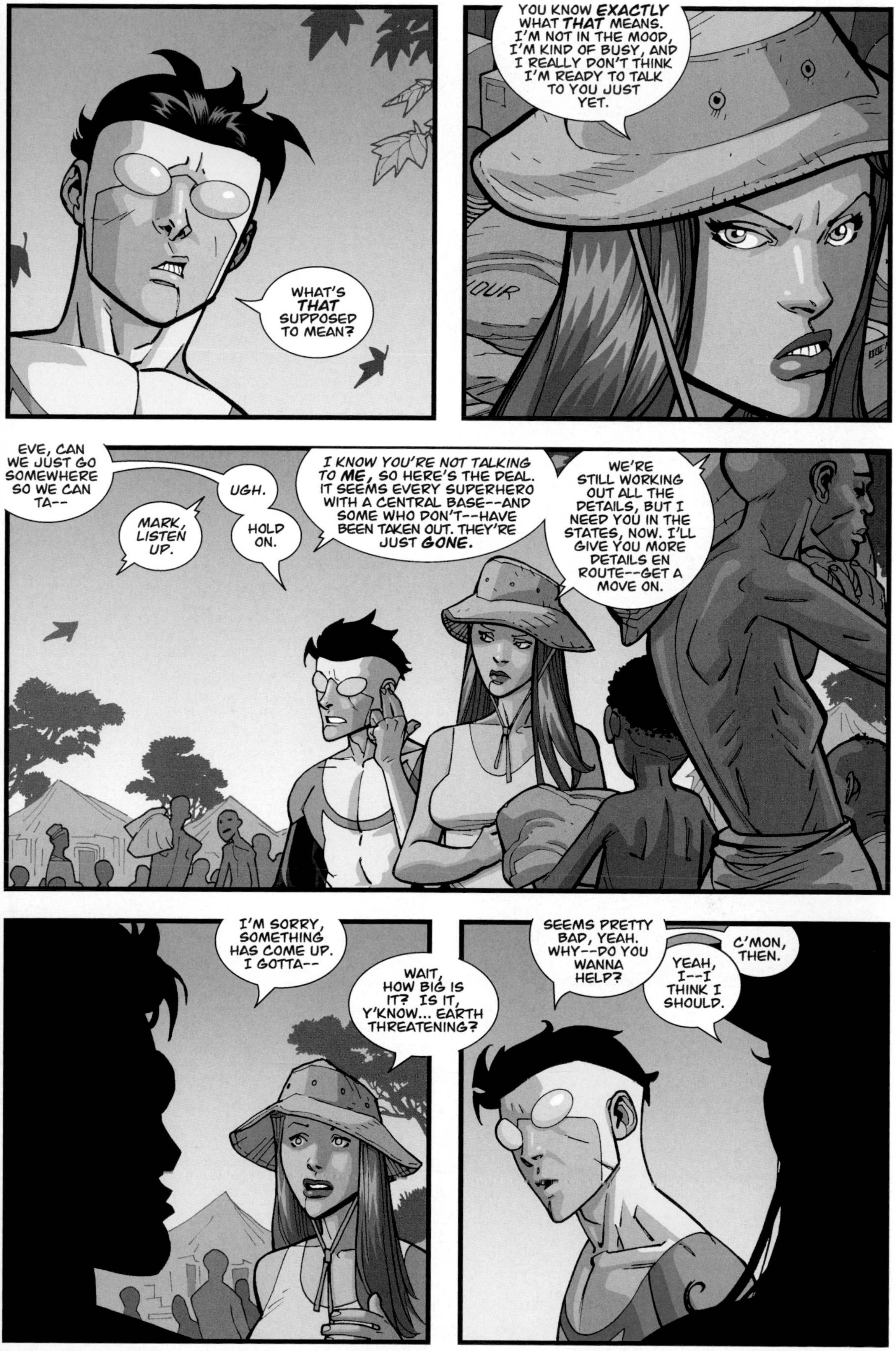
WHAT'S THAT SUPPOSED TO MEAN?
YOU KNOW EXACTLY WHAT THAT MEANS. I'M NOT IN THE MOOD, I'M KIND OF BUSY, AND I REALLY DON'T THINK I'M READY TO TALK TO YOU JUST YET.
EVE, CAN WE JUST GO SOMEWHERE SO WE CAN TA--
MARK, LISTEN UP.
UGH.
HOLD ON.
I KNOW YOU'RE NOT TALKING TO ME, SO HERE'S THE DEAL. IT SEEMS EVERY SUPERHERO WITH A CENTRAL BASE--AND SOME WHO DON'T--HAVE BEEN TAKEN OUT. THEY'RE JUST GONE.
WE'RE STILL WORKING OUT ALL THE DETAILS, BUT I NEED YOU IN THE STATES, NOW. I'LL GIVE YOU MORE DETAILS EN ROUTE--GET A MOVE ON.
I'M SORRY, SOMETHING HAS COME UP. I GOTTA--
WAIT, HOW BIG IS IT? IS IT, Y'KNOW... EARTH THREATENING?
SEEMS PRETTY BAD, YEAH. WHY--DO YOU WANNA HELP?
YEAH, I--I THINK I SHOULD.
C'MON, THEN.

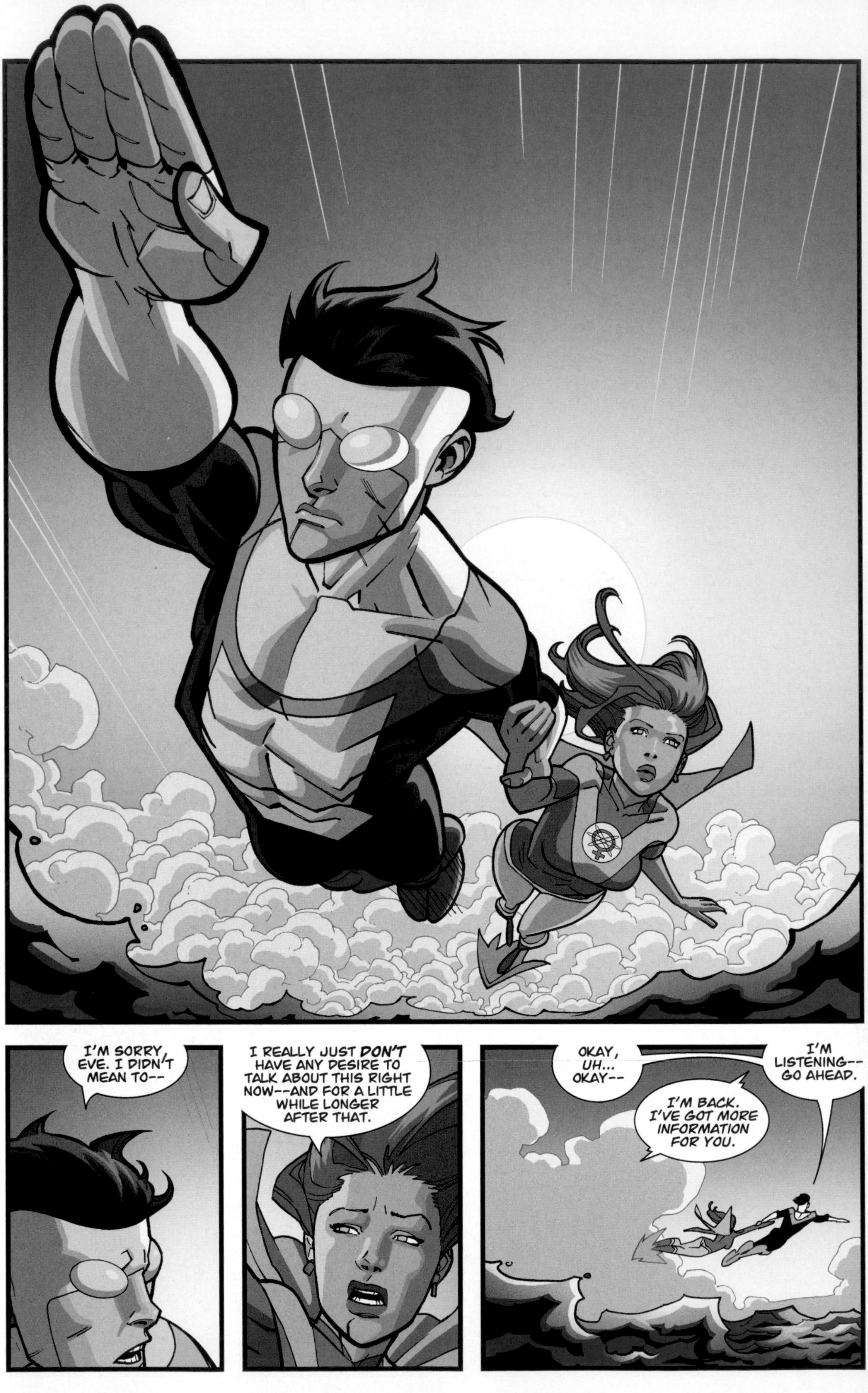
I'M SORRY, EVE. I DIDN'T MEAN TO--
I REALLY JUST **DON'T** HAVE ANY DESIRE TO TALK ABOUT THIS RIGHT NOW--AND FOR A LITTLE WHILE LONGER AFTER THAT.
OKAY, UH... OKAY--
I'M BACK. I'VE GOT MORE INFORMATION FOR YOU.
I'M LISTENING-- GO AHEAD.

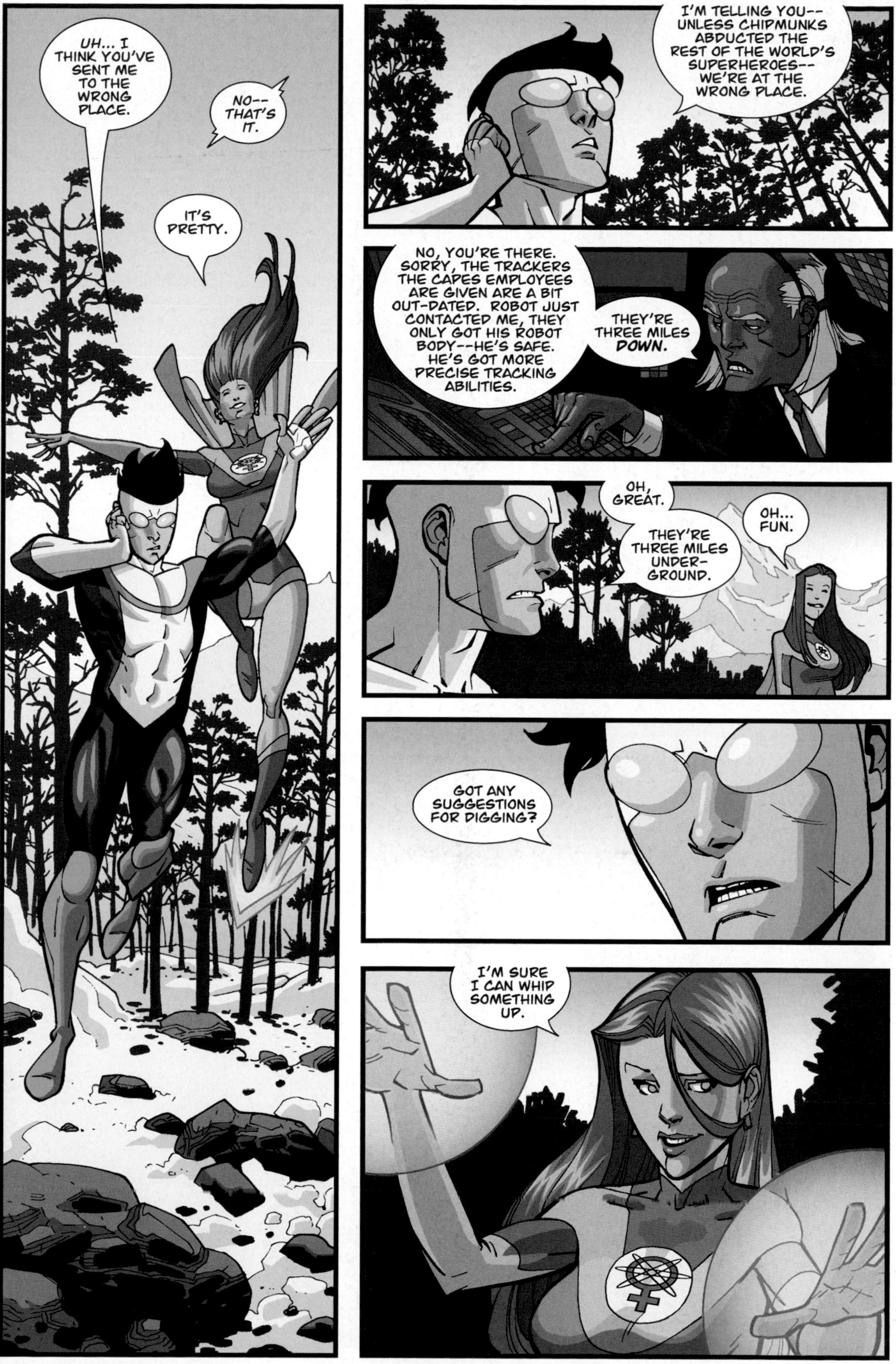
UH... I THINK YOU'VE SENT ME TO THE WRONG PLACE.
NO--THAT'S IT.
IT'S PRETTY.
I'M TELLING YOU--UNLESS CHIPMUNKS ABDUCTED THE REST OF THE WORLD'S SUPERHEROES--WE'RE AT THE WRONG PLACE.
NO, YOU'RE THERE. SORRY, THE TRACKERS THE CAPES EMPLOYEES ARE GIVEN ARE A BIT OUT-DATED. ROBOT JUST CONTACTED ME, THEY ONLY GOT HIS ROBOT BODY--HE'S SAFE. HE'S GOT MORE PRECISE TRACKING ABILITIES.
THEY'RE THREE MILES DOWN.
OH, GREAT.
THEY'RE THREE MILES UNDERGROUND.
OH... FUN.
GOT ANY SUGGESTIONS FOR DIGGING?
I'M SURE I CAN WHIP SOMETHING UP.

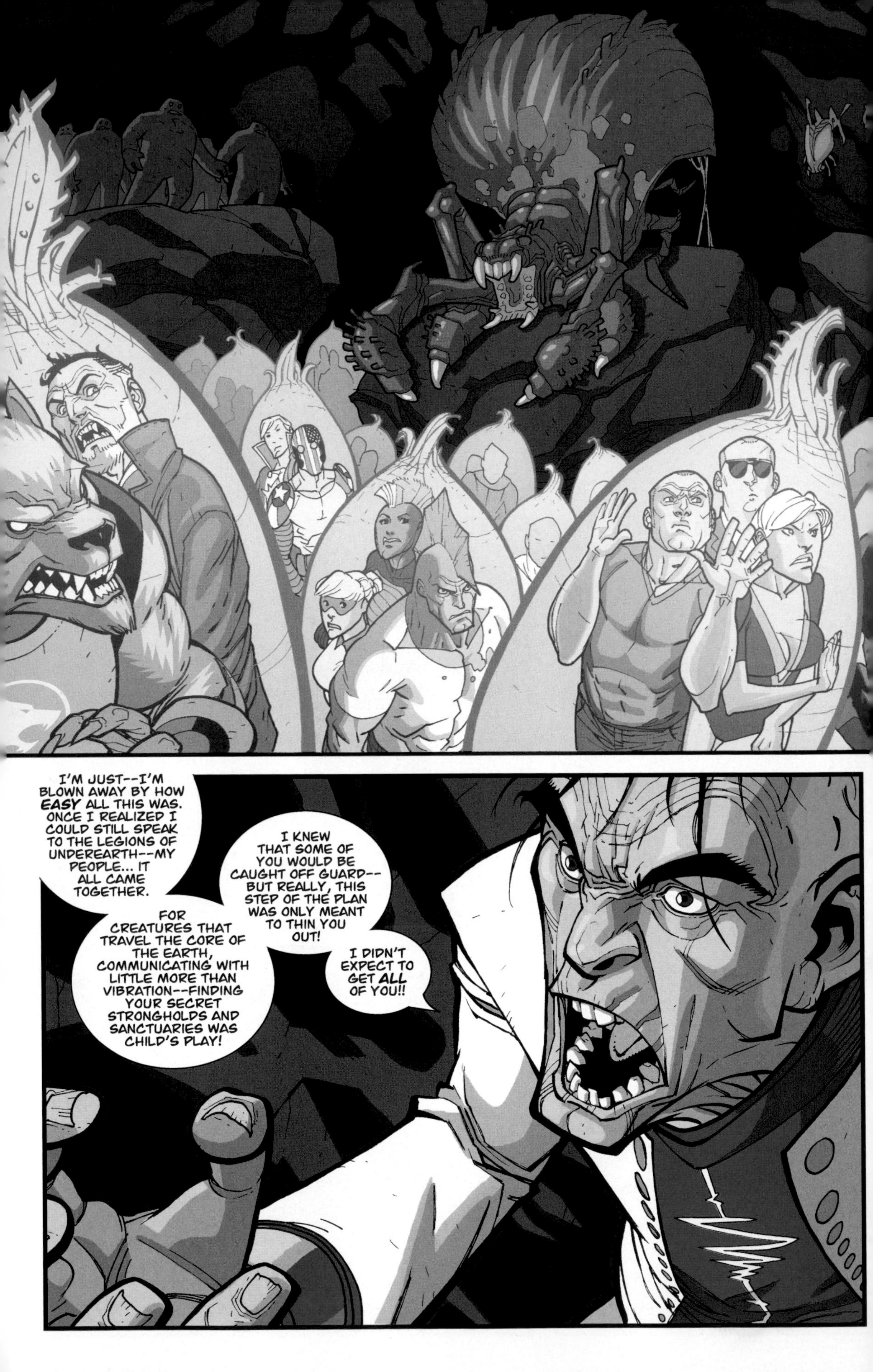
I'M JUST--I'M BLOWN AWAY BY HOW EASY ALL THIS WAS. ONCE I REALIZED I COULD STILL SPEAK TO THE LEGIONS OF UNDEREARTH--MY PEOPLE... IT ALL CAME TOGETHER.
FOR CREATURES THAT TRAVEL THE CORE OF THE EARTH, COMMUNICATING WITH LITTLE MORE THAN VIBRATION--FINDING YOUR SECRET STRONGHOLDS AND SANCTUARIES WAS CHILD'S PLAY!
I KNEW THAT SOME OF YOU WOULD BE CAUGHT OFF GUARD--BUT REALLY, THIS STEP OF THE PLAN WAS ONLY MEANT TO THIN YOU OUT!
I DIDN'T EXPECT TO GET ALL OF YOU!!

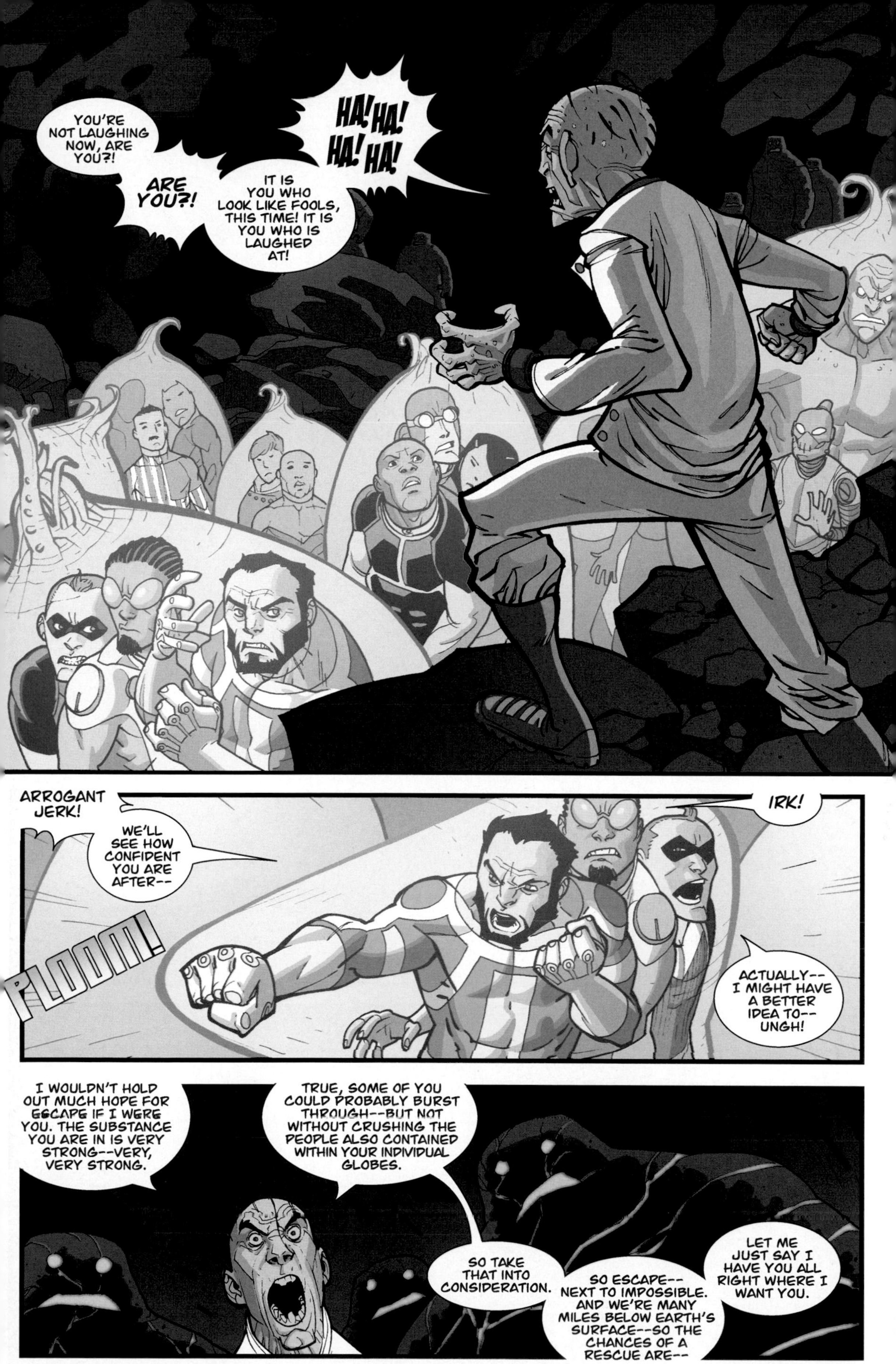
YOU'RE NOT LAUGHING NOW, ARE YOU?!
ARE YOU?!
IT IS YOU WHO LOOK LIKE FOOLS, THIS TIME! IT IS YOU WHO IS LAUGHED AT!
HA! HA! HA! HA!
ARROGANT JERK!
WE'LL SEE HOW CONFIDENT YOU ARE AFTER--
PLOOM!
IRK!
ACTUALLY-- I MIGHT HAVE A BETTER IDEA TO-- UNGH!
I WOULDN'T HOLD OUT MUCH HOPE FOR ESCAPE IF I WERE YOU. THE SUBSTANCE YOU ARE IN IS VERY STRONG--VERY, VERY STRONG.
TRUE, SOME OF YOU COULD PROBABLY BURST THROUGH--BUT NOT WITHOUT CRUSHING THE PEOPLE ALSO CONTAINED WITHIN YOUR INDIVIDUAL GLOBES.
SO TAKE THAT INTO CONSIDERATION.
SO ESCAPE-- NEXT TO IMPOSSIBLE. AND WE'RE MANY MILES BELOW EARTH'S SURFACE--SO THE CHANCES OF A RESCUE ARE--
LET ME JUST SAY I HAVE YOU ALL RIGHT WHERE I WANT YOU.

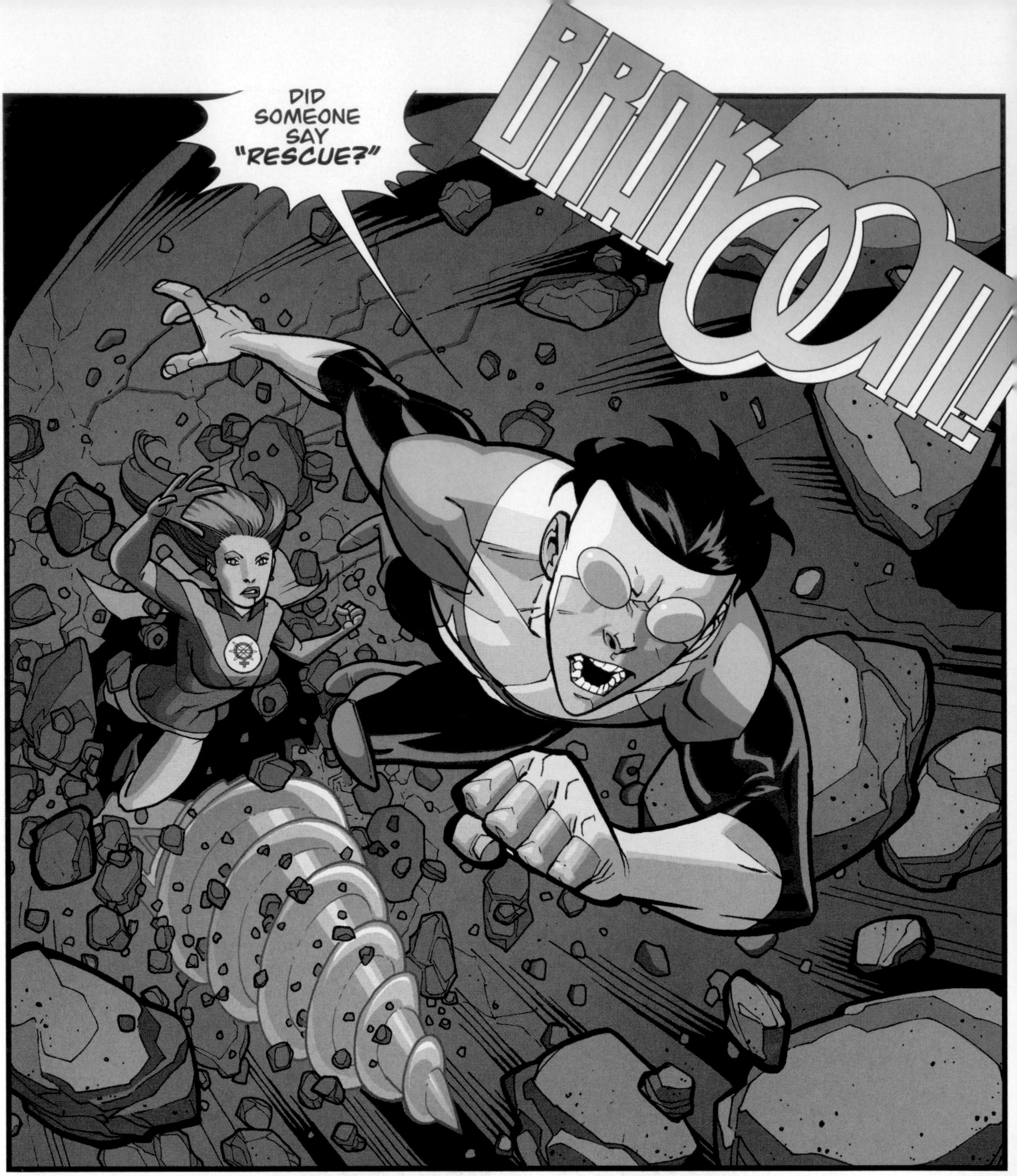
DID SOMEONE SAY "RESCUE?"
BRAKOOM!!

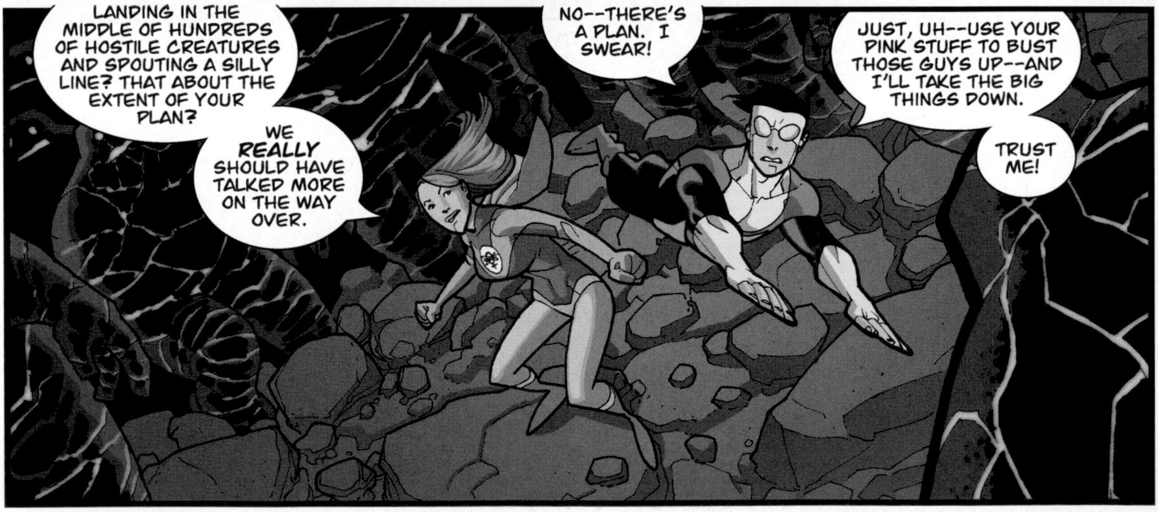
LANDING IN THE MIDDLE OF HUNDREDS OF HOSTILE CREATURES AND SPOUTING A SILLY LINE? THAT ABOUT THE EXTENT OF YOUR PLAN?
WE REALLY SHOULD HAVE TALKED MORE ON THE WAY OVER.
NO--THERE'S A PLAN. I SWEAR!
JUST, UH--USE YOUR PINK STUFF TO BUST THOSE GUYS UP--AND I'LL TAKE THE BIG THINGS DOWN.
TRUST ME!

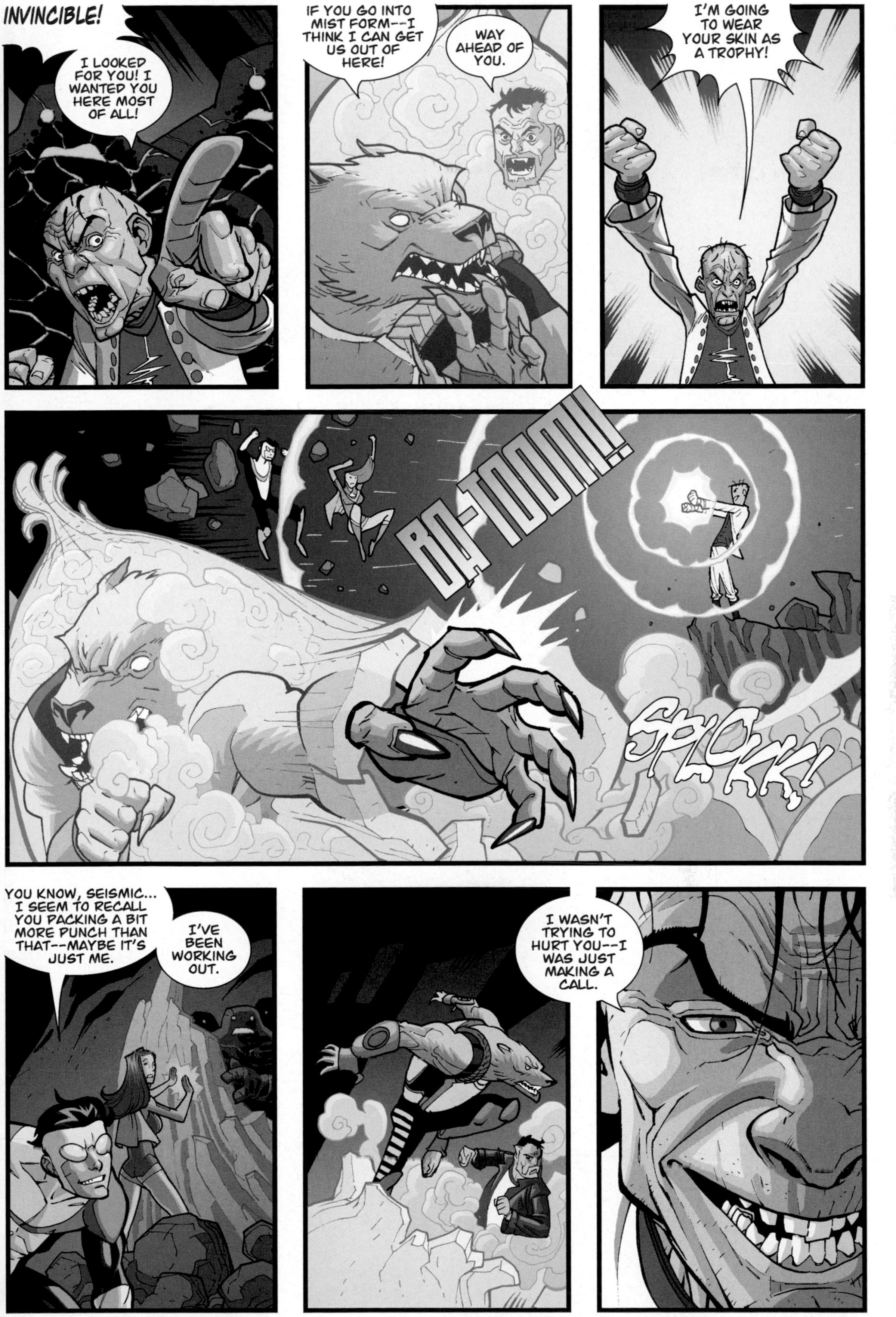
INVINCIBLE!
I LOOKED FOR YOU! I WANTED YOU HERE MOST OF ALL!
IF YOU GO INTO MIST FORM--I THINK I CAN GET US OUT OF HERE!
WAY AHEAD OF YOU.
I'M GOING TO WEAR YOUR SKIN AS A TROPHY!
BA-TOOM!!
SPLOKK!
YOU KNOW, SEISMIC... I SEEM TO RECALL YOU PACKING A BIT MORE PUNCH THAN THAT--MAYBE IT'S JUST ME.
I'VE BEEN WORKING OUT.
I WASN'T TRYING TO HURT YOU--I WAS JUST MAKING A CALL.

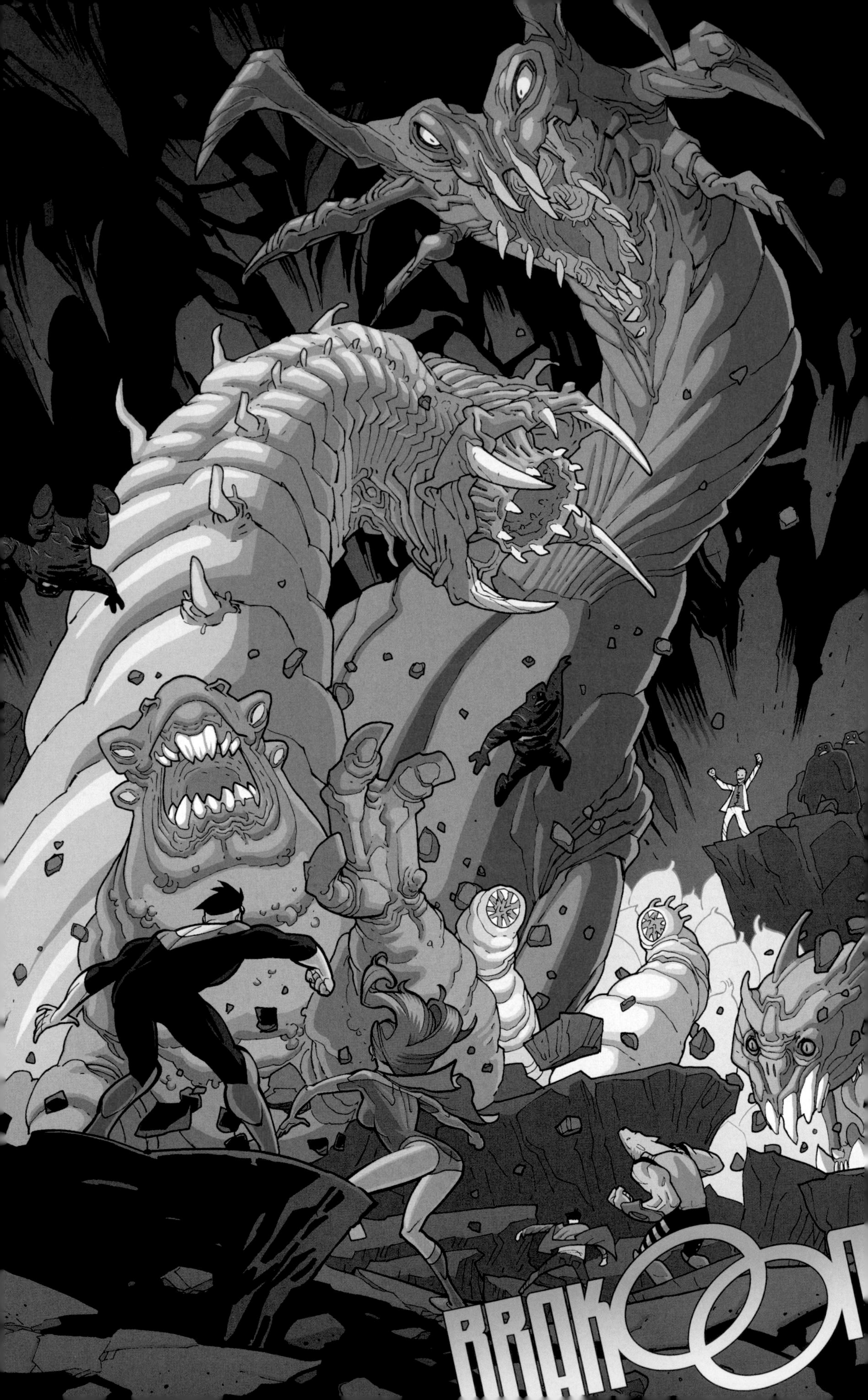
BRAKOO

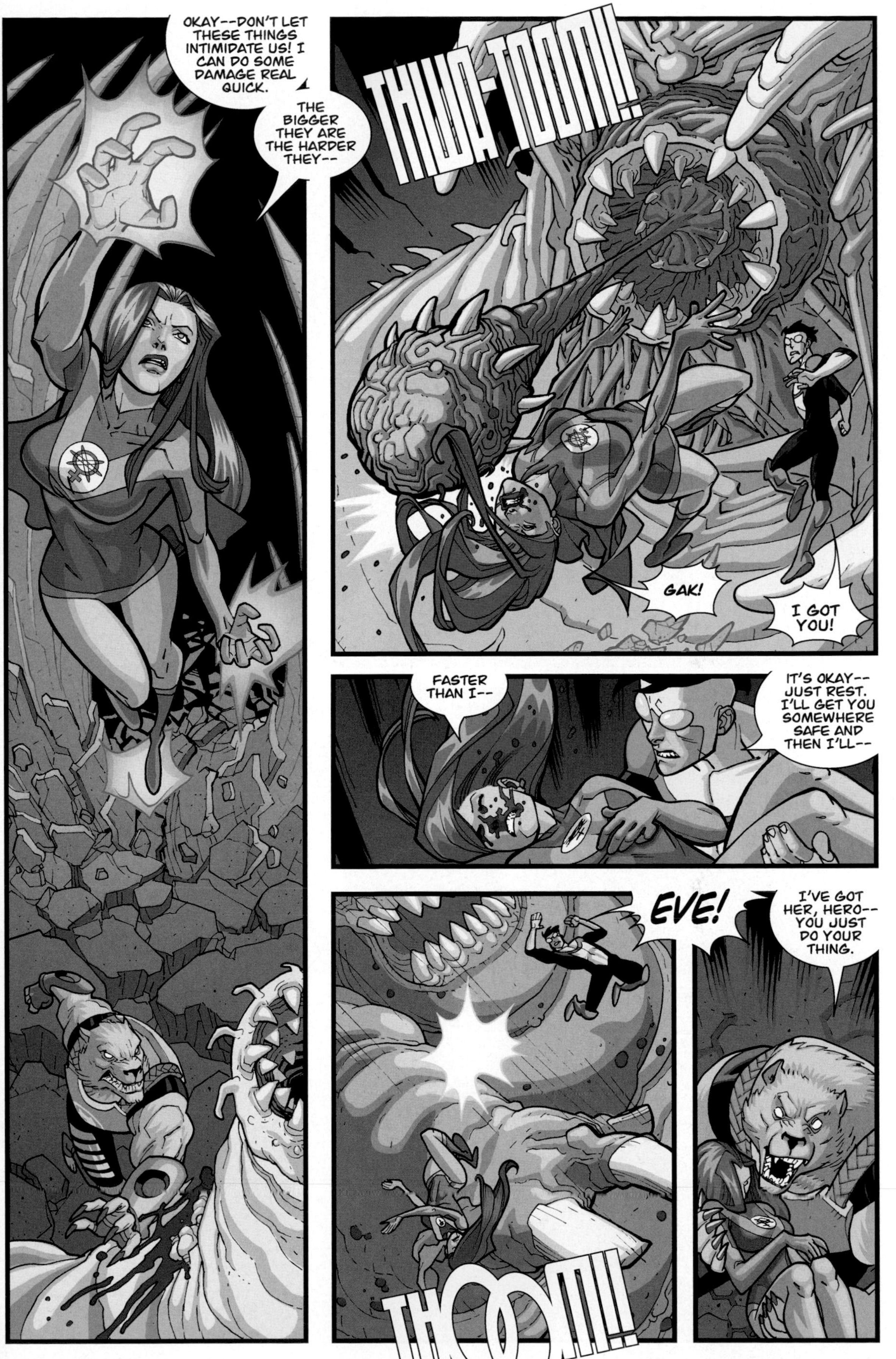
OKAY--DON'T LET THESE THINGS INTIMIDATE US! I CAN DO SOME DAMAGE REAL QUICK.
THE BIGGER THEY ARE THE HARDER THEY--
THWA-TOOM!!
GAK!
I GOT YOU!
FASTER THAN I--
IT'S OKAY--JUST REST. I'LL GET YOU SOMEWHERE SAFE AND THEN I'LL--
EVE!
I'VE GOT HER, HERO--YOU JUST DO YOUR THING.
THOOM!!

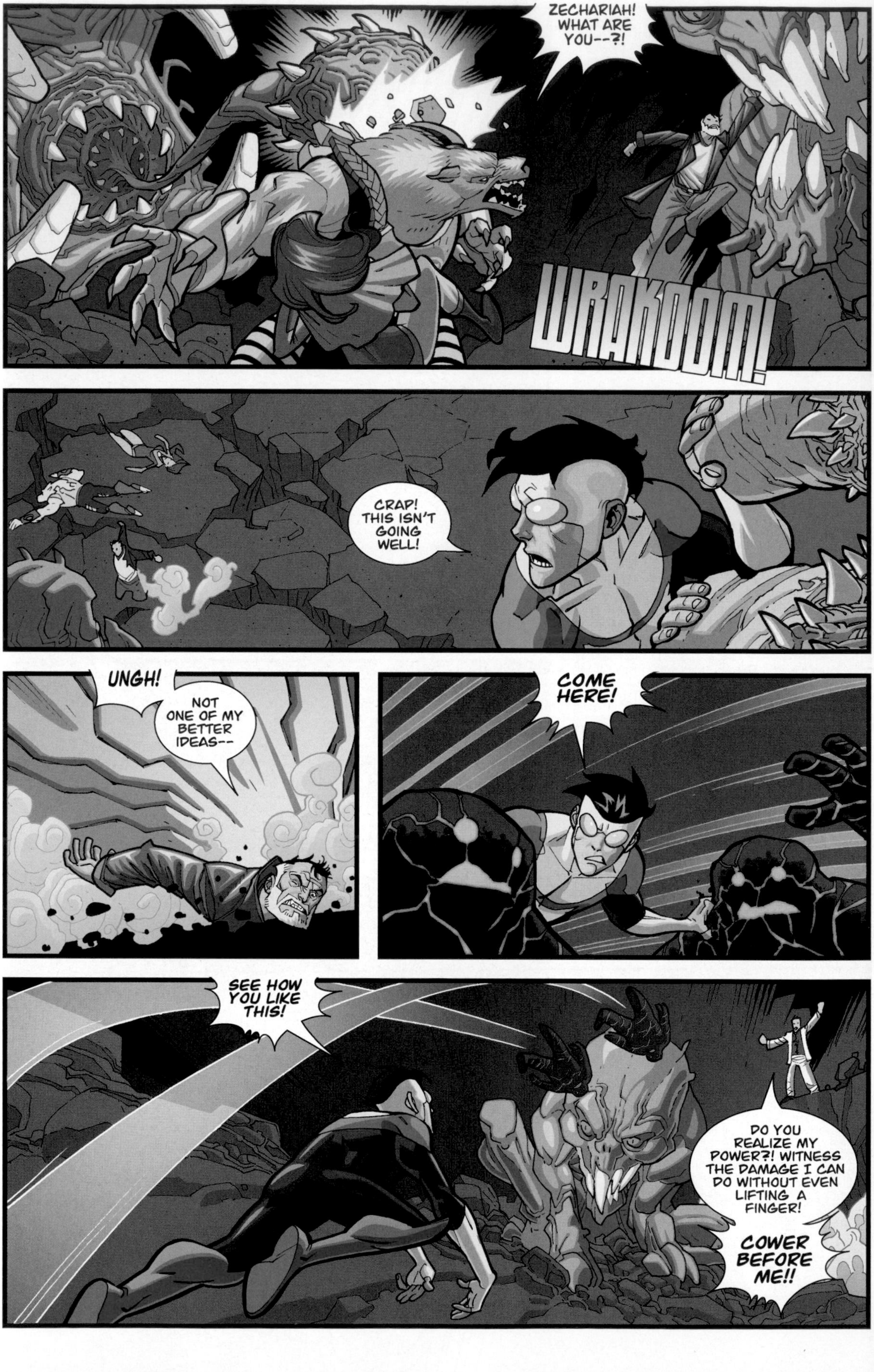
ZECHARIAH! WHAT ARE YOU--?!
WRAKOOM!
CRAP! THIS ISN'T GOING WELL!
UNGH!
NOT ONE OF MY BETTER IDEAS--
COME HERE!
SEE HOW YOU LIKE THIS!
DO YOU REALIZE MY POWER?! WITNESS THE DAMAGE I CAN DO WITHOUT EVEN LIFTING A FINGER!
COWER BEFORE ME!!

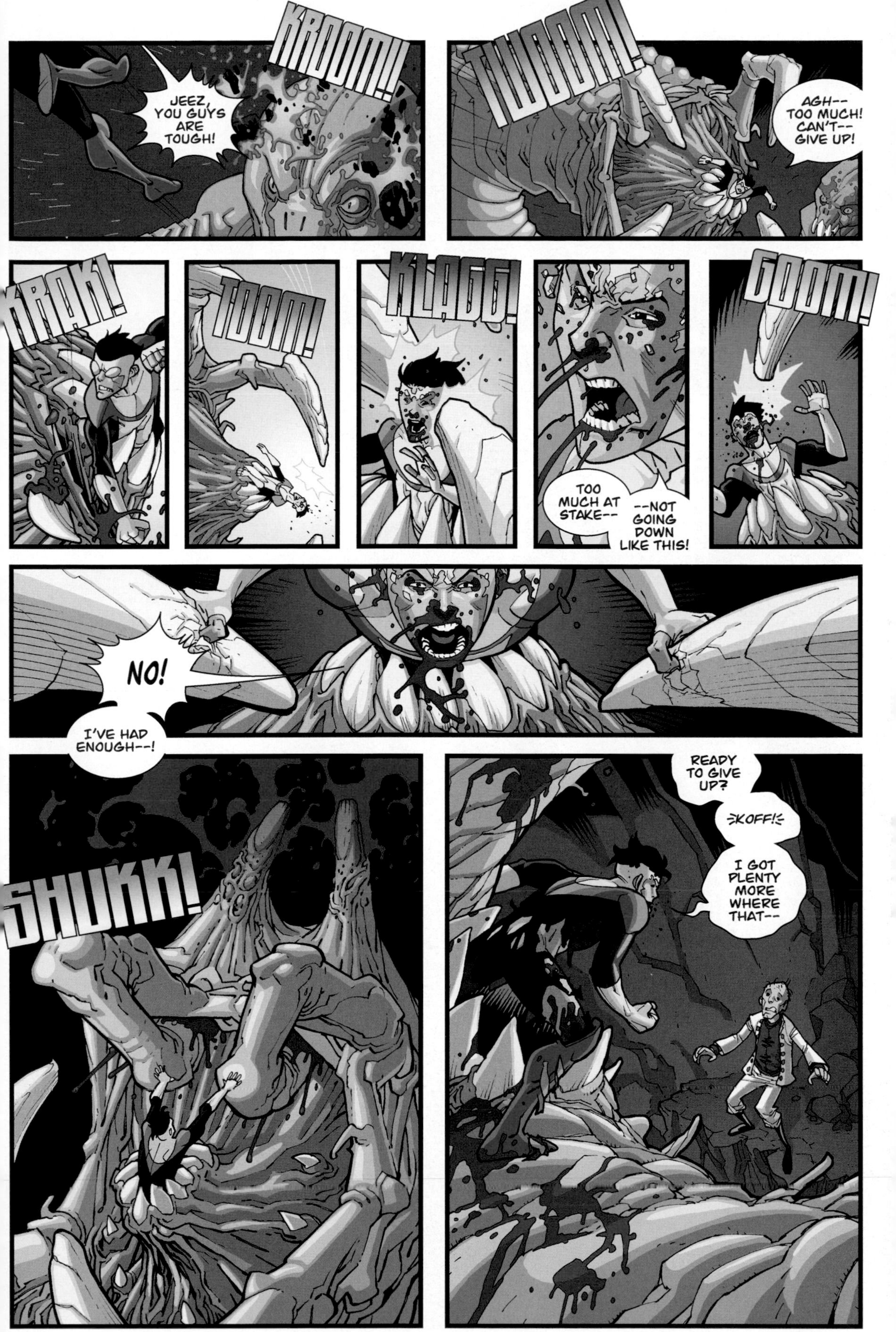
KROOM!!
JEEZ, YOU GUYS ARE TOUGH!
TWOOM!
AGH-- TOO MUCH! CAN'T-- GIVE UP!
KRAK!
TOOM!
KLAGG!
TOO MUCH AT STAKE--
--NOT GOING DOWN LIKE THIS!
GOOM!
NO!
I'VE HAD ENOUGH--!
SHUKK!
READY TO GIVE UP?
KOFF!
I GOT PLENTY MORE WHERE THAT--

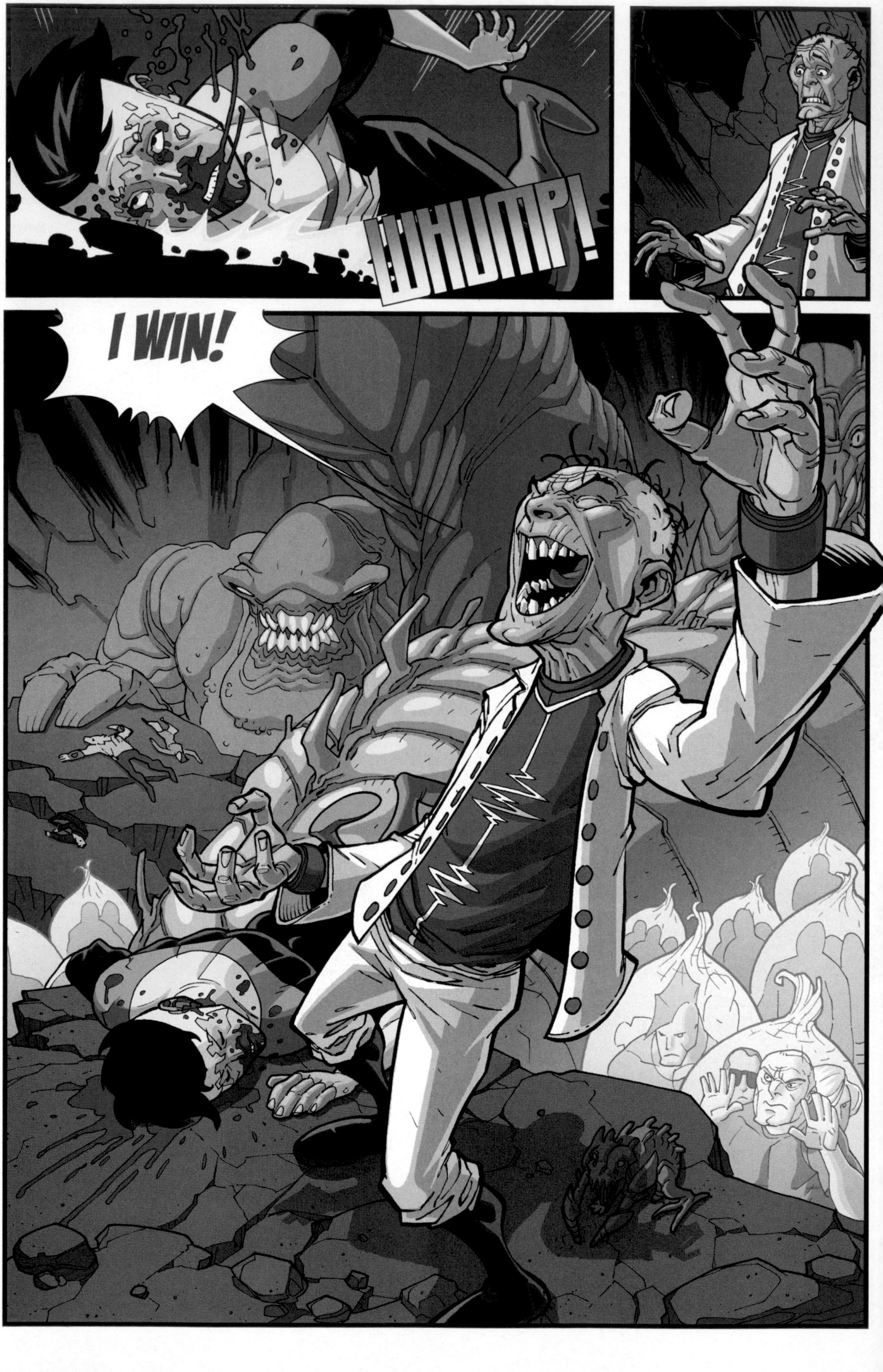
WHUMP!
I WIN!

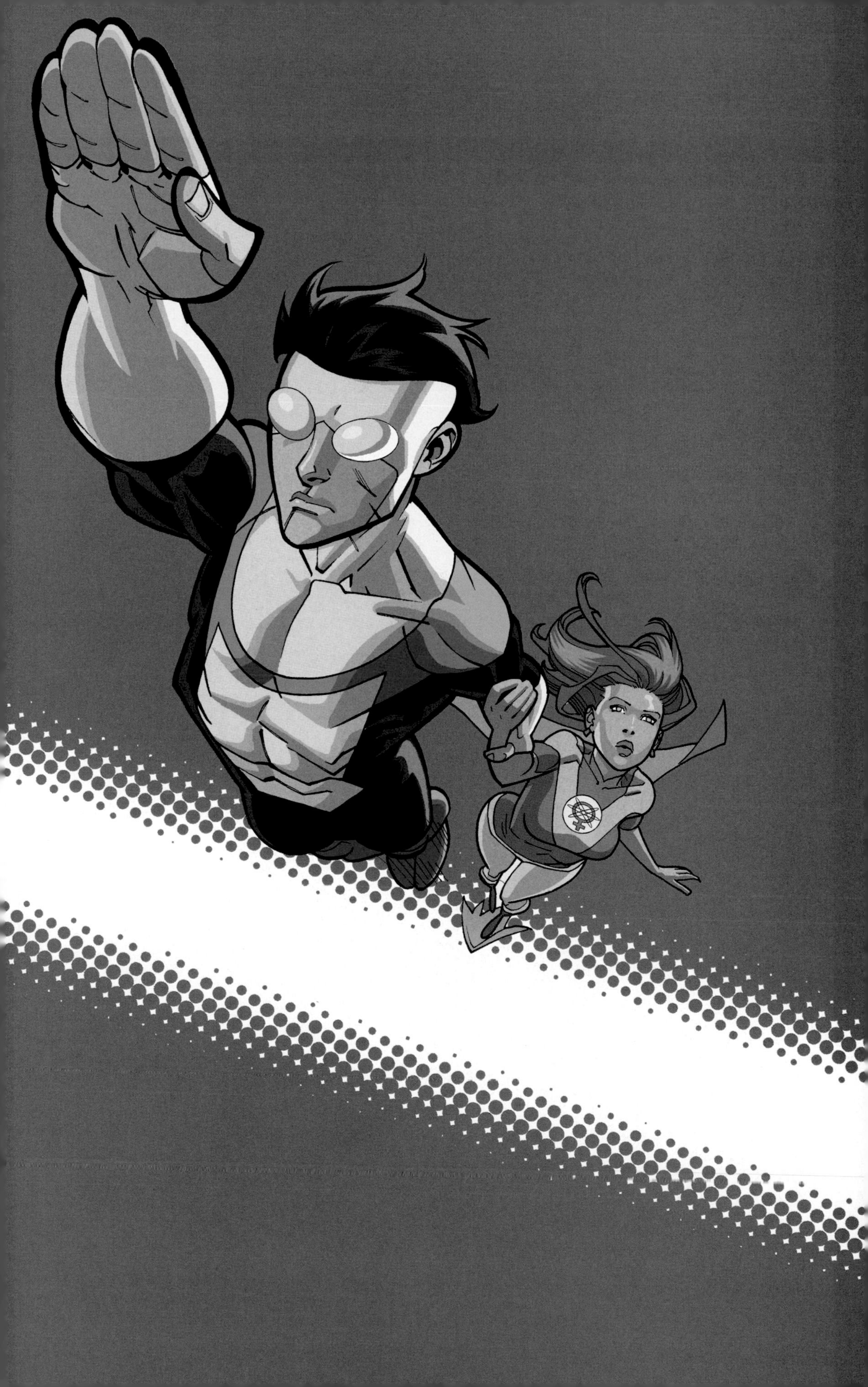

CHAPTER TWO

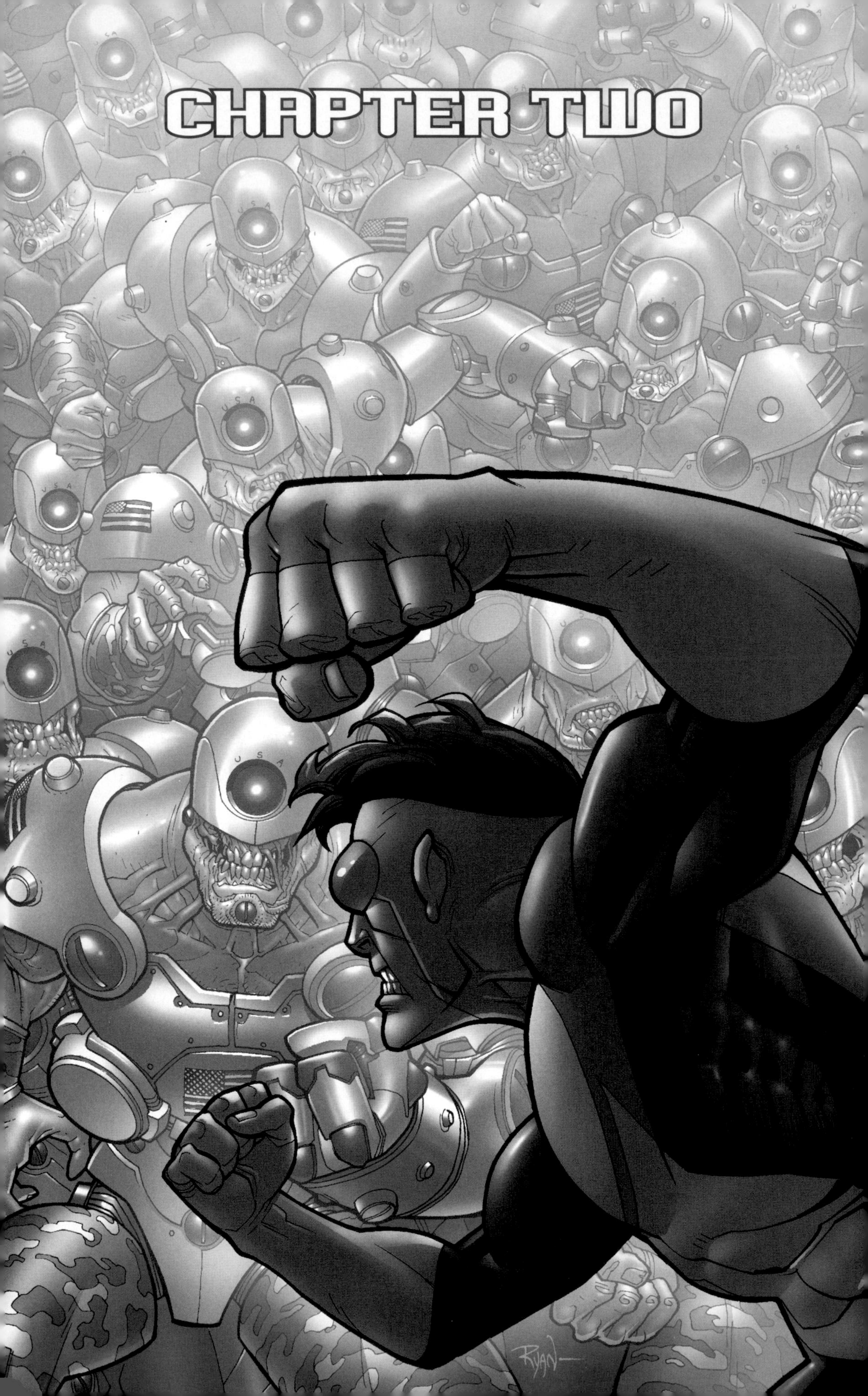

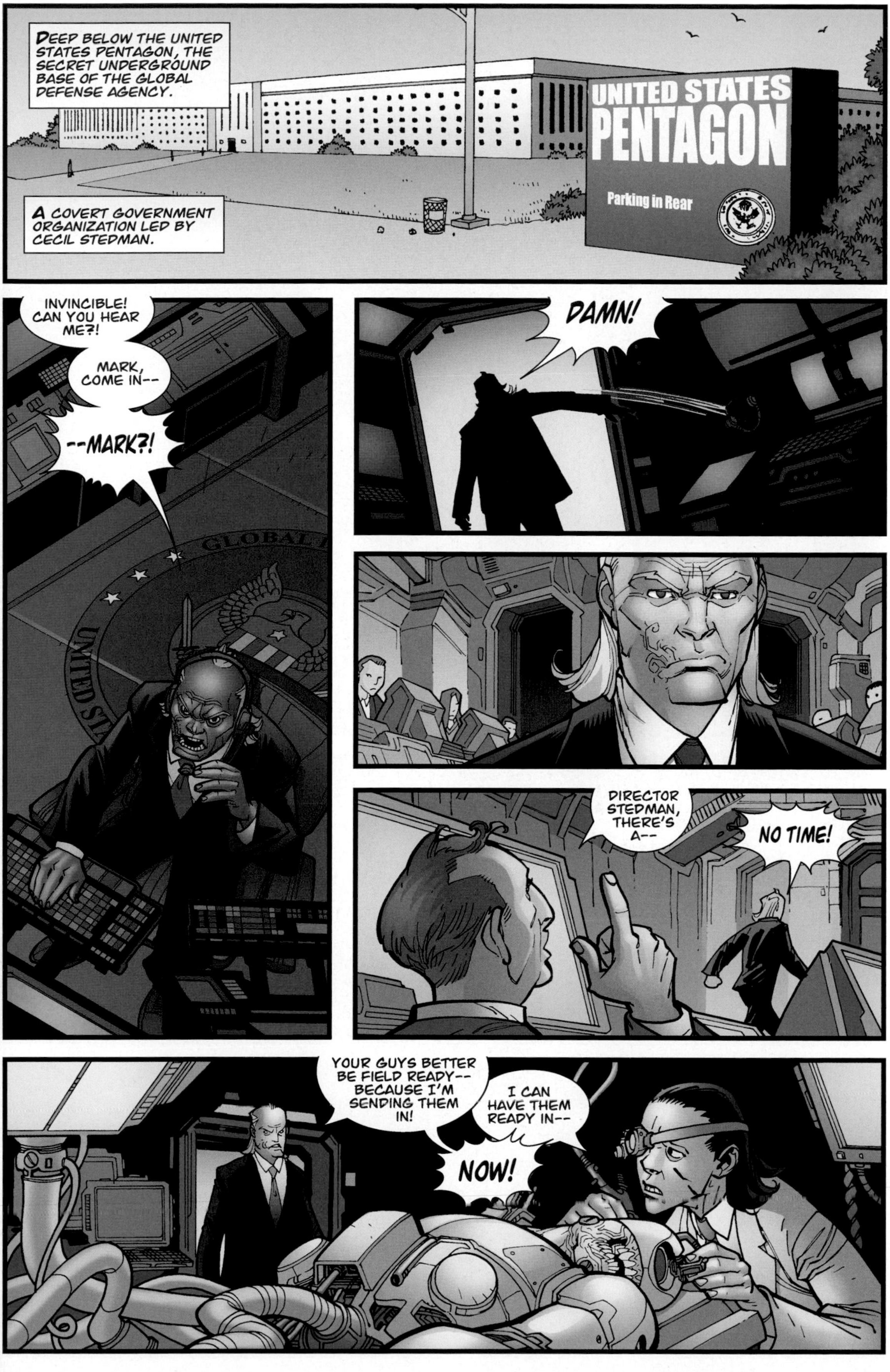

DEEP BELOW THE UNITED STATES PENTAGON, THE SECRET UNDERGROUND BASE OF THE GLOBAL DEFENSE AGENCY.
UNITED STATES PENTAGON
Parking in Rear
A COVERT GOVERNMENT ORGANIZATION LED BY CECIL STEDMAN.
INVINCIBLE! CAN YOU HEAR ME?!
MARK, COME IN--
--MARK?!
GLOBAL
UNITED ST
DAMN!
DIRECTOR STEDMAN, THERE'S A--
NO TIME!
YOUR GUYS BETTER BE FIELD READY--BECAUSE I'M SENDING THEM IN!
I CAN HAVE THEM READY IN--
NOW!

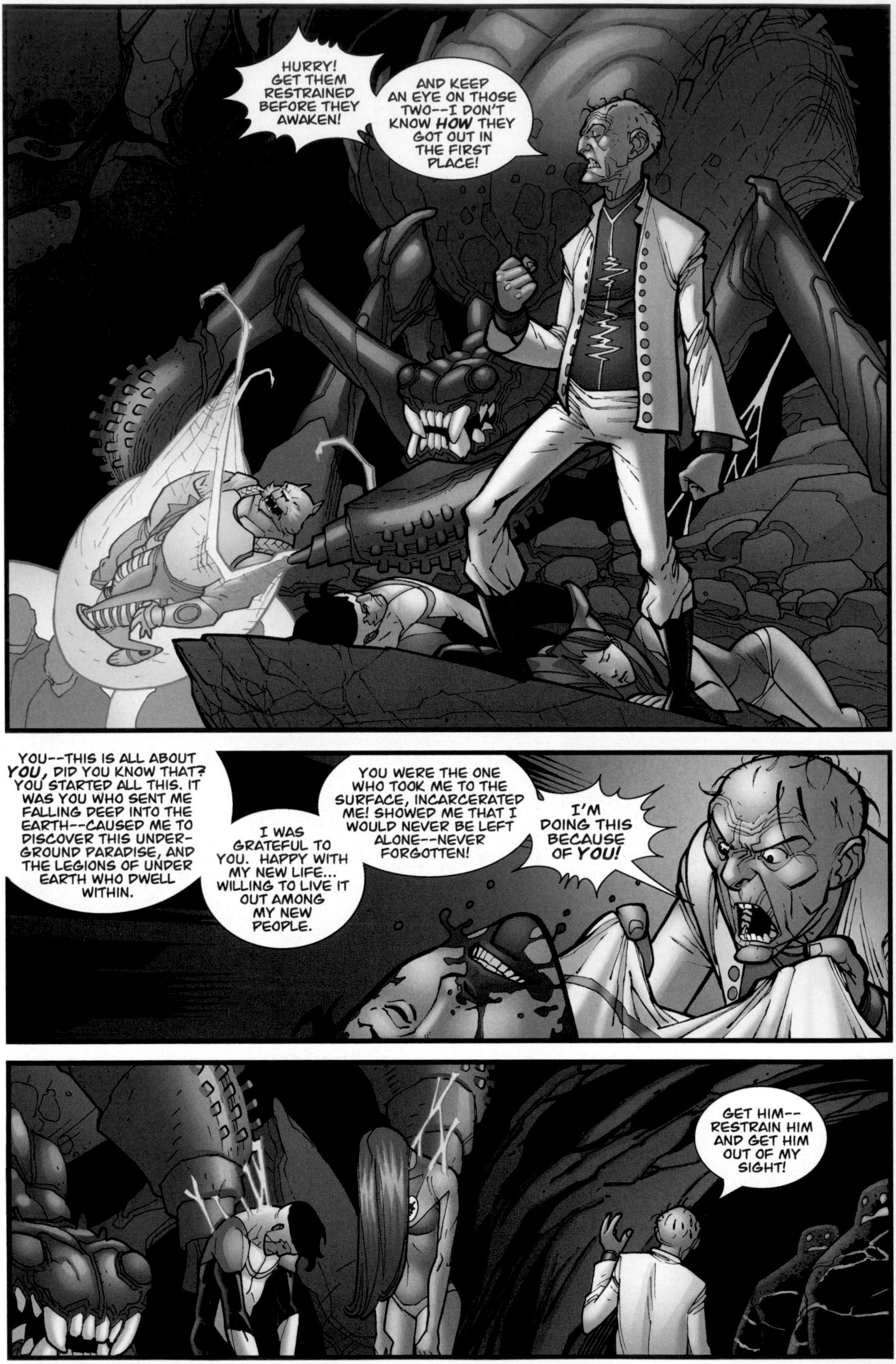
HURRY! GET THEM RESTRAINED BEFORE THEY AWAKEN!
AND KEEP AN EYE ON THOSE TWO--I DON'T KNOW HOW THEY GOT OUT IN THE FIRST PLACE!
YOU--THIS IS ALL ABOUT YOU, DID YOU KNOW THAT? YOU STARTED ALL THIS. IT WAS YOU WHO SENT ME FALLING DEEP INTO THE EARTH--CAUSED ME TO DISCOVER THIS UNDERGROUND PARADISE, AND THE LEGIONS OF UNDER EARTH WHO DWELL WITHIN.
I WAS GRATEFUL TO YOU. HAPPY WITH MY NEW LIFE... WILLING TO LIVE IT OUT AMONG MY NEW PEOPLE.
YOU WERE THE ONE WHO TOOK ME TO THE SURFACE, INCARCERATED ME! SHOWED ME THAT I WOULD NEVER BE LEFT ALONE--NEVER FORGOTTEN!
I'M DOING THIS BECAUSE OF YOU!
GET HIM--RESTRAIN HIM AND GET HIM OUT OF MY SIGHT!

UNGH...

HUNGH? WHA--?

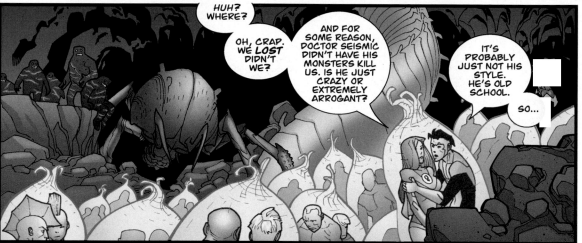

HUH? WHERE?

OH, CRAP. WE *LOST* DIDN'T WE?

AND FOR SOME REASON, DOCTOR SEISMIC DIDN'T HAVE HIS MONSTERS KILL US. IS HE JUST CRAZY OR EXTREMELY ARROGANT?

IT'S PROBABLY JUST NOT HIS STYLE. HE'S OLD SCHOOL.

SO...

JUST GIVE ME A MINUTE AND I'LL HAVE US OUT OF HERE.

NO. WAIT.

WE GET OUT OF HERE-- THEN WHAT? IT'LL BE JUST LIKE BEFORE--WE'LL BE OVERPOWERED LIKE BEFORE AND THEN HE MIGHT PUT US IN SOMETHING STRONGER.

WE'VE GOT TO THINK ABOUT THIS.

WE'RE SURROUNDED BY THE MOST POWERFUL SUPERHEROES ON THE PLANET--I MEAN, THIS ISN'T EVERYONE BUT IT'S CLOSE--I THINK I'VE GOT AN IDEA.

WE NEED TO FOCUS ON FREEING EVERYONE--IGNORE THE MONSTERS, DON'T TRY TO DEFEAT THEM OURSELVES.

WE GET EVERYONE OUT--AND THEN FIGHT AS A GROUP, WE'LL--

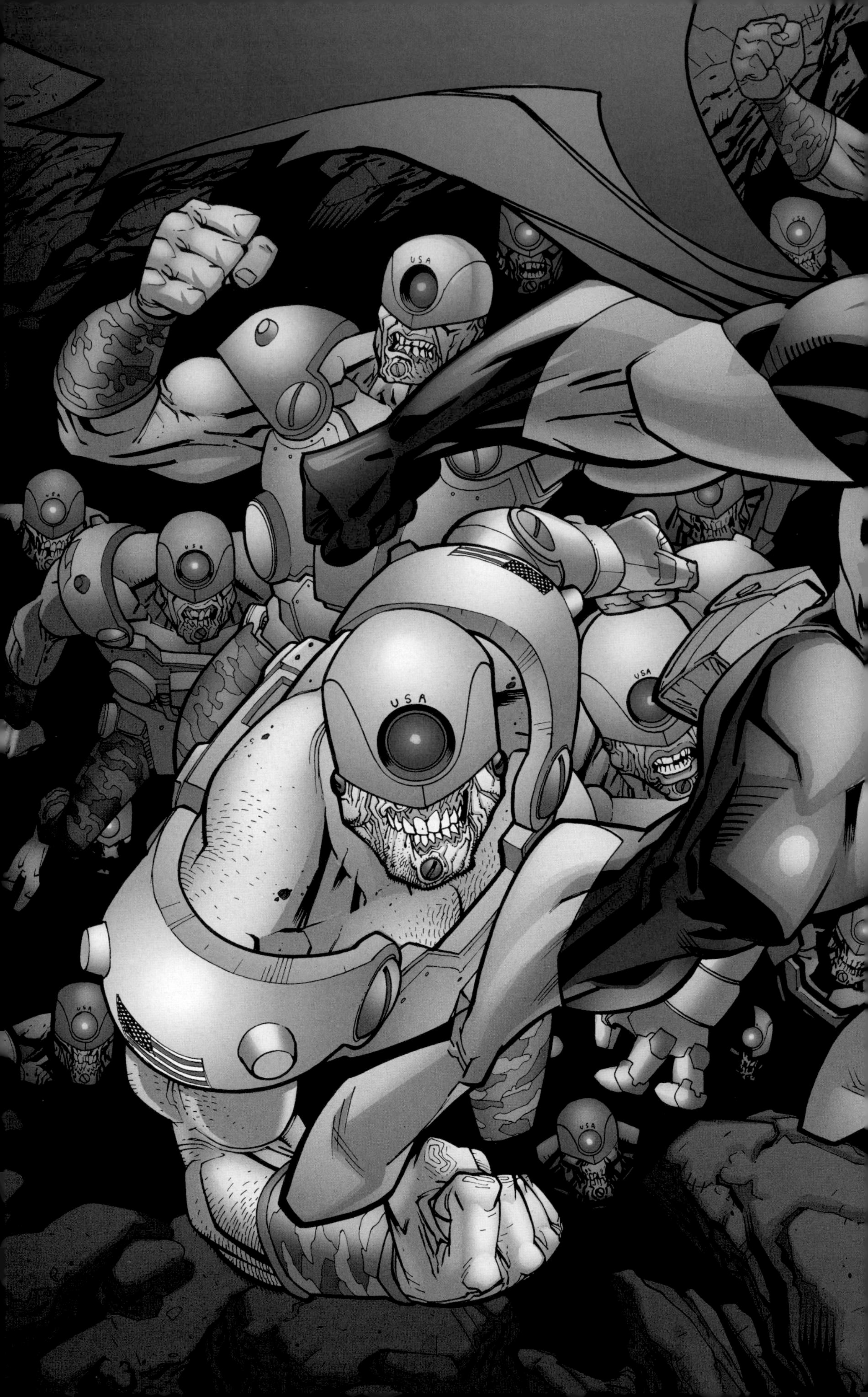
USA

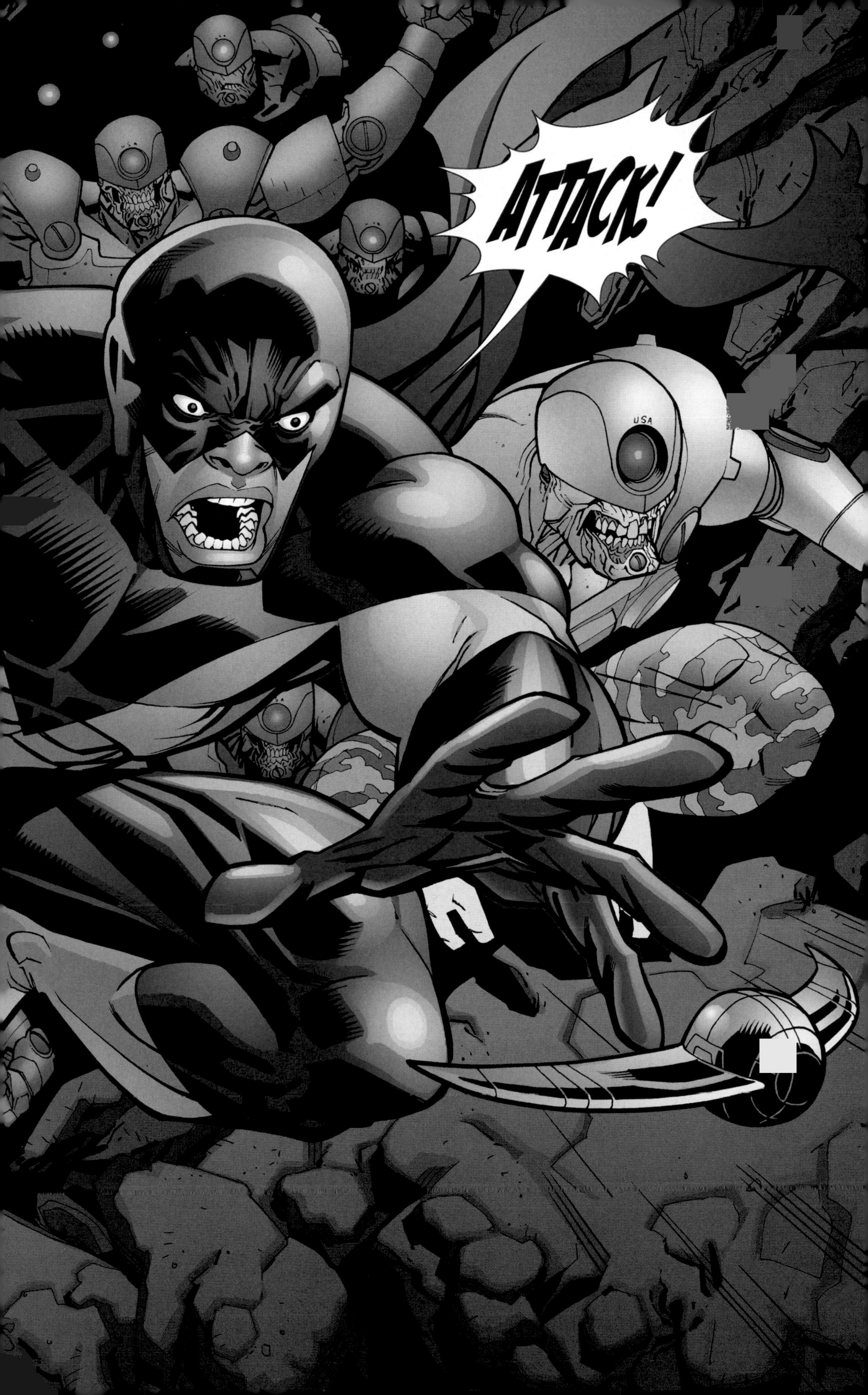
ATTACK!
USA

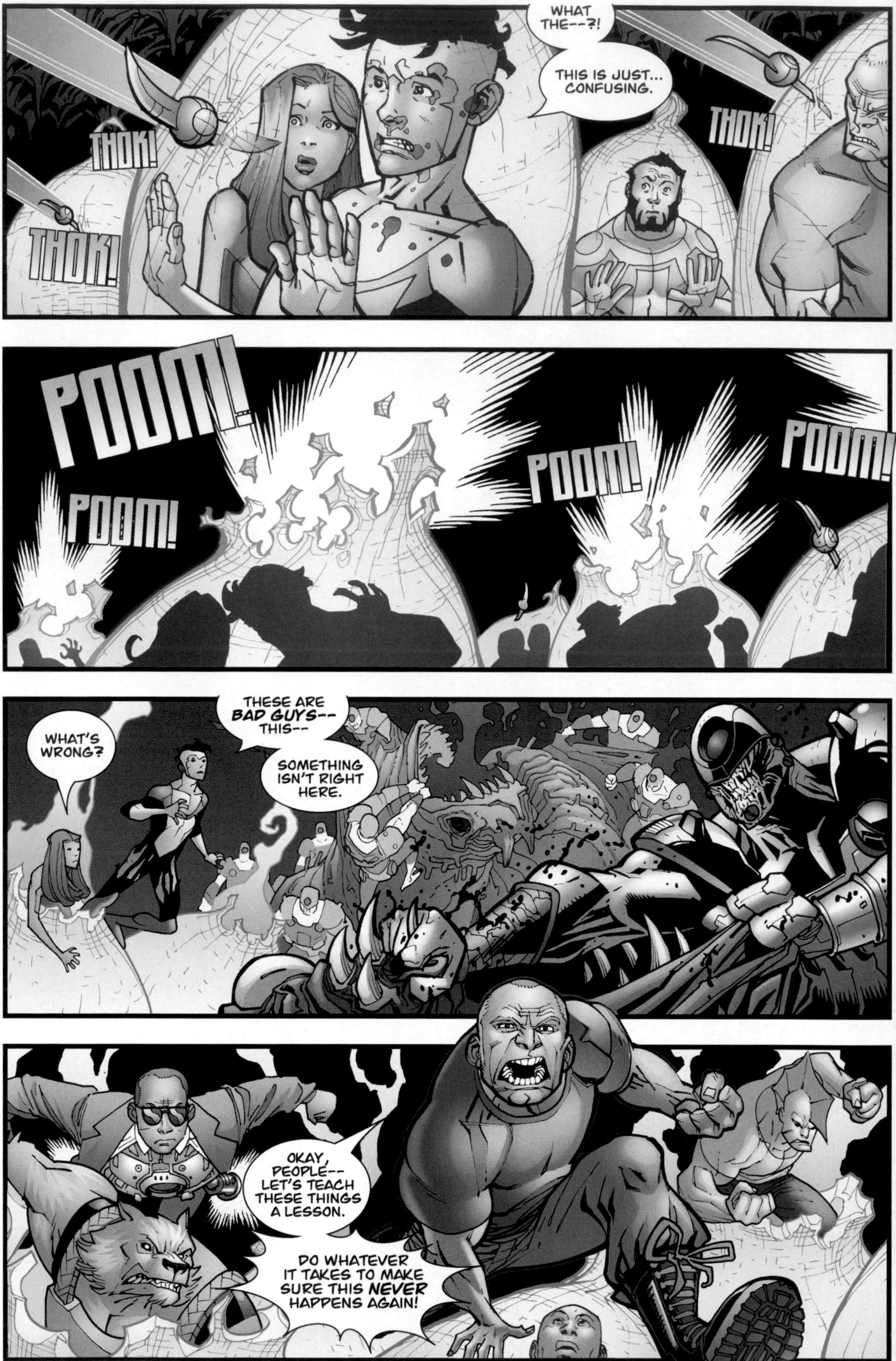
THOK!
THOK!
WHAT THE--?!
THIS IS JUST... CONFUSING.
THOK!
POOM!
POOM!
POOM!
POOM!
WHAT'S WRONG?
THESE ARE BAD GUYS-- THIS--
SOMETHING ISN'T RIGHT HERE.
OKAY, PEOPLE-- LET'S TEACH THESE THINGS A LESSON.
DO WHATEVER IT TAKES TO MAKE SURE THIS NEVER HAPPENS AGAIN!

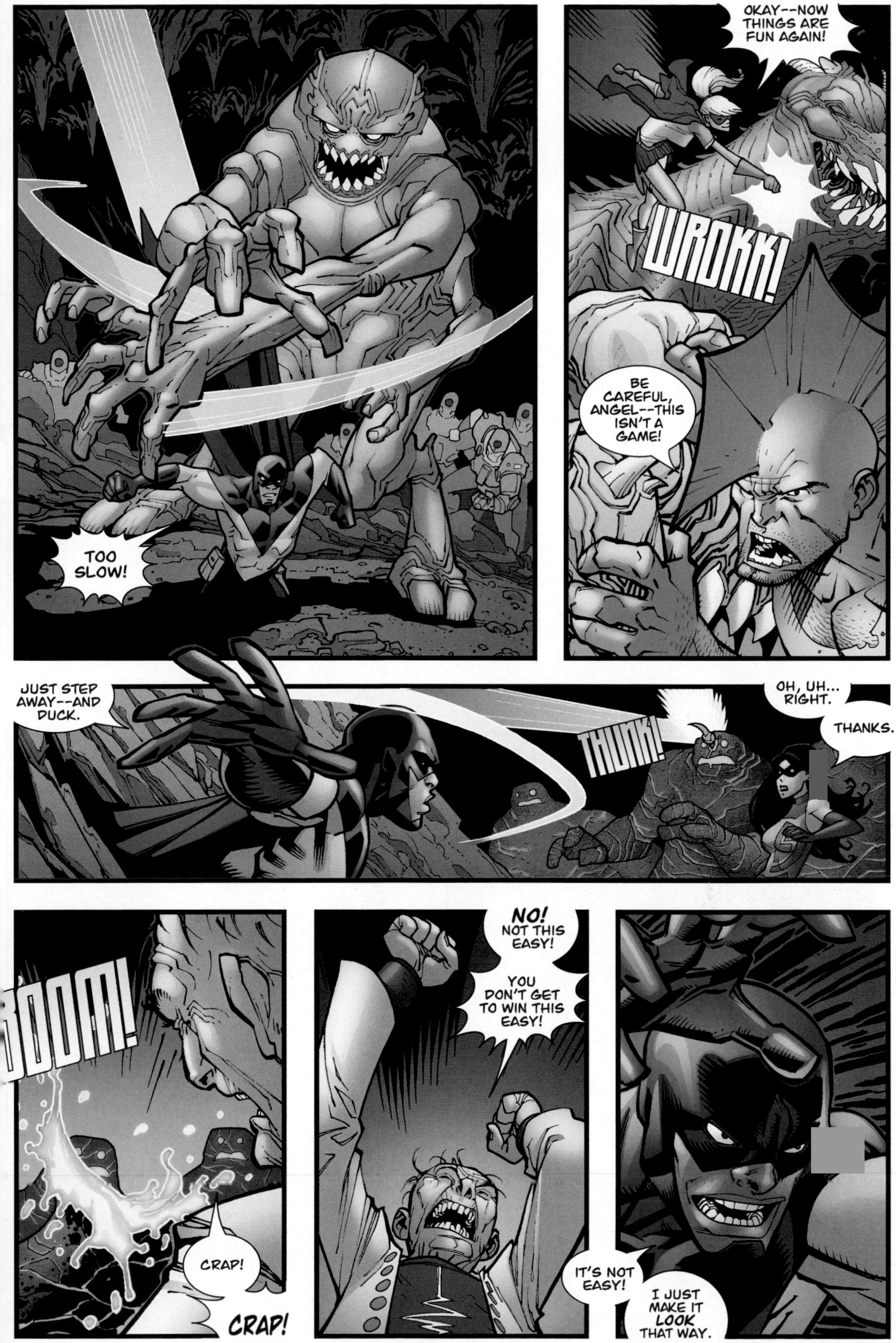
TOO SLOW!
OKAY--NOW THINGS ARE FUN AGAIN!
WROKK!
BE CAREFUL, ANGEL--THIS ISN'T A GAME!
JUST STEP AWAY--AND DUCK.
THUNK!
OH, UH... RIGHT.
THANKS.
BOOM!
CRAP!
CRAP!
NO! NOT THIS EASY!
YOU DON'T GET TO WIN THIS EASY!
IT'S NOT EASY!
I JUST MAKE IT LOOK THAT WAY.

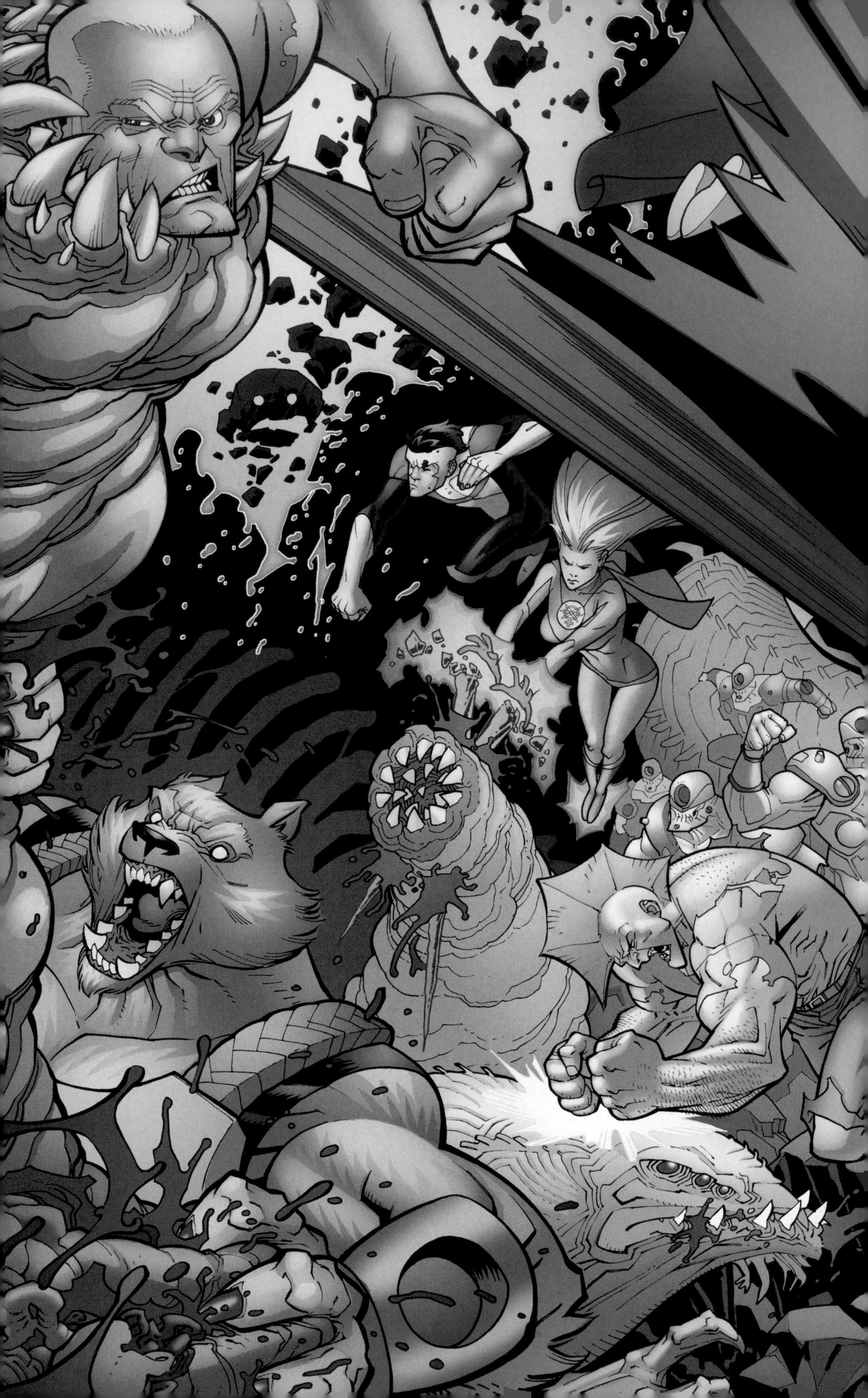

WRAAAMM!!

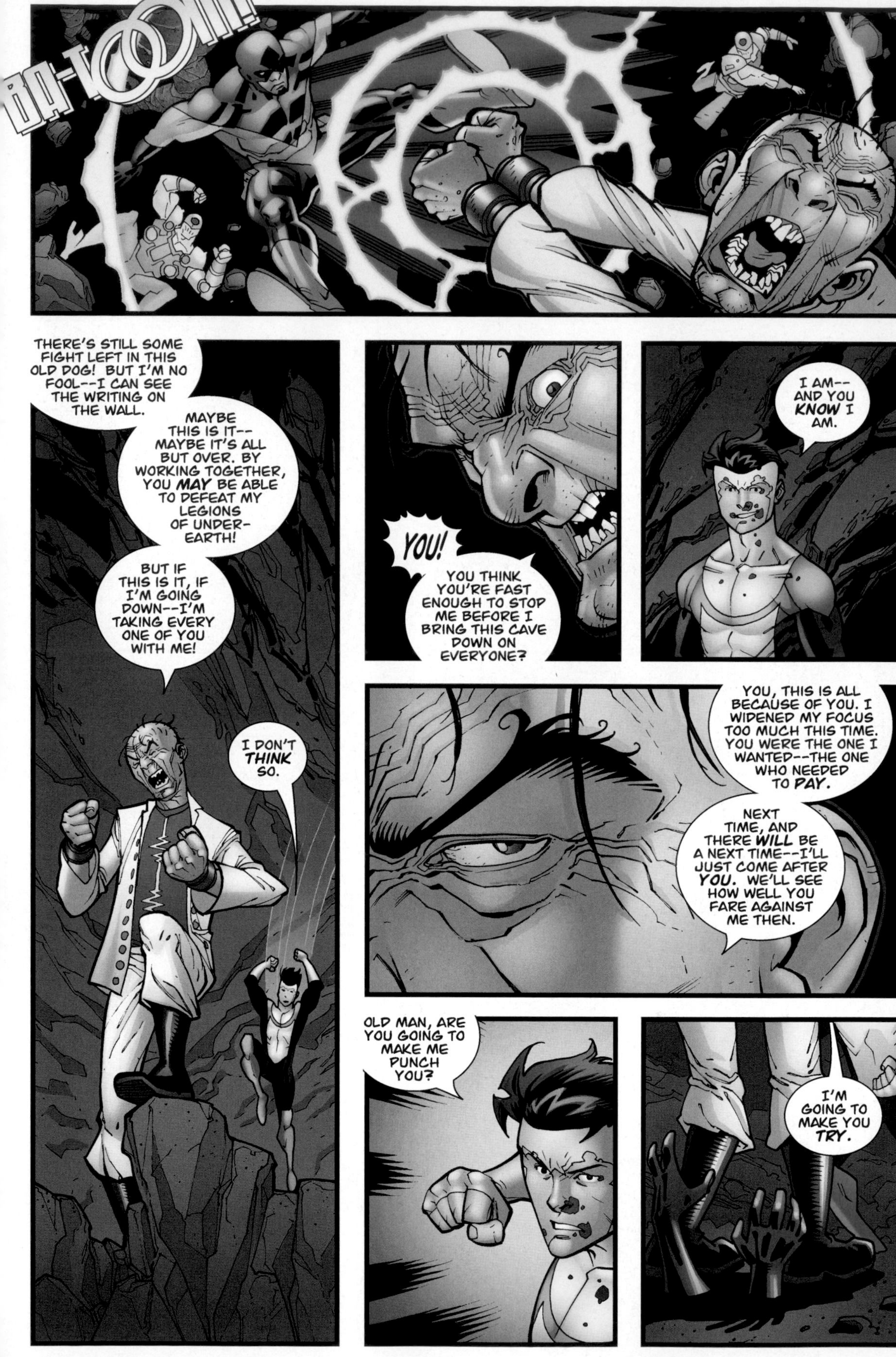
BA-TOOM!
THERE'S STILL SOME FIGHT LEFT IN THIS OLD DOG! BUT I'M NO FOOL--I CAN SEE THE WRITING ON THE WALL.
MAYBE THIS IS IT-- MAYBE IT'S ALL BUT OVER. BY WORKING TOGETHER, YOU MAY BE ABLE TO DEFEAT MY LEGIONS OF UNDER-EARTH!
BUT IF THIS IS IT, IF I'M GOING DOWN--I'M TAKING EVERY ONE OF YOU WITH ME!
I DON'T THINK SO.
YOU!
YOU THINK YOU'RE FAST ENOUGH TO STOP ME BEFORE I BRING THIS CAVE DOWN ON EVERYONE?
I AM-- AND YOU KNOW I AM.
YOU, THIS IS ALL BECAUSE OF YOU. I WIDENED MY FOCUS TOO MUCH THIS TIME. YOU WERE THE ONE I WANTED--THE ONE WHO NEEDED TO PAY.
NEXT TIME, AND THERE WILL BE A NEXT TIME--I'LL JUST COME AFTER YOU. WE'LL SEE HOW WELL YOU FARE AGAINST ME THEN.
OLD MAN, ARE YOU GOING TO MAKE ME PUNCH YOU?
I'M GOING TO MAKE YOU TRY.

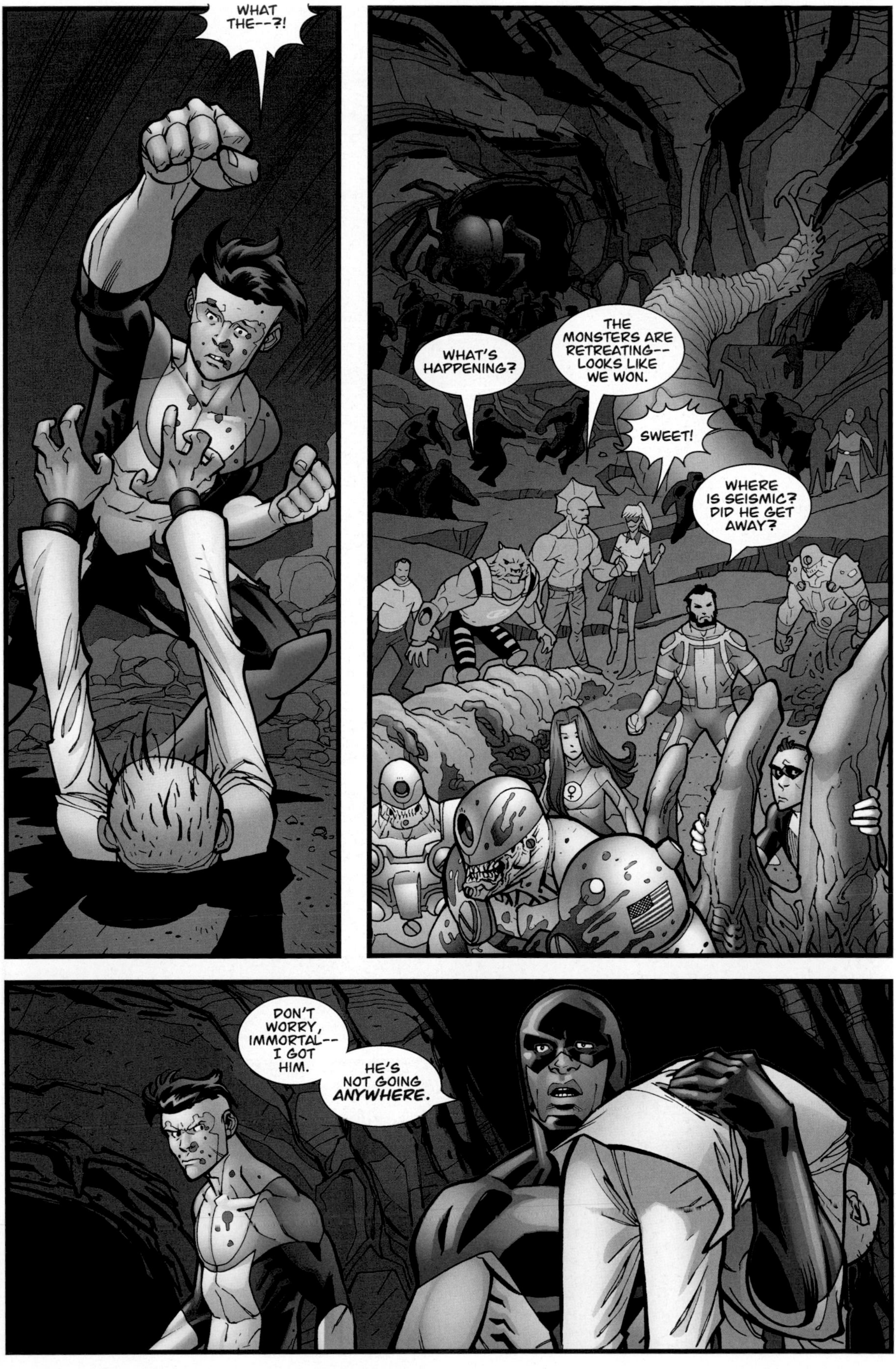
WHAT THE--?!
WHAT'S HAPPENING?
THE MONSTERS ARE RETREATING-- LOOKS LIKE WE WON.
SWEET!
WHERE IS SEISMIC? DID HE GET AWAY?
DON'T WORRY, IMMORTAL-- I GOT HIM.
HE'S NOT GOING ANYWHERE.

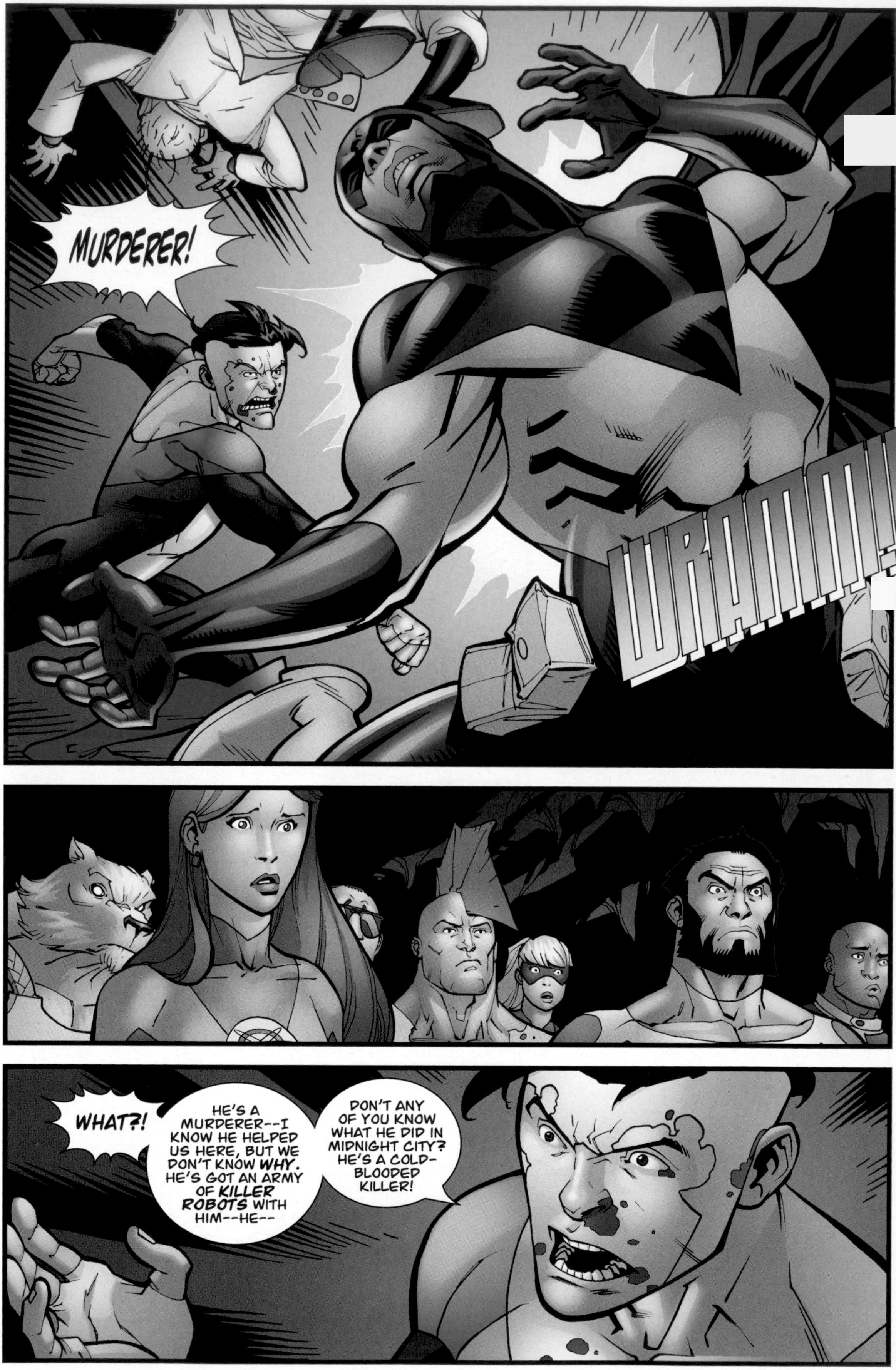
MURDERER!
WRAMM!!
WHAT?!
HE'S A MURDERER--I KNOW HE HELPED US HERE, BUT WE DON'T KNOW WHY. HE'S GOT AN ARMY OF KILLER ROBOTS WITH HIM--HE--
DON'T ANY OF YOU KNOW WHAT HE DID IN MIDNIGHT CITY? HE'S A COLD-BLOODED KILLER!

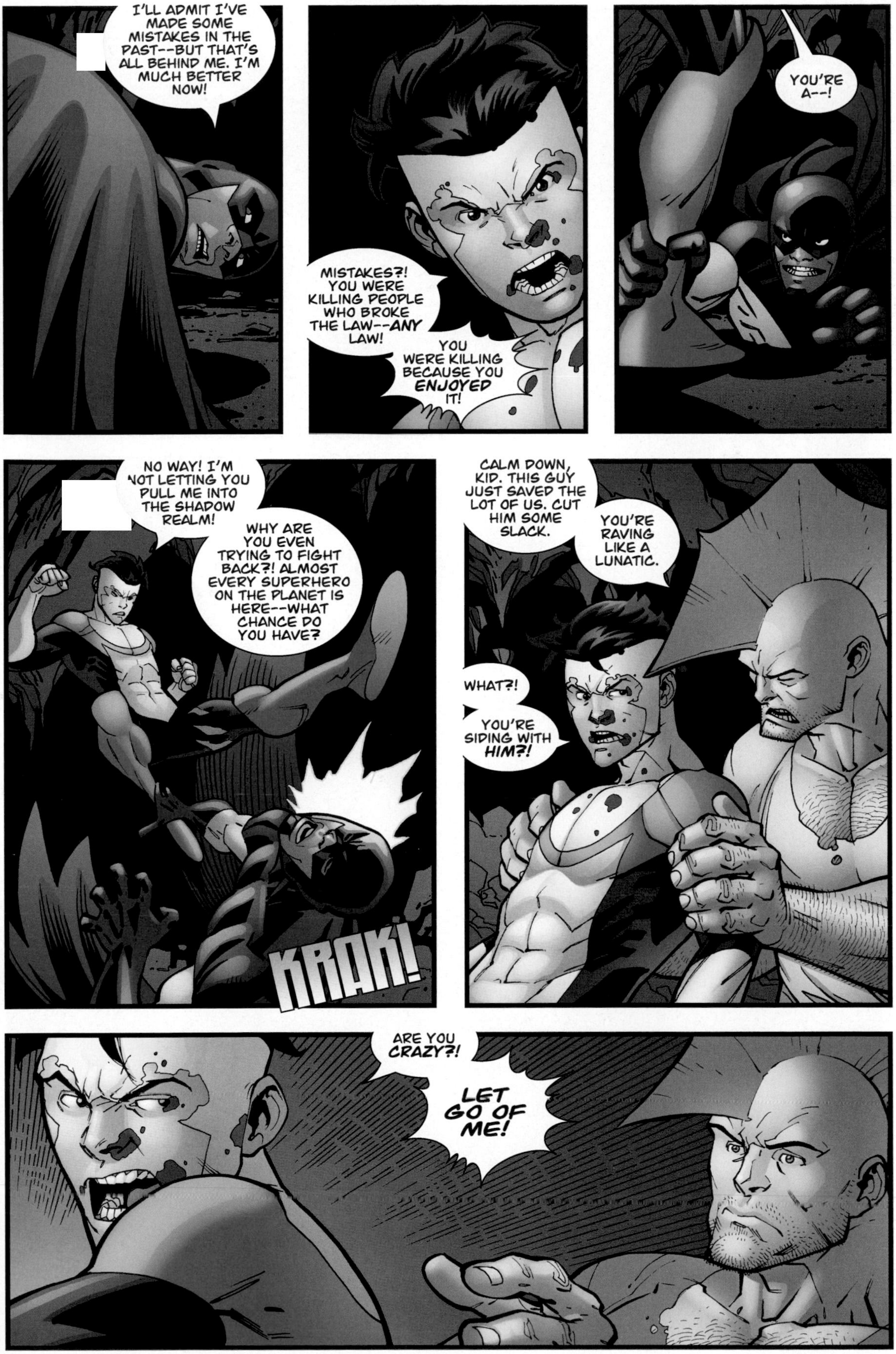
I'LL ADMIT I'VE MADE SOME MISTAKES IN THE PAST--BUT THAT'S ALL BEHIND ME. I'M MUCH BETTER NOW!
MISTAKES?! YOU WERE KILLING PEOPLE WHO BROKE THE LAW--ANY LAW!
YOU WERE KILLING BECAUSE YOU ENJOYED IT!
YOU'RE A--!
NO WAY! I'M NOT LETTING YOU PULL ME INTO THE SHADOW REALM!
WHY ARE YOU EVEN TRYING TO FIGHT BACK?! ALMOST EVERY SUPERHERO ON THE PLANET IS HERE--WHAT CHANCE DO YOU HAVE?
KRAK!
CALM DOWN, KID. THIS GUY JUST SAVED THE LOT OF US. CUT HIM SOME SLACK.
YOU'RE RAVING LIKE A LUNATIC.
WHAT?!
YOU'RE SIDING WITH HIM?!
ARE YOU CRAZY?!
LET GO OF ME!

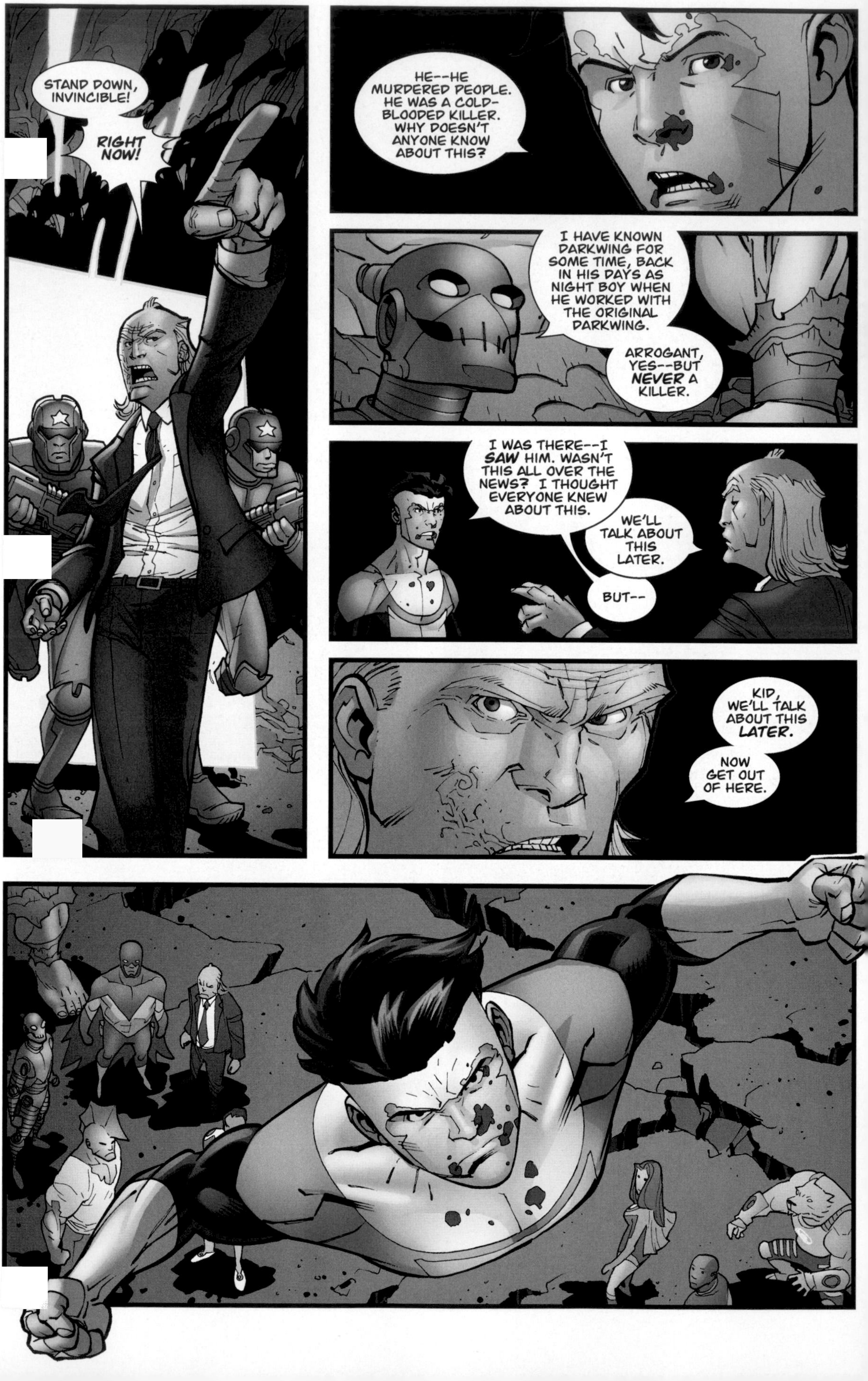
STAND DOWN, INVINCIBLE!
RIGHT NOW!
HE--HE MURDERED PEOPLE. HE WAS A COLD-BLOODED KILLER. WHY DOESN'T ANYONE KNOW ABOUT THIS?
I HAVE KNOWN DARKWING FOR SOME TIME, BACK IN HIS DAYS AS NIGHT BOY WHEN HE WORKED WITH THE ORIGINAL DARKWING.
ARROGANT, YES--BUT NEVER A KILLER.
I WAS THERE--I SAW HIM. WASN'T THIS ALL OVER THE NEWS? I THOUGHT EVERYONE KNEW ABOUT THIS.
WE'LL TALK ABOUT THIS LATER.
BUT--
KID, WE'LL TALK ABOUT THIS LATER.
NOW GET OUT OF HERE.

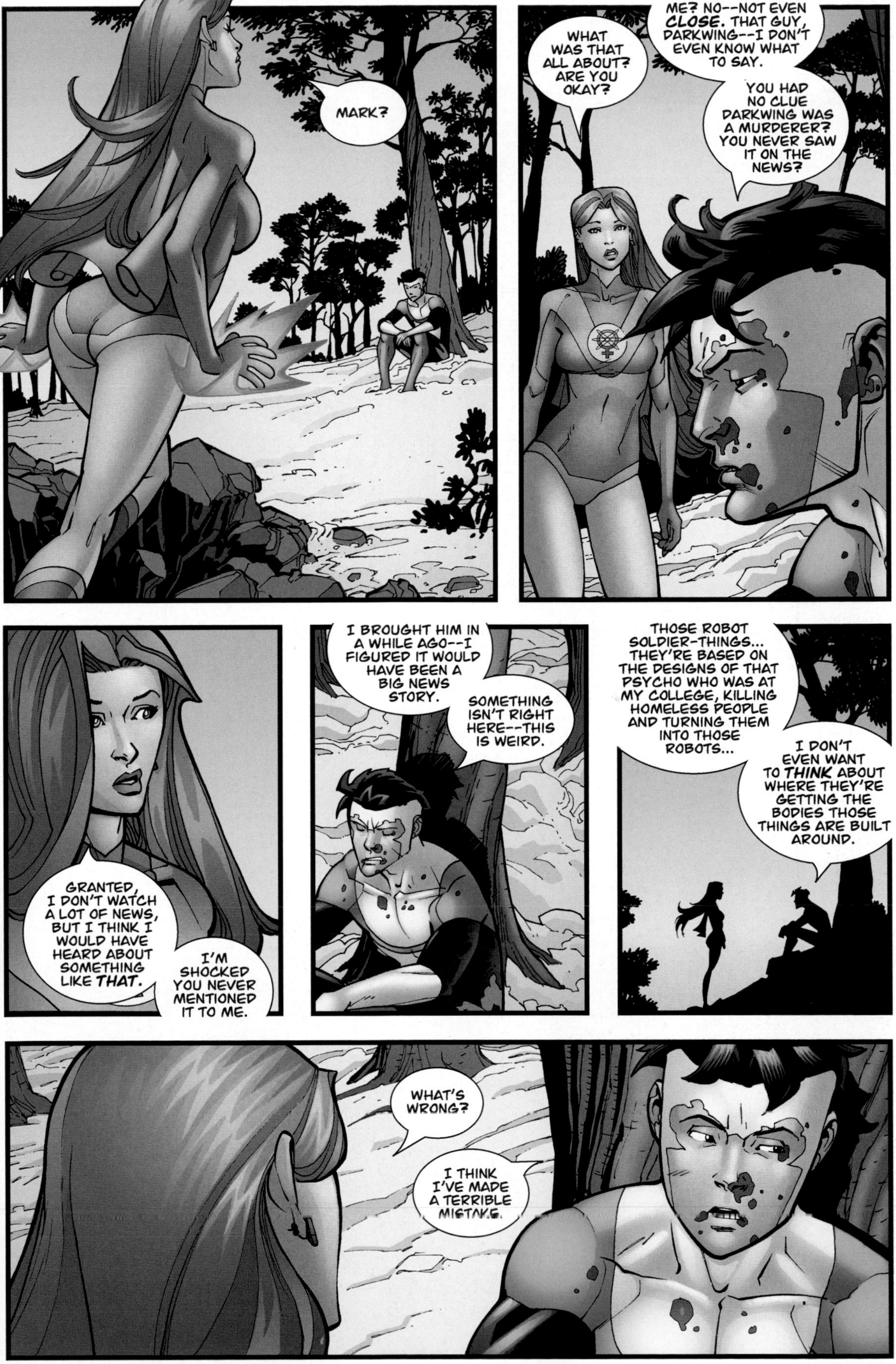

MARK?
WHAT WAS THAT ALL ABOUT? ARE YOU OKAY?
ME? NO--NOT EVEN CLOSE. THAT GUY, DARKWING--I DON'T EVEN KNOW WHAT TO SAY.
YOU HAD NO CLUE DARKWING WAS A MURDERER? YOU NEVER SAW IT ON THE NEWS?
GRANTED, I DON'T WATCH A LOT OF NEWS, BUT I THINK I WOULD HAVE HEARD ABOUT SOMETHING LIKE THAT.
I'M SHOCKED YOU NEVER MENTIONED IT TO ME.
I BROUGHT HIM IN A WHILE AGO--I FIGURED IT WOULD HAVE BEEN A BIG NEWS STORY.
SOMETHING ISN'T RIGHT HERE--THIS IS WEIRD.
THOSE ROBOT SOLDIER-THINGS... THEY'RE BASED ON THE DESIGNS OF THAT PSYCHO WHO WAS AT MY COLLEGE, KILLING HOMELESS PEOPLE AND TURNING THEM INTO THOSE ROBOTS...
I DON'T EVEN WANT TO THINK ABOUT WHERE THEY'RE GETTING THE BODIES THOSE THINGS ARE BUILT AROUND.
WHAT'S WRONG?
I THINK I'VE MADE A TERRIBLE MISTAKE.

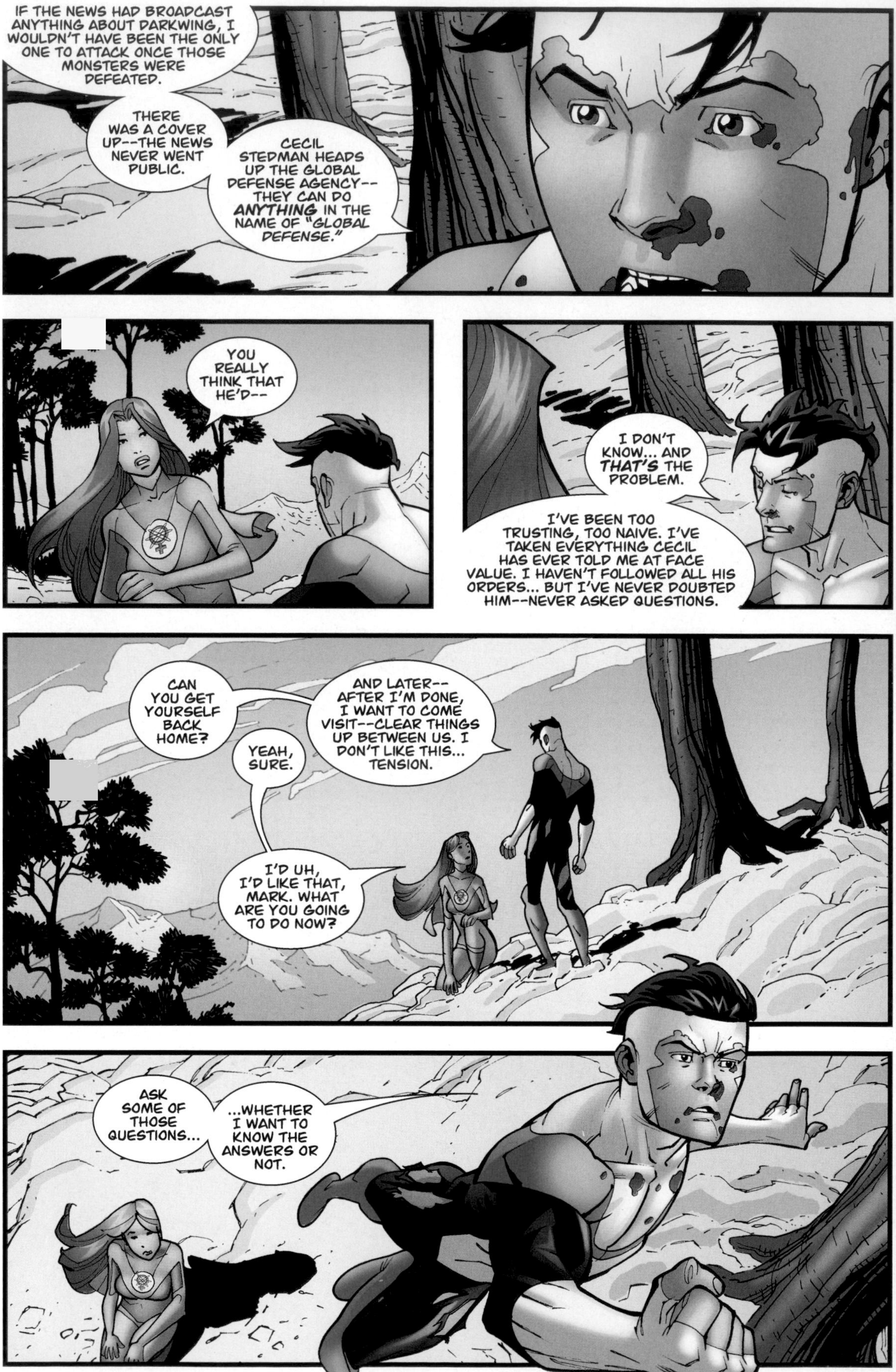
IF THE NEWS HAD BROADCAST ANYTHING ABOUT DARKWING, I WOULDN'T HAVE BEEN THE ONLY ONE TO ATTACK ONCE THOSE MONSTERS WERE DEFEATED.
THERE WAS A COVER UP--THE NEWS NEVER WENT PUBLIC.
CECIL STEDMAN HEADS UP THE GLOBAL DEFENSE AGENCY--THEY CAN DO ANYTHING IN THE NAME OF "GLOBAL DEFENSE."
YOU REALLY THINK THAT HE'D--
I DON'T KNOW... AND THAT'S THE PROBLEM.
I'VE BEEN TOO TRUSTING, TOO NAIVE. I'VE TAKEN EVERYTHING CECIL HAS EVER TOLD ME AT FACE VALUE. I HAVEN'T FOLLOWED ALL HIS ORDERS... BUT I'VE NEVER DOUBTED HIM--NEVER ASKED QUESTIONS.
CAN YOU GET YOURSELF BACK HOME?
AND LATER--AFTER I'M DONE, I WANT TO COME VISIT--CLEAR THINGS UP BETWEEN US. I DON'T LIKE THIS... TENSION.
YEAH, SURE.
I'D UH, I'D LIKE THAT, MARK. WHAT ARE YOU GOING TO DO NOW?
ASK SOME OF THOSE QUESTIONS...
...WHETHER I WANT TO KNOW THE ANSWERS OR NOT.

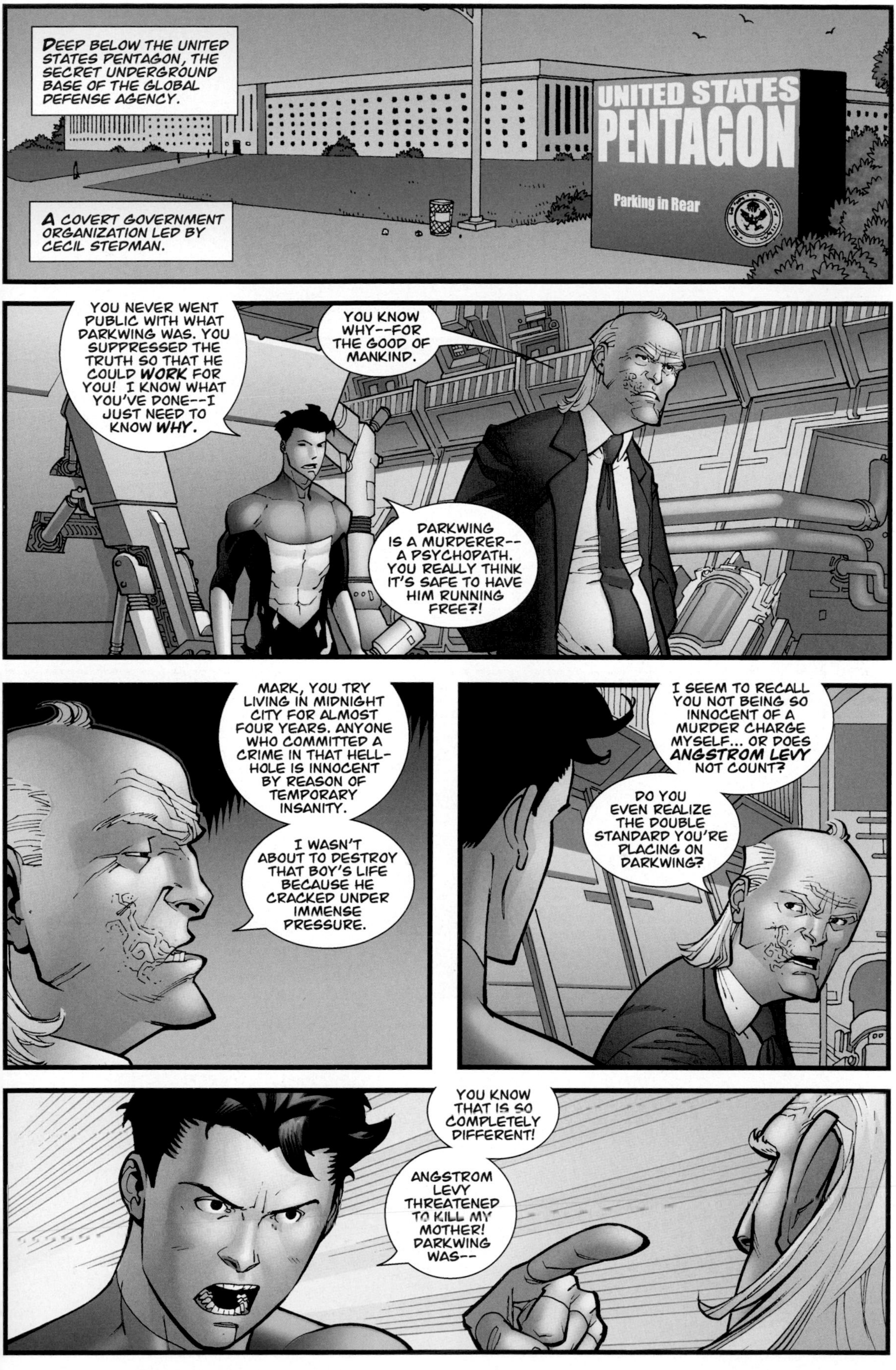
DEEP BELOW THE UNITED STATES PENTAGON, THE SECRET UNDERGROUND BASE OF THE GLOBAL DEFENSE AGENCY.
UNITED STATES PENTAGON
Parking in Rear
A COVERT GOVERNMENT ORGANIZATION LED BY CECIL STEDMAN.
YOU NEVER WENT PUBLIC WITH WHAT DARKWING WAS. YOU SUPPRESSED THE TRUTH SO THAT HE COULD WORK FOR YOU! I KNOW WHAT YOU'VE DONE--I JUST NEED TO KNOW WHY.
YOU KNOW WHY--FOR THE GOOD OF MANKIND.
DARKWING IS A MURDERER--A PSYCHOPATH. YOU REALLY THINK IT'S SAFE TO HAVE HIM RUNNING FREE?!
MARK, YOU TRY LIVING IN MIDNIGHT CITY FOR ALMOST FOUR YEARS. ANYONE WHO COMMITTED A CRIME IN THAT HELL-HOLE IS INNOCENT BY REASON OF TEMPORARY INSANITY.
I WASN'T ABOUT TO DESTROY THAT BOY'S LIFE BECAUSE HE CRACKED UNDER IMMENSE PRESSURE.
I SEEM TO RECALL YOU NOT BEING SO INNOCENT OF A MURDER CHARGE MYSELF... OR DOES ANGSTROM LEVY NOT COUNT?
DO YOU EVEN REALIZE THE DOUBLE STANDARD YOU'RE PLACING ON DARKWING?
YOU KNOW THAT IS SO COMPLETELY DIFFERENT!
ANGSTROM LEVY THREATENED TO KILL MY MOTHER! DARKWING WAS--

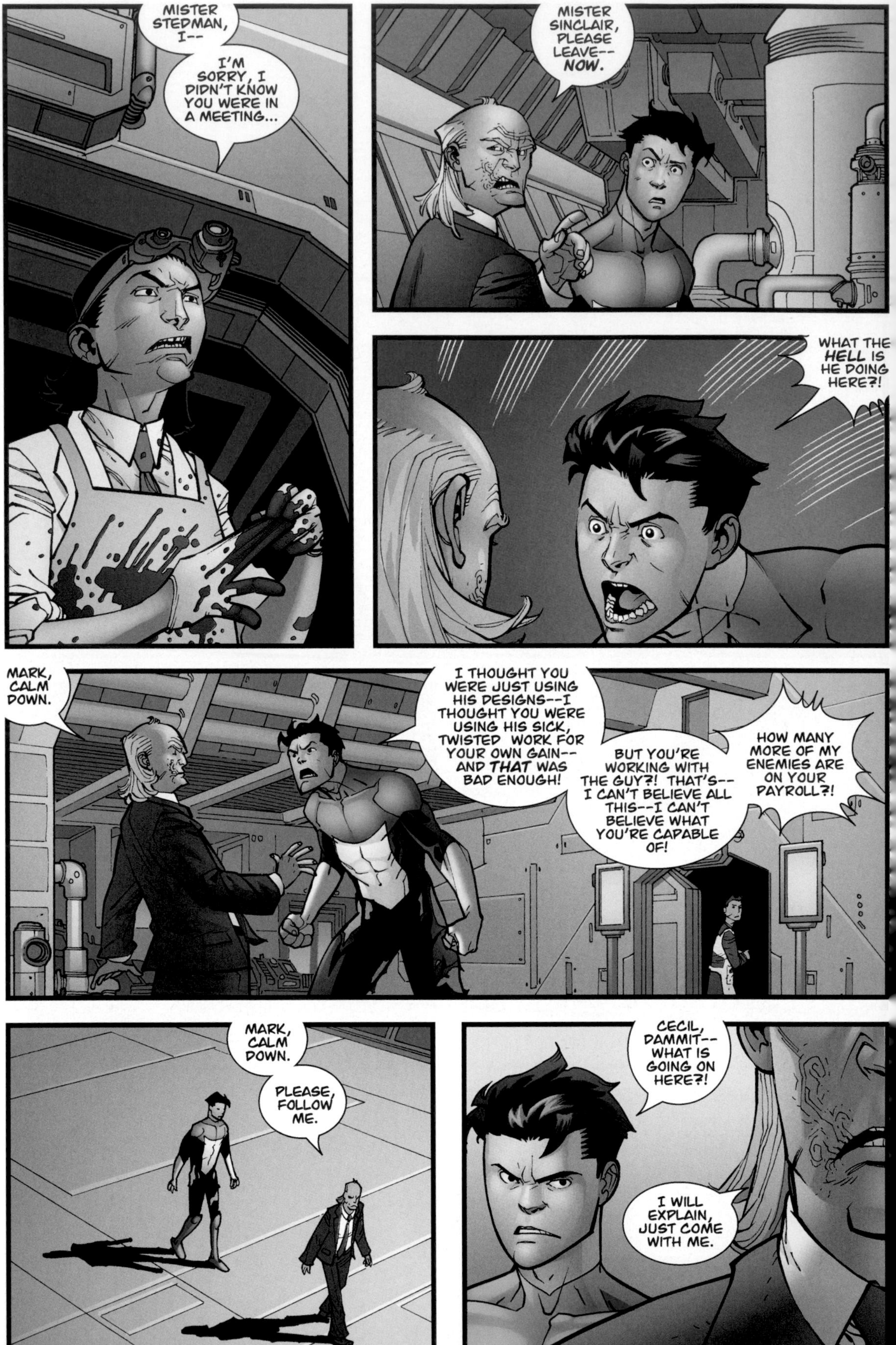

MISTER STEDMAN, I--
I'M SORRY, I DIDN'T KNOW YOU WERE IN A MEETING...
MISTER SINCLAIR, PLEASE LEAVE-- NOW.
WHAT THE HELL IS HE DOING HERE?!
MARK, CALM DOWN.
I THOUGHT YOU WERE JUST USING HIS DESIGNS--I THOUGHT YOU WERE USING HIS SICK, TWISTED WORK FOR YOUR OWN GAIN-- AND THAT WAS BAD ENOUGH!
BUT YOU'RE WORKING WITH THE GUY?! THAT'S-- I CAN'T BELIEVE ALL THIS--I CAN'T BELIEVE WHAT YOU'RE CAPABLE OF!
HOW MANY MORE OF MY ENEMIES ARE ON YOUR PAYROLL?!
MARK, CALM DOWN.
PLEASE, FOLLOW ME.
CECIL, DAMMIT-- WHAT IS GOING ON HERE?!
I WILL EXPLAIN, JUST COME WITH ME.

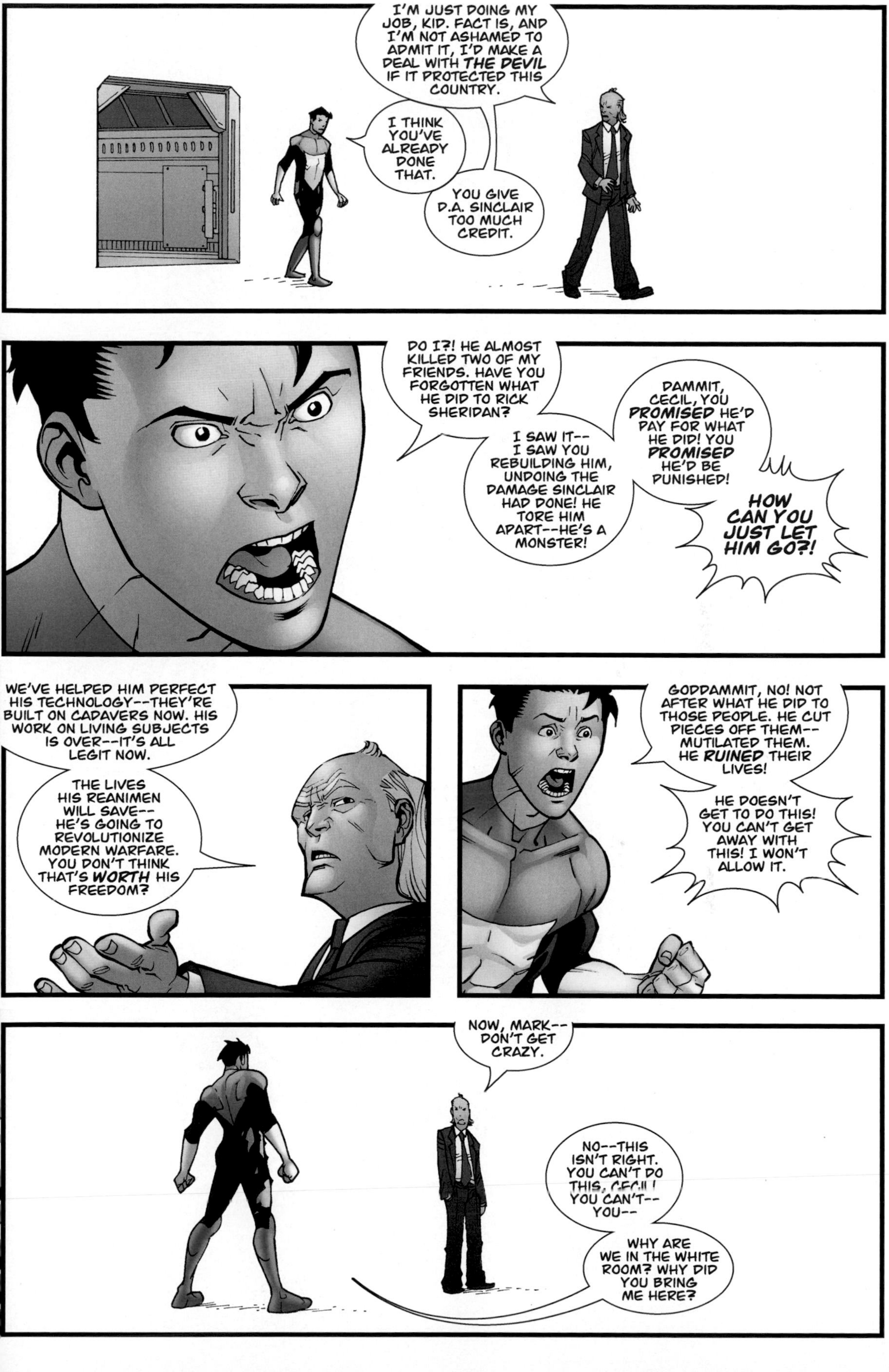

I'M JUST DOING MY JOB, KID. FACT IS, AND I'M NOT ASHAMED TO ADMIT IT, I'D MAKE A DEAL WITH THE DEVIL IF IT PROTECTED THIS COUNTRY.
I THINK YOU'VE ALREADY DONE THAT.
YOU GIVE D.A. SINCLAIR TOO MUCH CREDIT.
DO I?! HE ALMOST KILLED TWO OF MY FRIENDS. HAVE YOU FORGOTTEN WHAT HE DID TO RICK SHERIDAN?
I SAW IT-- I SAW YOU REBUILDING HIM, UNDOING THE DAMAGE SINCLAIR HAD DONE! HE TORE HIM APART--HE'S A MONSTER!
DAMMIT, CECIL, YOU PROMISED HE'D PAY FOR WHAT HE DID! YOU PROMISED HE'D BE PUNISHED!
HOW CAN YOU JUST LET HIM GO?!
WE'VE HELPED HIM PERFECT HIS TECHNOLOGY--THEY'RE BUILT ON CADAVERS NOW. HIS WORK ON LIVING SUBJECTS IS OVER--IT'S ALL LEGIT NOW.
THE LIVES HIS REANIMEN WILL SAVE-- HE'S GOING TO REVOLUTIONIZE MODERN WARFARE. YOU DON'T THINK THAT'S WORTH HIS FREEDOM?
GODDAMMIT, NO! NOT AFTER WHAT HE DID TO THOSE PEOPLE. HE CUT PIECES OFF THEM-- MUTILATED THEM. HE RUINED THEIR LIVES!
HE DOESN'T GET TO DO THIS! YOU CAN'T GET AWAY WITH THIS! I WON'T ALLOW IT.
NOW, MARK-- DON'T GET CRAZY.
NO--THIS ISN'T RIGHT. YOU CAN'T DO THIS, CECIL! YOU CAN'T-- YOU--
WHY ARE WE IN THE WHITE ROOM? WHY DID YOU BRING ME HERE?

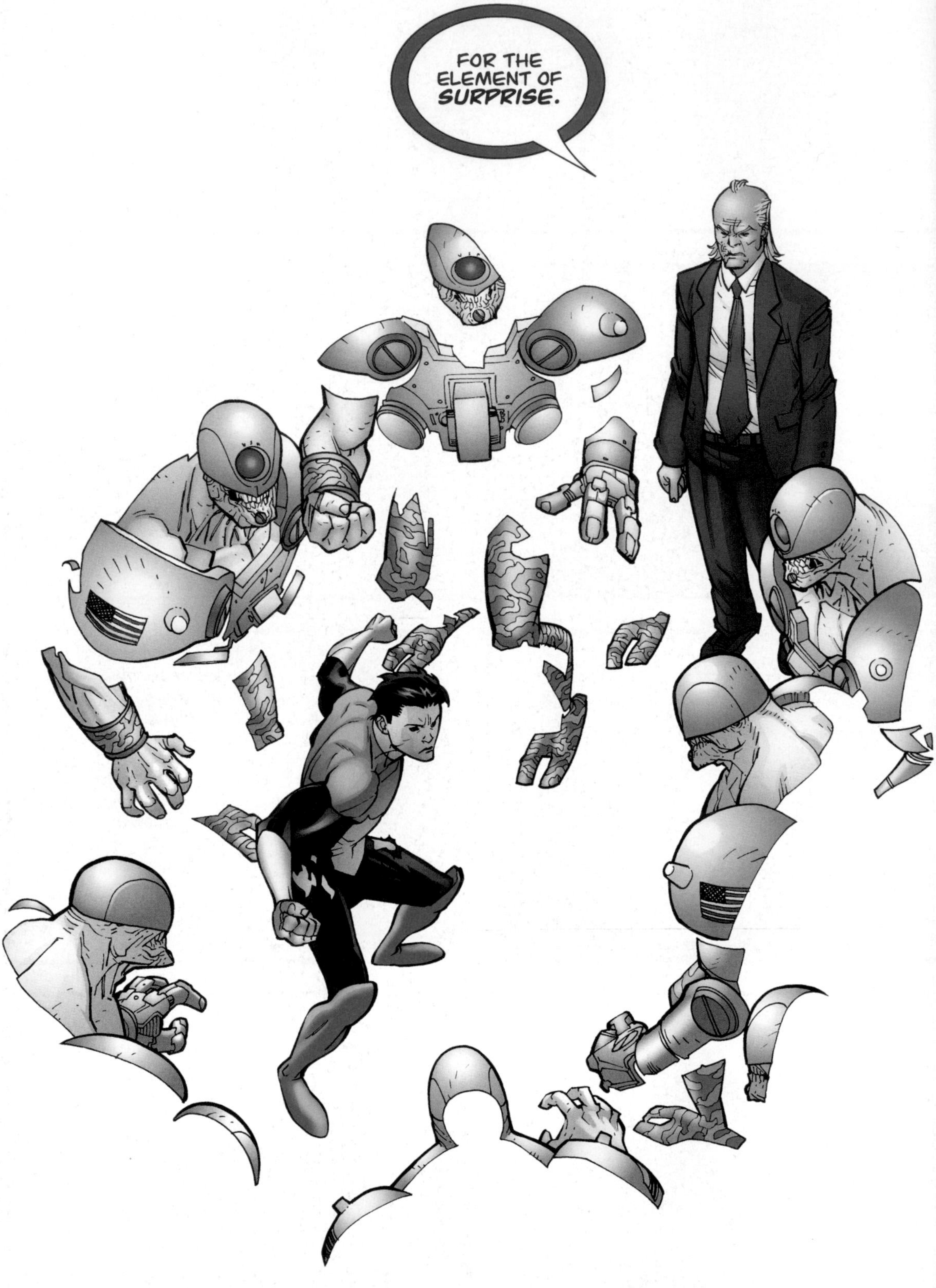
FOR THE ELEMENT OF SURPRISE.

CHAPTER THREE

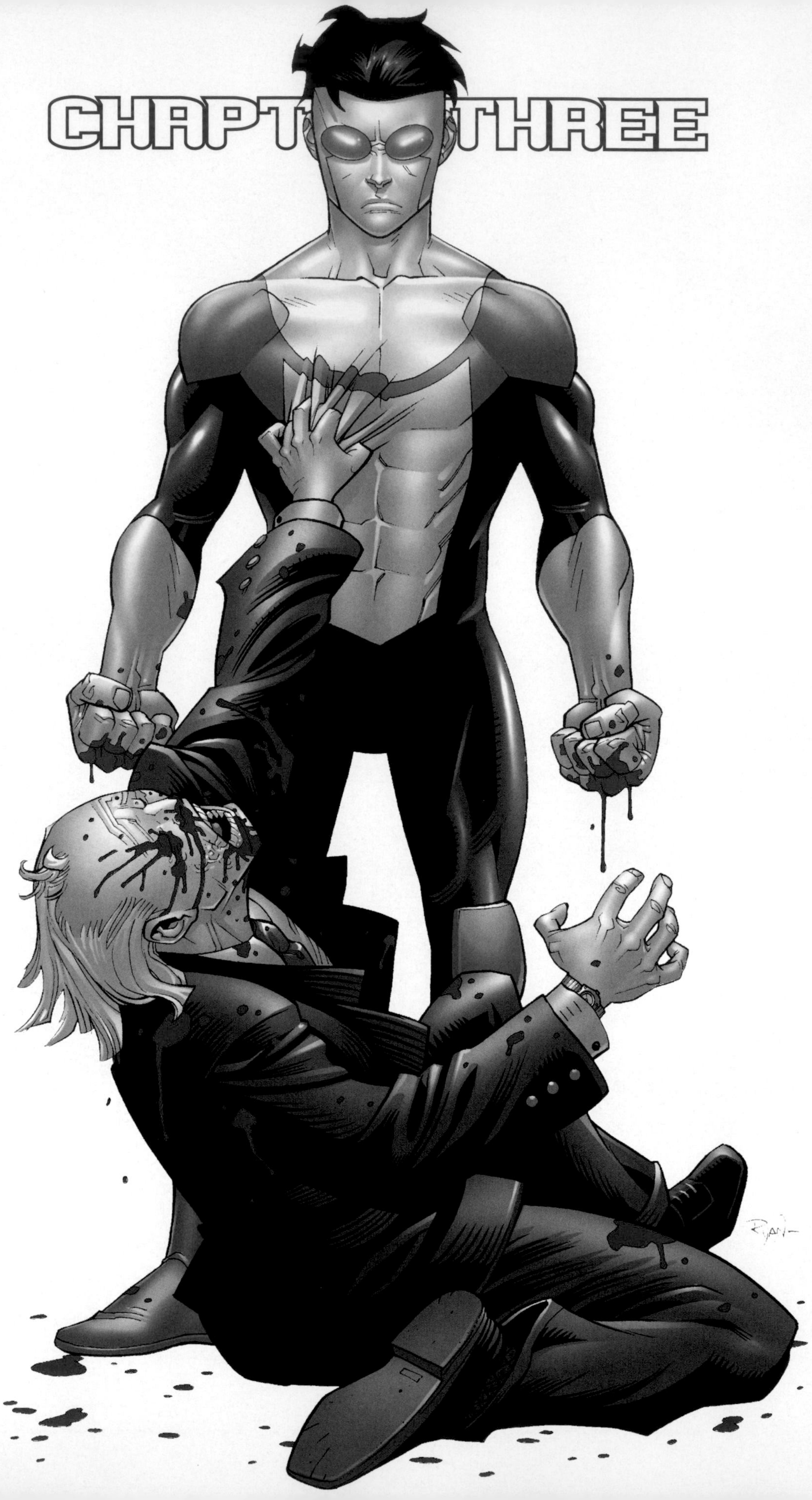

WHAT IS *THIS*?!

YOU THINK I DON'T *KNOW* WHAT COMES NEXT? YOU TALK LIKE YOU'RE TALKING-- THEN YOU FLIP OUT. YOU'RE A LOOSE CANNON, MARK.

I DON'T PARTICULARLY WISH TO END UP LIKE ANGSTROM LEVY.

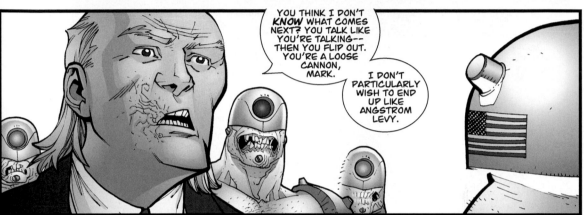

ANGSTROM LEVY WAS AN ACCIDENT!!

VRAKOOM!!

I CAME HERE TO CONFRONT YOU FOR WORKING WITH EVIL, MURDEROUS PEOPLE--AND YOU'RE ATTACKING *ME* FOR IT?! MAKING ME OUT TO BE THE BAD GUY?!

THIS ISN'T RIGHT!

VRAMM!!

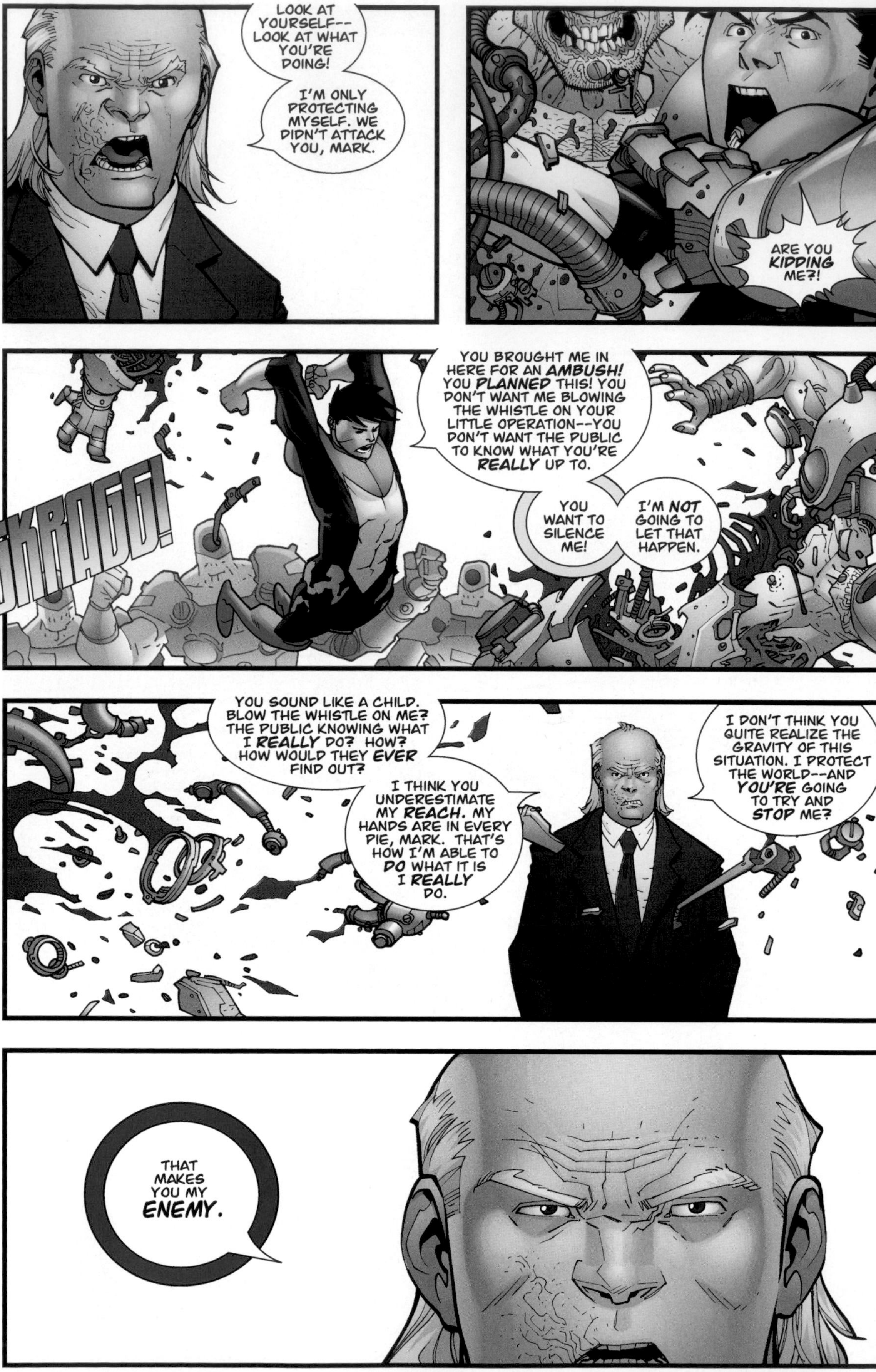

LOOK AT YOURSELF--LOOK AT WHAT YOU'RE DOING!
I'M ONLY PROTECTING MYSELF. WE DIDN'T ATTACK YOU, MARK.
ARE YOU KIDDING ME?!
SKRAGG!
YOU BROUGHT ME IN HERE FOR AN AMBUSH! YOU PLANNED THIS! YOU DON'T WANT ME BLOWING THE WHISTLE ON YOUR LITTLE OPERATION--YOU DON'T WANT THE PUBLIC TO KNOW WHAT YOU'RE REALLY UP TO.
YOU WANT TO SILENCE ME!
I'M NOT GOING TO LET THAT HAPPEN.
YOU SOUND LIKE A CHILD. BLOW THE WHISTLE ON ME? THE PUBLIC KNOWING WHAT I REALLY DO? HOW? HOW WOULD THEY EVER FIND OUT?
I THINK YOU UNDERESTIMATE MY REACH. MY HANDS ARE IN EVERY PIE, MARK. THAT'S HOW I'M ABLE TO DO WHAT IT IS I REALLY DO.
I DON'T THINK YOU QUITE REALIZE THE GRAVITY OF THIS SITUATION. I PROTECT THE WORLD--AND YOU'RE GOING TO TRY AND STOP ME?
THAT MAKES YOU MY ENEMY.

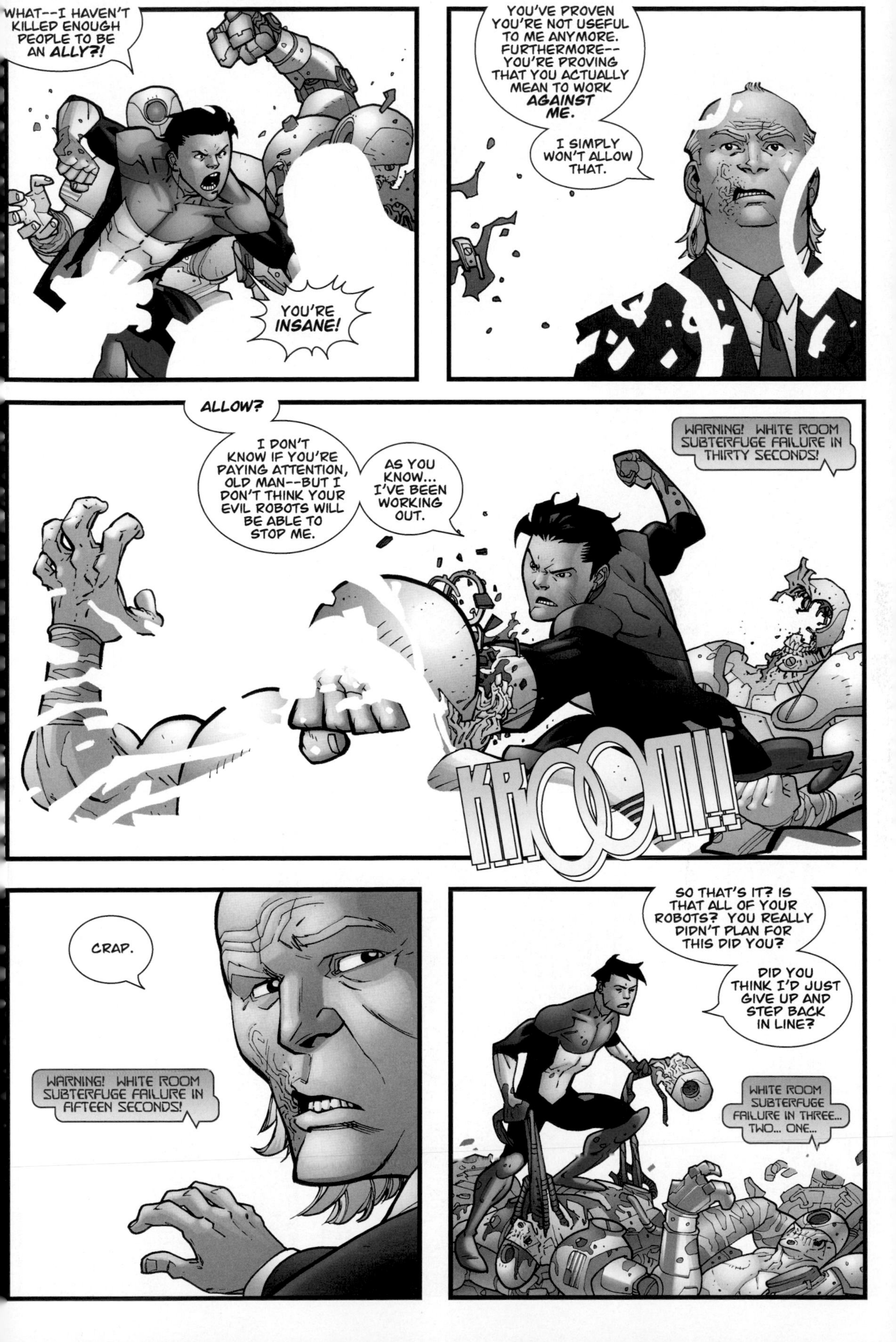
WHAT--I HAVEN'T KILLED ENOUGH PEOPLE TO BE AN ALLY?!
YOU'RE INSANE!
YOU'VE PROVEN YOU'RE NOT USEFUL TO ME ANYMORE. FURTHERMORE-- YOU'RE PROVING THAT YOU ACTUALLY MEAN TO WORK AGAINST ME.
I SIMPLY WON'T ALLOW THAT.
ALLOW?
I DON'T KNOW IF YOU'RE PAYING ATTENTION, OLD MAN--BUT I DON'T THINK YOUR EVIL ROBOTS WILL BE ABLE TO STOP ME.
AS YOU KNOW... I'VE BEEN WORKING OUT.
WARNING! WHITE ROOM SUBTERFUGE FAILURE IN THIRTY SECONDS!
KROOOM!!
CRAP.
WARNING! WHITE ROOM SUBTERFUGE FAILURE IN FIFTEEN SECONDS!
SO THAT'S IT? IS THAT ALL OF YOUR ROBOTS? YOU REALLY DIDN'T PLAN FOR THIS DID YOU?
DID YOU THINK I'D JUST GIVE UP AND STEP BACK IN LINE?
WHITE ROOM SUBTERFUGE FAILURE IN THREE... TWO... ONE...

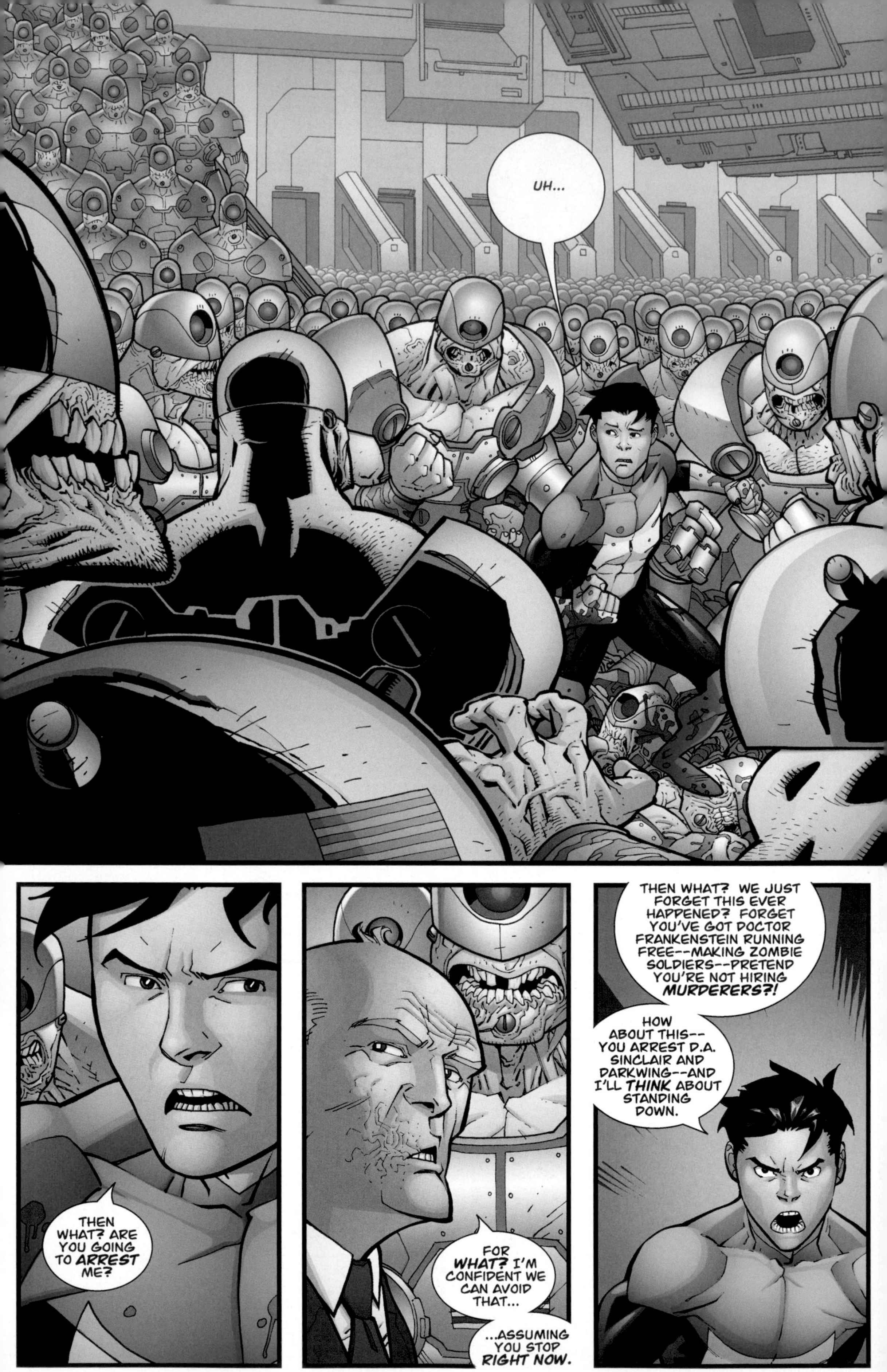
UH...
THEN WHAT? ARE YOU GOING TO ARREST ME?
FOR WHAT? I'M CONFIDENT WE CAN AVOID THAT...
...ASSUMING YOU STOP RIGHT NOW.
THEN WHAT? WE JUST FORGET THIS EVER HAPPENED? FORGET YOU'VE GOT DOCTOR FRANKENSTEIN RUNNING FREE--MAKING ZOMBIE SOLDIERS--PRETEND YOU'RE NOT HIRING MURDERERS?!
HOW ABOUT THIS--YOU ARREST D.A. SINCLAIR AND DARKWING--AND I'LL THINK ABOUT STANDING DOWN.

YEAH, WE COULD BE HERE ALL DAY AT THE RATE YOU'RE GOING.

SO WHY DON'T YOU JUST GIVE UP?

IF YOU'RE NOT GOING TO CONTINUE WORKING FOR ME--THEN I'LL NEED THEM MORE THAN EVER.

NO, I'M SORRY THAT ME WORKING WITH THEM INTERFERES WITH YOUR STRICT VIEWS ON RIGHT AND WRONG THAT ARE BORN OUT OF A NEED TO PROVE YOU'RE NOT YOUR FATHER--BUT I WON'T STOP WORKING WITH THEM ANY TIME SOON.

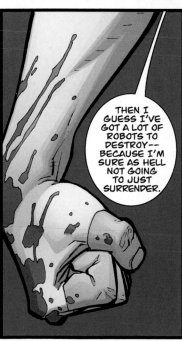

THEN I GUESS I'VE GOT A LOT OF ROBOTS TO DESTROY-- BECAUSE I'M SURE AS HELL NOT GOING TO JUST SURRENDER.

ACTUALLY, I THINK YOU'VE COST THE AMERICAN TAXPAYERS QUITE ENOUGH ALREADY. I'VE GOT A MUCH MORE EFFICIENT WAY OF KEEPING YOU IN CHECK.

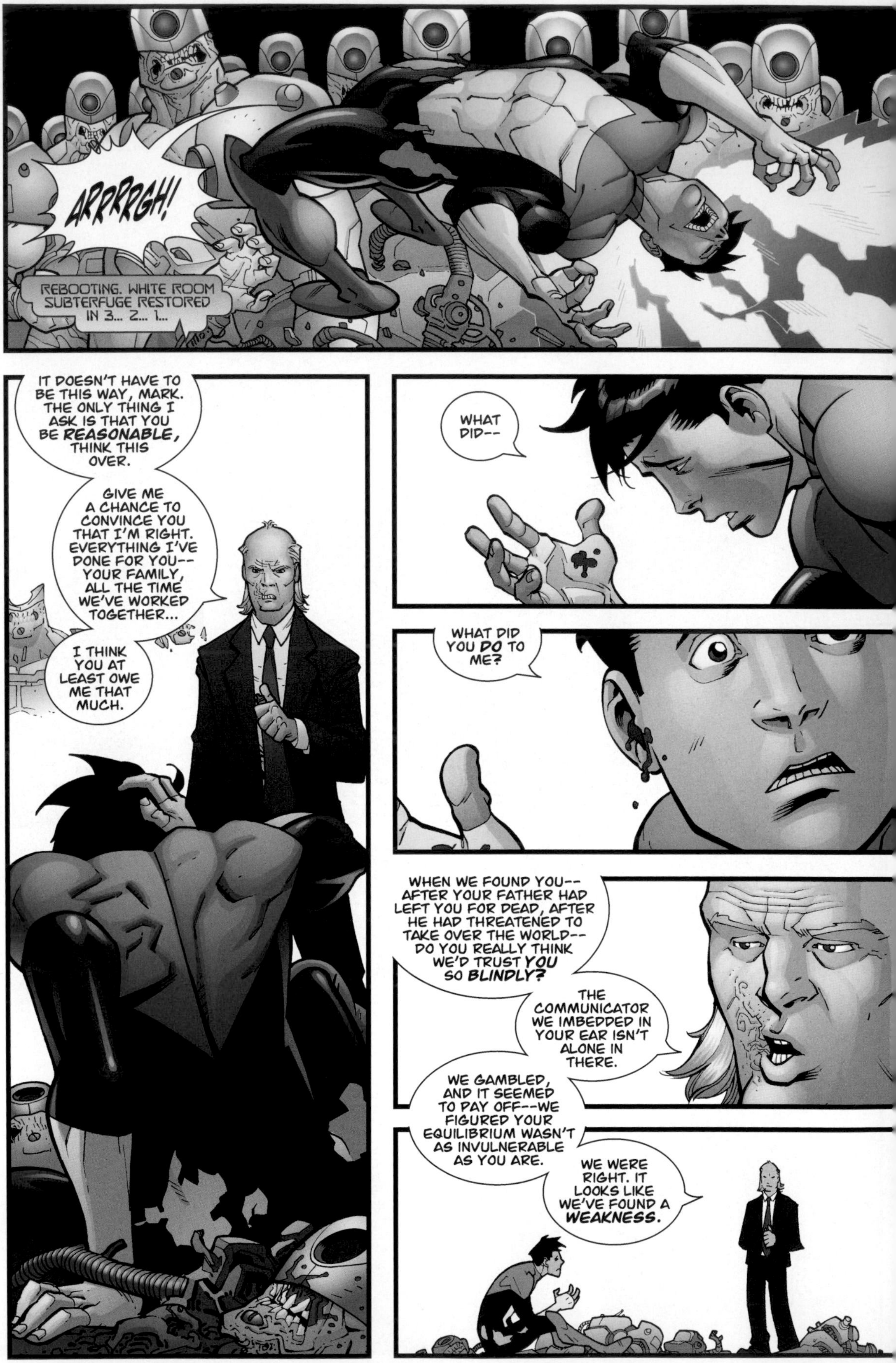
ARRRRGH!
REBOOTING. WHITE ROOM SUBTERFUGE RESTORED IN 3... 2... 1...
IT DOESN'T HAVE TO BE THIS WAY, MARK. THE ONLY THING I ASK IS THAT YOU BE REASONABLE, THINK THIS OVER.
GIVE ME A CHANCE TO CONVINCE YOU THAT I'M RIGHT. EVERYTHING I'VE DONE FOR YOU-- YOUR FAMILY, ALL THE TIME WE'VE WORKED TOGETHER...
I THINK YOU AT LEAST OWE ME THAT MUCH.
WHAT DID--
WHAT DID YOU DO TO ME?
WHEN WE FOUND YOU-- AFTER YOUR FATHER HAD LEFT YOU FOR DEAD, AFTER HE HAD THREATENED TO TAKE OVER THE WORLD-- DO YOU REALLY THINK WE'D TRUST YOU SO BLINDLY?
THE COMMUNICATOR WE IMBEDDED IN YOUR EAR ISN'T ALONE IN THERE.
WE GAMBLED, AND IT SEEMED TO PAY OFF--WE FIGURED YOUR EQUILIBRIUM WASN'T AS INVULNERABLE AS YOU ARE.
WE WERE RIGHT. IT LOOKS LIKE WE'VE FOUND A WEAKNESS.

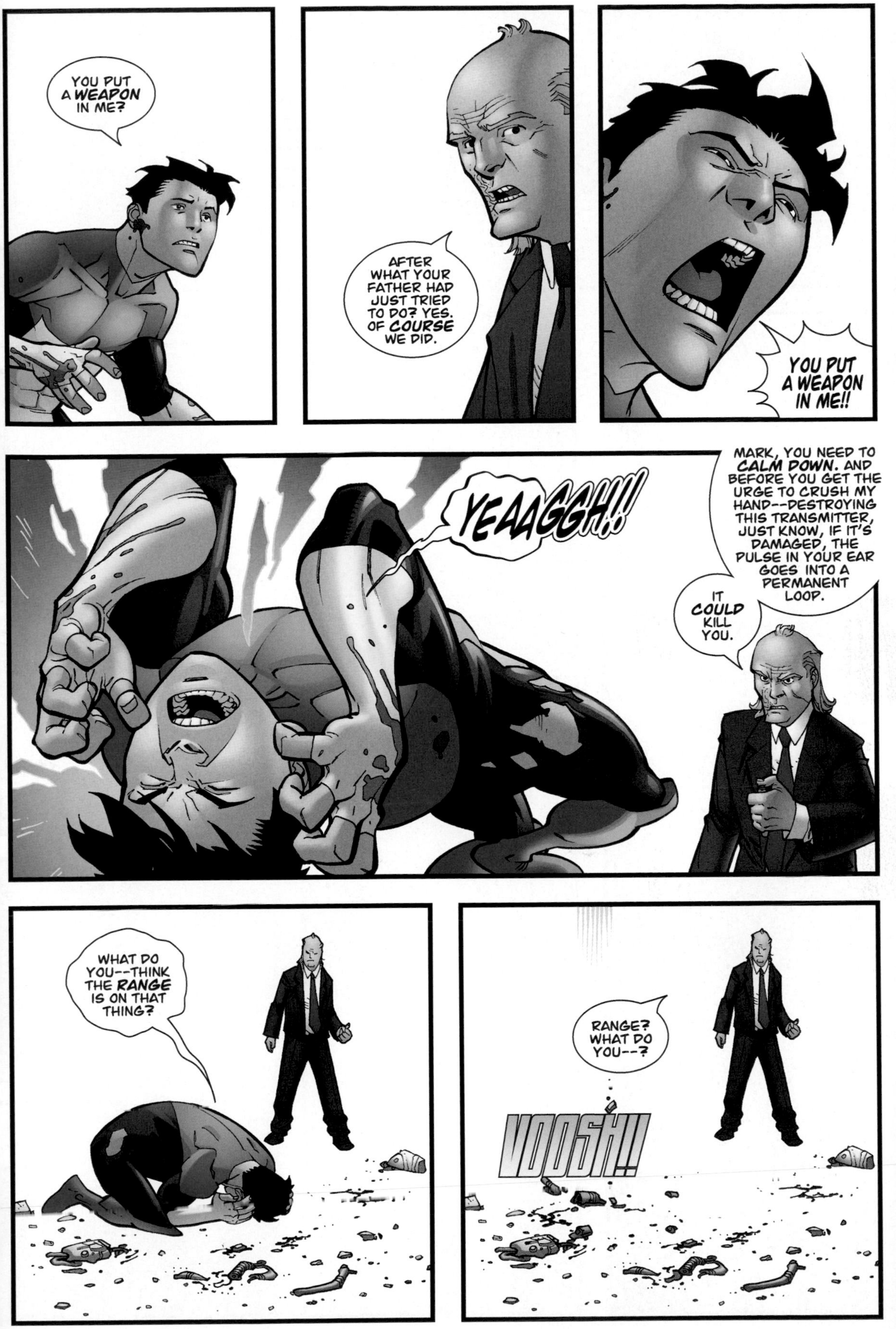
YOU PUT A WEAPON IN ME?
AFTER WHAT YOUR FATHER HAD JUST TRIED TO DO? YES. OF COURSE WE DID.
YOU PUT A WEAPON IN ME!!
YEAAGGH!!
MARK, YOU NEED TO CALM DOWN. AND BEFORE YOU GET THE URGE TO CRUSH MY HAND--DESTROYING THIS TRANSMITTER, JUST KNOW, IF IT'S DAMAGED, THE PULSE IN YOUR EAR GOES INTO A PERMANENT LOOP.
IT COULD KILL YOU.
WHAT DO YOU--THINK THE RANGE IS ON THAT THING?
RANGE? WHAT DO YOU--?
VOOSH!!

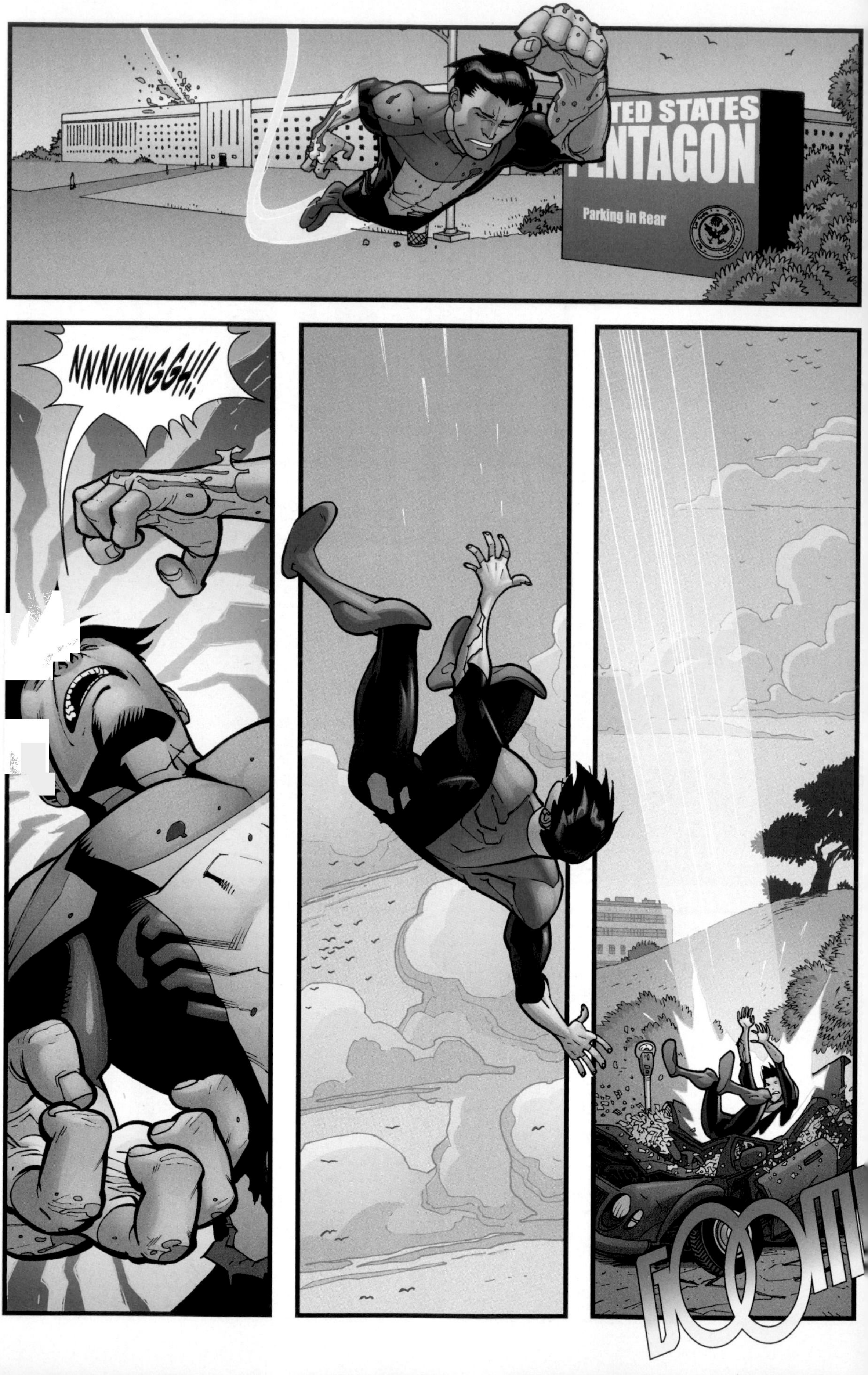
TED STATES
PENTAGON
Parking in Rear
NNNNNNGGH!!
GOOM

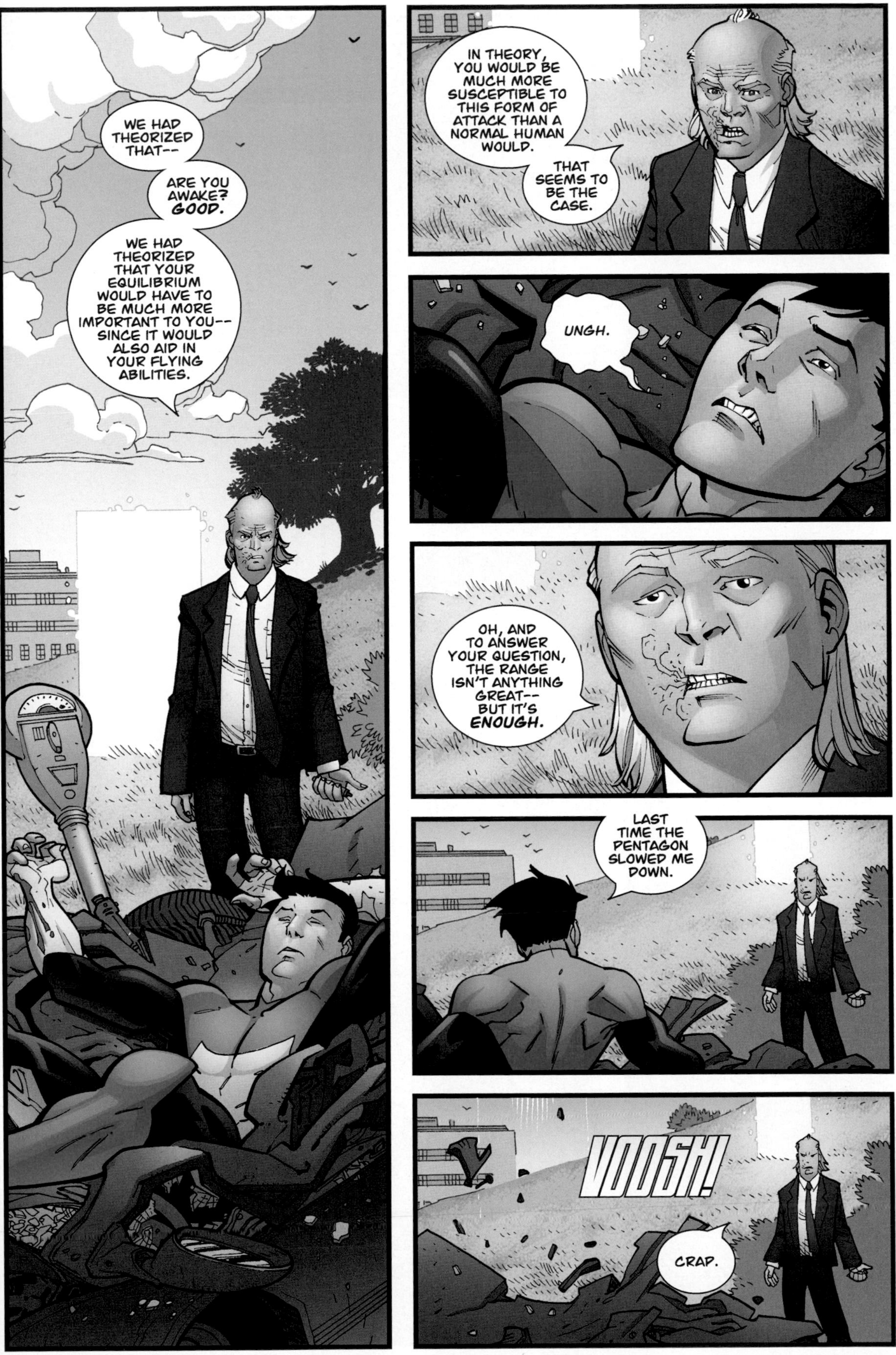
WE HAD THEORIZED THAT--
ARE YOU AWAKE? GOOD.
WE HAD THEORIZED THAT YOUR EQUILIBRIUM WOULD HAVE TO BE MUCH MORE IMPORTANT TO YOU-- SINCE IT WOULD ALSO AID IN YOUR FLYING ABILITIES.
IN THEORY, YOU WOULD BE MUCH MORE SUSCEPTIBLE TO THIS FORM OF ATTACK THAN A NORMAL HUMAN WOULD.
THAT SEEMS TO BE THE CASE.
UNGH.
OH, AND TO ANSWER YOUR QUESTION, THE RANGE ISN'T ANYTHING GREAT-- BUT IT'S ENOUGH.
LAST TIME THE PENTAGON SLOWED ME DOWN.
VOOSH!
CRAP.

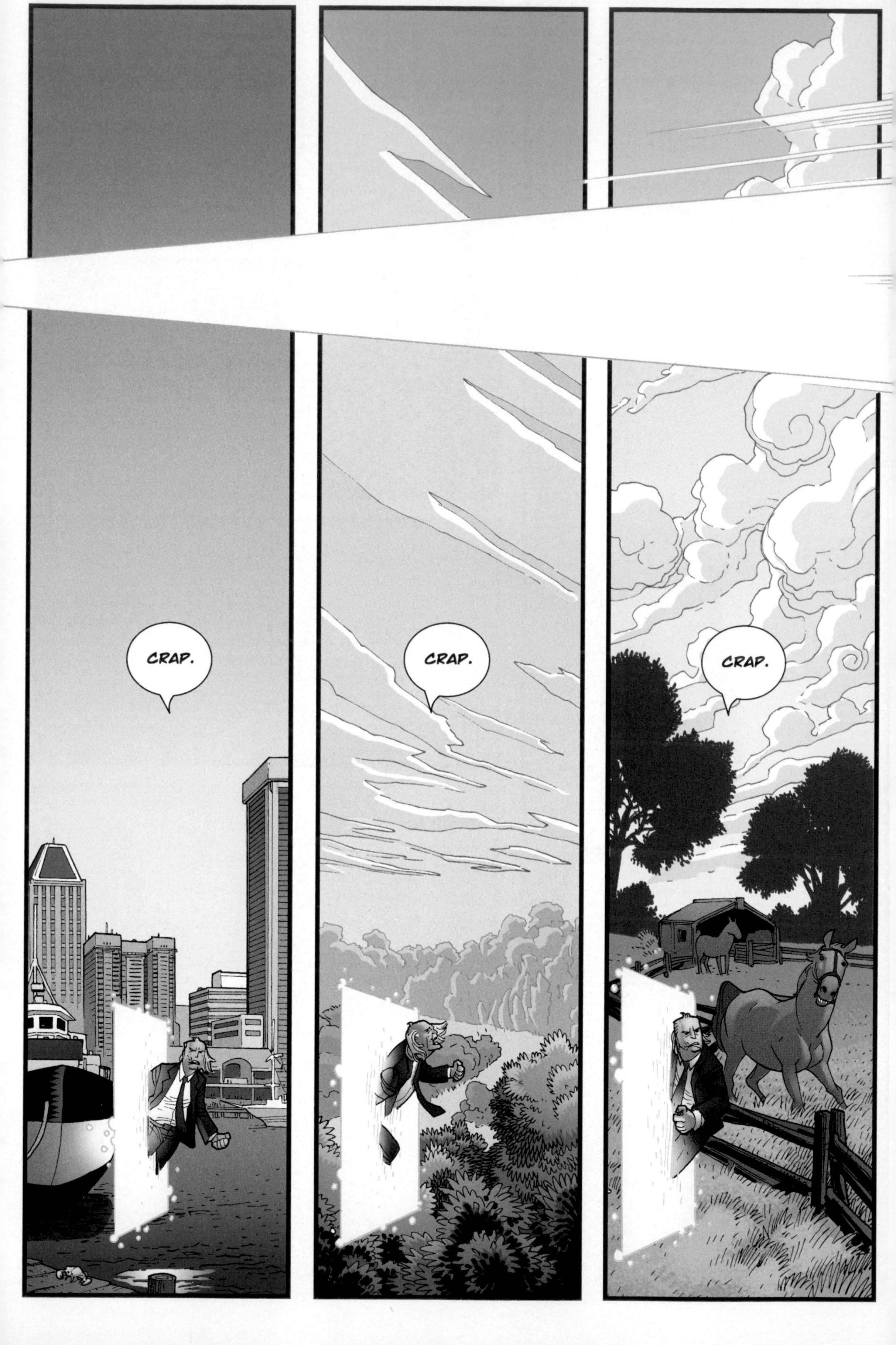
CRAP.
CRAP.
CRAP.

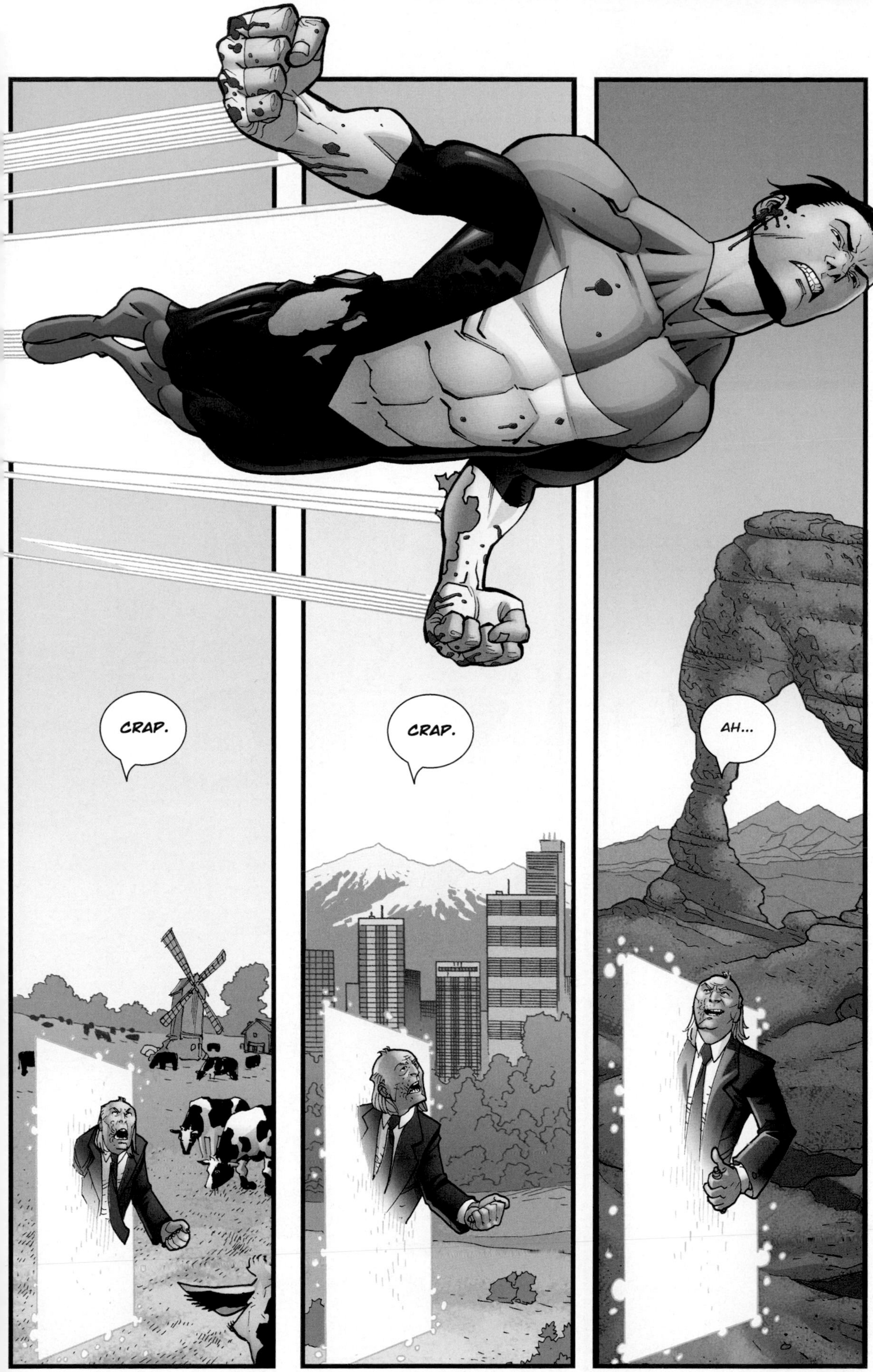
CRAP.
CRAP.
AH...

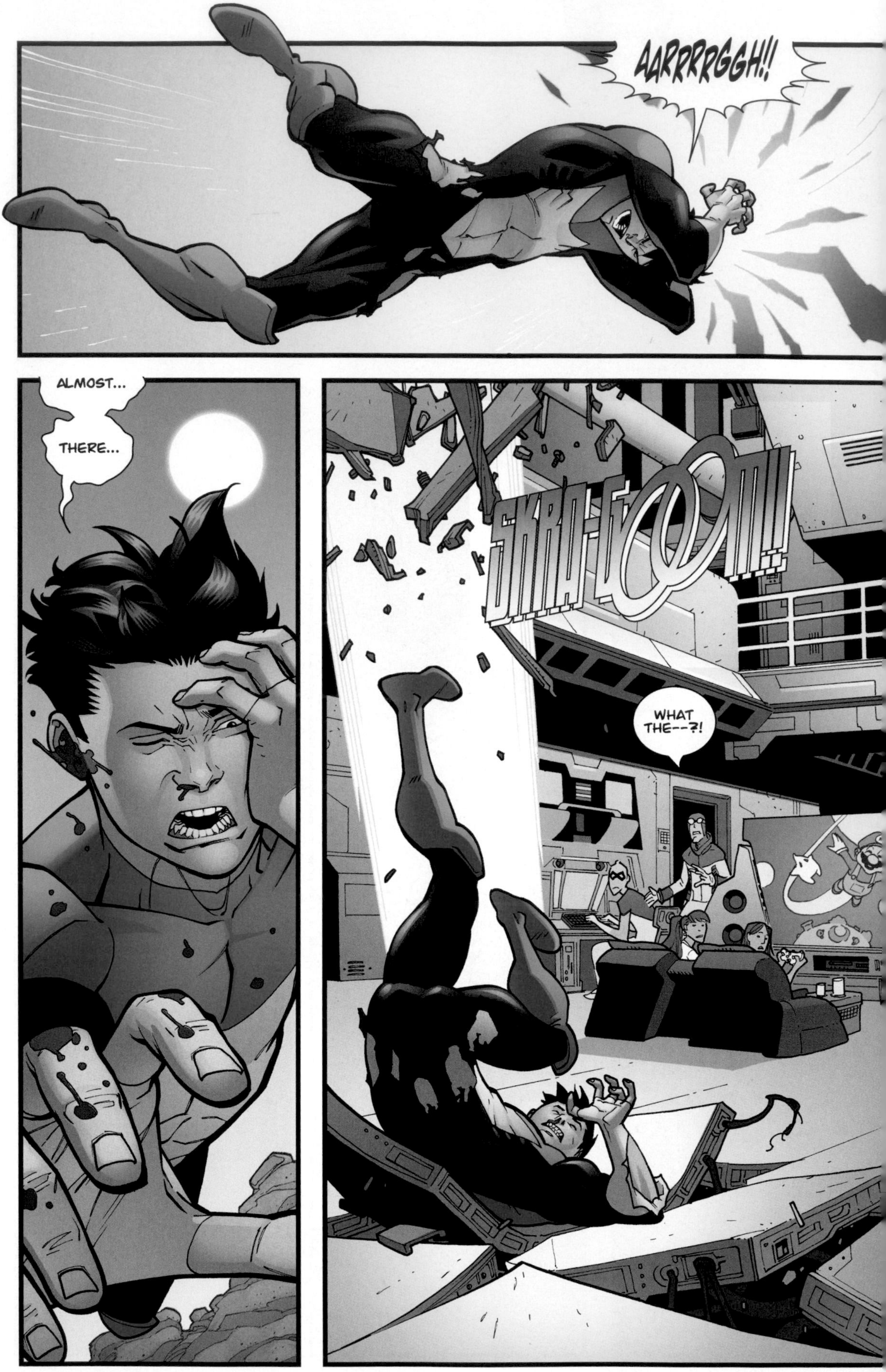
AARRRRGGH!!
ALMOST...
THERE...
SKRA-KOOM!!
WHAT THE--?!

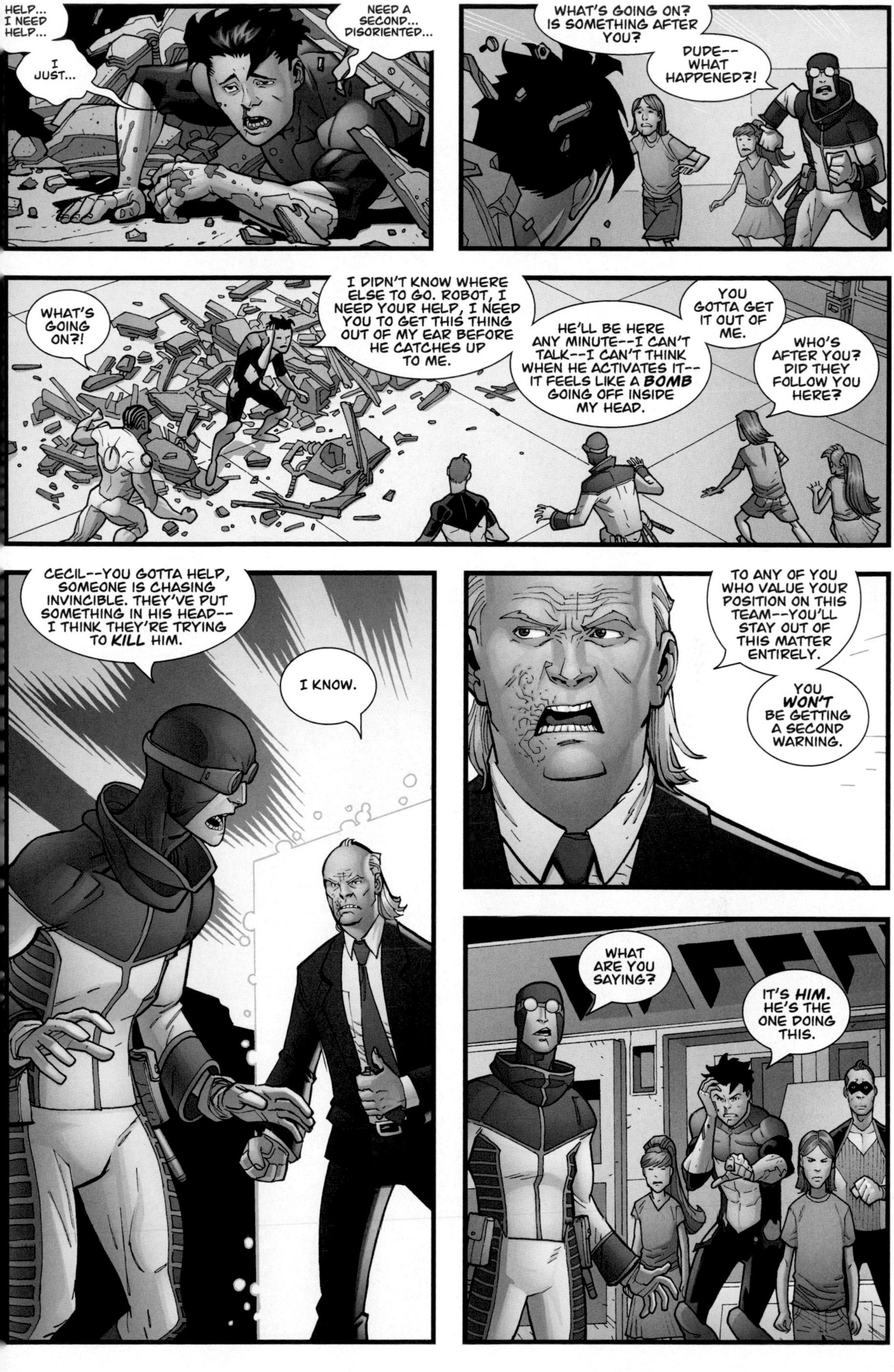
HELP... I NEED HELP...
I JUST...
NEED A SECOND... DISORIENTED...
WHAT'S GOING ON? IS SOMETHING AFTER YOU?
DUDE-- WHAT HAPPENED?!
WHAT'S GOING ON?!
I DIDN'T KNOW WHERE ELSE TO GO. ROBOT, I NEED YOUR HELP, I NEED YOU TO GET THIS THING OUT OF MY EAR BEFORE HE CATCHES UP TO ME.
HE'LL BE HERE ANY MINUTE--I CAN'T TALK--I CAN'T THINK WHEN HE ACTIVATES IT-- IT FEELS LIKE A BOMB GOING OFF INSIDE MY HEAD.
YOU GOTTA GET IT OUT OF ME.
WHO'S AFTER YOU? DID THEY FOLLOW YOU HERE?
CECIL--YOU GOTTA HELP, SOMEONE IS CHASING INVINCIBLE. THEY'VE PUT SOMETHING IN HIS HEAD-- I THINK THEY'RE TRYING TO KILL HIM.
I KNOW.
TO ANY OF YOU WHO VALUE YOUR POSITION ON THIS TEAM--YOU'LL STAY OUT OF THIS MATTER ENTIRELY.
YOU WON'T BE GETTING A SECOND WARNING.
WHAT ARE YOU SAYING?
IT'S HIM. HE'S THE ONE DOING THIS.

I KNOW SOME OF YOU CONSIDER YOURSELVES TO BE FRIENDS WITH INVINCIBLE, I WOULD HAVE DONE THE SAME BEFORE TODAY--BUT LISTEN TO ME WHEN I SAY THIS--HE IS NO FRIEND TO ANY OF US NOW.

HE IS DOING EVERYTHING HE CAN TO COMPROMISE THE SECURITY OF THIS PLANET. HE IS UNDERMINING ME AND MY ORGANIZATION-- THE ORGANIZATION THAT FUNDS THIS TEAM.

I HATE THAT IT'S COME TO THIS, BUT I MUST ASK YOU TO HELP ME RESTRAIN HIM.

WHAT HAPPENED TO YOU, INVINCIBLE? YOU'VE BEEN ACTING LIKE A MANIAC SINCE WE DEFEATED DOC SEISMIC EARLIER.

DON'T LISTEN TO HIM--HE'S NOT TELLING YOU THE WHOLE STORY!

HE'S EMPLOYING MURDERERS! THE MAN WHO HELPED US STOP DOC SEISMIC, DARKWING, HE'S A MURDERER--I KNOW YOU DON'T BELIEVE ME BUT IT'S TRUE.

I WAS SENT INTO MIDNIGHT CITY BY CECIL-- SENT IN TO STOP A MURDERER. I FOUND OUT IT WAS DARKWING, HE'D SNAPPED, HE WAS KILLING ANYONE WHO BROKE THE LAW.

I ARRESTED HIM--I THOUGHT HE WAS IN JAIL. CECIL SUPPRESSED THE TRUTH--PUT HIM ON THE PAYROLL!

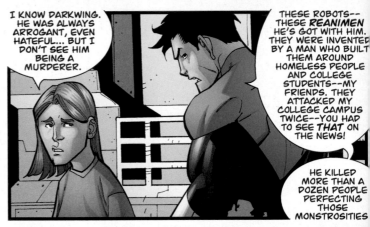

I KNOW DARKWING. HE WAS ALWAYS ARROGANT, EVEN HATEFUL... BUT I DON'T SEE HIM BEING A MURDERER.

THESE ROBOTS-- THESE REANIMEN HE'S GOT WITH HIM. THEY WERE INVENTED BY A MAN WHO BUILT THEM AROUND HOMELESS PEOPLE AND COLLEGE STUDENTS--MY FRIENDS. THEY ATTACKED MY COLLEGE CAMPUS TWICE--YOU HAD TO SEE THAT ON THE NEWS!

HE KILLED MORE THAN A DOZEN PEOPLE PERFECTING THOSE MONSTROSITIES

I SAW THAT... I THOUGHT THOSE THINGS LOOKED FAMILIAR.

THIS ISN'T WHAT WE SIGNED UP FOR!

CECIL, IS... IS INVINCIBLE TELLING THE TRUTH ABOUT THESE THINGS?

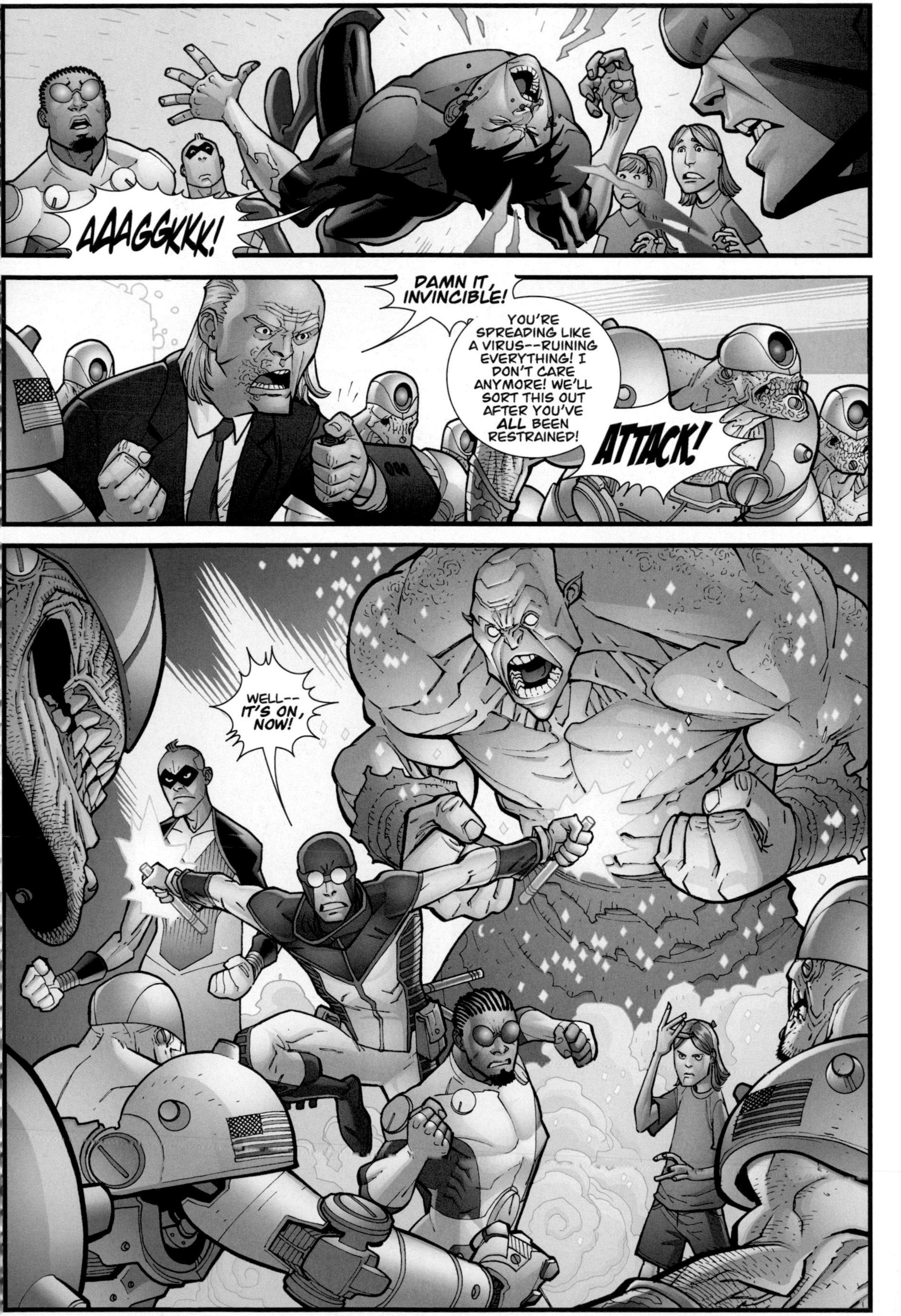
AAAGGKKK!
DAMN IT, INVINCIBLE!
YOU'RE SPREADING LIKE A VIRUS--RUINING EVERYTHING! I DON'T CARE ANYMORE! WE'LL SORT THIS OUT AFTER YOU'VE ALL BEEN RESTRAINED!
ATTACK!
WELL-- IT'S ON, NOW!

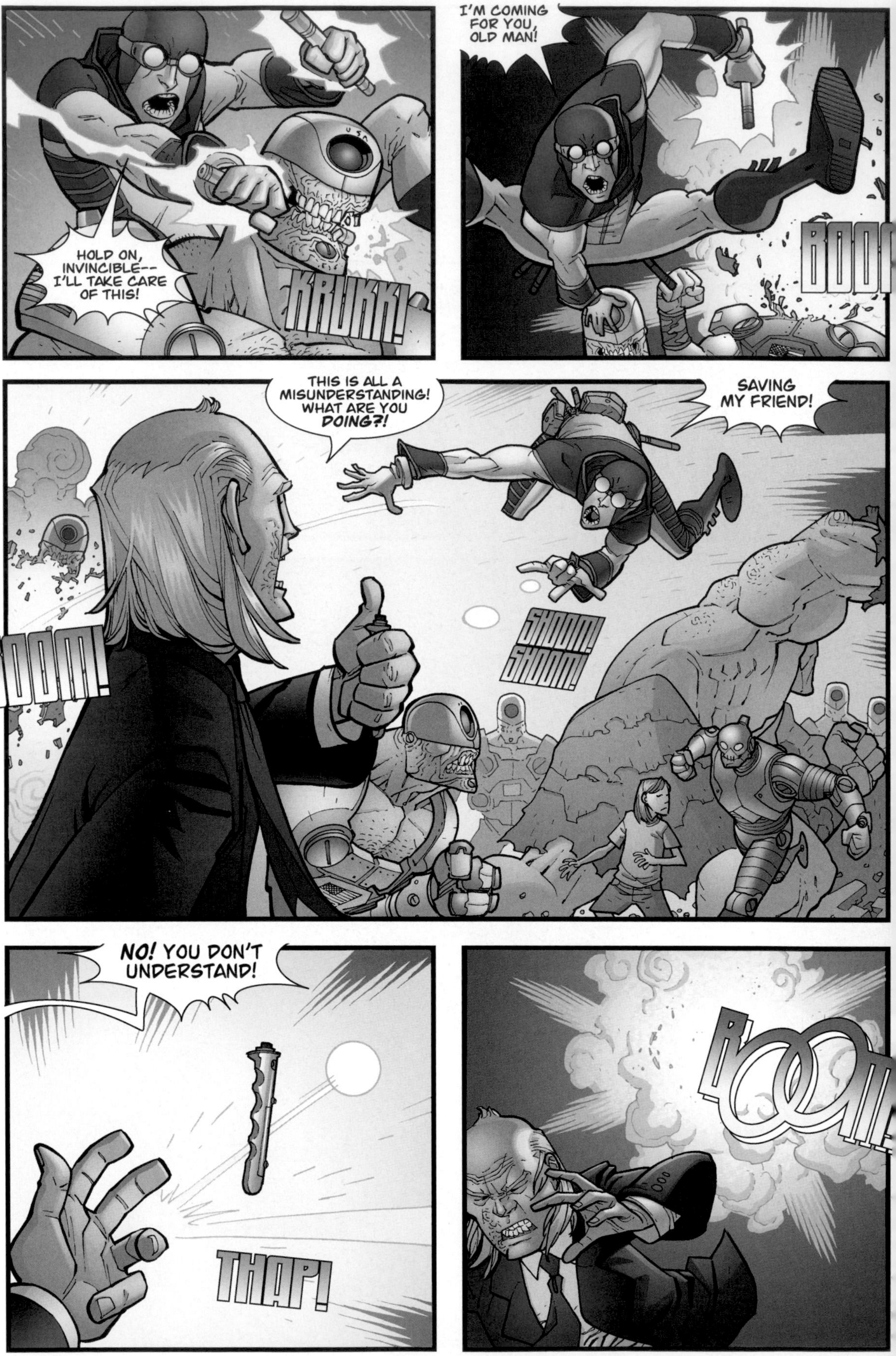
HOLD ON, INVINCIBLE-- I'LL TAKE CARE OF THIS!
KRUKK!
I'M COMING FOR YOU, OLD MAN!
BOOM
THIS IS ALL A MISUNDERSTANDING! WHAT ARE YOU DOING?!
SAVING MY FRIEND!
BOOM!
SHOOM! SHOOM!
NO! YOU DON'T UNDERSTAND!
THAP!
BOOM

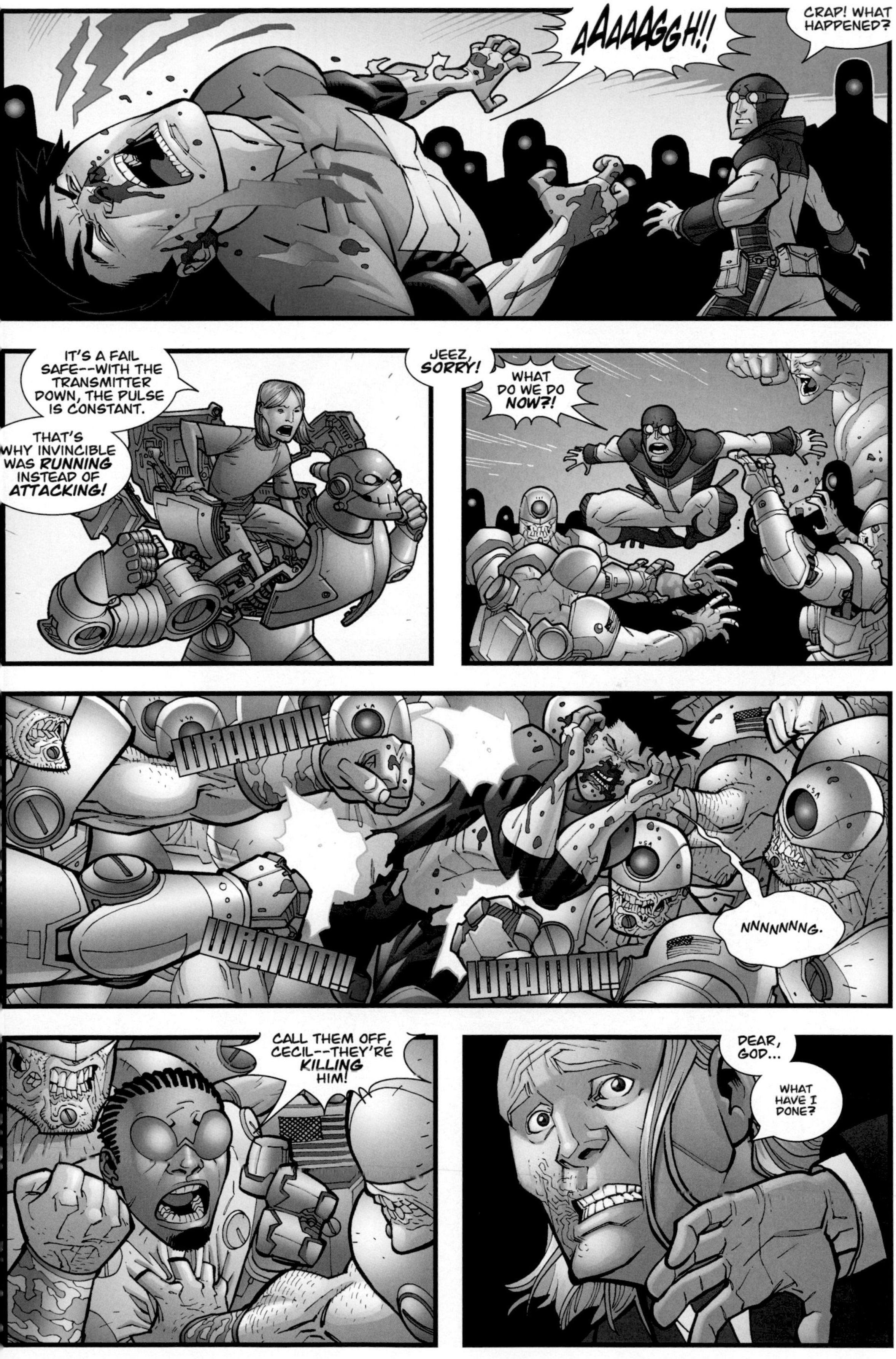
AAAAAGGH!!
CRAP! WHAT HAPPENED?
IT'S A FAIL SAFE--WITH THE TRANSMITTER DOWN, THE PULSE IS CONSTANT.
THAT'S WHY INVINCIBLE WAS RUNNING INSTEAD OF ATTACKING!
JEEZ, SORRY!
WHAT DO WE DO NOW?!
WRAMM!
WRAMM!
WRAMM!
NNNNNNNG.
CALL THEM OFF, CECIL--THEY'RE KILLING HIM!
DEAR, GOD...
WHAT HAVE I DONE?

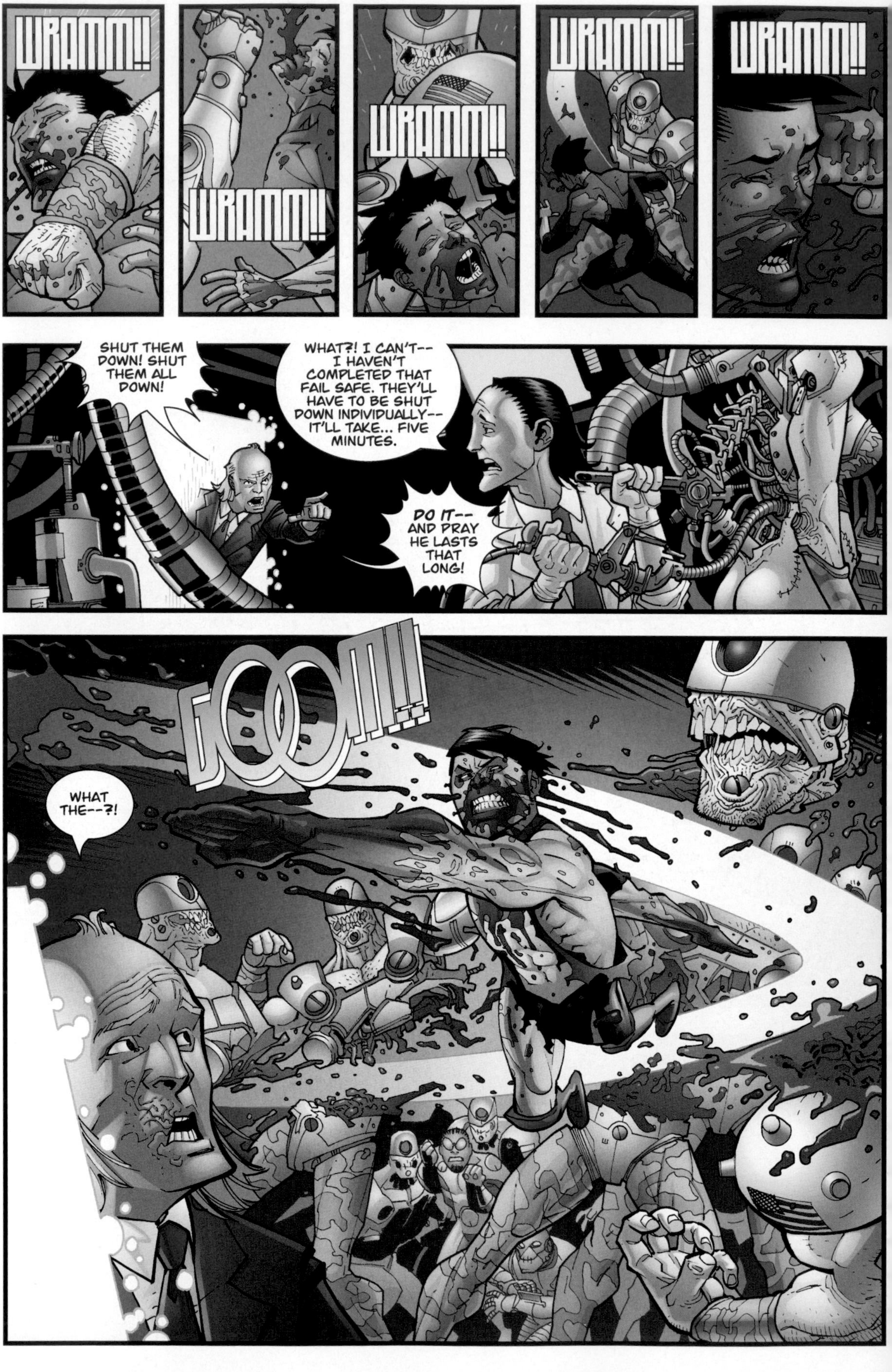
WRAMM!!
WRAMM!!
WRAMM!!
WRAMM!!
WRAMM!!
SHUT THEM DOWN! SHUT THEM ALL DOWN!
WHAT?! I CAN'T-- I HAVEN'T COMPLETED THAT FAIL SAFE. THEY'LL HAVE TO BE SHUT DOWN INDIVIDUALLY-- IT'LL TAKE... FIVE MINUTES.
DO IT-- AND PRAY HE LASTS THAT LONG!
GOOM!!
WHAT THE--?!

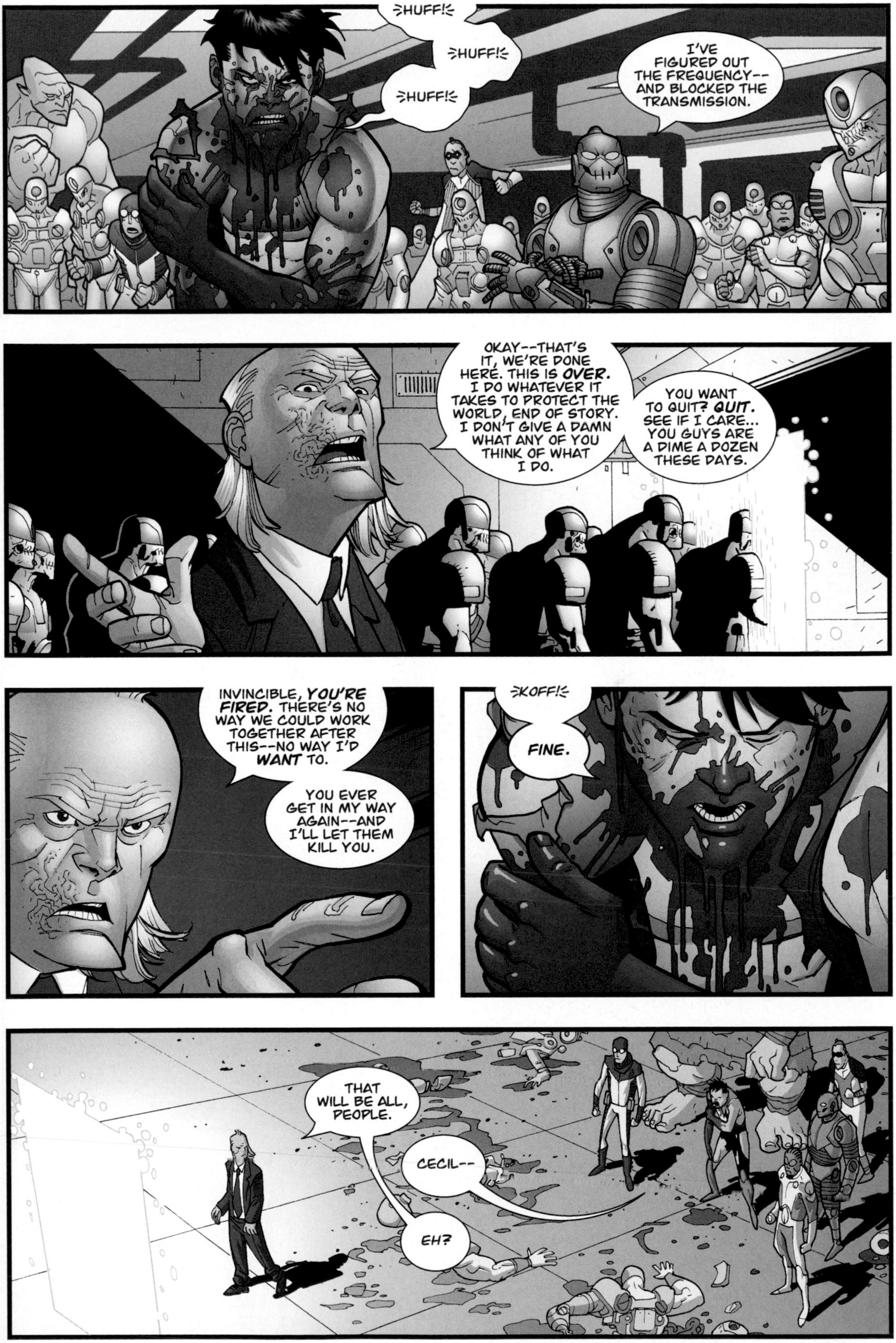

HUFF!
HUFF!
HUFF!
I'VE FIGURED OUT THE FREQUENCY-- AND BLOCKED THE TRANSMISSION.
OKAY--THAT'S IT, WE'RE DONE HERE. THIS IS OVER. I DO WHATEVER IT TAKES TO PROTECT THE WORLD, END OF STORY. I DON'T GIVE A DAMN WHAT ANY OF YOU THINK OF WHAT I DO.
YOU WANT TO QUIT? QUIT. SEE IF I CARE... YOU GUYS ARE A DIME A DOZEN THESE DAYS.
INVINCIBLE, YOU'RE FIRED. THERE'S NO WAY WE COULD WORK TOGETHER AFTER THIS--NO WAY I'D WANT TO.
YOU EVER GET IN MY WAY AGAIN--AND I'LL LET THEM KILL YOU.
KOFF!
FINE.
THAT WILL BE ALL, PEOPLE.
CECIL--
EH?

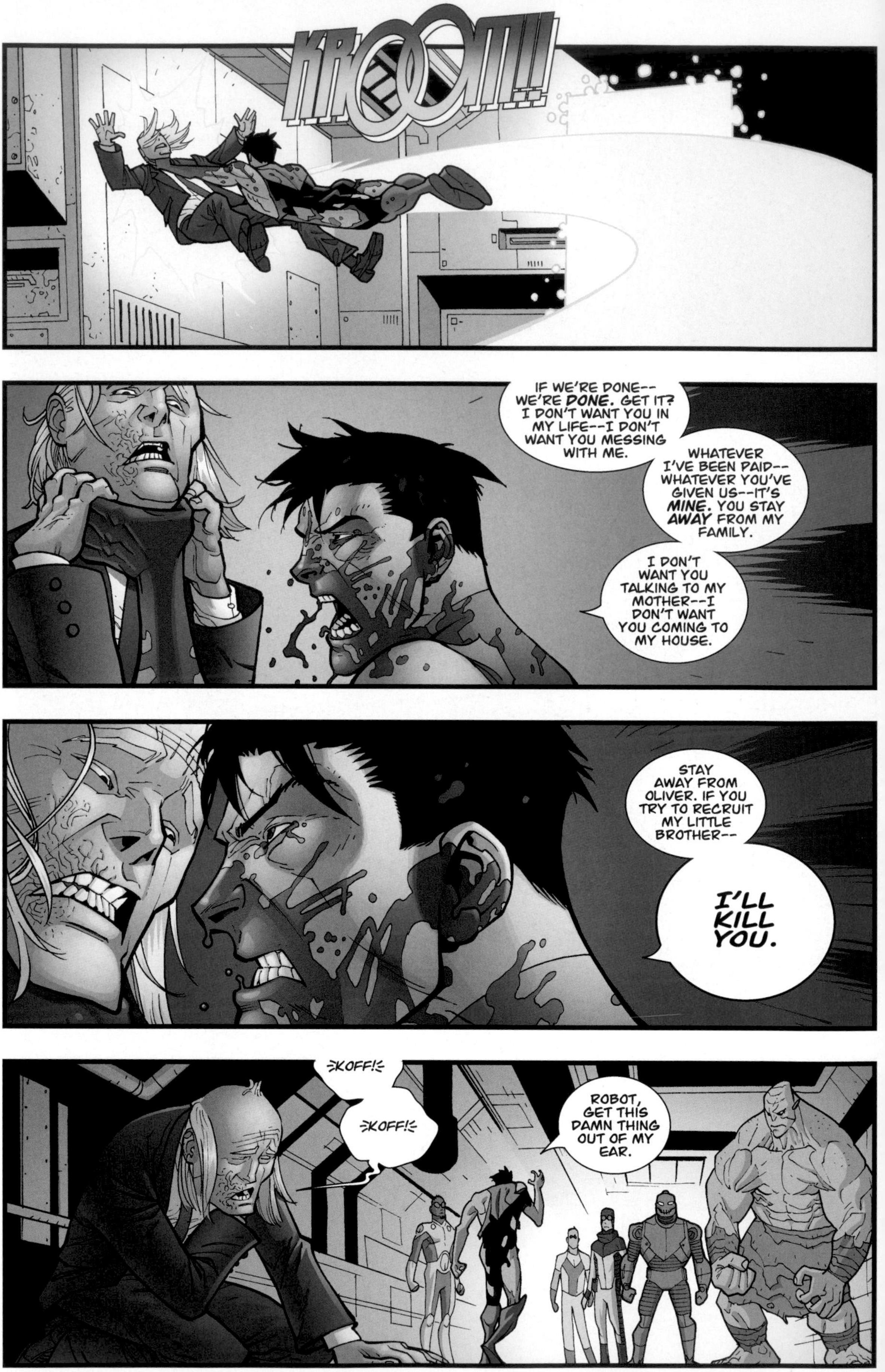
KROOM!!
IF WE'RE DONE-- WE'RE DONE. GET IT? I DON'T WANT YOU IN MY LIFE--I DON'T WANT YOU MESSING WITH ME.
WHATEVER I'VE BEEN PAID-- WHATEVER YOU'VE GIVEN US--IT'S MINE. YOU STAY AWAY FROM MY FAMILY.
I DON'T WANT YOU TALKING TO MY MOTHER--I DON'T WANT YOU COMING TO MY HOUSE.
STAY AWAY FROM OLIVER. IF YOU TRY TO RECRUIT MY LITTLE BROTHER--
I'LL KILL YOU.
KOFF!
KOFF!
ROBOT, GET THIS DAMN THING OUT OF MY EAR.

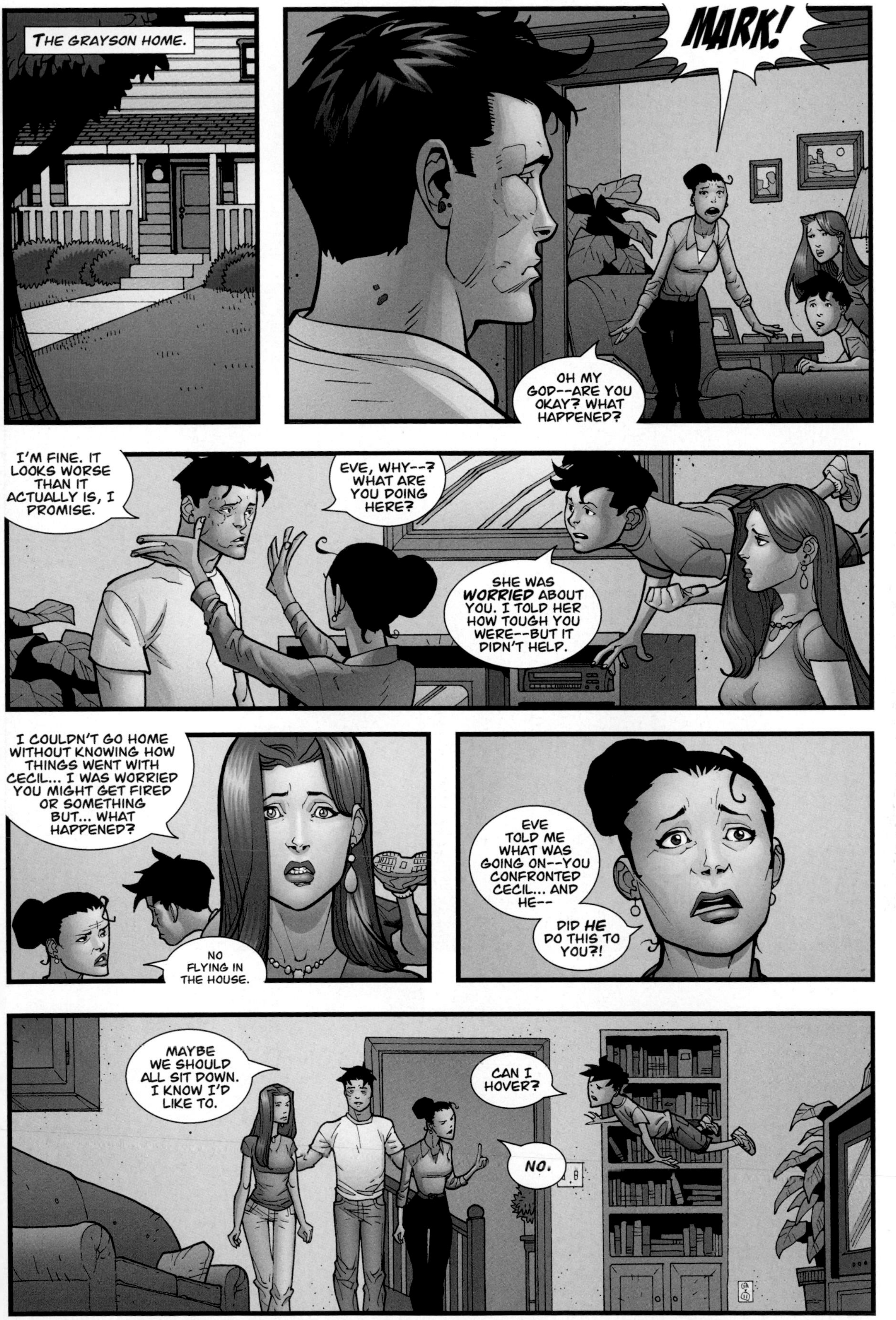
THE GRAYSON HOME.
MARK!
OH MY GOD--ARE YOU OKAY? WHAT HAPPENED?
I'M FINE. IT LOOKS WORSE THAN IT ACTUALLY IS, I PROMISE.
EVE, WHY--? WHAT ARE YOU DOING HERE?
SHE WAS WORRIED ABOUT YOU. I TOLD HER HOW TOUGH YOU WERE--BUT IT DIDN'T HELP.
I COULDN'T GO HOME WITHOUT KNOWING HOW THINGS WENT WITH CECIL... I WAS WORRIED YOU MIGHT GET FIRED OR SOMETHING BUT... WHAT HAPPENED?
NO FLYING IN THE HOUSE.
EVE TOLD ME WHAT WAS GOING ON--YOU CONFRONTED CECIL... AND HE--
DID HE DO THIS TO YOU?!
MAYBE WE SHOULD ALL SIT DOWN. I KNOW I'D LIKE TO.
CAN I HOVER?
NO.

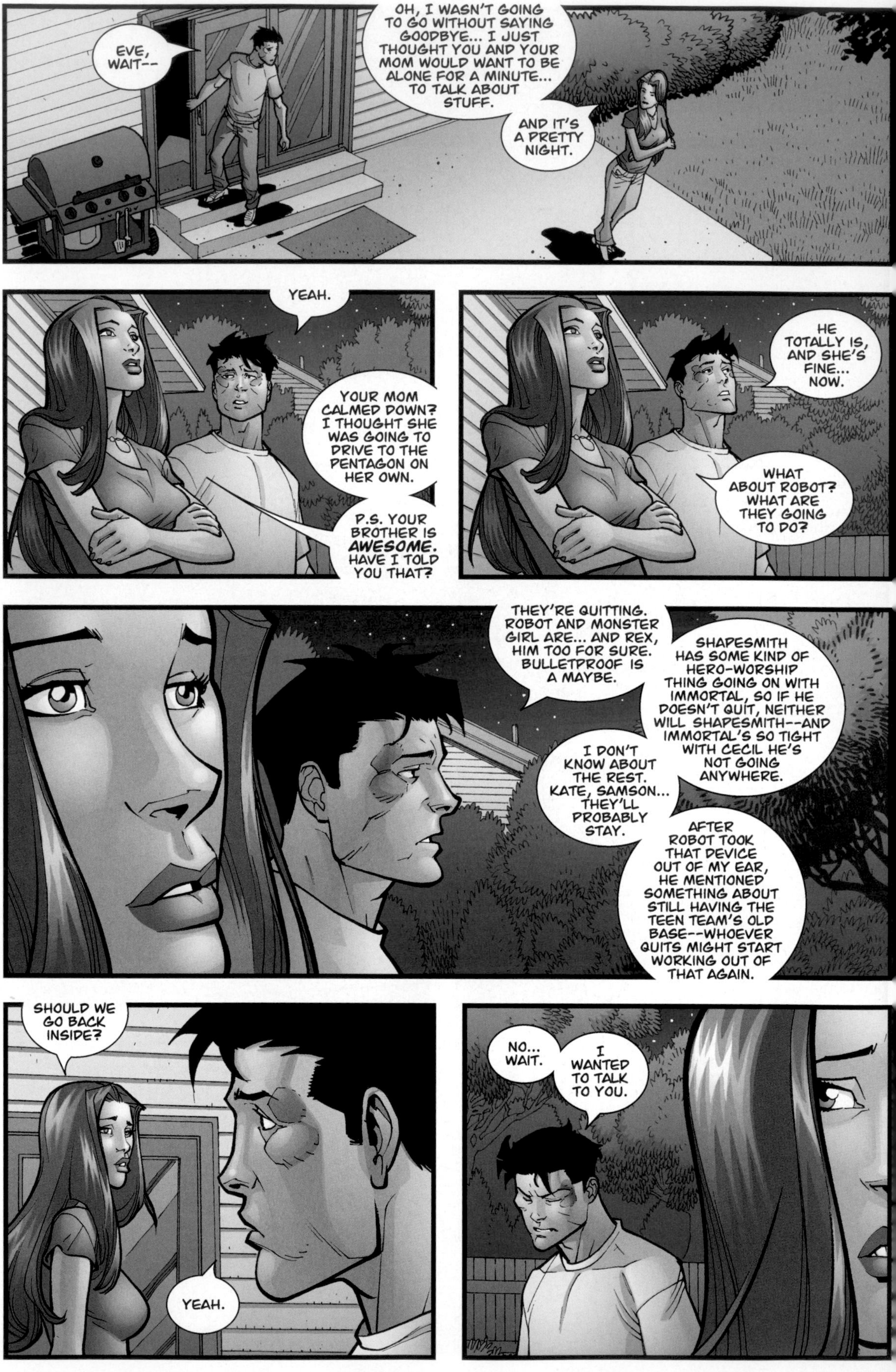
EVE, WAIT--
OH, I WASN'T GOING TO GO WITHOUT SAYING GOODBYE... I JUST THOUGHT YOU AND YOUR MOM WOULD WANT TO BE ALONE FOR A MINUTE... TO TALK ABOUT STUFF.
AND IT'S A PRETTY NIGHT.
YEAH.
YOUR MOM CALMED DOWN? I THOUGHT SHE WAS GOING TO DRIVE TO THE PENTAGON ON HER OWN.
P.S. YOUR BROTHER IS AWESOME. HAVE I TOLD YOU THAT?
HE TOTALLY IS, AND SHE'S FINE... NOW.
WHAT ABOUT ROBOT? WHAT ARE THEY GOING TO DO?
THEY'RE QUITTING. ROBOT AND MONSTER GIRL ARE... AND REX, HIM TOO FOR SURE. BULLETPROOF IS A MAYBE.
SHAPESMITH HAS SOME KIND OF HERO-WORSHIP THING GOING ON WITH IMMORTAL, SO IF HE DOESN'T QUIT, NEITHER WILL SHAPESMITH--AND IMMORTAL'S SO TIGHT WITH CECIL HE'S NOT GOING ANYWHERE.
I DON'T KNOW ABOUT THE REST. KATE, SAMSON... THEY'LL PROBABLY STAY.
AFTER ROBOT TOOK THAT DEVICE OUT OF MY EAR, HE MENTIONED SOMETHING ABOUT STILL HAVING THE TEEN TEAM'S OLD BASE--WHOEVER QUITS MIGHT START WORKING OUT OF THAT AGAIN.
SHOULD WE GO BACK INSIDE?
YEAH.
NO... WAIT.
I WANTED TO TALK TO YOU.

OH, YEAH?

OKAY. WHEN THOSE THINGS WERE BEATING ON ME-- WHEN THE PULSE WAS GOING OFF IN MY HEAD NON-STOP... I COULDN'T THINK, I COULDN'T MOVE, I COULDN'T FIGHT BACK.

THERE WAS A MOMENT, A TIME WHEN I THOUGHT-- THIS IS IT. I'M GOING TO DIE... AND IN THAT MOMENT I KEPT GETTING FLASHES... LITTLE THOUGHTS, POPPING UP THROUGH THE DARKNESS.

THOUGHTS OF *YOU*.

I KNOW WHAT I SAID BEFORE... BUT THIS IS *REAL*-- WHAT I FEEL ABOUT YOU. I WAS GOING TO DIE AND ALL I COULD THINK OF WAS YOU.

THE WAY YOU SMELL, YOUR SMILE, THE SOUND OF YOUR VOICE, THE WAY--

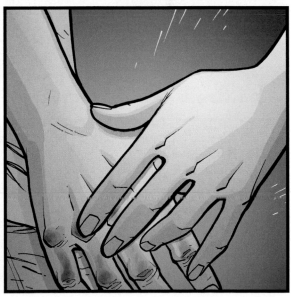

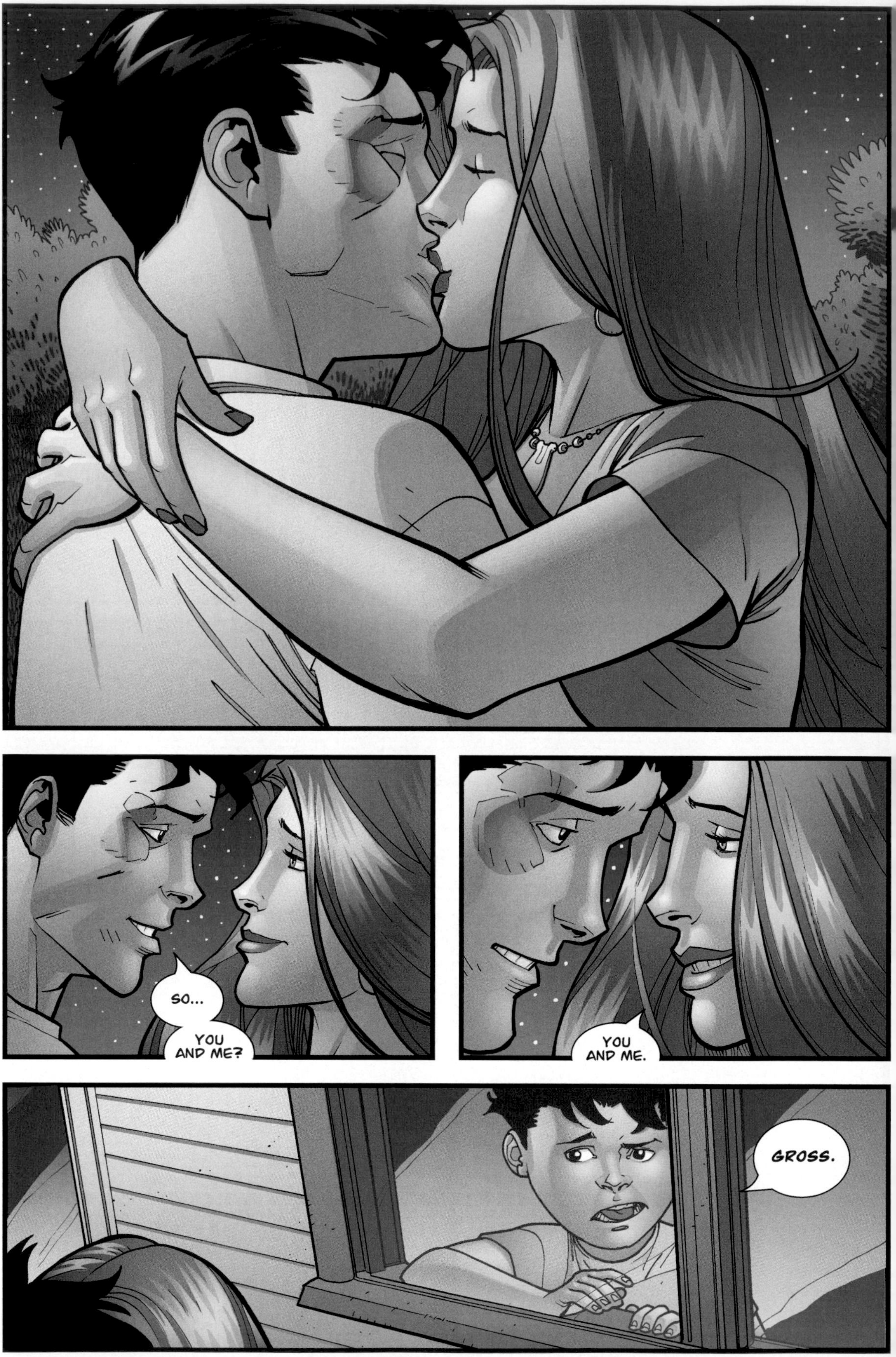
SO...
YOU AND ME?
YOU AND ME.
GROSS.

AT LONG LAST--THE SECRET ORIGIN OF CECIL STEDMAN!

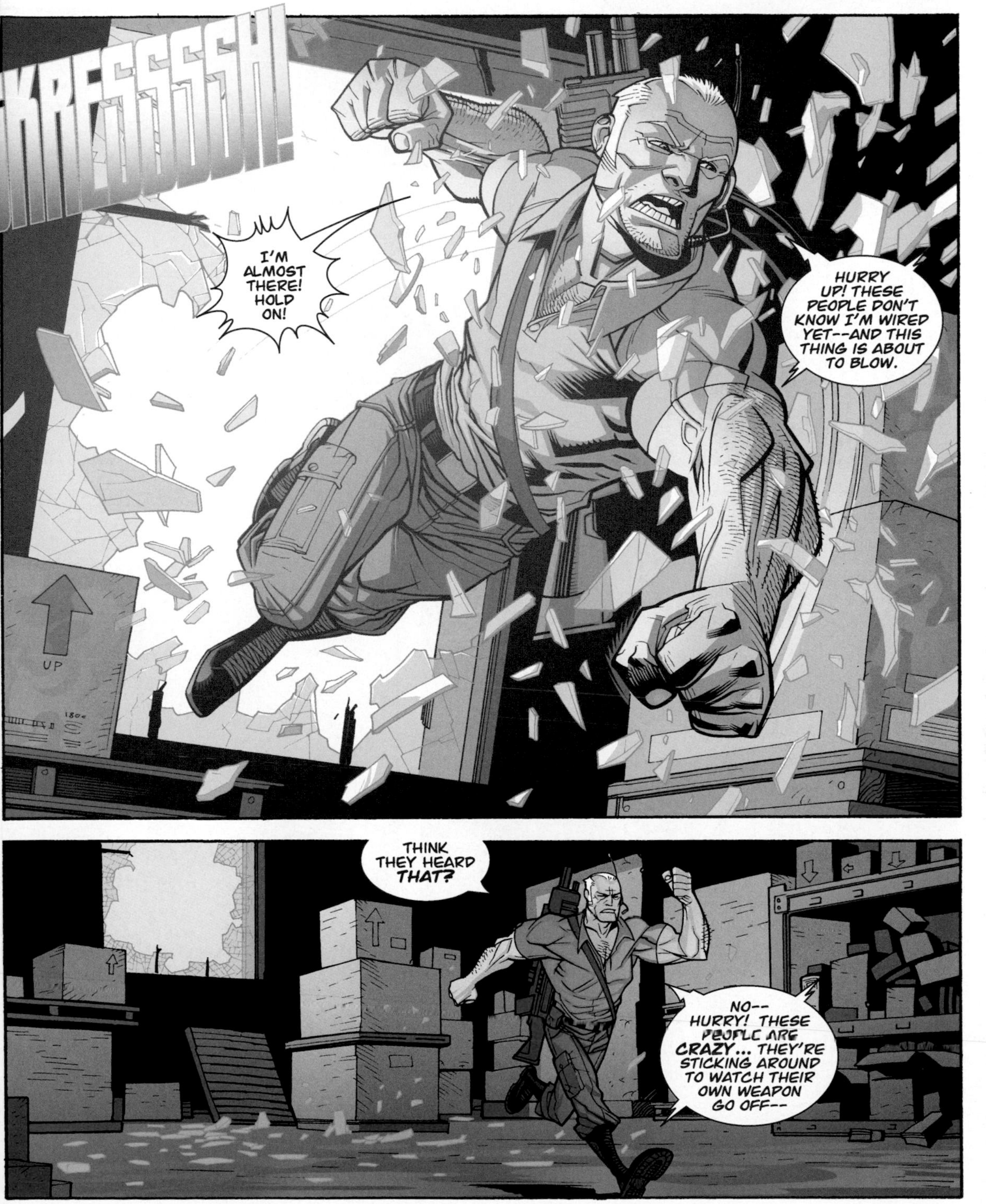
KRESSSSSH!
I'M ALMOST THERE! HOLD ON!
HURRY UP! THESE PEOPLE DON'T KNOW I'M WIRED YET--AND THIS THING IS ABOUT TO BLOW.
UP
THINK THEY HEARD THAT?
NO-- HURRY! THESE PEOPLE ARE CRAZY... THEY'RE STICKING AROUND TO WATCH THEIR OWN WEAPON GO OFF--

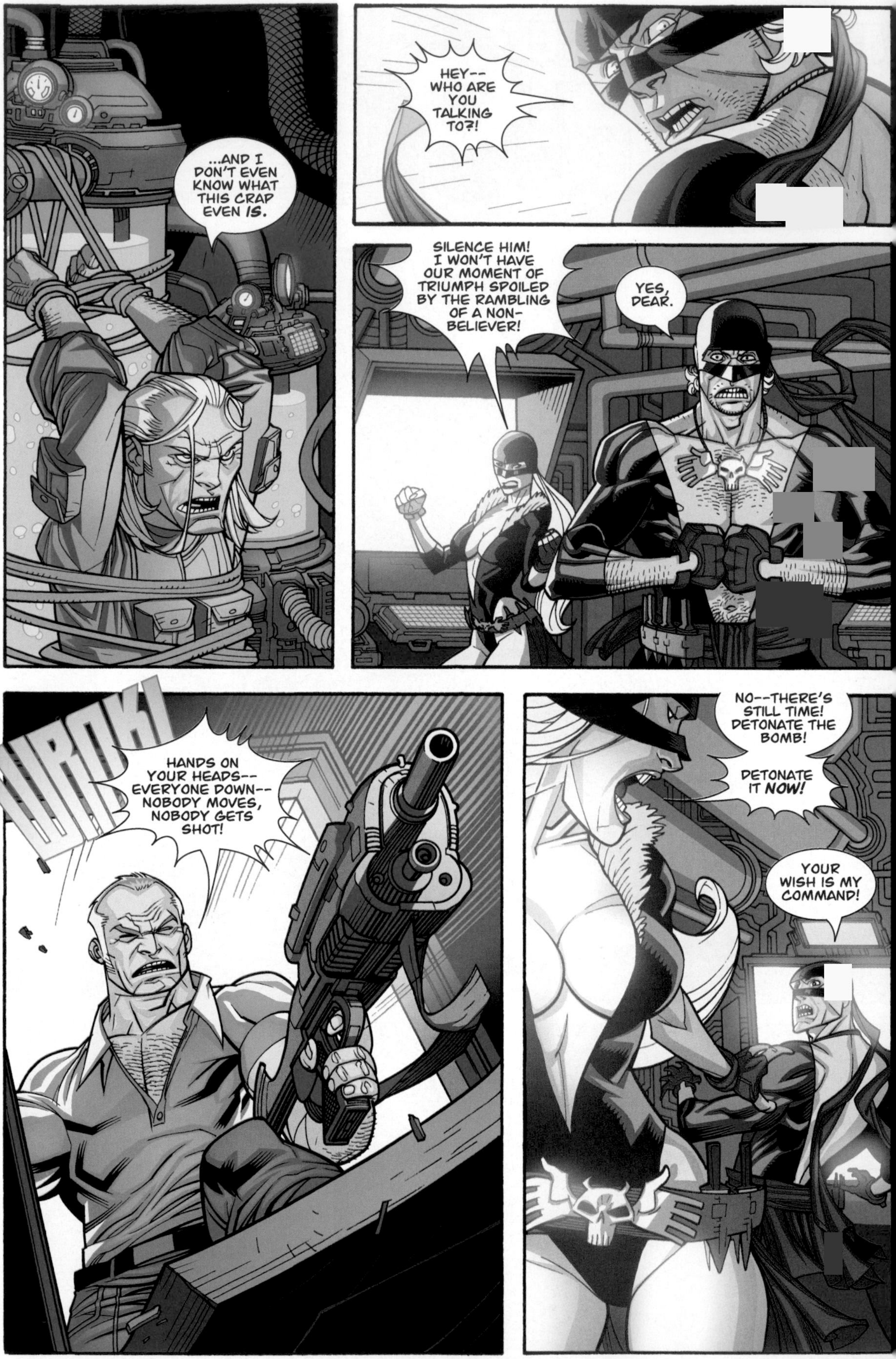
...AND I DON'T EVEN KNOW WHAT THIS CRAP EVEN *IS.*
HEY-- WHO ARE YOU TALKING TO?!
SILENCE HIM! I WON'T HAVE OUR MOMENT OF TRIUMPH SPOILED BY THE RAMBLING OF A NON-BELIEVER!
YES, DEAR.
WROK!
HANDS ON YOUR HEADS-- EVERYONE DOWN-- NOBODY MOVES, NOBODY GETS SHOT!
NO--THERE'S STILL TIME! DETONATE THE BOMB!
DETONATE IT *NOW!*
YOUR WISH IS MY COMMAND!

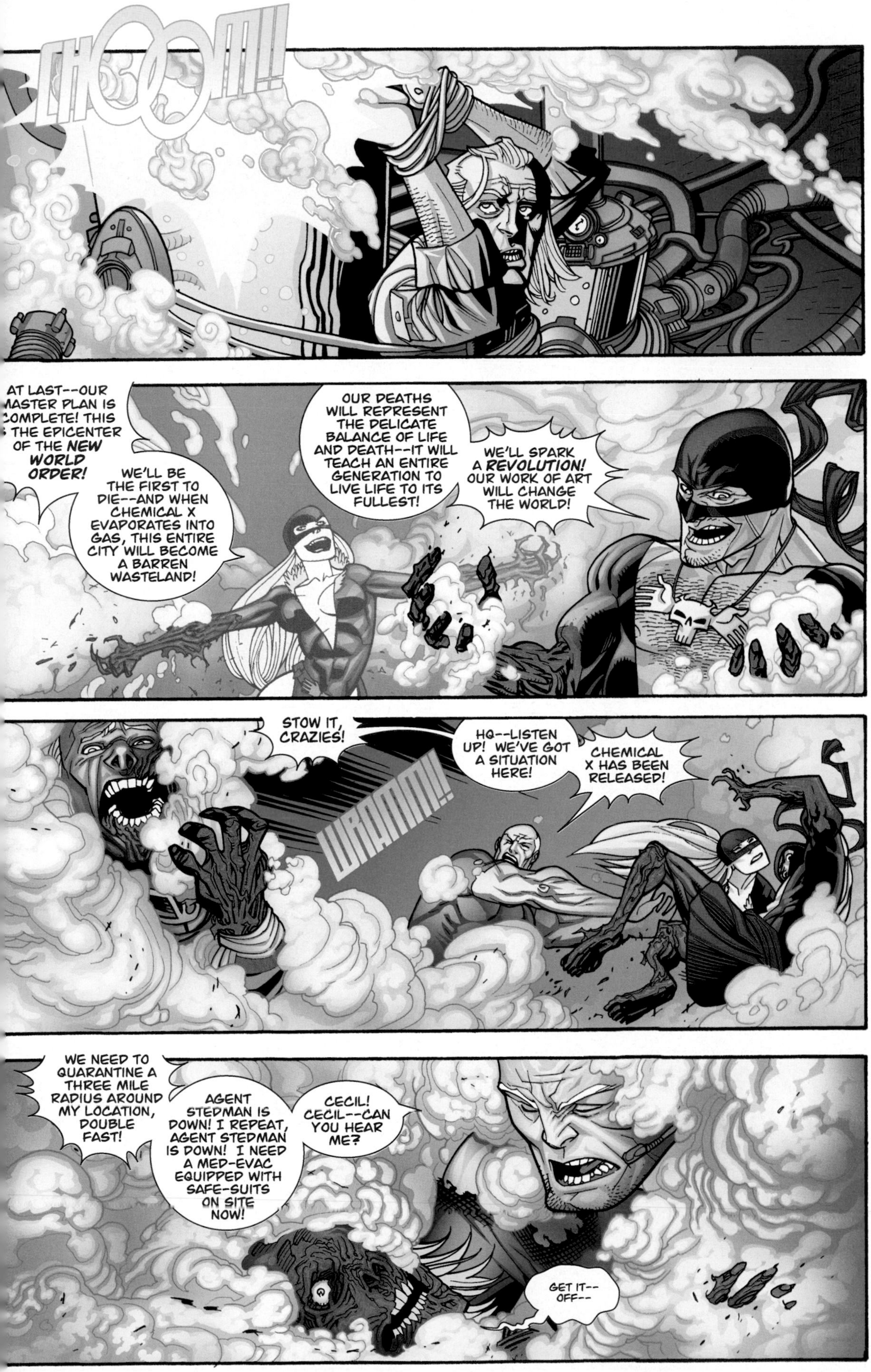
CHOOM!!
AT LAST--OUR MASTER PLAN IS COMPLETE! THIS IS THE EPICENTER OF THE NEW WORLD ORDER!
WE'LL BE THE FIRST TO DIE--AND WHEN CHEMICAL X EVAPORATES INTO GAS, THIS ENTIRE CITY WILL BECOME A BARREN WASTELAND!
OUR DEATHS WILL REPRESENT THE DELICATE BALANCE OF LIFE AND DEATH--IT WILL TEACH AN ENTIRE GENERATION TO LIVE LIFE TO ITS FULLEST!
WE'LL SPARK A REVOLUTION! OUR WORK OF ART WILL CHANGE THE WORLD!
STOW IT, CRAZIES!
WRAMM!!
HQ--LISTEN UP! WE'VE GOT A SITUATION HERE!
CHEMICAL X HAS BEEN RELEASED!
WE NEED TO QUARANTINE A THREE MILE RADIUS AROUND MY LOCATION, DOUBLE FAST!
AGENT STEDMAN IS DOWN! I REPEAT, AGENT STEDMAN IS DOWN! I NEED A MED-EVAC EQUIPPED WITH SAFE-SUITS ON SITE NOW!
CECIL! CECIL--CAN YOU HEAR ME?
GET IT-- OFF--

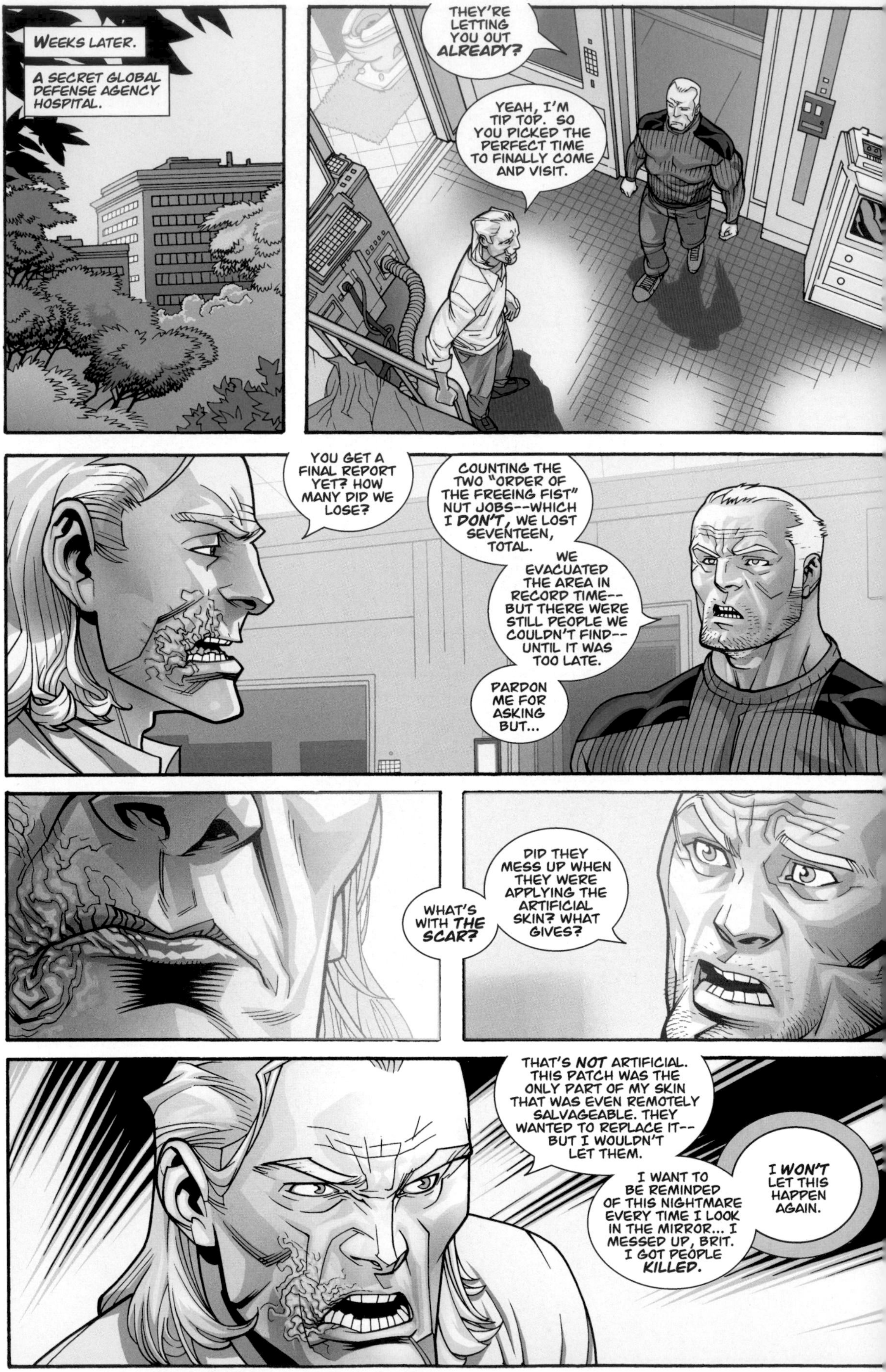
WEEKS LATER.
A SECRET GLOBAL DEFENSE AGENCY HOSPITAL.
THEY'RE LETTING YOU OUT ALREADY?
YEAH, I'M TIP TOP. SO YOU PICKED THE PERFECT TIME TO FINALLY COME AND VISIT.
YOU GET A FINAL REPORT YET? HOW MANY DID WE LOSE?
COUNTING THE TWO "ORDER OF THE FREEING FIST" NUT JOBS--WHICH I DON'T, WE LOST SEVENTEEN, TOTAL.
WE EVACUATED THE AREA IN RECORD TIME--BUT THERE WERE STILL PEOPLE WE COULDN'T FIND--UNTIL IT WAS TOO LATE.
PARDON ME FOR ASKING BUT...
WHAT'S WITH THE SCAR?
DID THEY MESS UP WHEN THEY WERE APPLYING THE ARTIFICIAL SKIN? WHAT GIVES?
THAT'S NOT ARTIFICIAL. THIS PATCH WAS THE ONLY PART OF MY SKIN THAT WAS EVEN REMOTELY SALVAGEABLE. THEY WANTED TO REPLACE IT--BUT I WOULDN'T LET THEM.
I WANT TO BE REMINDED OF THIS NIGHTMARE EVERY TIME I LOOK IN THE MIRROR... I MESSED UP, BRIT. I GOT PEOPLE KILLED.
I WON'T LET THIS HAPPEN AGAIN.

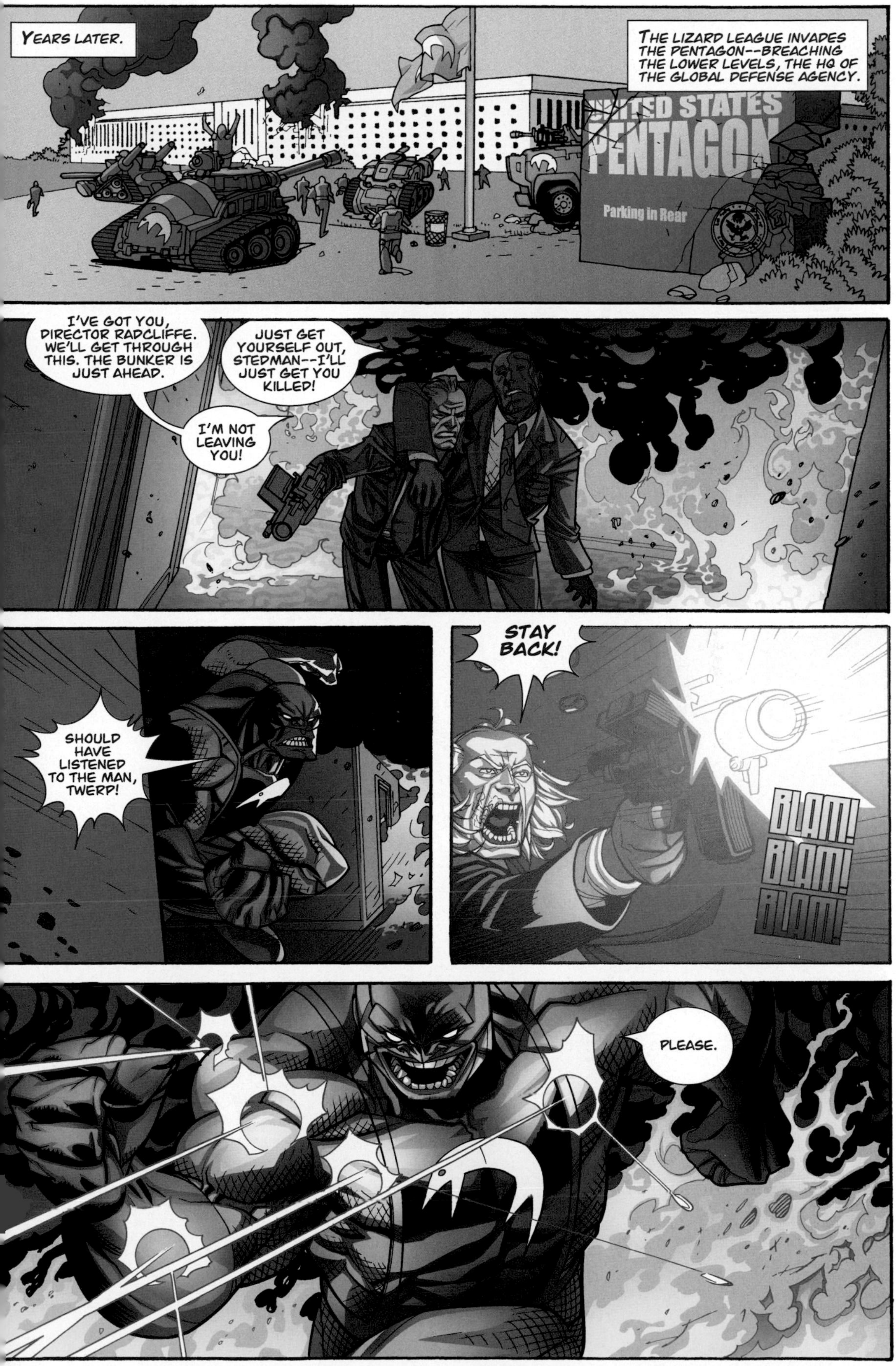

YEARS LATER.
THE LIZARD LEAGUE INVADES THE PENTAGON--BREACHING THE LOWER LEVELS, THE HQ OF THE GLOBAL DEFENSE AGENCY.
UNITED STATES PENTAGON
Parking in Rear
I'VE GOT YOU, DIRECTOR RADCLIFFE. WE'LL GET THROUGH THIS. THE BUNKER IS JUST AHEAD.
JUST GET YOURSELF OUT, STEDMAN--I'LL JUST GET YOU KILLED!
I'M NOT LEAVING YOU!
SHOULD HAVE LISTENED TO THE MAN, TWERP!
STAY BACK!
BLAM! BLAM! BLAM!
PLEASE.

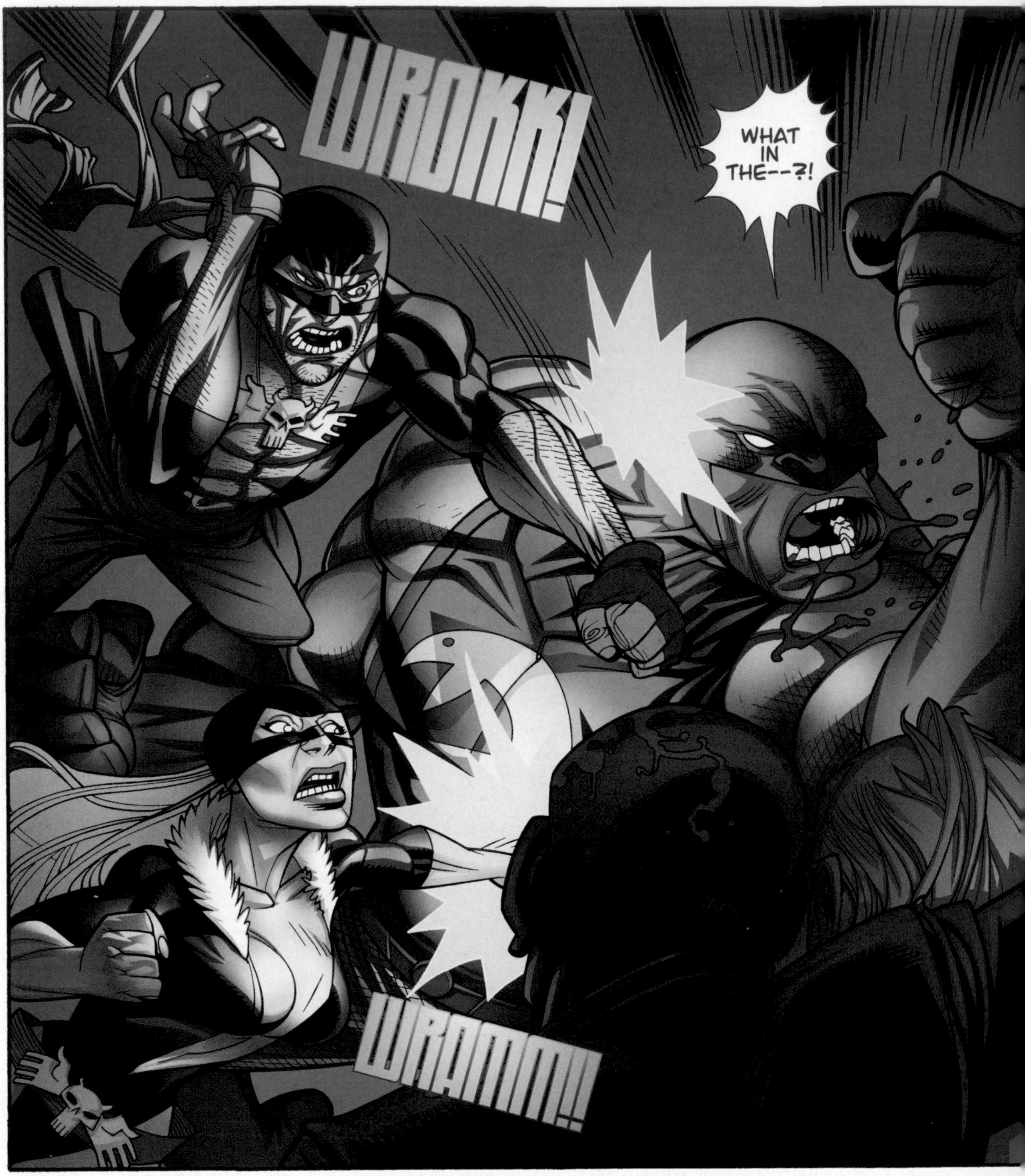
WROKK!
WHAT IN THE--?!
WRAMM!!

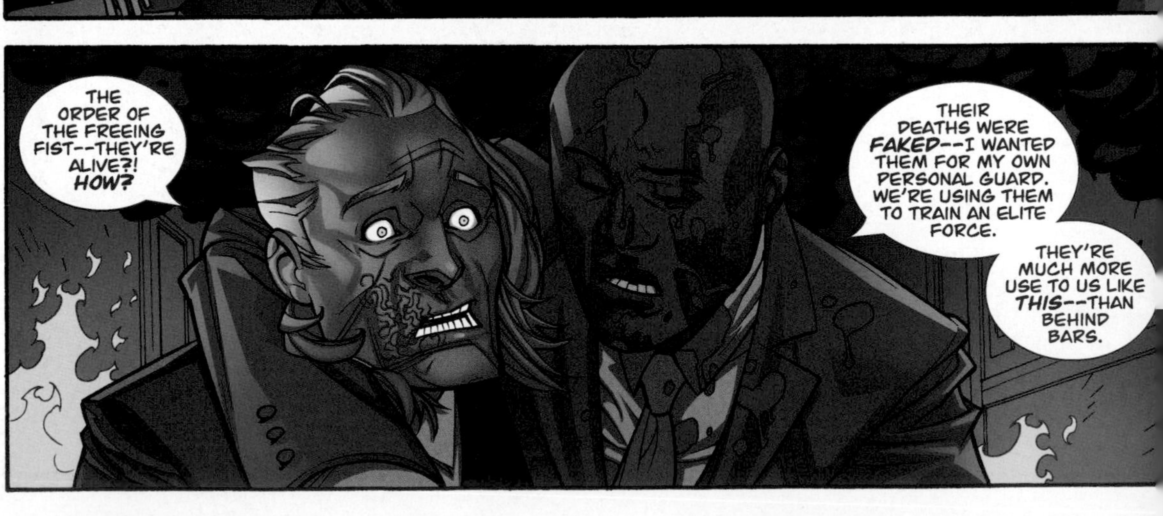
THE ORDER OF THE FREEING FIST--THEY'RE ALIVE?! HOW?
THEIR DEATHS WERE FAKED--I WANTED THEM FOR MY OWN PERSONAL GUARD. WE'RE USING THEM TO TRAIN AN ELITE FORCE.
THEY'RE MUCH MORE USE TO US LIKE THIS--THAN BEHIND BARS.

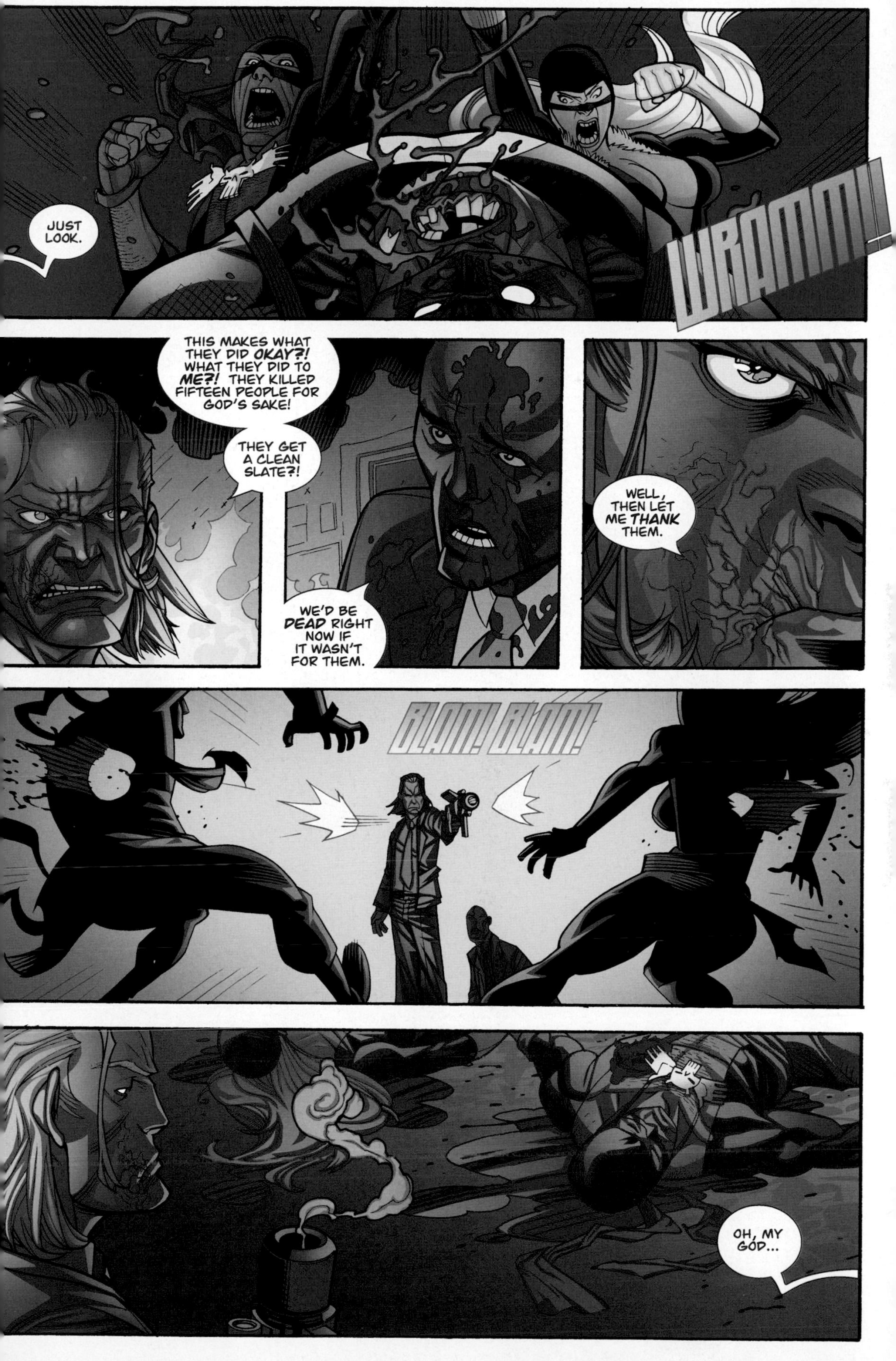

JUST LOOK.
WRAMM!!
THIS MAKES WHAT THEY DID OKAY?! WHAT THEY DID TO ME?! THEY KILLED FIFTEEN PEOPLE FOR GOD'S SAKE!
THEY GET A CLEAN SLATE?!
WE'D BE DEAD RIGHT NOW IF IT WASN'T FOR THEM.
WELL, THEN LET ME THANK THEM.
BLAM! BLAM!
OH, MY GOD...

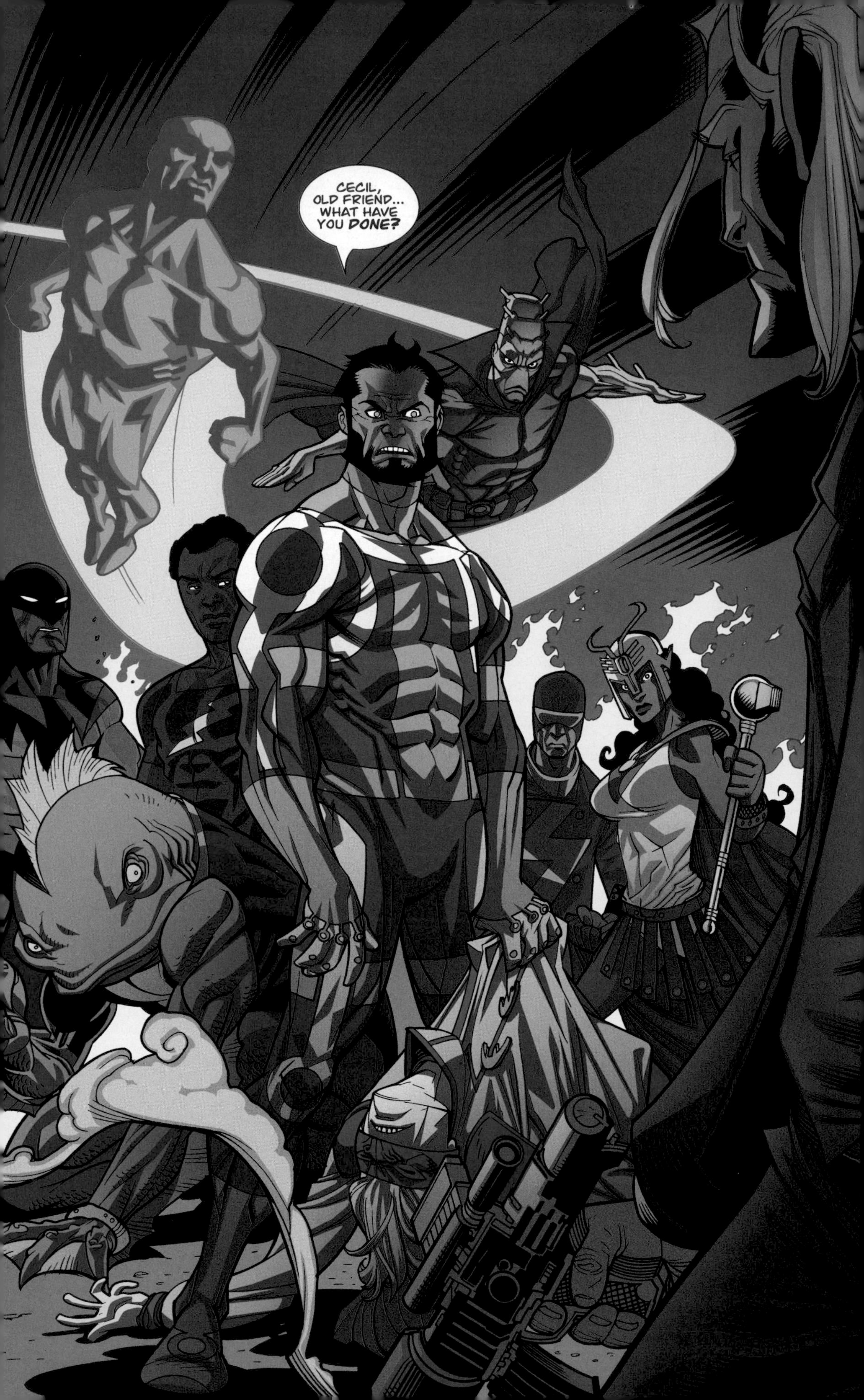
CECIL, OLD FRIEND... WHAT HAVE YOU DONE?

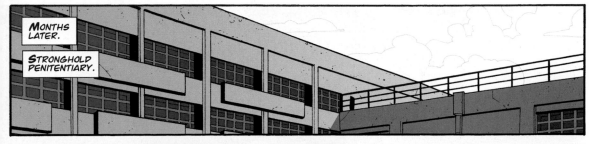

MONTHS LATER.

STRONGHOLD PENITENTIARY.

WHAT DO *YOU* WANT?

AS MUCH AS I'D LIKE TO SAY THIS IS JUST A VISIT FROM AN OLD FRIEND... I CAN'T. WE *NEED* YOU, CECIL. YOUR COUNTRY NEEDS YOU...

I NEED YOU.

I'VE GOTTEN MYSELF INVOLVED IN A SIDE PROJECT--IT'S TAKING UP A LOT OF MY TIME AND IT'S ENTERING INTO GRAY AREAS I CAN'T DIRECTLY ASSOCIATE WITH THE GLOBAL DEFENSE AGENCY.

I NEED TO STEP DOWN-- DISTANCE MY PROJECT AND MYSELF FROM THE AGENCY.

YOU ARE THE ONLY MAN ALIVE WHO COULD REPLACE ME.

NO. I'M NOT INTERESTED.

STILL BITTER OVER OUR LAST CONFRONTATION? CAN'T YOU JUST LEARN FROM *YOUR* SITUATION? YOU DID A BAD THING-- BUT YOU'RE MORE GOOD TO US OUTSIDE OF THIS CELL THAN IN.

SHOULD WE LEAVE *YOU* HERE TO ROT?

THE TRUTH IS, YOU CAN BE THE GOOD GUY-- OR YOU CAN BE THE GUY WHO SAVED THE WORLD. THEY'RE NOT ALWAYS THE SAME GUY.

CONSIDER MY OFFER. YOU DON'T HAVE TO DECIDE NOW, BUT *SOON*.

I DON'T HAVE A LOT OF TIME.

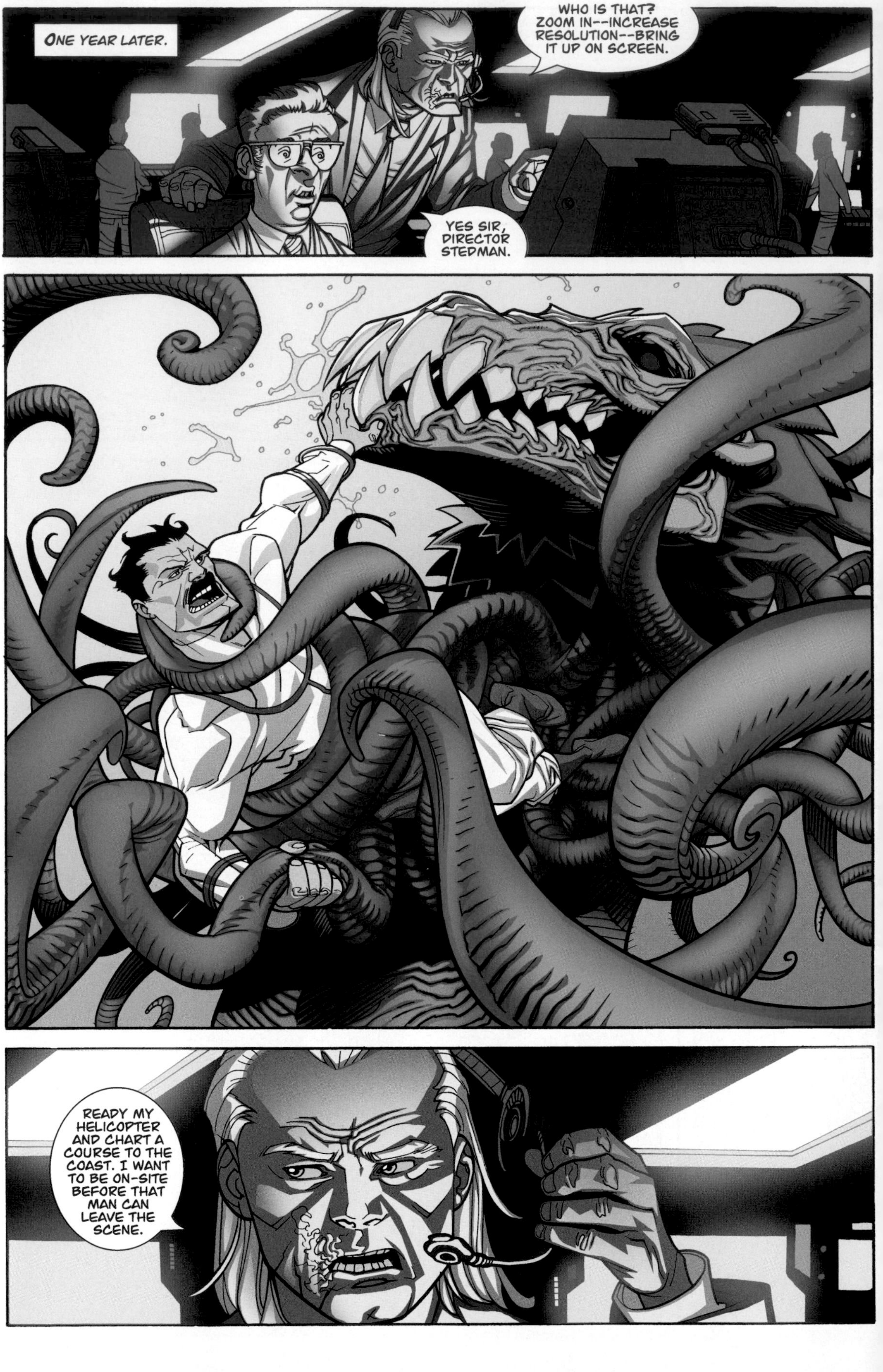
ONE YEAR LATER.
WHO IS THAT? ZOOM IN--INCREASE RESOLUTION--BRING IT UP ON SCREEN.
YES SIR, DIRECTOR STEDMAN.
READY MY HELICOPTER AND CHART A COURSE TO THE COAST. I WANT TO BE ON-SITE BEFORE THAT MAN CAN LEAVE THE SCENE.

HMN?

WHO ARE YOU?

MY NAME IS CECIL STEDMAN, I'M THE HEAD OF THE GLOBAL DEFENSE AGENCY. YOU'VE DISPLAYED A RANGE OF ABILITIES HERE TODAY THAT MY AGENCY WOULD DEEM--

EXCUSE ME, SIR. COULD I HAVE A WORD WITH YOU?

GLOBAL DEFENSE AGENCY? YOU REPRESENT THE INTERESTS OF THIS PLANET?

YES. YES I DO.

THEN I WOULD LIKE TO SPEAK WITH YOU AS WELL. I'VE COME HERE TO PROTECT THIS PLANET.

I WOULD VERY MUCH APPRECIATE YOUR ASSISTANCE IN LEARNING THE CUSTOMS AND BEHAVIORS OF ITS PEOPLE.

THAT, I CAN DEFINITELY HELP YOU WITH--AS WELL AS YOUR MISSION IN GENERAL. YOU SEE, WE HAVE THE SAME JOB. COME BACK TO MY HEADQUARTERS WITH ME--IT'LL BE EASIER TO TALK THERE.

OKAY, BUT--

DON'T WORRY ABOUT THAT. MY PEOPLE WILL CLEAN IT UP.

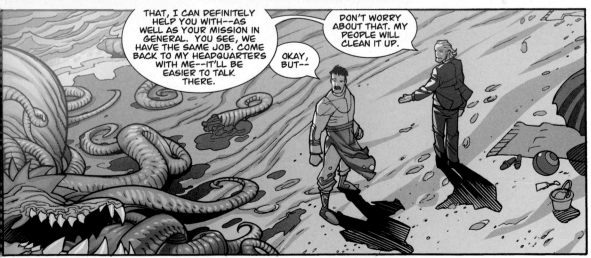

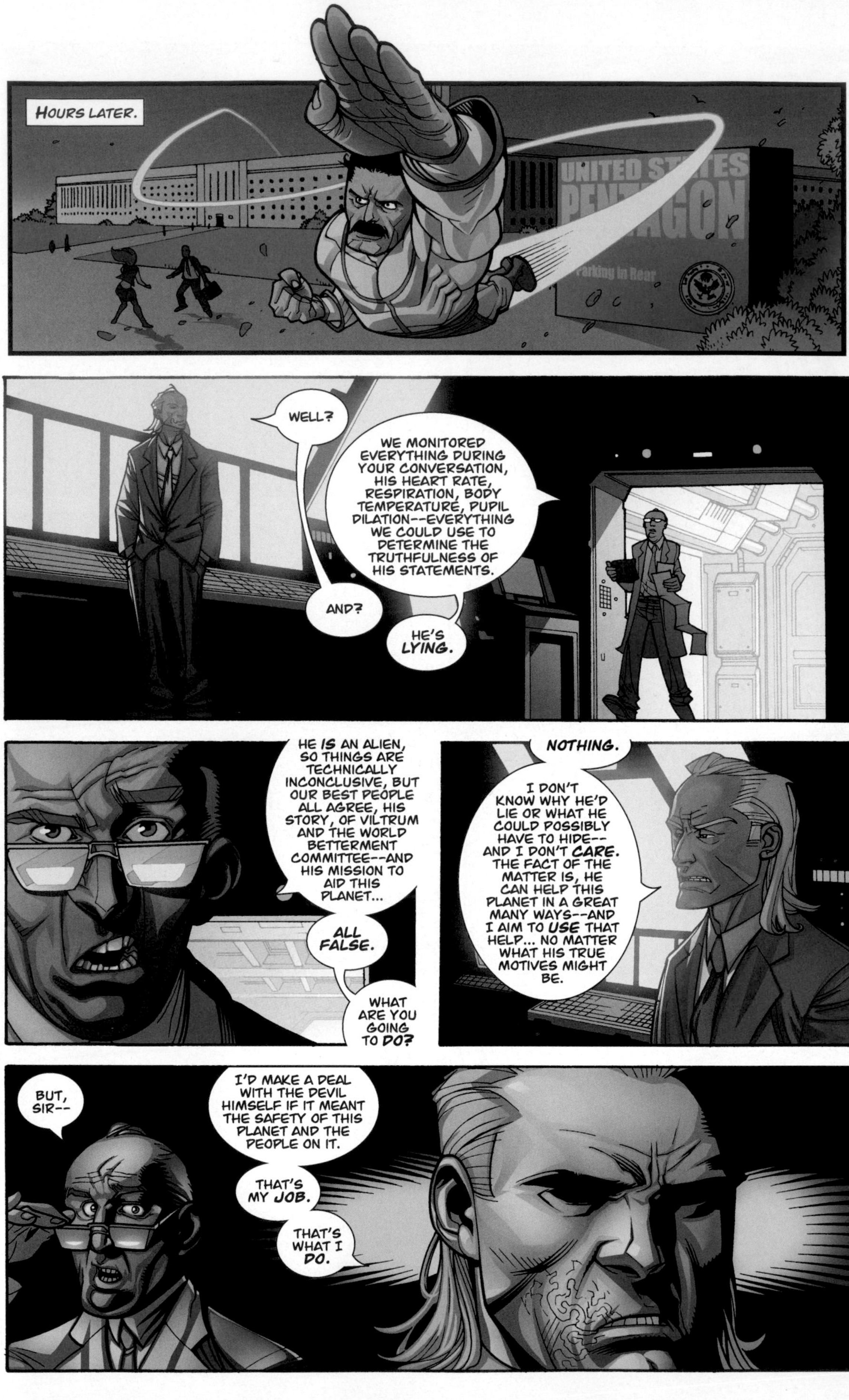
HOURS LATER.
UNITED STATES PENTAGON
Parking in Rear
WELL?
WE MONITORED EVERYTHING DURING YOUR CONVERSATION, HIS HEART RATE, RESPIRATION, BODY TEMPERATURE, PUPIL DILATION--EVERYTHING WE COULD USE TO DETERMINE THE TRUTHFULNESS OF HIS STATEMENTS.
AND?
HE'S LYING.
HE IS AN ALIEN, SO THINGS ARE TECHNICALLY INCONCLUSIVE, BUT OUR BEST PEOPLE ALL AGREE, HIS STORY, OF VILTRUM AND THE WORLD BETTERMENT COMMITTEE--AND HIS MISSION TO AID THIS PLANET...
ALL FALSE.
WHAT ARE YOU GOING TO DO?
NOTHING.
I DON'T KNOW WHY HE'D LIE OR WHAT HE COULD POSSIBLY HAVE TO HIDE--AND I DON'T CARE. THE FACT OF THE MATTER IS, HE CAN HELP THIS PLANET IN A GREAT MANY WAYS--AND I AIM TO USE THAT HELP... NO MATTER WHAT HIS TRUE MOTIVES MIGHT BE.
BUT, SIR--
I'D MAKE A DEAL WITH THE DEVIL HIMSELF IF IT MEANT THE SAFETY OF THIS PLANET AND THE PEOPLE ON IT.
THAT'S MY JOB.
THAT'S WHAT I DO.

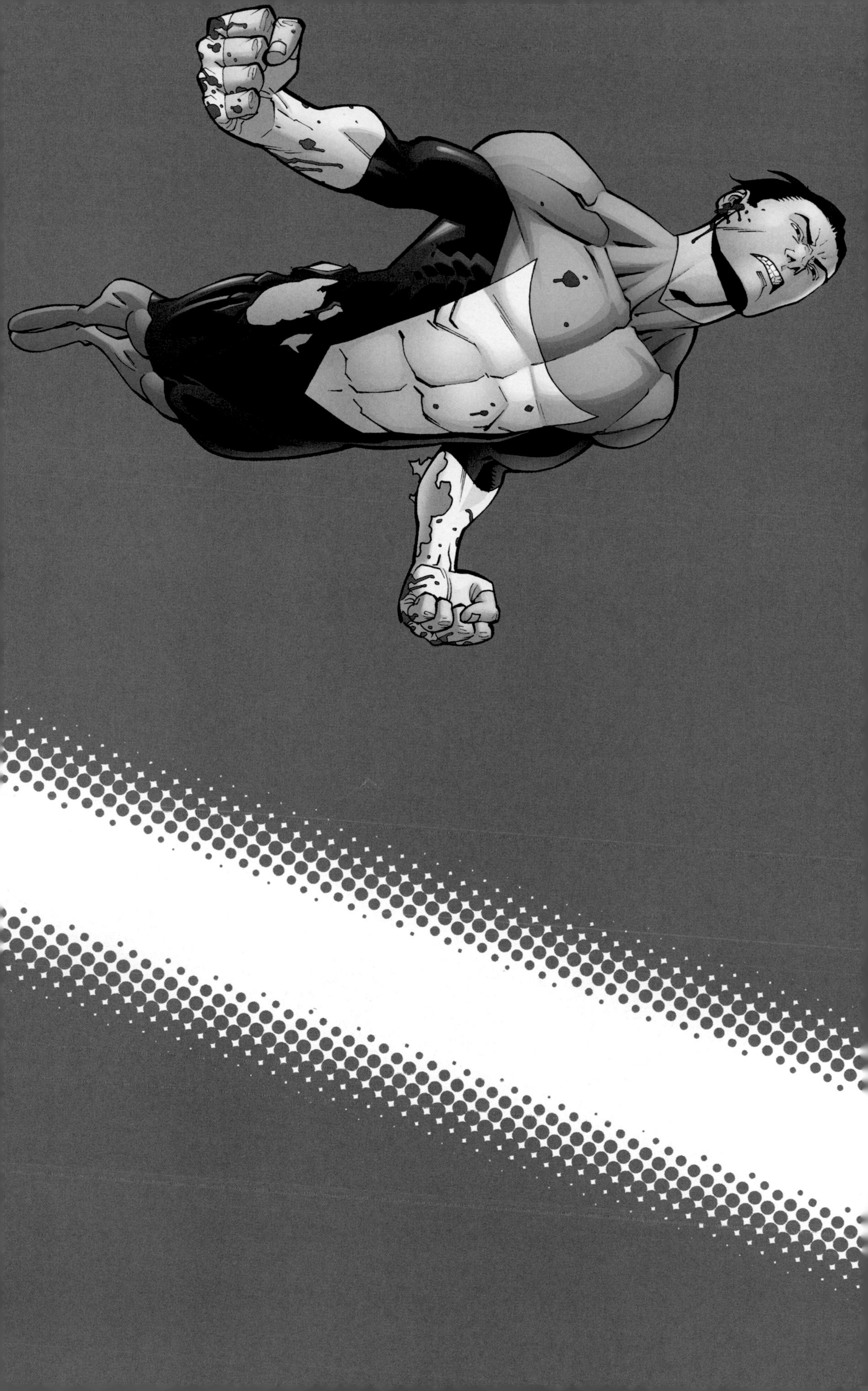

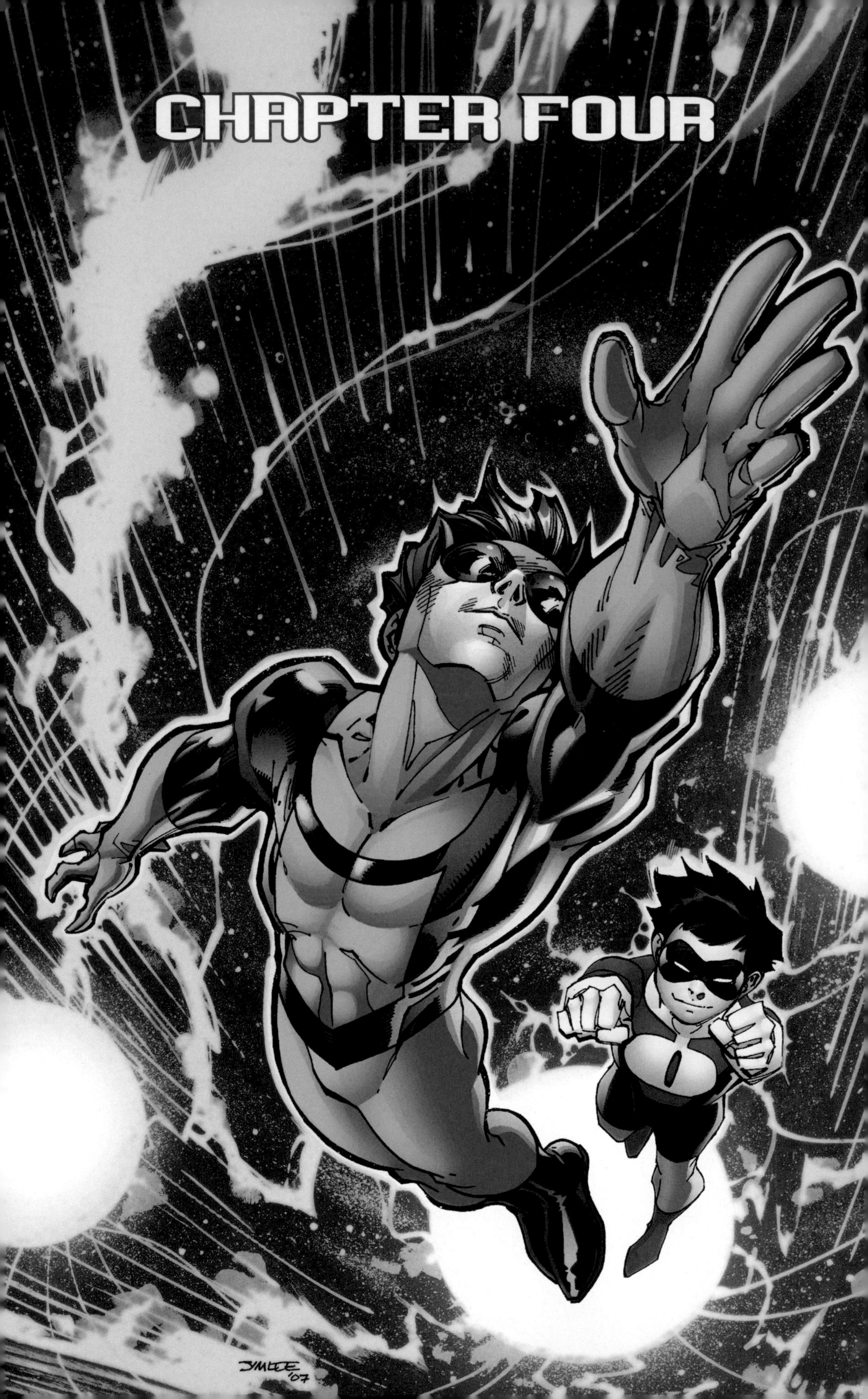
CHAPTER FOUR

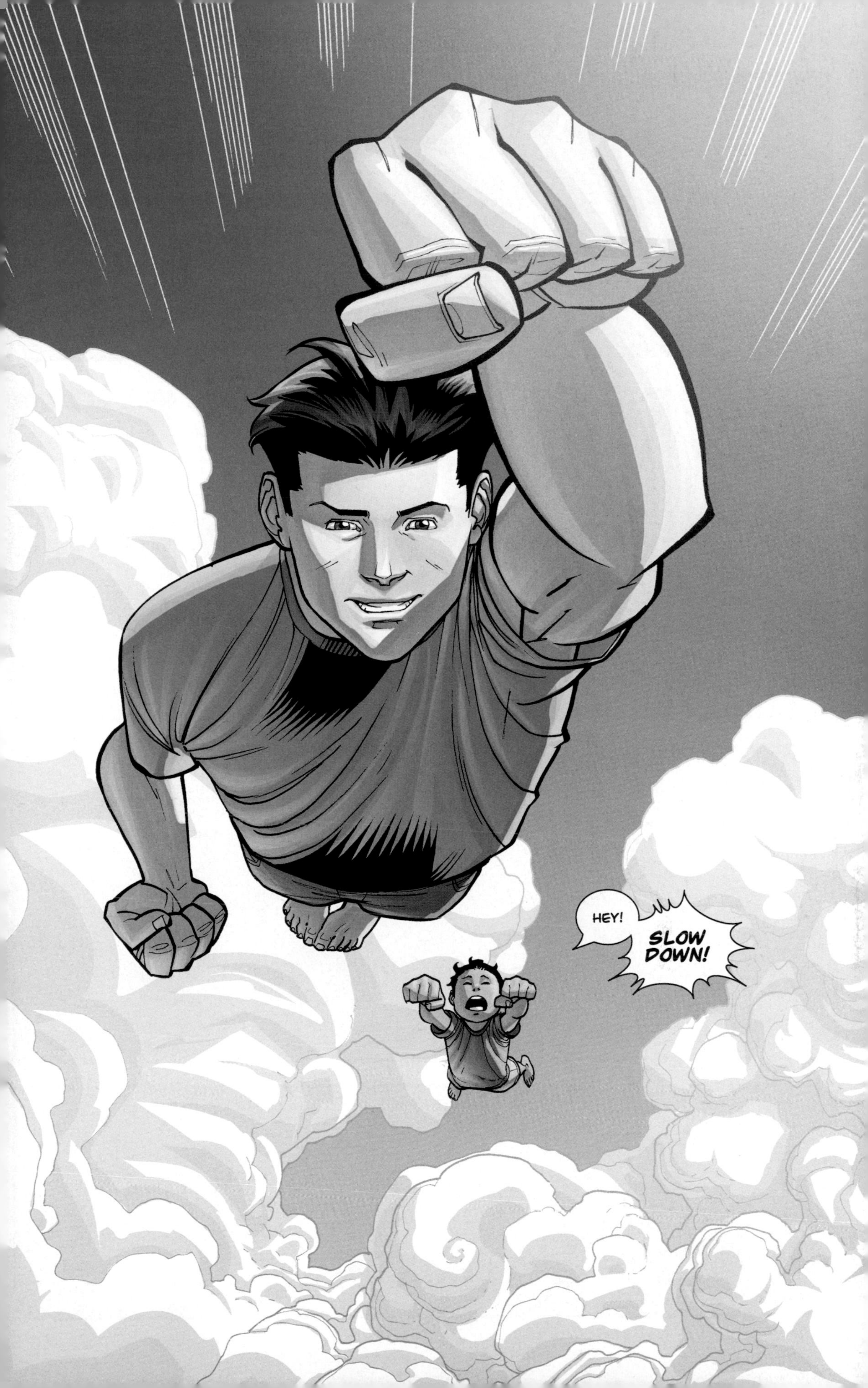
HEY!
SLOW DOWN!

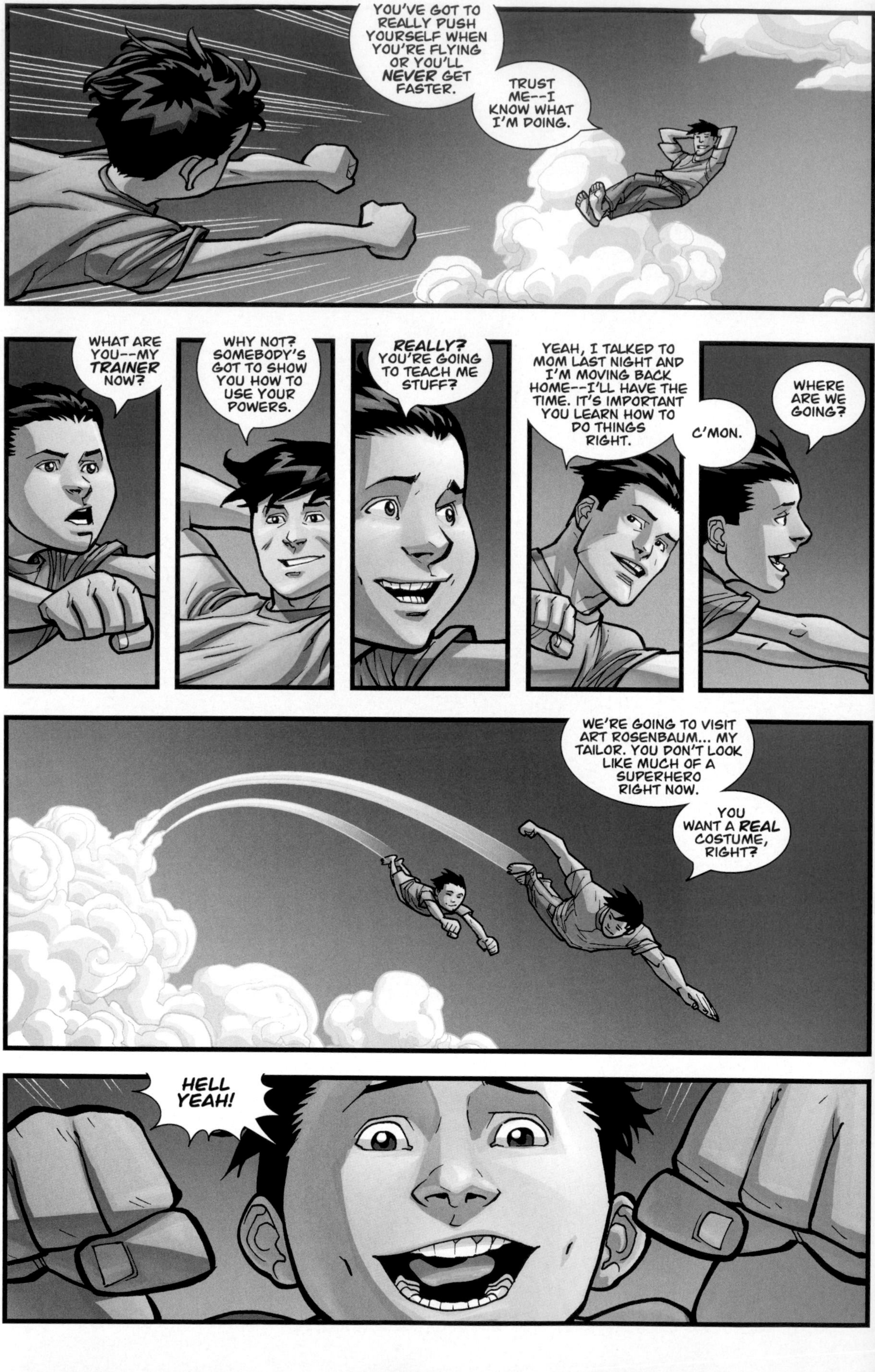
YOU'VE GOT TO REALLY PUSH YOURSELF WHEN YOU'RE FLYING OR YOU'LL NEVER GET FASTER.
TRUST ME--I KNOW WHAT I'M DOING.
WHAT ARE YOU--MY TRAINER NOW?
WHY NOT? SOMEBODY'S GOT TO SHOW YOU HOW TO USE YOUR POWERS.
REALLY? YOU'RE GOING TO TEACH ME STUFF?
YEAH, I TALKED TO MOM LAST NIGHT AND I'M MOVING BACK HOME--I'LL HAVE THE TIME. IT'S IMPORTANT YOU LEARN HOW TO DO THINGS RIGHT.
C'MON.
WHERE ARE WE GOING?
WE'RE GOING TO VISIT ART ROSENBAUM... MY TAILOR. YOU DON'T LOOK LIKE MUCH OF A SUPERHERO RIGHT NOW.
YOU WANT A REAL COSTUME, RIGHT?
HELL YEAH!

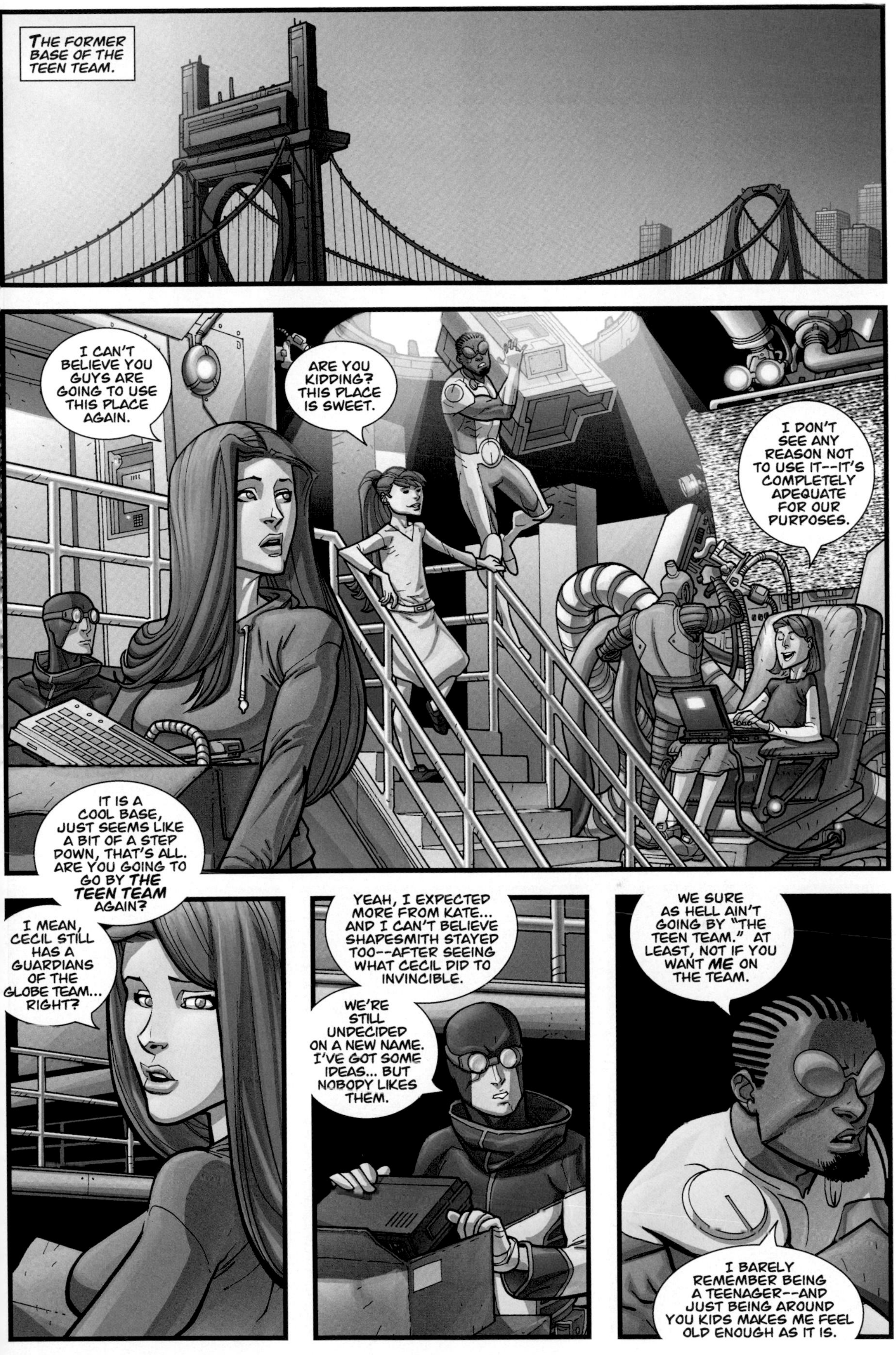
THE FORMER BASE OF THE TEEN TEAM.
I CAN'T BELIEVE YOU GUYS ARE GOING TO USE THIS PLACE AGAIN.
ARE YOU KIDDING? THIS PLACE IS SWEET.
I DON'T SEE ANY REASON NOT TO USE IT--IT'S COMPLETELY ADEQUATE FOR OUR PURPOSES.
IT IS A COOL BASE, JUST SEEMS LIKE A BIT OF A STEP DOWN, THAT'S ALL. ARE YOU GOING TO GO BY THE TEEN TEAM AGAIN?
I MEAN, CECIL STILL HAS A GUARDIANS OF THE GLOBE TEAM... RIGHT?
YEAH, I EXPECTED MORE FROM KATE... AND I CAN'T BELIEVE SHAPESMITH STAYED TOO--AFTER SEEING WHAT CECIL DID TO INVINCIBLE.
WE'RE STILL UNDECIDED ON A NEW NAME. I'VE GOT SOME IDEAS... BUT NOBODY LIKES THEM.
WE SURE AS HELL AIN'T GOING BY "THE TEEN TEAM." AT LEAST, NOT IF YOU WANT ME ON THE TEAM.
I BARELY REMEMBER BEING A TEENAGER--AND JUST BEING AROUND YOU KIDS MAKES ME FEEL OLD ENOUGH AS IT IS.

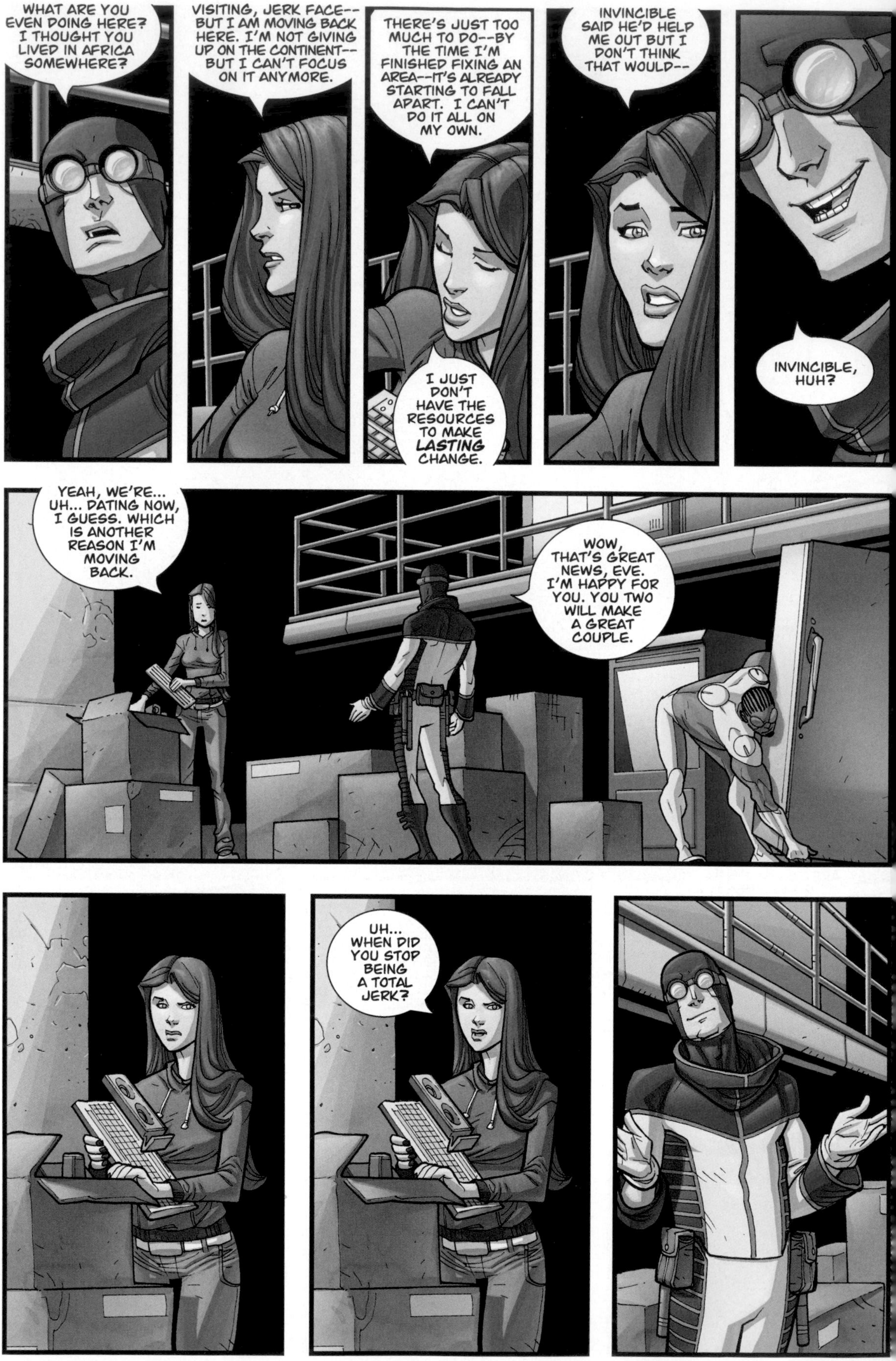
WHAT ARE YOU EVEN DOING HERE? I THOUGHT YOU LIVED IN AFRICA SOMEWHERE?
VISITING, JERK FACE-- BUT I AM MOVING BACK HERE. I'M NOT GIVING UP ON THE CONTINENT-- BUT I CAN'T FOCUS ON IT ANYMORE.
THERE'S JUST TOO MUCH TO DO--BY THE TIME I'M FINISHED FIXING AN AREA--IT'S ALREADY STARTING TO FALL APART. I CAN'T DO IT ALL ON MY OWN.
I JUST DON'T HAVE THE RESOURCES TO MAKE LASTING CHANGE.
INVINCIBLE SAID HE'D HELP ME OUT BUT I DON'T THINK THAT WOULD--
INVINCIBLE, HUH?
YEAH, WE'RE... UH... DATING NOW, I GUESS. WHICH IS ANOTHER REASON I'M MOVING BACK.
WOW, THAT'S GREAT NEWS, EVE. I'M HAPPY FOR YOU. YOU TWO WILL MAKE A GREAT COUPLE.
UH... WHEN DID YOU STOP BEING A TOTAL JERK?

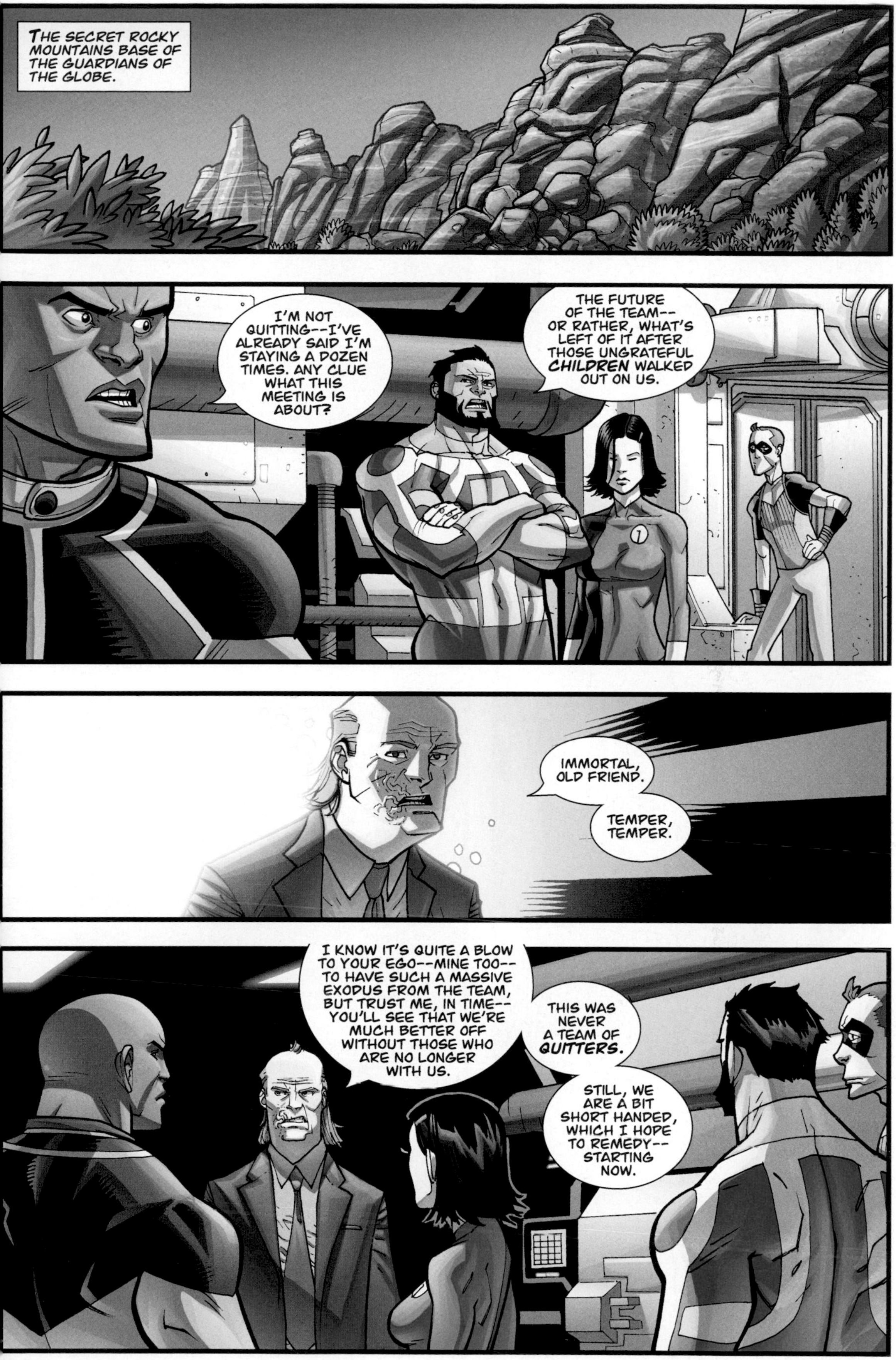
THE SECRET ROCKY MOUNTAINS BASE OF THE GUARDIANS OF THE GLOBE.
I'M NOT QUITTING--I'VE ALREADY SAID I'M STAYING A DOZEN TIMES. ANY CLUE WHAT THIS MEETING IS ABOUT?
THE FUTURE OF THE TEAM-- OR RATHER, WHAT'S LEFT OF IT AFTER THOSE UNGRATEFUL CHILDREN WALKED OUT ON US.
IMMORTAL, OLD FRIEND.
TEMPER, TEMPER.
I KNOW IT'S QUITE A BLOW TO YOUR EGO--MINE TOO-- TO HAVE SUCH A MASSIVE EXODUS FROM THE TEAM, BUT TRUST ME, IN TIME-- YOU'LL SEE THAT WE'RE MUCH BETTER OFF WITHOUT THOSE WHO ARE NO LONGER WITH US.
THIS WAS NEVER A TEAM OF QUITTERS.
STILL, WE ARE A BIT SHORT HANDED, WHICH I HOPE TO REMEDY-- STARTING NOW.

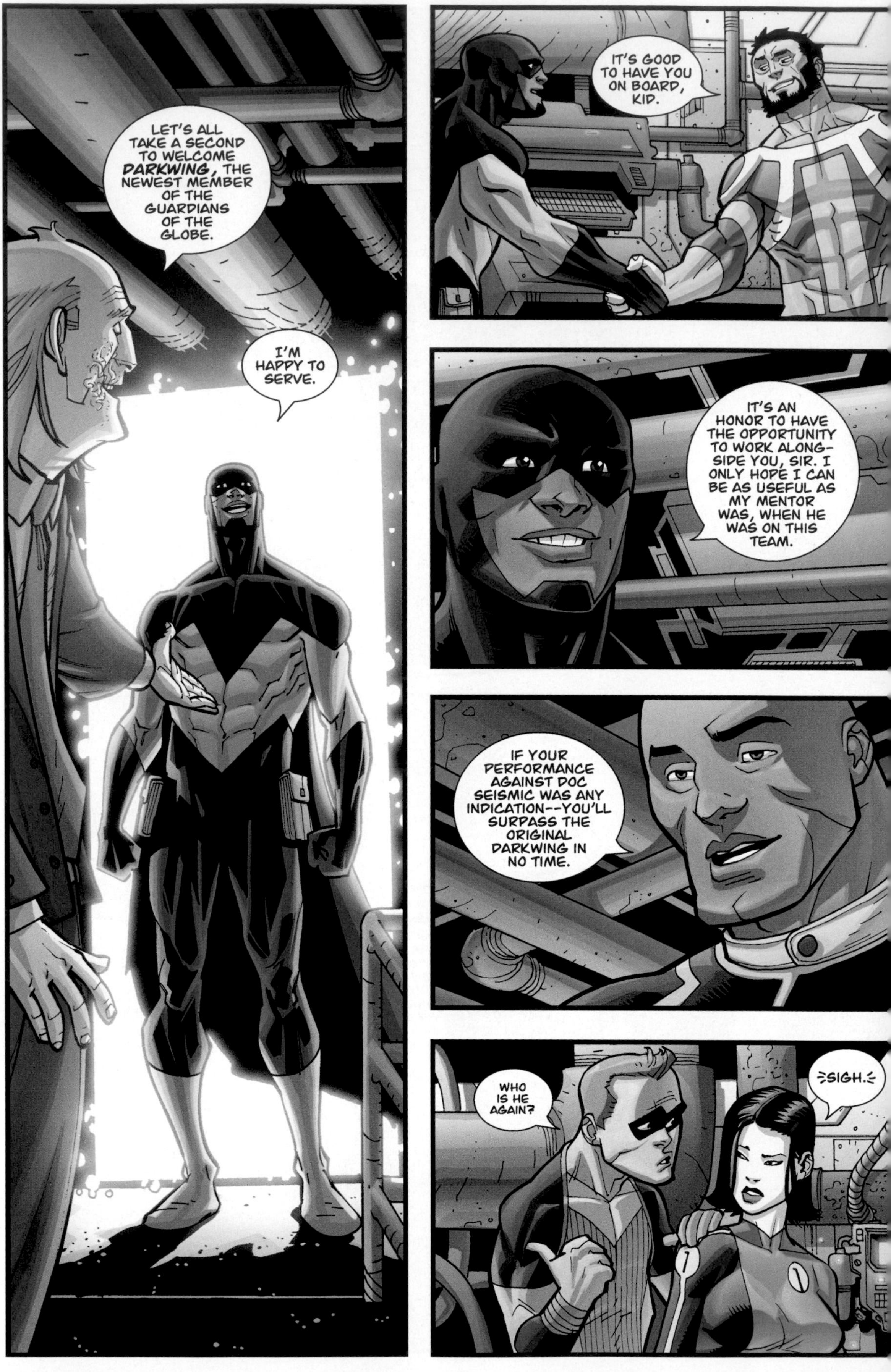
LET'S ALL TAKE A SECOND TO WELCOME DARKWING, THE NEWEST MEMBER OF THE GUARDIANS OF THE GLOBE.
I'M HAPPY TO SERVE.
IT'S GOOD TO HAVE YOU ON BOARD, KID.
IT'S AN HONOR TO HAVE THE OPPORTUNITY TO WORK ALONG-SIDE YOU, SIR. I ONLY HOPE I CAN BE AS USEFUL AS MY MENTOR WAS, WHEN HE WAS ON THIS TEAM.
IF YOUR PERFORMANCE AGAINST DOC SEISMIC WAS ANY INDICATION--YOU'LL SURPASS THE ORIGINAL DARKWING IN NO TIME.
WHO IS HE AGAIN?
SIGH.

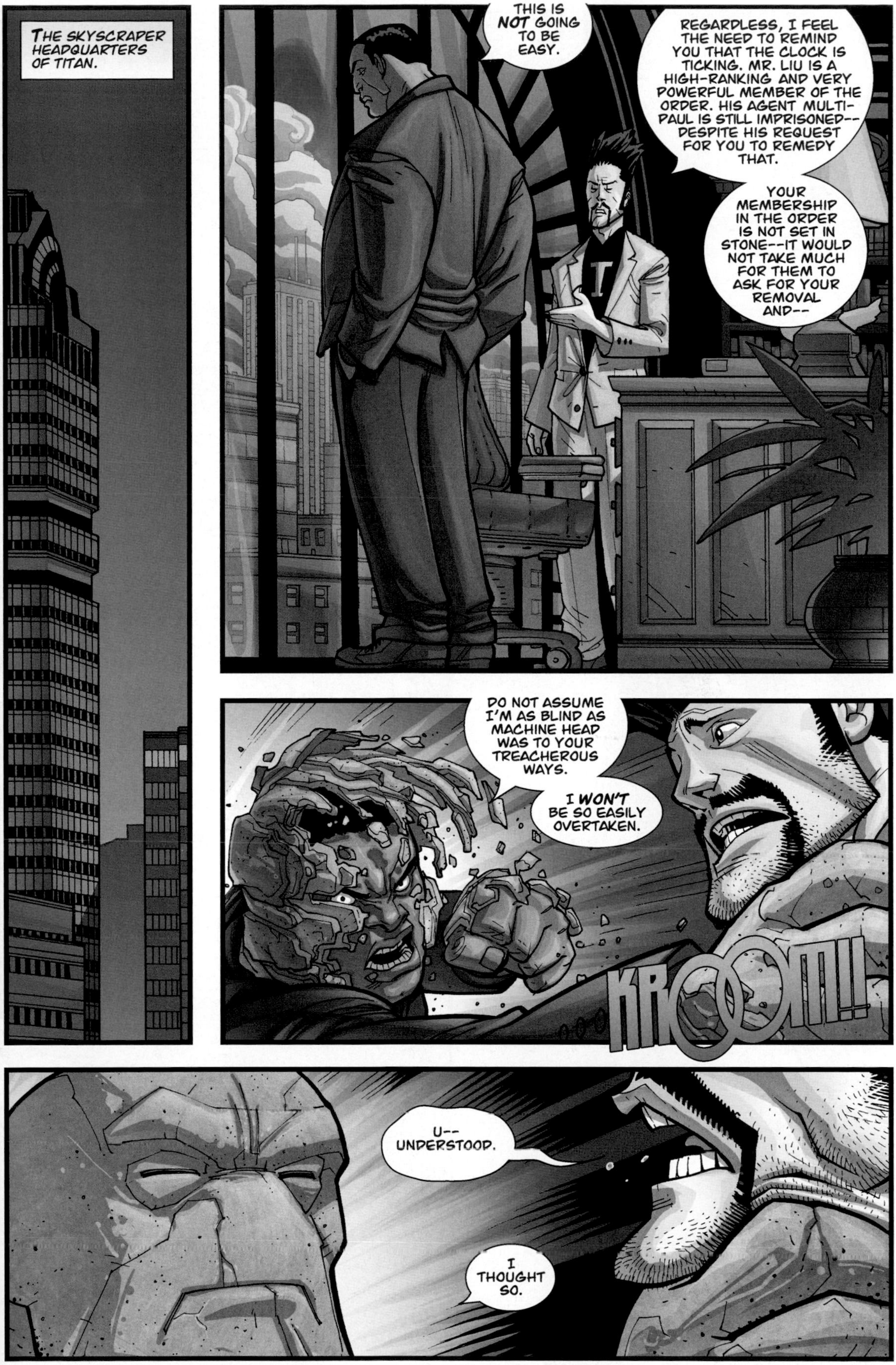
THE SKYSCRAPER HEADQUARTERS OF TITAN.
THIS IS NOT GOING TO BE EASY.
REGARDLESS, I FEEL THE NEED TO REMIND YOU THAT THE CLOCK IS TICKING. MR. LIU IS A HIGH-RANKING AND VERY POWERFUL MEMBER OF THE ORDER. HIS AGENT MULTI-PAUL IS STILL IMPRISONED-- DESPITE HIS REQUEST FOR YOU TO REMEDY THAT.
YOUR MEMBERSHIP IN THE ORDER IS NOT SET IN STONE--IT WOULD NOT TAKE MUCH FOR THEM TO ASK FOR YOUR REMOVAL AND--
DO NOT ASSUME I'M AS BLIND AS MACHINE HEAD WAS TO YOUR TREACHEROUS WAYS.
I WON'T BE SO EASILY OVERTAKEN.
KROOOM!!
U-- UNDERSTOOD.
I THOUGHT SO.

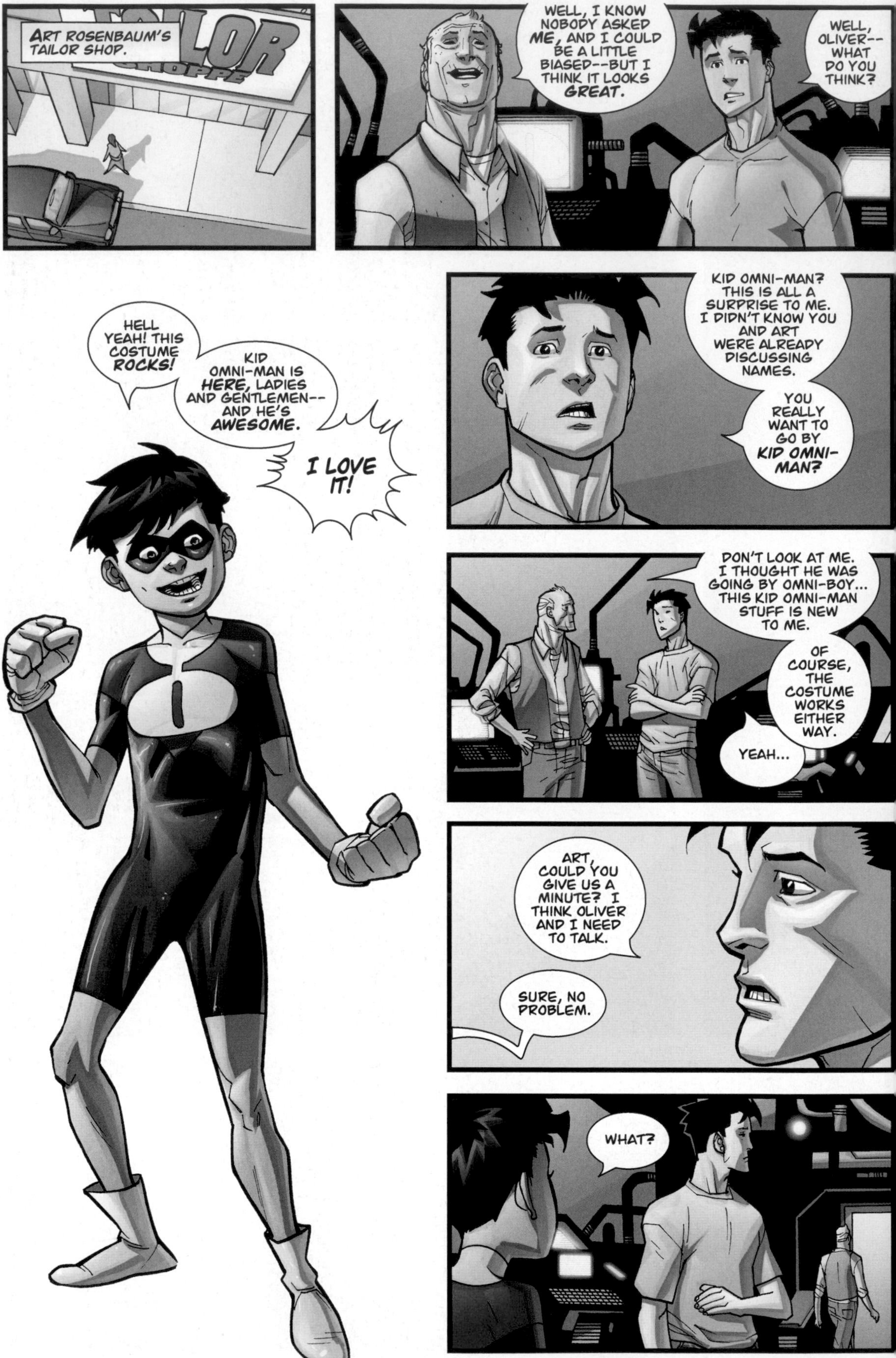
ART ROSENBAUM'S TAILOR SHOP.
WELL, I KNOW NOBODY ASKED ME, AND I COULD BE A LITTLE BIASED--BUT I THINK IT LOOKS GREAT.
WELL, OLIVER--WHAT DO YOU THINK?
HELL YEAH! THIS COSTUME ROCKS!
KID OMNI-MAN IS HERE, LADIES AND GENTLEMEN--AND HE'S AWESOME.
I LOVE IT!
KID OMNI-MAN? THIS IS ALL A SURPRISE TO ME. I DIDN'T KNOW YOU AND ART WERE ALREADY DISCUSSING NAMES.
YOU REALLY WANT TO GO BY KID OMNI-MAN?
DON'T LOOK AT ME. I THOUGHT HE WAS GOING BY OMNI-BOY... THIS KID OMNI-MAN STUFF IS NEW TO ME.
OF COURSE, THE COSTUME WORKS EITHER WAY.
YEAH...
ART, COULD YOU GIVE US A MINUTE? I THINK OLIVER AND I NEED TO TALK.
SURE, NO PROBLEM.
WHAT?

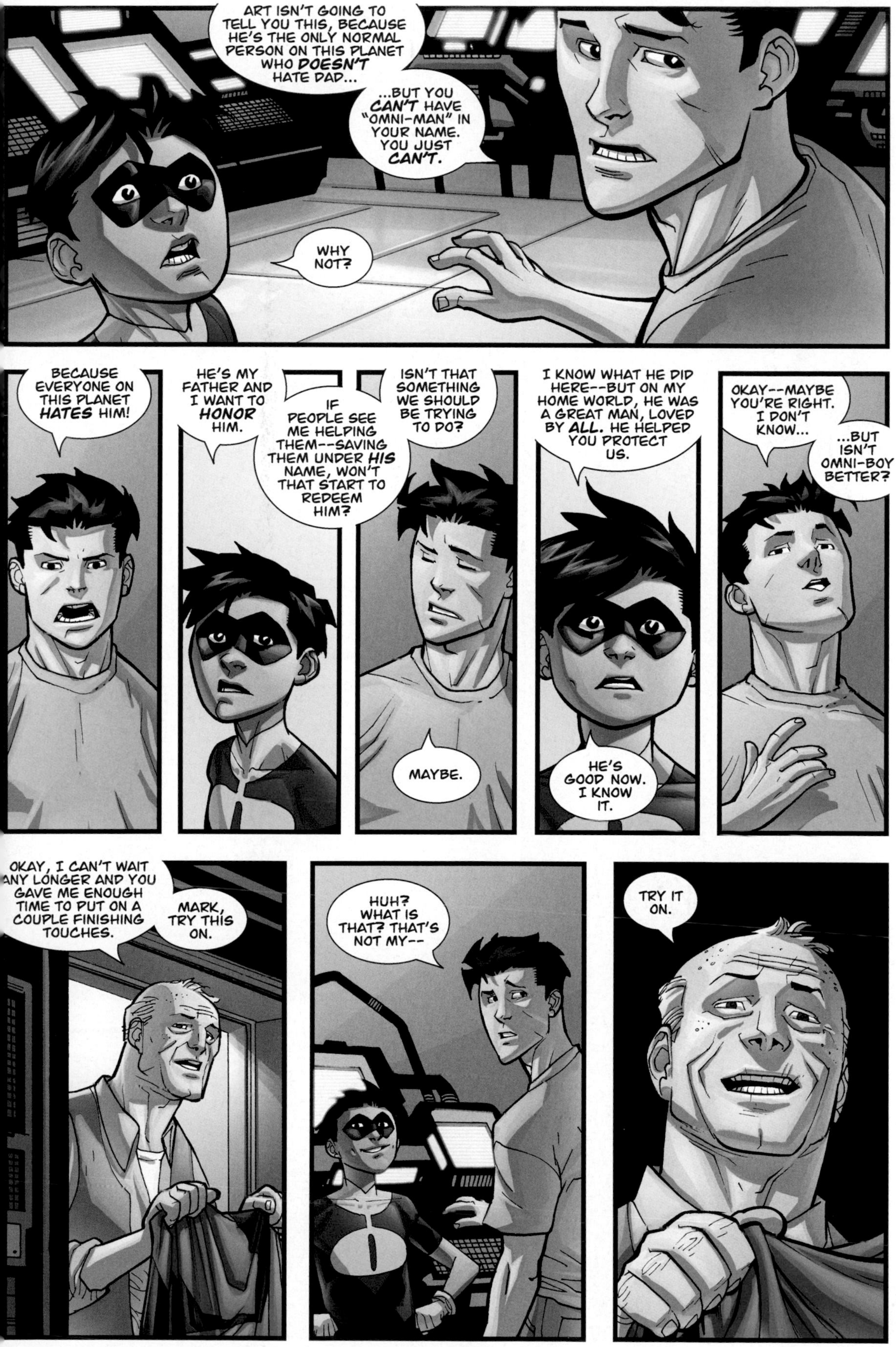
ART ISN'T GOING TO TELL YOU THIS, BECAUSE HE'S THE ONLY NORMAL PERSON ON THIS PLANET WHO DOESN'T HATE DAD...
...BUT YOU CAN'T HAVE "OMNI-MAN" IN YOUR NAME. YOU JUST CAN'T.
WHY NOT?
BECAUSE EVERYONE ON THIS PLANET HATES HIM!
HE'S MY FATHER AND I WANT TO HONOR HIM.
IF PEOPLE SEE ME HELPING THEM--SAVING THEM UNDER HIS NAME, WON'T THAT START TO REDEEM HIM?
ISN'T THAT SOMETHING WE SHOULD BE TRYING TO DO?
MAYBE.
I KNOW WHAT HE DID HERE--BUT ON MY HOME WORLD, HE WAS A GREAT MAN, LOVED BY ALL. HE HELPED YOU PROTECT US.
HE'S GOOD NOW. I KNOW IT.
OKAY--MAYBE YOU'RE RIGHT. I DON'T KNOW...
...BUT ISN'T OMNI-BOY BETTER?
OKAY, I CAN'T WAIT ANY LONGER AND YOU GAVE ME ENOUGH TIME TO PUT ON A COUPLE FINISHING TOUCHES.
MARK, TRY THIS ON.
HUH? WHAT IS THAT? THAT'S NOT MY--
TRY IT ON.

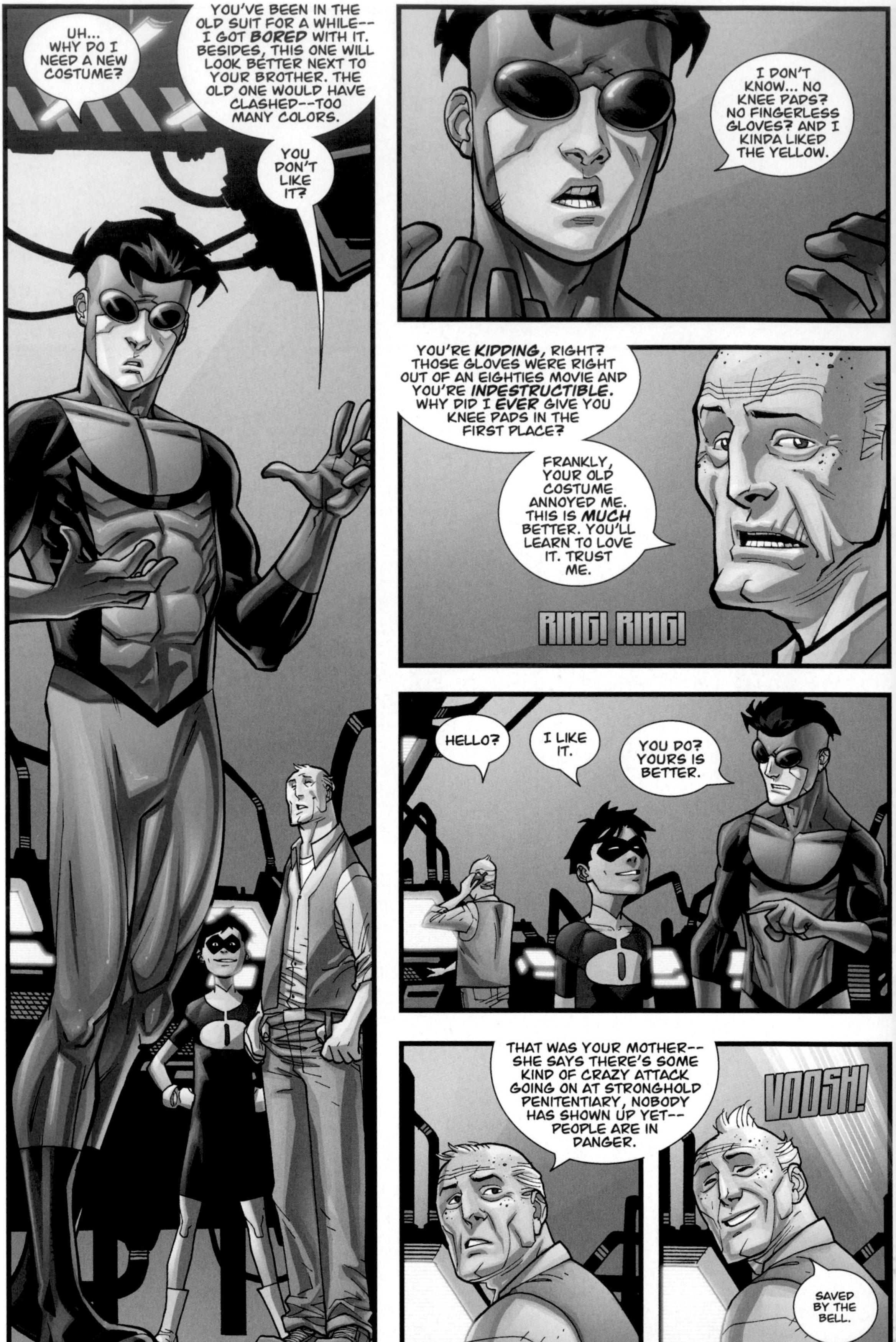

UH... WHY DO I NEED A NEW COSTUME?
YOU'VE BEEN IN THE OLD SUIT FOR A WHILE-- I GOT BORED WITH IT. BESIDES, THIS ONE WILL LOOK BETTER NEXT TO YOUR BROTHER. THE OLD ONE WOULD HAVE CLASHED--TOO MANY COLORS.
YOU DON'T LIKE IT?
I DON'T KNOW... NO KNEE PADS? NO FINGERLESS GLOVES? AND I KINDA LIKED THE YELLOW.
YOU'RE KIDDING, RIGHT? THOSE GLOVES WERE RIGHT OUT OF AN EIGHTIES MOVIE AND YOU'RE INDESTRUCTIBLE. WHY DID I EVER GIVE YOU KNEE PADS IN THE FIRST PLACE?
FRANKLY, YOUR OLD COSTUME ANNOYED ME. THIS IS MUCH BETTER. YOU'LL LEARN TO LOVE IT. TRUST ME.
RING! RING!
HELLO?
I LIKE IT.
YOU DO? YOURS IS BETTER.
THAT WAS YOUR MOTHER-- SHE SAYS THERE'S SOME KIND OF CRAZY ATTACK GOING ON AT STRONGHOLD PENITENTIARY, NOBODY HAS SHOWN UP YET-- PEOPLE ARE IN DANGER.
VOOSH!
SAVED BY THE BELL.

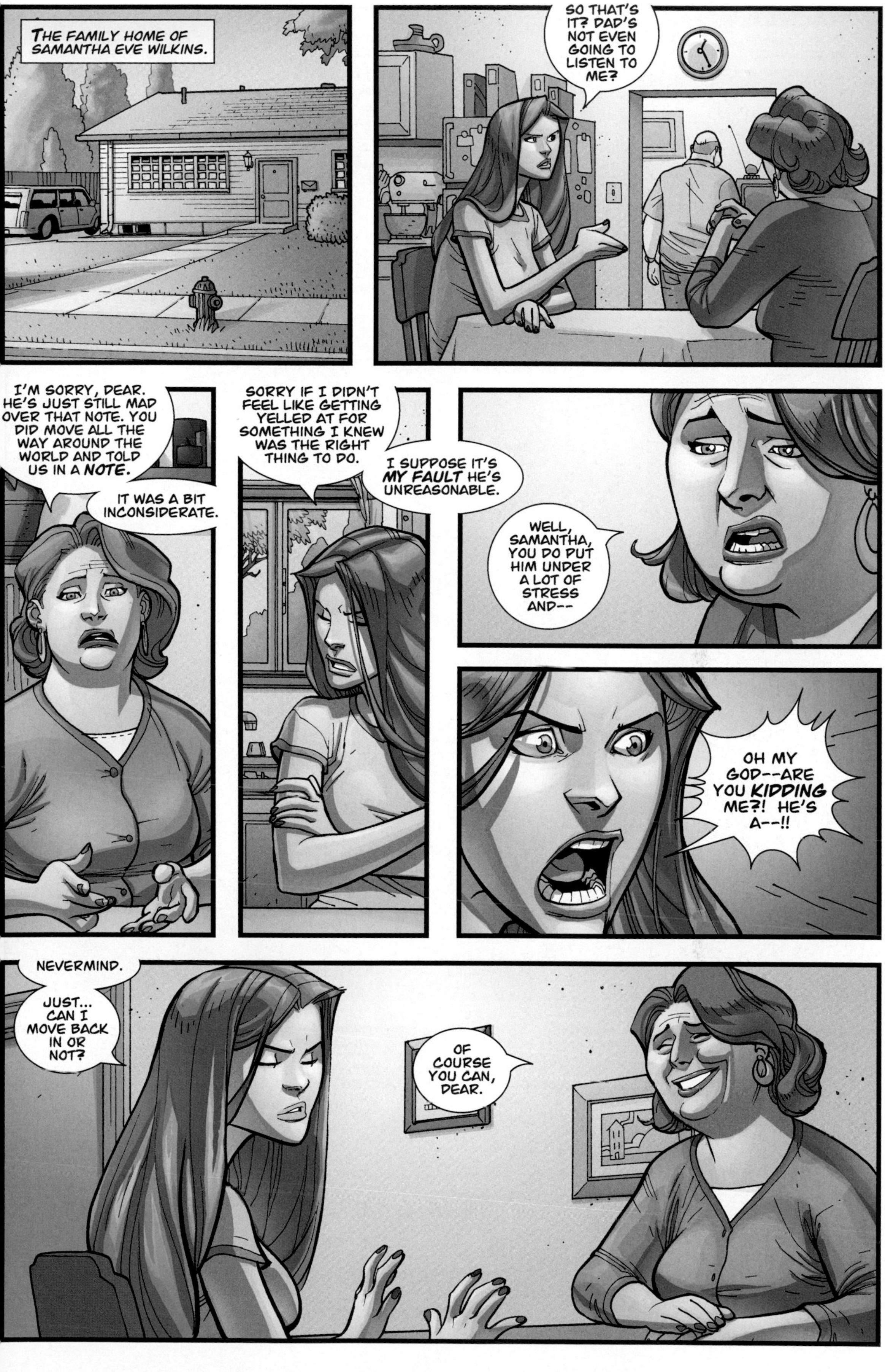
THE FAMILY HOME OF SAMANTHA EVE WILKINS.
SO THAT'S IT? DAD'S NOT EVEN GOING TO LISTEN TO ME?
I'M SORRY, DEAR. HE'S JUST STILL MAD OVER THAT NOTE. YOU DID MOVE ALL THE WAY AROUND THE WORLD AND TOLD US IN A NOTE.
IT WAS A BIT INCONSIDERATE.
SORRY IF I DIDN'T FEEL LIKE GETTING YELLED AT FOR SOMETHING I KNEW WAS THE RIGHT THING TO DO.
I SUPPOSE IT'S MY FAULT HE'S UNREASONABLE.
WELL, SAMANTHA, YOU DO PUT HIM UNDER A LOT OF STRESS AND--
OH MY GOD--ARE YOU KIDDING ME?! HE'S A--!!
NEVERMIND.
JUST... CAN I MOVE BACK IN OR NOT?
OF COURSE YOU CAN, DEAR.

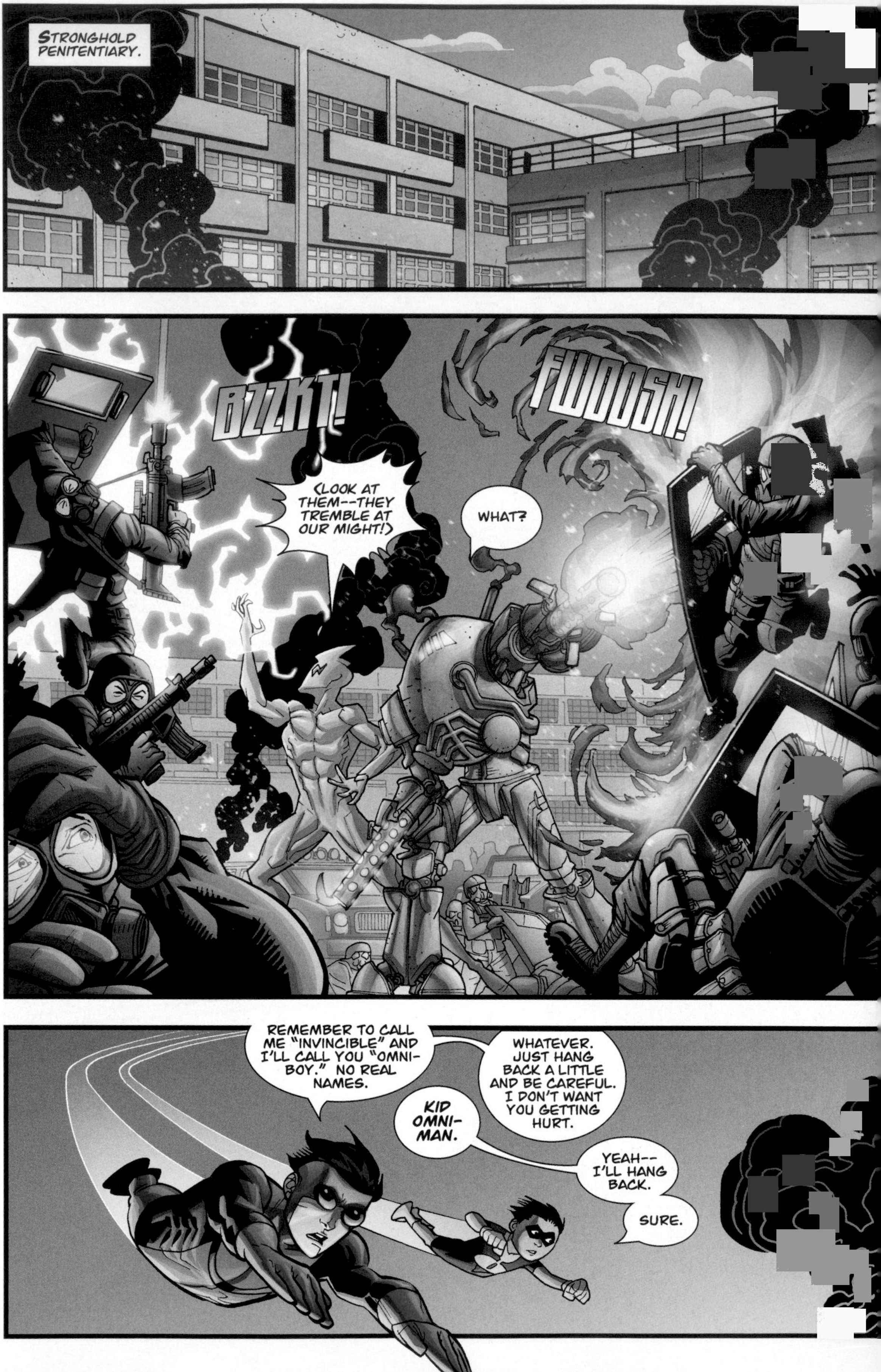
STRONGHOLD PENITENTIARY.
BZZKT!
FWOOSH!
<LOOK AT THEM--THEY TREMBLE AT OUR MIGHT!>
WHAT?
REMEMBER TO CALL ME "INVINCIBLE" AND I'LL CALL YOU "OMNI-BOY." NO REAL NAMES.
KID OMNI-MAN.
WHATEVER. JUST HANG BACK A LITTLE AND BE CAREFUL. I DON'T WANT YOU GETTING HURT.
YEAH-- I'LL HANG BACK.
SURE.

WILL DO!

OLIV-- OMNI-B-- KID-OM-- JUST STOP!!

FINALLY-- I THOUGHT THE ORDER WAS GOING TO LET ME ROT IN HERE FOREVER.

LOCK DOWN! LOCK DOWN!

‹WHY ARE YOU WASTING YOUR TIME OUT HERE? OUR ORDERS ARE TO FREE ONE PRISONER--WE SHOULD BE FIGHTING OUR WAY INSIDE! I NEED YOU TO COVER ME!›

FWOOSH!

ARE YOU SPEAKING RUSSIAN AGAIN? I CAN'T UNDERSTAND A DAMN WORD YOU'RE SAYING!

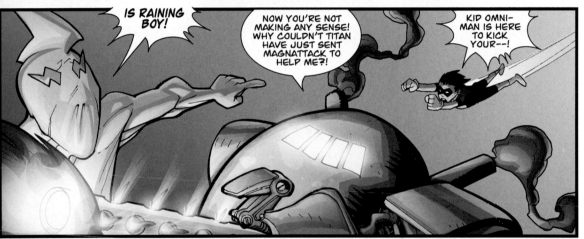

IS RAINING BOY!

NOW YOU'RE NOT MAKING ANY SENSE! WHY COULDN'T TITAN HAVE JUST SENT MAGNATTACK TO HELP ME?!

KID OMNI-MAN IS HERE TO KICK YOUR--!

YEEAAGHH!

RZZZKKT!

‹HEAD STRONG AMERICAN BOY MUST DIE!›

BOOM!!

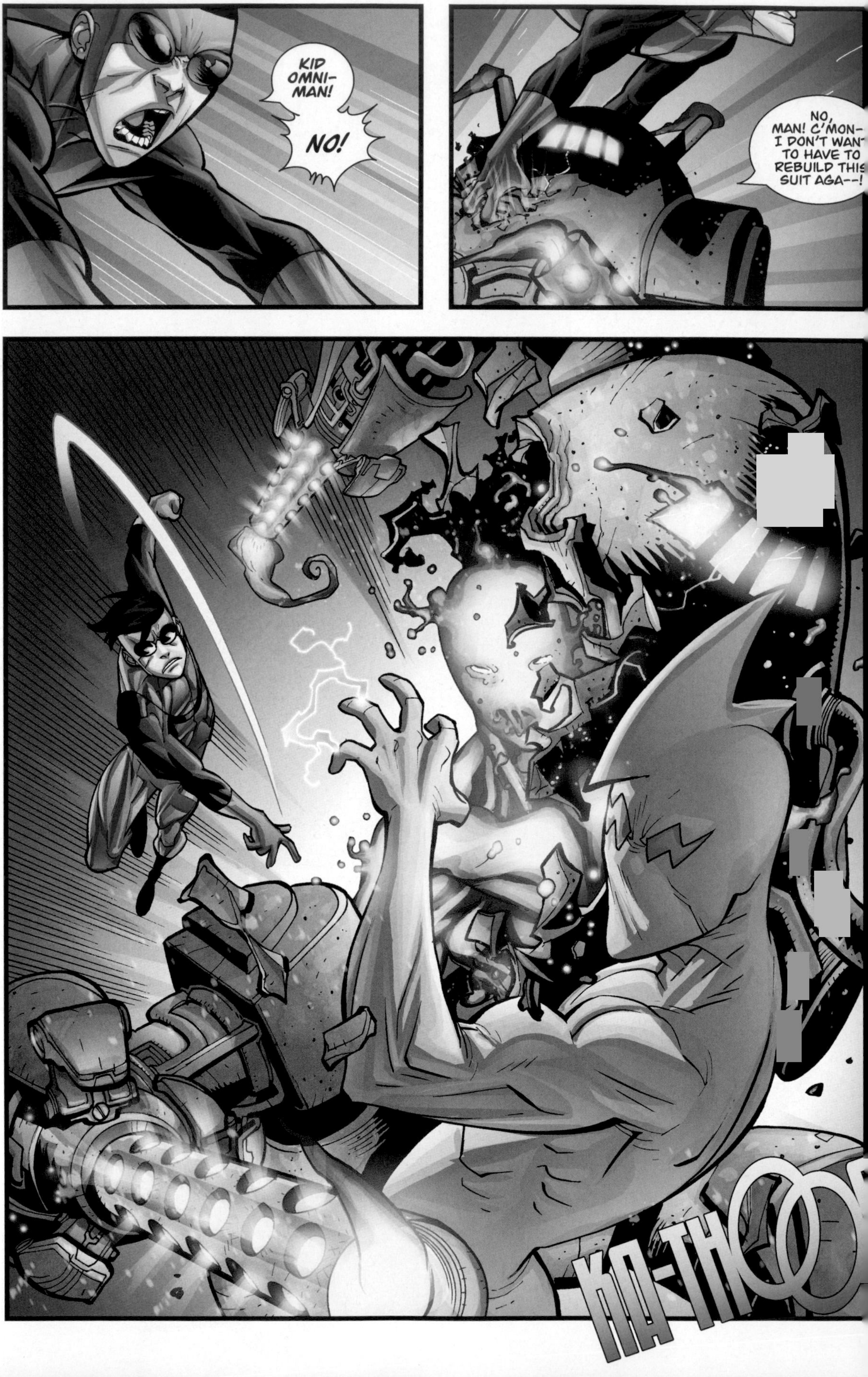
KID OMNI-MAN!
NO!
NO, MAN! C'MON— I DON'T WANT TO HAVE TO REBUILD THIS SUIT AGA--!
KA-THOO

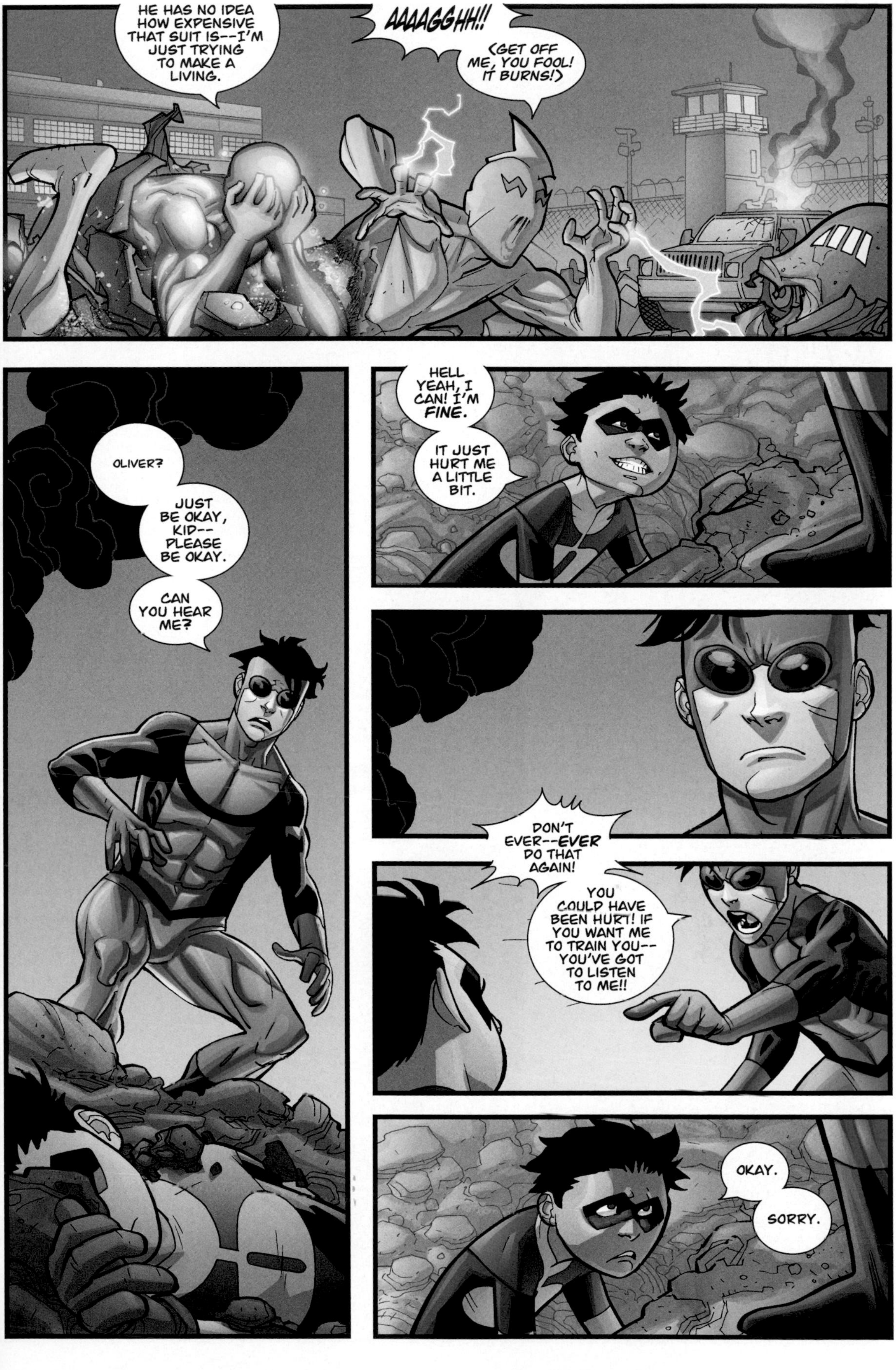
HE HAS NO IDEA HOW EXPENSIVE THAT SUIT IS--I'M JUST TRYING TO MAKE A LIVING.
AAAAGGHH!!
(GET OFF ME, YOU FOOL! IT BURNS!)
OLIVER?
JUST BE OKAY, KID-- PLEASE BE OKAY.
CAN YOU HEAR ME?
HELL YEAH, I CAN! I'M FINE.
IT JUST HURT ME A LITTLE BIT.
DON'T EVER--EVER DO THAT AGAIN!
YOU COULD HAVE BEEN HURT! IF YOU WANT ME TO TRAIN YOU-- YOU'VE GOT TO LISTEN TO ME!!
OKAY.
SORRY.

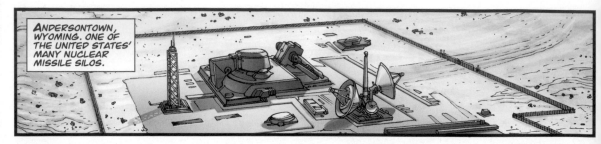

ANDERSONTOWN, WYOMING. ONE OF THE UNITED STATES' MANY NUCLEAR MISSILE SILOS.

I CAN'T BELIEVE THEY STILL HAVEN'T FINISHED THE REPAIRS AFTER THE ATTACK FROM THE LIZARD LEAGUE. OUR TAX DOLLARS AT WORK, HUH?

NO KIDDING-- THIS PLACE IS A WRECK.

THANKFULLY-- MOST OF THOSE GUYS ARE DEAD NOW. SO THE CHANCES OF SOMETHING LIKE THAT HAPPENING AGAIN ARE SLIM AND--

BOOM!!

SO SORRY FOR THE INTERRUPTION. PLEASE, CONTINUE.

YOU WERE SAYING...?

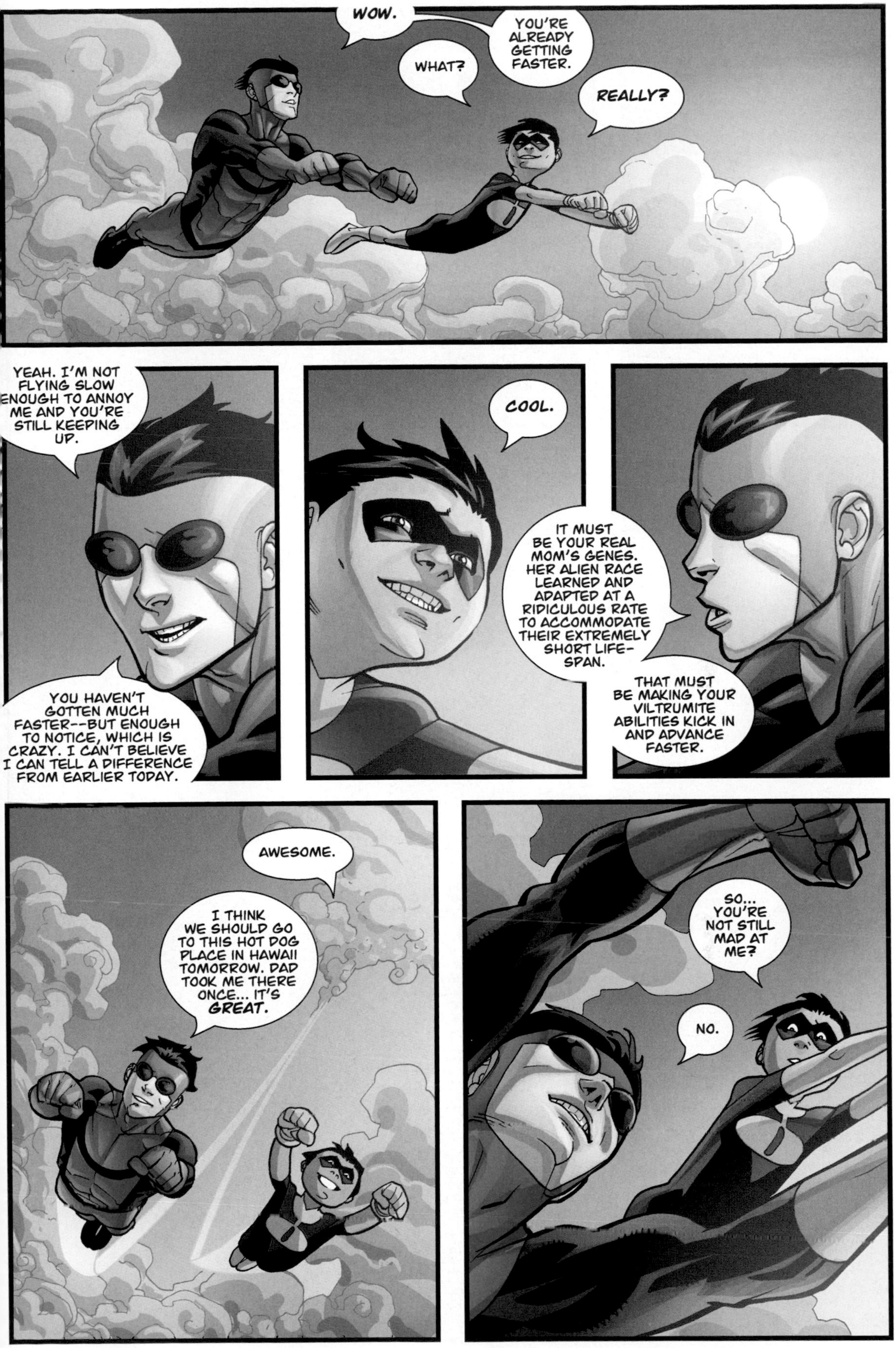
WOW.
YOU'RE ALREADY GETTING FASTER.
WHAT?
REALLY?
YEAH. I'M NOT FLYING SLOW ENOUGH TO ANNOY ME AND YOU'RE STILL KEEPING UP.
YOU HAVEN'T GOTTEN MUCH FASTER--BUT ENOUGH TO NOTICE, WHICH IS CRAZY. I CAN'T BELIEVE I CAN TELL A DIFFERENCE FROM EARLIER TODAY.
COOL.
IT MUST BE YOUR REAL MOM'S GENES. HER ALIEN RACE LEARNED AND ADAPTED AT A RIDICULOUS RATE TO ACCOMMODATE THEIR EXTREMELY SHORT LIFE-SPAN.
THAT MUST BE MAKING YOUR VILTRUMITE ABILITIES KICK IN AND ADVANCE FASTER.
AWESOME.
I THINK WE SHOULD GO TO THIS HOT DOG PLACE IN HAWAII TOMORROW. DAD TOOK ME THERE ONCE... IT'S GREAT.
SO... YOU'RE NOT STILL MAD AT ME?
NO.

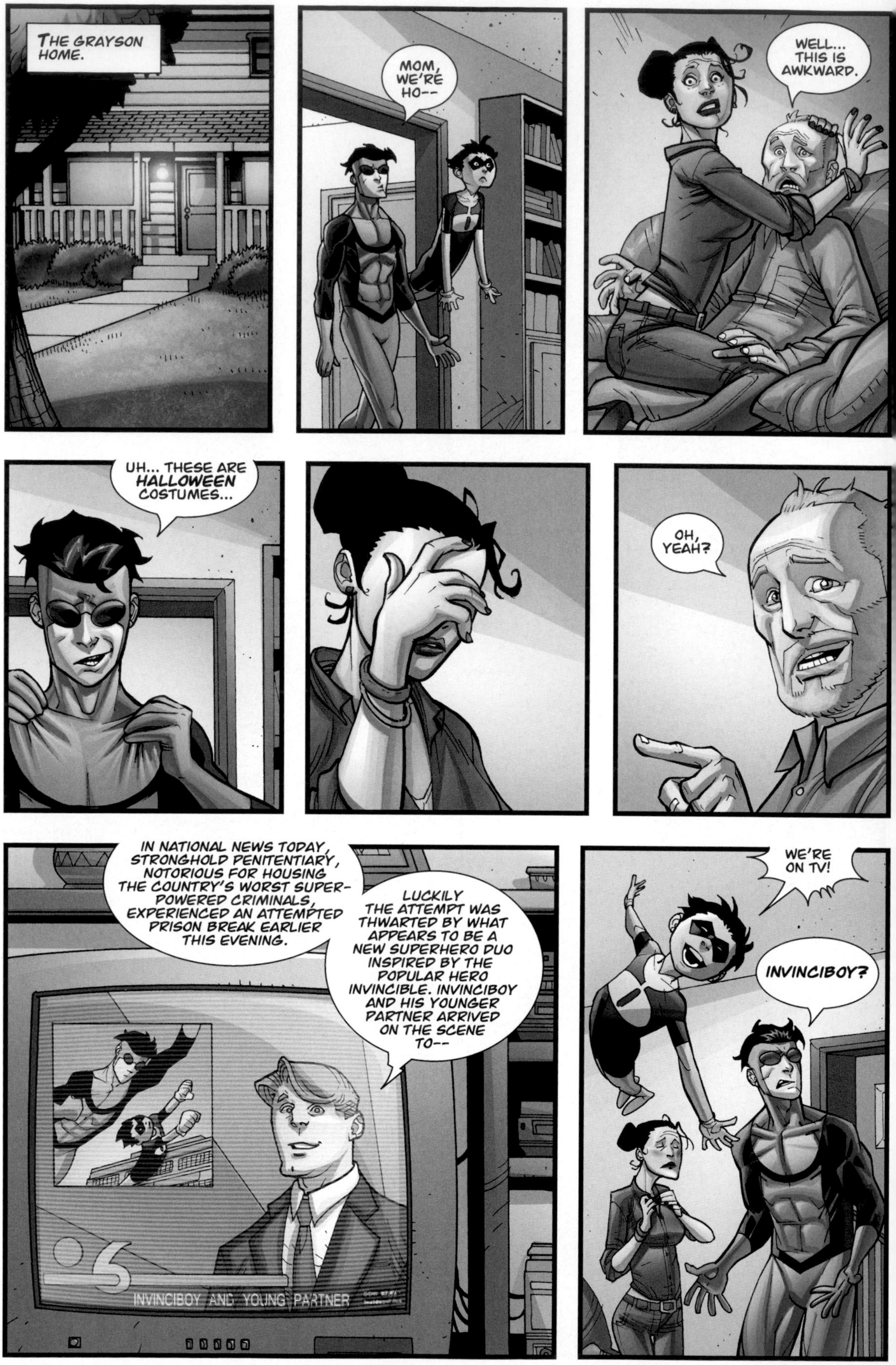
THE GRAYSON HOME.
MOM, WE'RE HO--
WELL... THIS IS AWKWARD.
UH... THESE ARE HALLOWEEN COSTUMES...
OH, YEAH?
IN NATIONAL NEWS TODAY, STRONGHOLD PENITENTIARY, NOTORIOUS FOR HOUSING THE COUNTRY'S WORST SUPER-POWERED CRIMINALS, EXPERIENCED AN ATTEMPTED PRISON BREAK EARLIER THIS EVENING.
LUCKILY THE ATTEMPT WAS THWARTED BY WHAT APPEARS TO BE A NEW SUPERHERO DUO INSPIRED BY THE POPULAR HERO INVINCIBLE. INVINCIBOY AND HIS YOUNGER PARTNER ARRIVED ON THE SCENE TO--
INVINCIBOY AND YOUNG PARTNER
WE'RE ON TV!
INVINCIBOY?

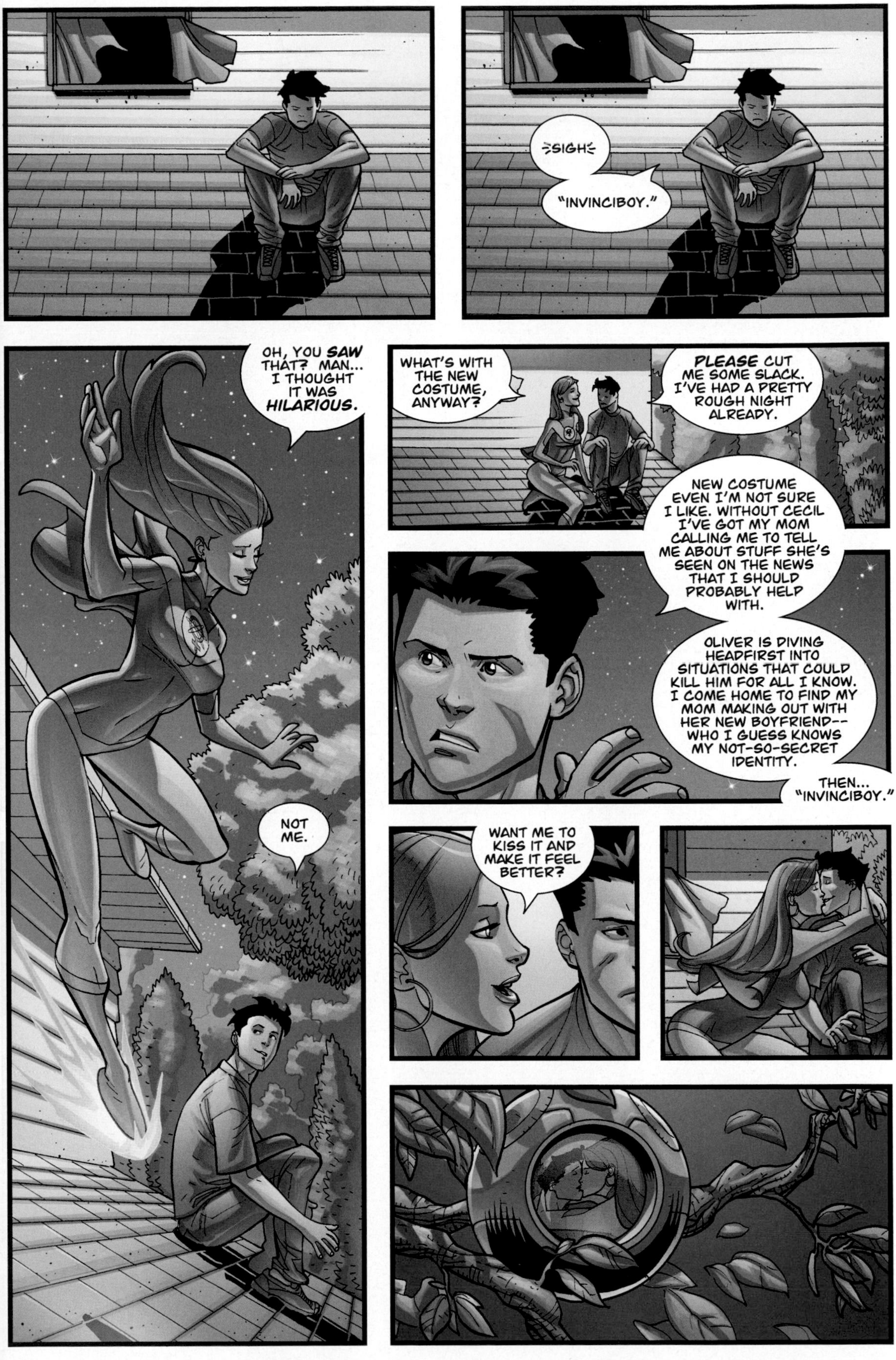

SIGH
"INVINCIBOY."
OH, YOU **SAW** THAT? MAN... I THOUGHT IT WAS **HILARIOUS.**
NOT ME.
WHAT'S WITH THE NEW COSTUME, ANYWAY?
PLEASE CUT ME SOME SLACK. I'VE HAD A PRETTY ROUGH NIGHT ALREADY.
NEW COSTUME EVEN I'M NOT SURE I LIKE. WITHOUT CECIL I'VE GOT MY MOM CALLING ME TO TELL ME ABOUT STUFF SHE'S SEEN ON THE NEWS THAT I SHOULD PROBABLY HELP WITH.
OLIVER IS DIVING HEADFIRST INTO SITUATIONS THAT COULD KILL HIM FOR ALL I KNOW. I COME HOME TO FIND MY MOM MAKING OUT WITH HER NEW BOYFRIEND-- WHO I GUESS KNOWS MY NOT-SO-SECRET IDENTITY.
THEN... "INVINCIBOY."
WANT ME TO KISS IT AND MAKE IT FEEL BETTER?

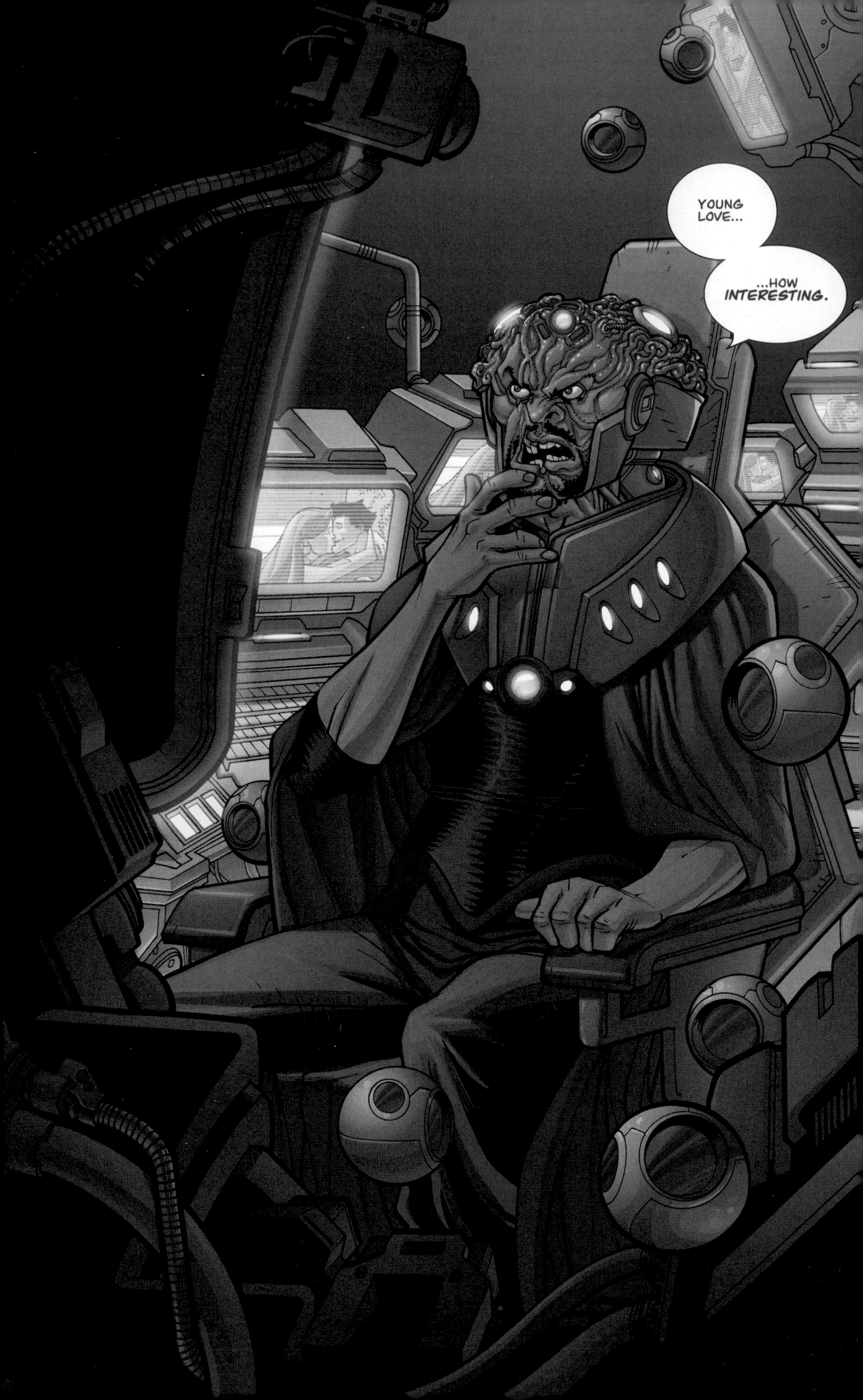
YOUNG LOVE...
...HOW INTERESTING.

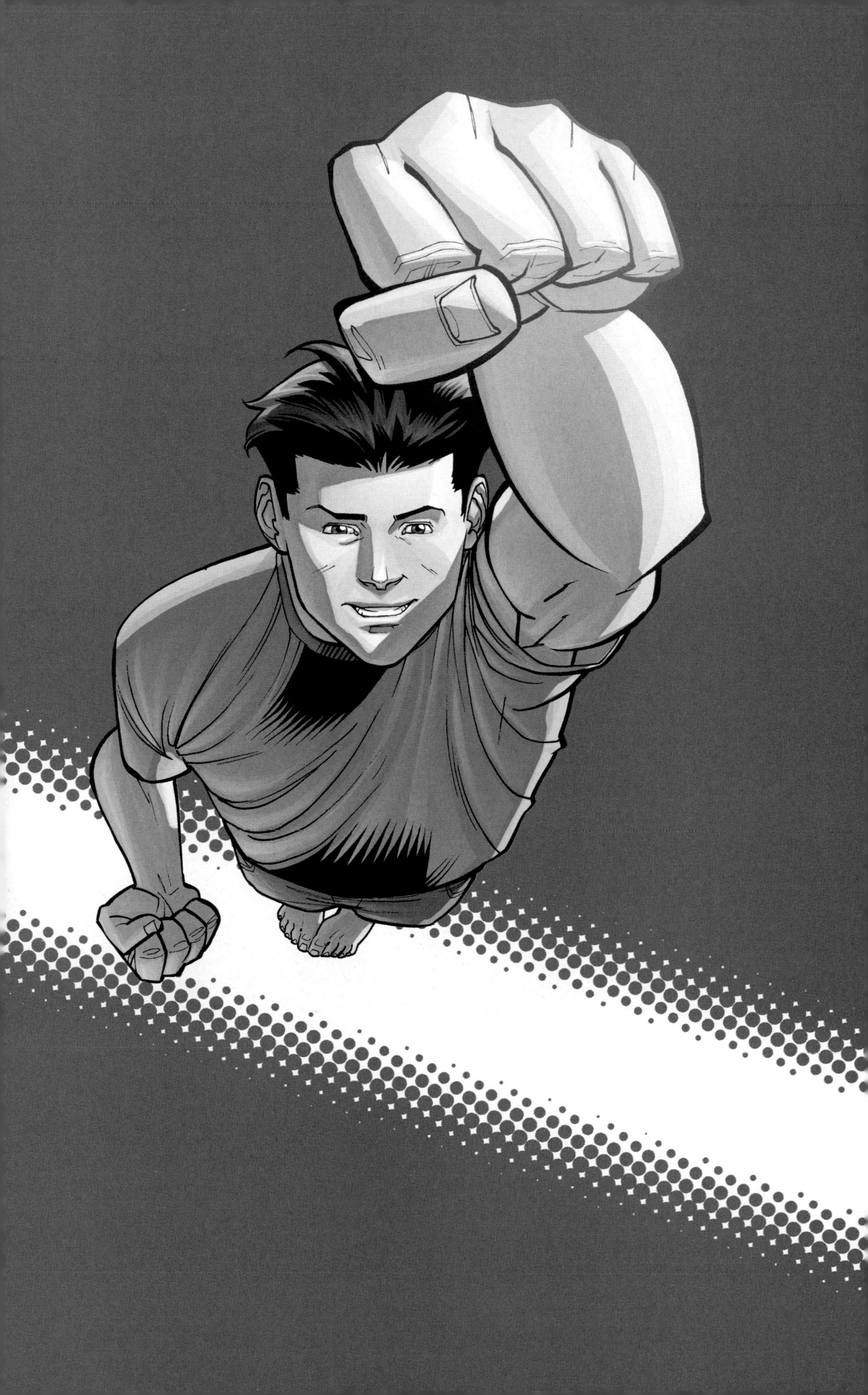

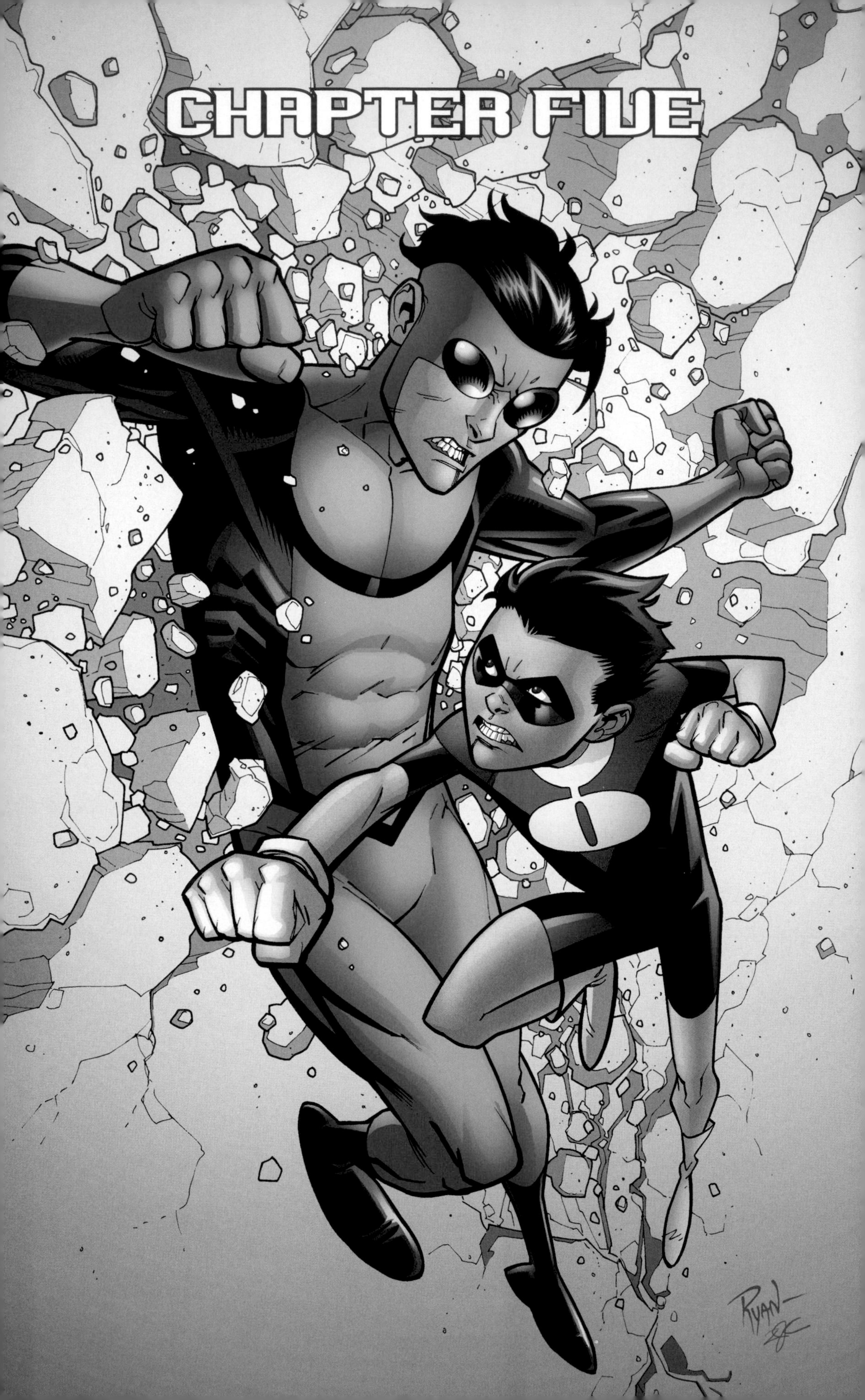
CHAPTER FIVE
RYAN

MARK! GET DOWN HERE, NOW!

WHAT IS IT? IS EVERYTHING OKAY?

LOOK.

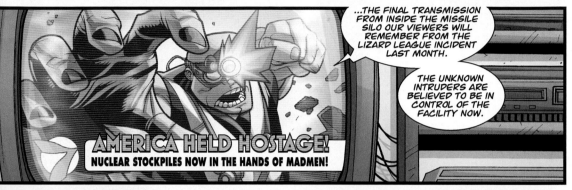

...THE FINAL TRANSMISSION FROM INSIDE THE MISSILE SILO OUR VIEWERS WILL REMEMBER FROM THE LIZARD LEAGUE INCIDENT LAST MONTH.

THE UNKNOWN INTRUDERS ARE BELIEVED TO BE IN CONTROL OF THE FACILITY NOW.

AMERICA HELD HOSTAGE!
NUCLEAR STOCKPILES NOW IN THE HANDS OF MADMEN!

THE MAULER TWINS-- *CRAP*. CALL EVE-- TELL HER I'LL BE LATE--AND THAT I *DON'T* NEED HELP. I'LL BE DONE BY THE TIME SHE COULD FLY OVER THERE.

OKAY, I'LL--

VOOSH!

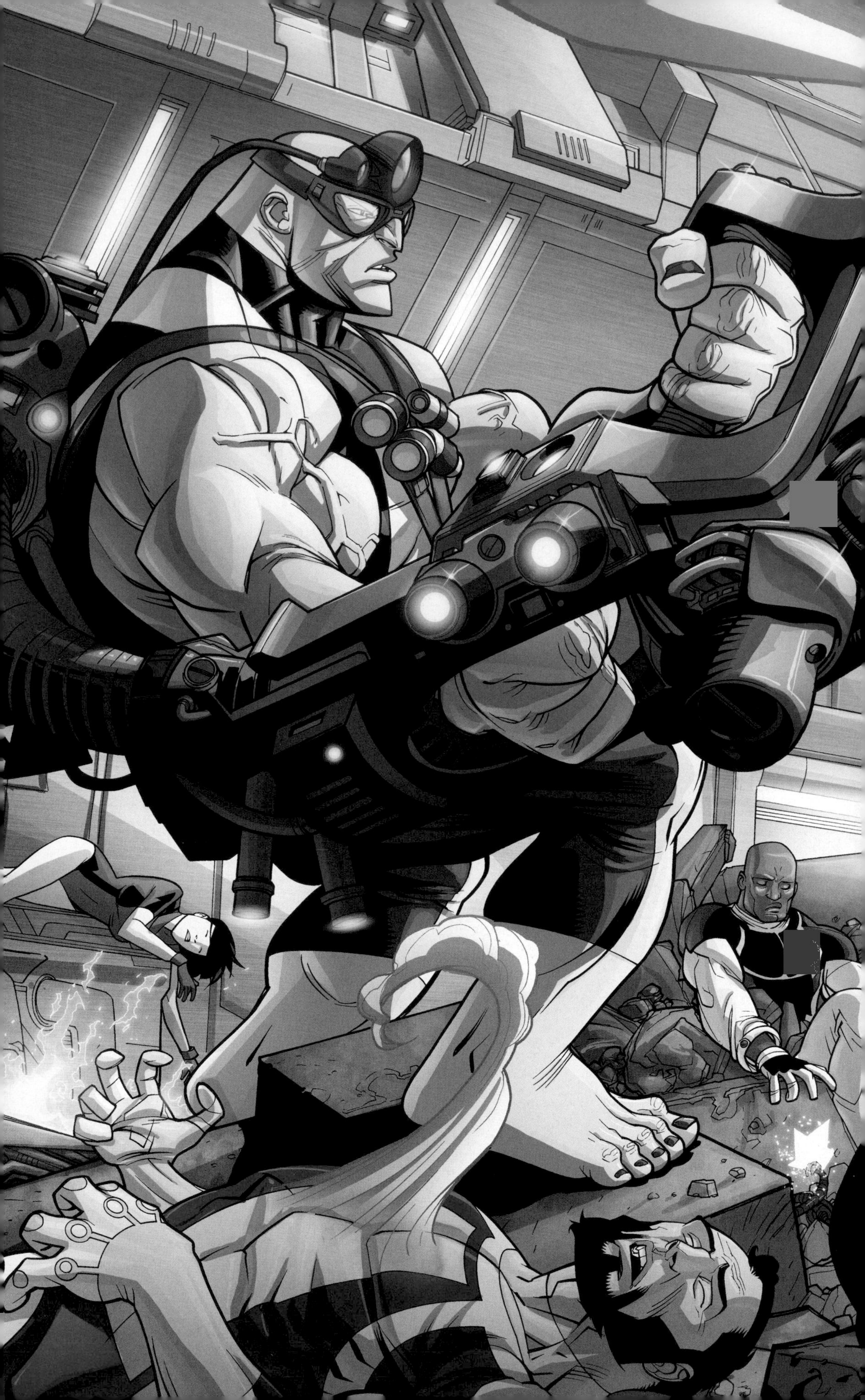

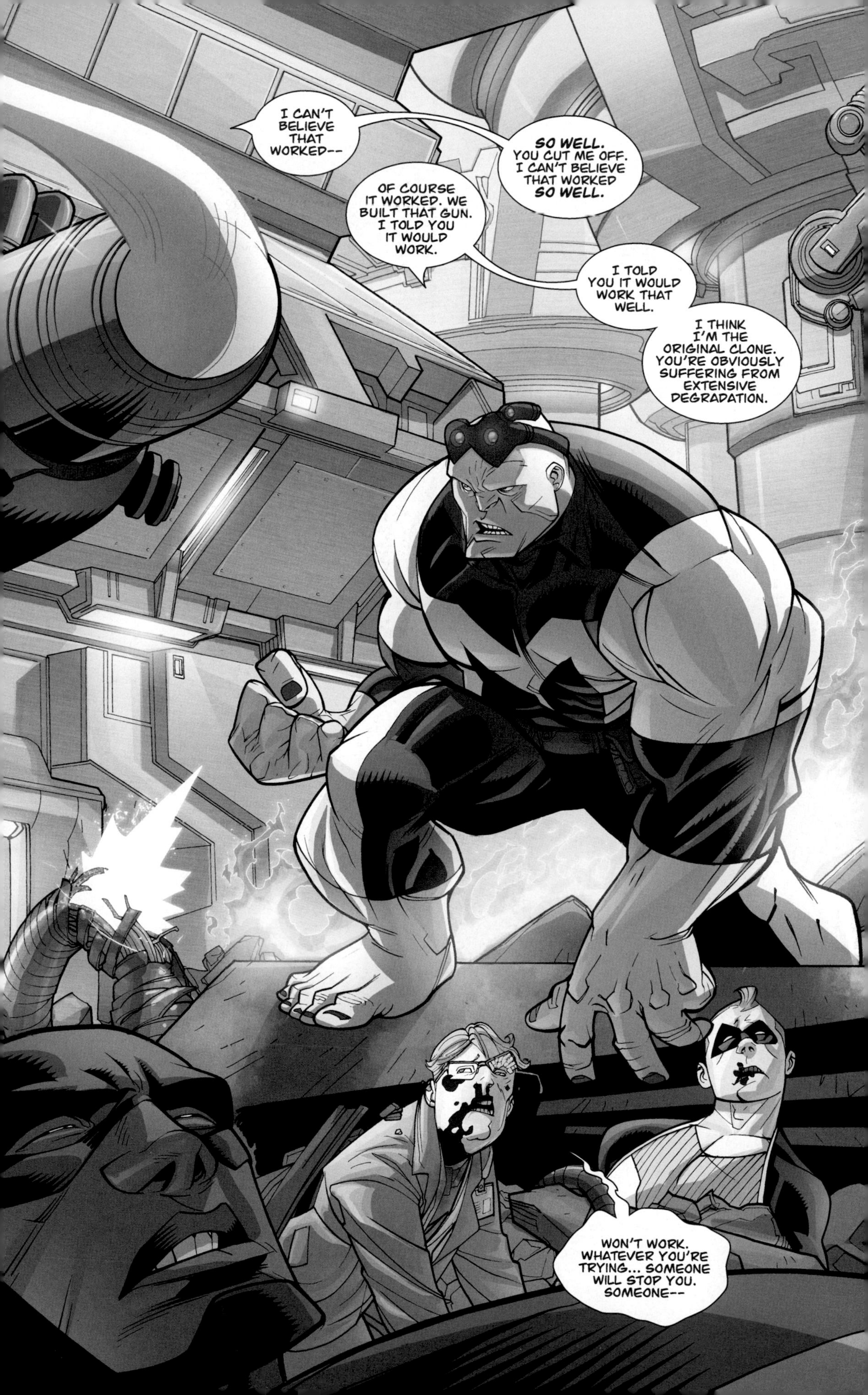
I CAN'T BELIEVE THAT WORKED--
SO WELL. YOU CUT ME OFF. I CAN'T BELIEVE THAT WORKED SO WELL.
OF COURSE IT WORKED. WE BUILT THAT GUN. I TOLD YOU IT WOULD WORK.
I TOLD YOU IT WOULD WORK THAT WELL.
I THINK I'M THE ORIGINAL CLONE. YOU'RE OBVIOUSLY SUFFERING FROM EXTENSIVE DEGRADATION.
WON'T WORK. WHATEVER YOU'RE TRYING... SOMEONE WILL STOP YOU. SOMEONE--

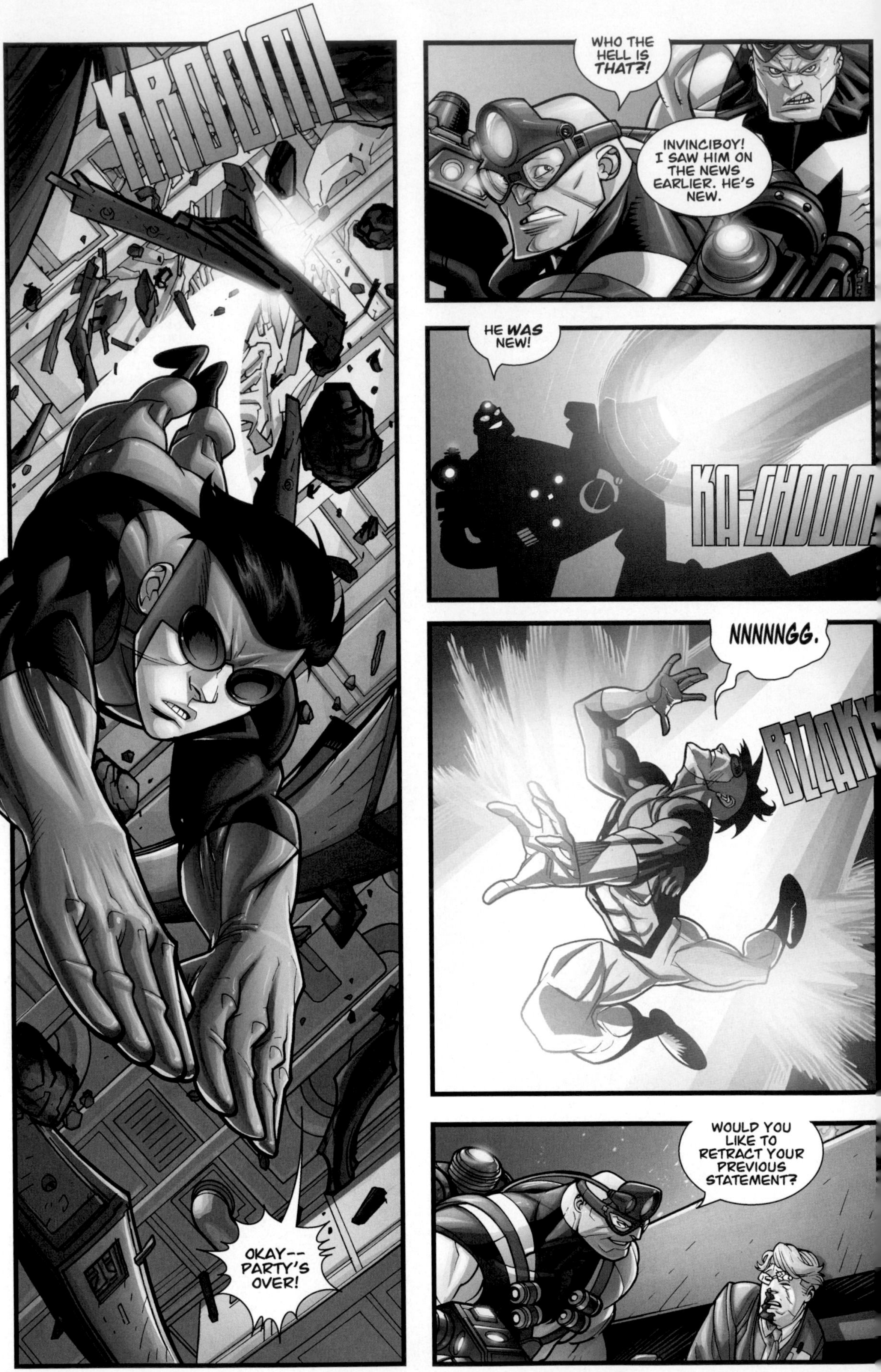
KROOM!
OKAY-- PARTY'S OVER!
WHO THE HELL IS THAT?!
INVINCIBOY! I SAW HIM ON THE NEWS EARLIER. HE'S NEW.
HE WAS NEW!
KA-CHOOM!
NNNNNGG.
WOULD YOU LIKE TO RETRACT YOUR PREVIOUS STATEMENT?

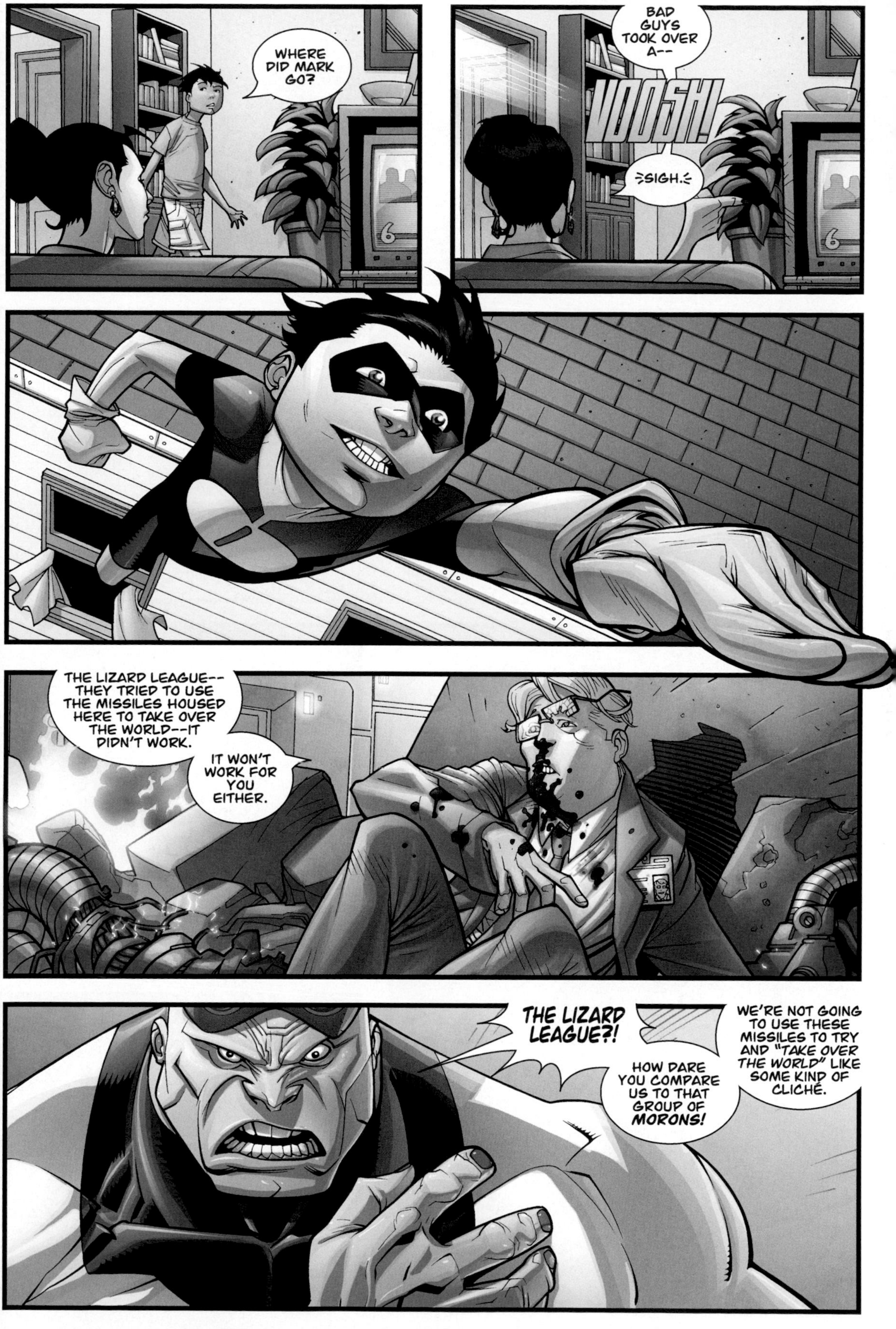
WHERE DID MARK GO?
BAD GUYS TOOK OVER A--
VOOSH!
SIGH.
THE LIZARD LEAGUE--THEY TRIED TO USE THE MISSILES HOUSED HERE TO TAKE OVER THE WORLD--IT DIDN'T WORK.
IT WON'T WORK FOR YOU EITHER.
THE LIZARD LEAGUE?!
HOW DARE YOU COMPARE US TO THAT GROUP OF MORONS!
WE'RE NOT GOING TO USE THESE MISSILES TO TRY AND "TAKE OVER THE WORLD" LIKE SOME KIND OF CLICHÉ.

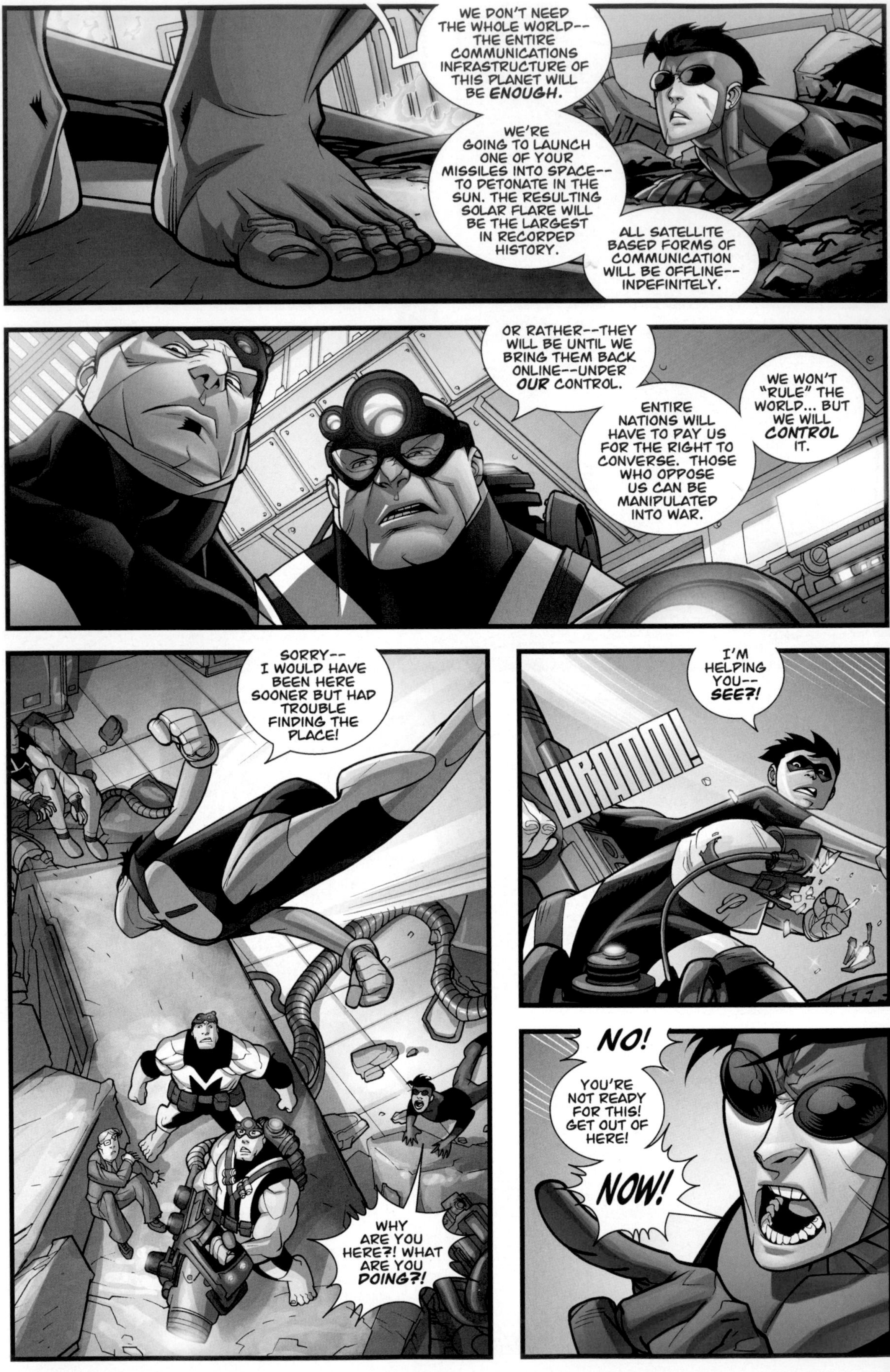
WE DON'T NEED THE WHOLE WORLD-- THE ENTIRE COMMUNICATIONS INFRASTRUCTURE OF THIS PLANET WILL BE ENOUGH.
WE'RE GOING TO LAUNCH ONE OF YOUR MISSILES INTO SPACE-- TO DETONATE IN THE SUN. THE RESULTING SOLAR FLARE WILL BE THE LARGEST IN RECORDED HISTORY.
ALL SATELLITE BASED FORMS OF COMMUNICATION WILL BE OFFLINE-- INDEFINITELY.
OR RATHER--THEY WILL BE UNTIL WE BRING THEM BACK ONLINE--UNDER OUR CONTROL.
ENTIRE NATIONS WILL HAVE TO PAY US FOR THE RIGHT TO CONVERSE. THOSE WHO OPPOSE US CAN BE MANIPULATED INTO WAR.
WE WON'T "RULE" THE WORLD... BUT WE WILL CONTROL IT.
SORRY-- I WOULD HAVE BEEN HERE SOONER BUT HAD TROUBLE FINDING THE PLACE!
WHY ARE YOU HERE?! WHAT ARE YOU DOING?!
I'M HELPING YOU-- SEE?!
WRAMM!
NO!
YOU'RE NOT READY FOR THIS! GET OUT OF HERE!
NOW!

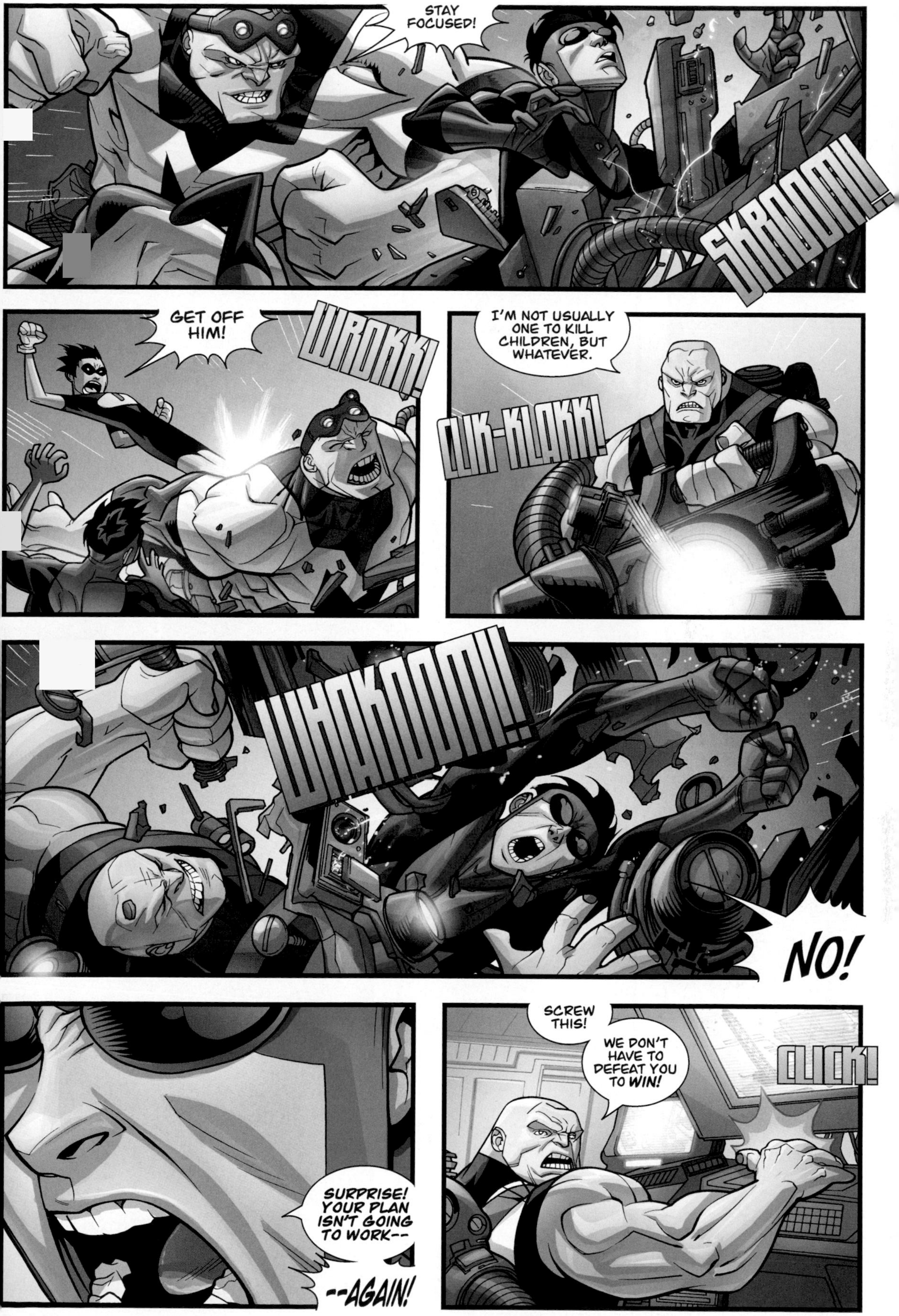

STAY FOCUSED!
SKROOM!!
GET OFF HIM!
WROKK!
I'M NOT USUALLY ONE TO KILL CHILDREN, BUT WHATEVER.
CLIK-KLAKK!
WHKOOM!!
NO!
SURPRISE! YOUR PLAN ISN'T GOING TO WORK--
--AGAIN!
SCREW THIS!
WE DON'T HAVE TO DEFEAT YOU TO WIN!
CLICK!

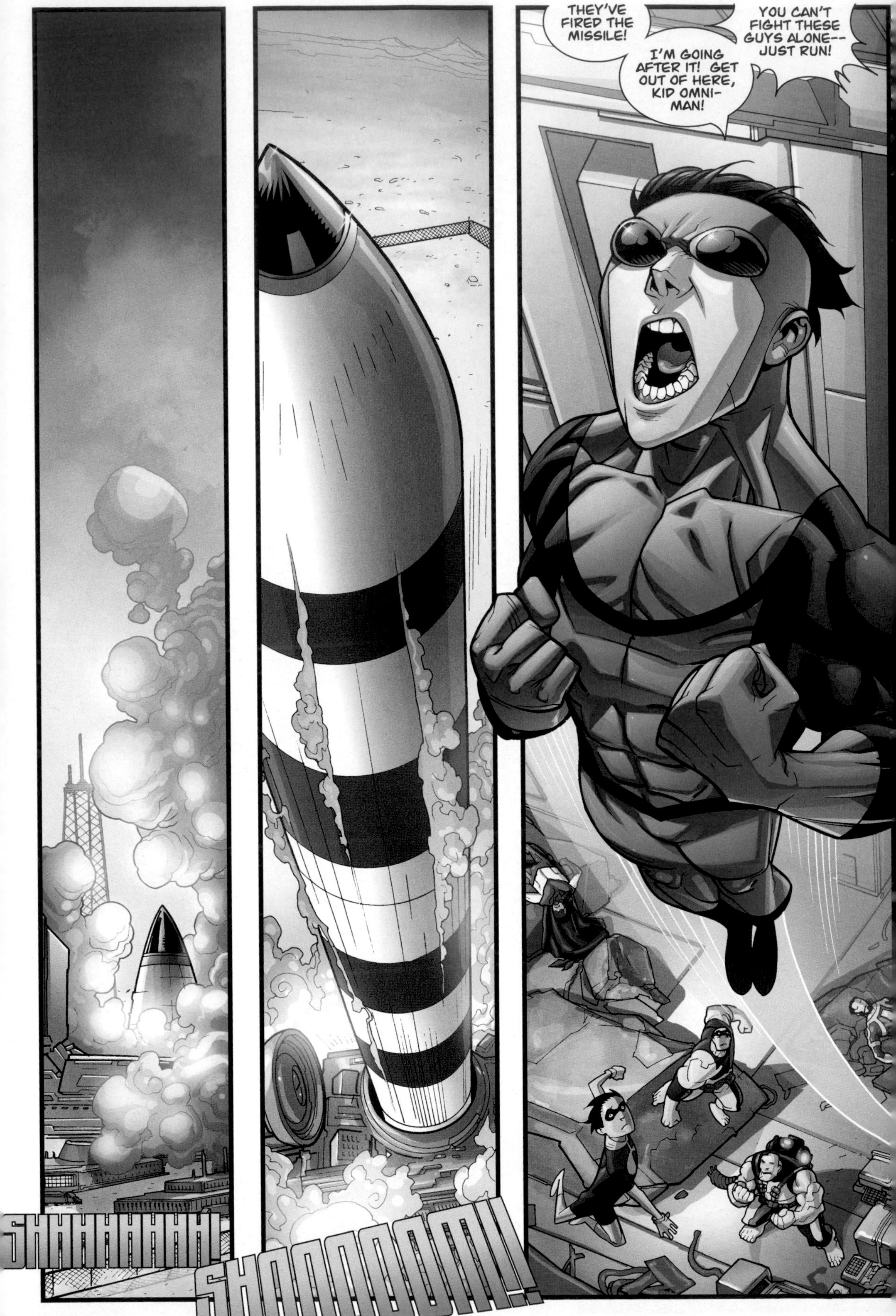

THEY'VE FIRED THE MISSILE!
I'M GOING AFTER IT! GET OUT OF HERE, KID OMNI-MAN!
YOU CAN'T FIGHT THESE GUYS ALONE-- JUST RUN!
SHHHHHHHH!
SHOOOOOM!!

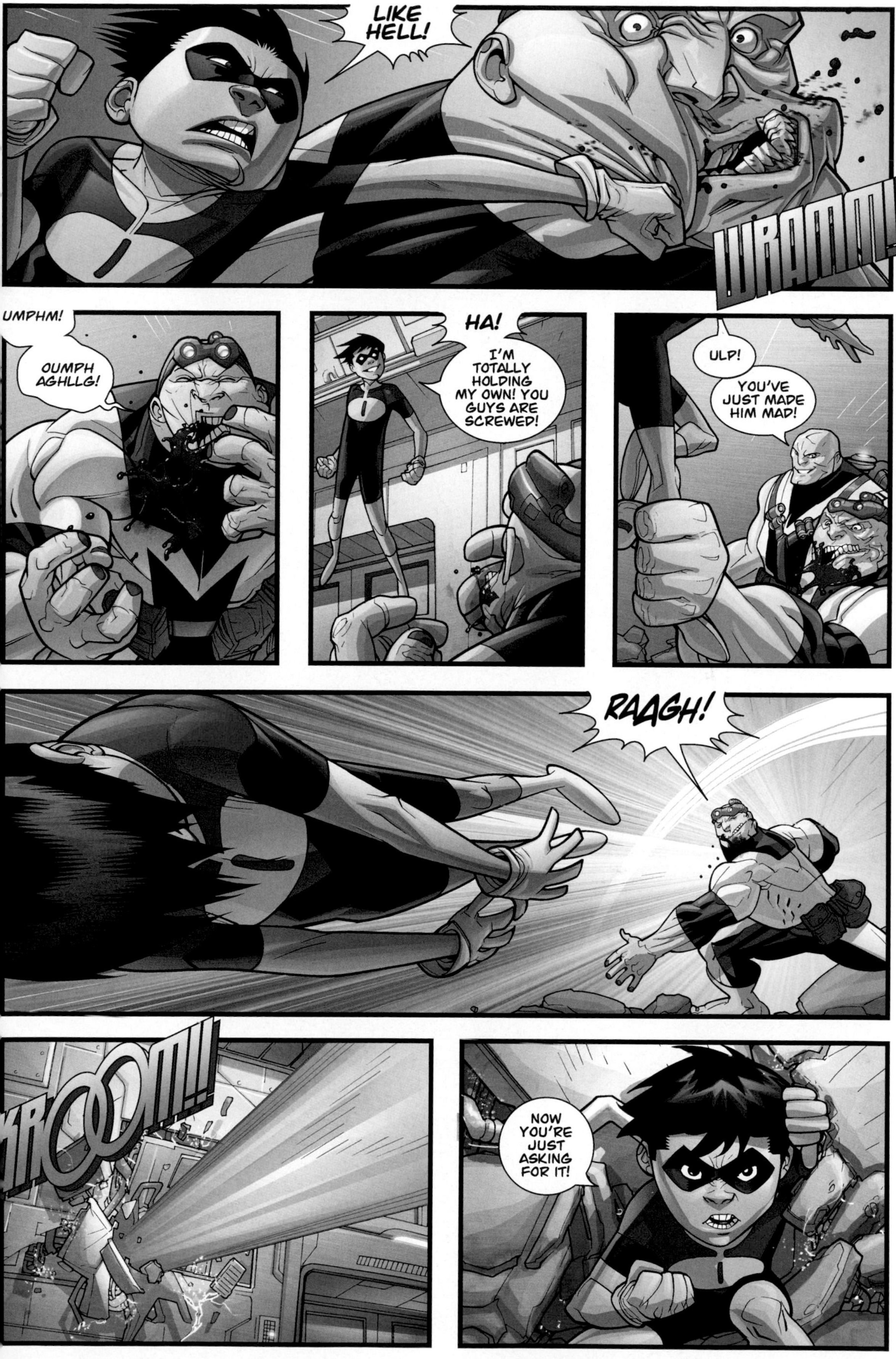
LIKE HELL!
WRAMM!!
UMPHM!
OUMPH AGHLLG!
HA!
I'M TOTALLY HOLDING MY OWN! YOU GUYS ARE SCREWED!
ULP!
YOU'VE JUST MADE HIM MAD!
RAAGH!
KROOOM!!
NOW YOU'RE JUST ASKING FOR IT!

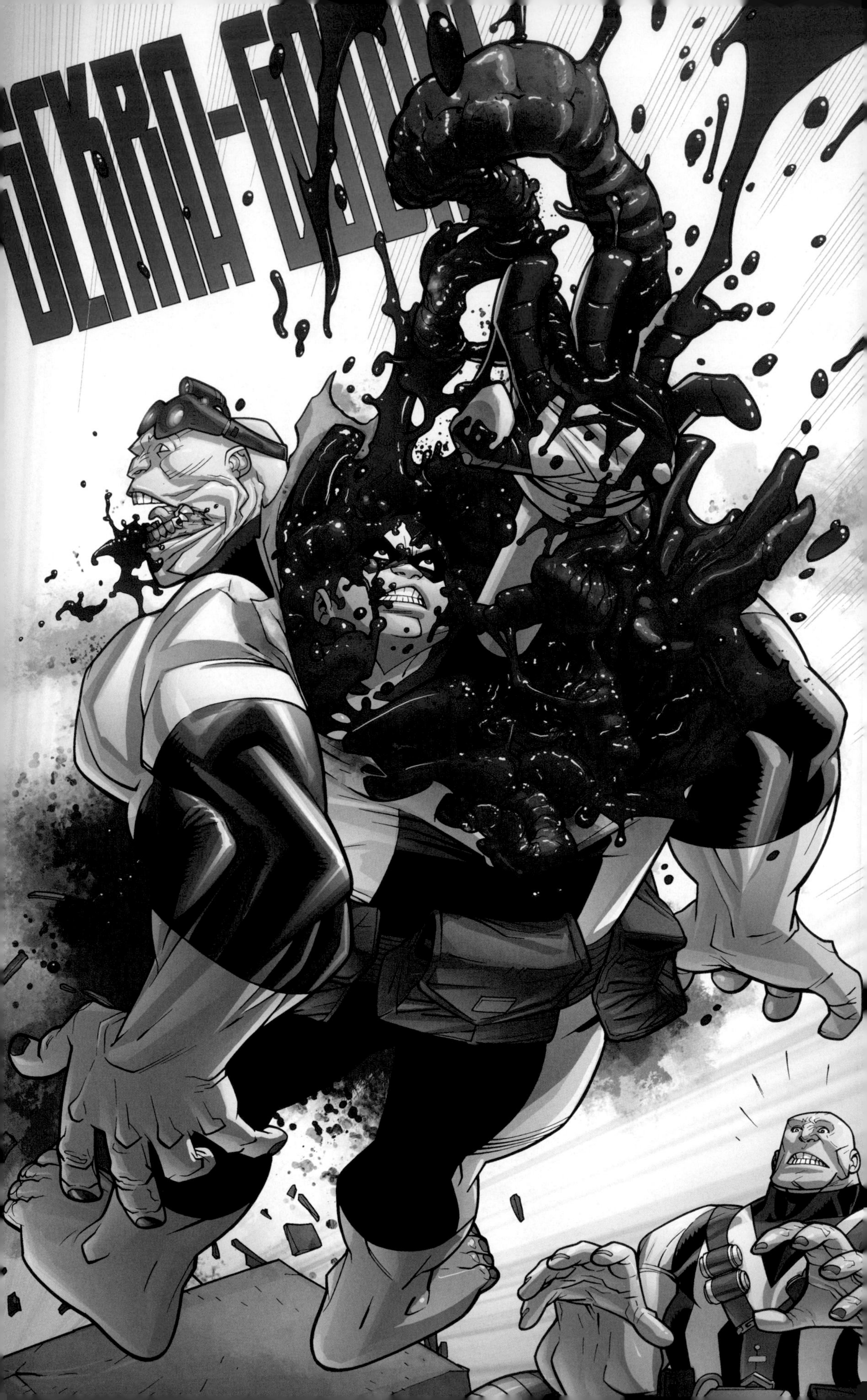

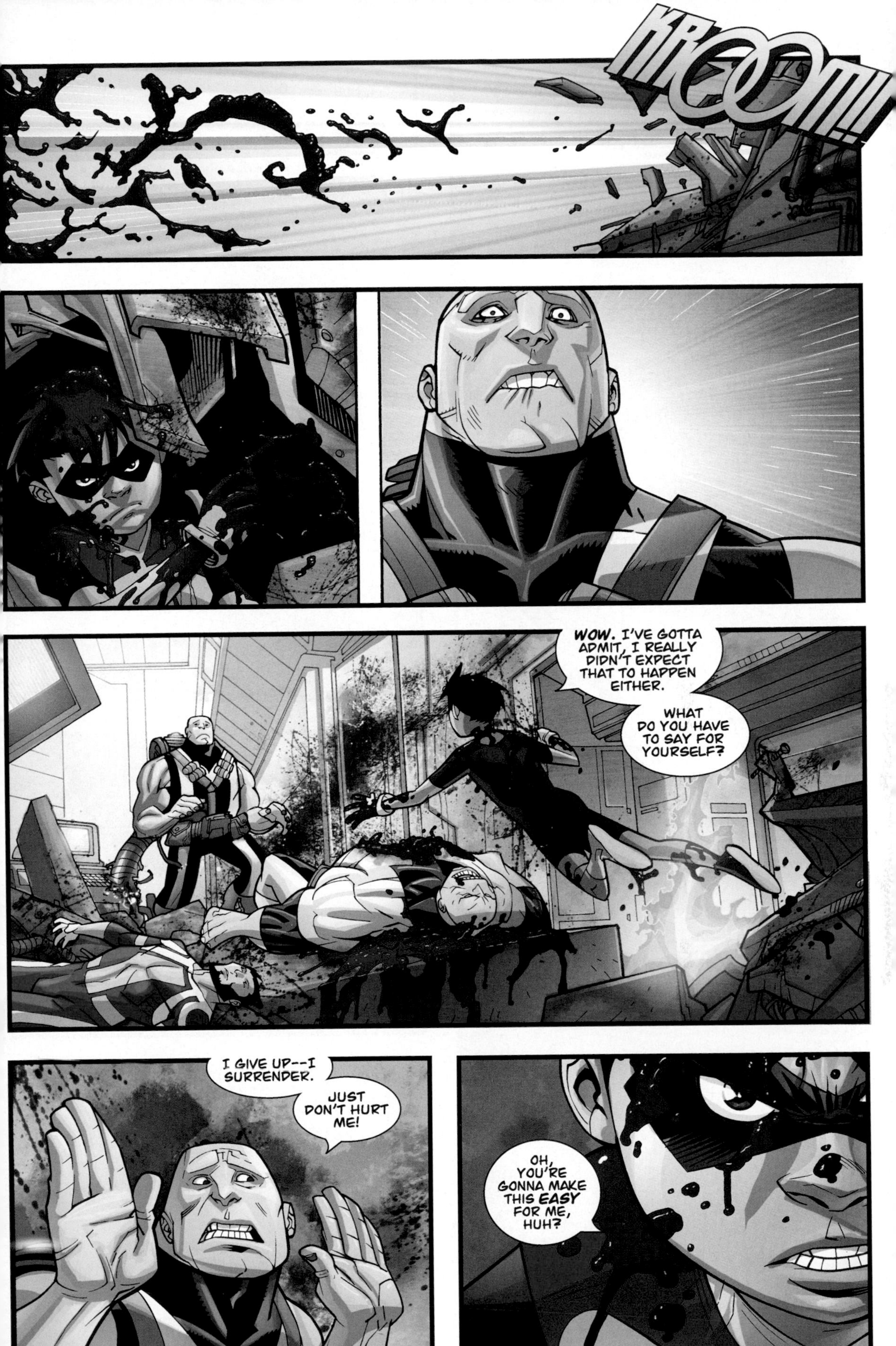
KROOM!!
WOW. I'VE GOTTA ADMIT, I REALLY DIDN'T EXPECT THAT TO HAPPEN EITHER.
WHAT DO YOU HAVE TO SAY FOR YOURSELF?
I GIVE UP--I SURRENDER.
JUST DON'T HURT ME!
OH, YOU'RE GONNA MAKE THIS EASY FOR ME, HUH?

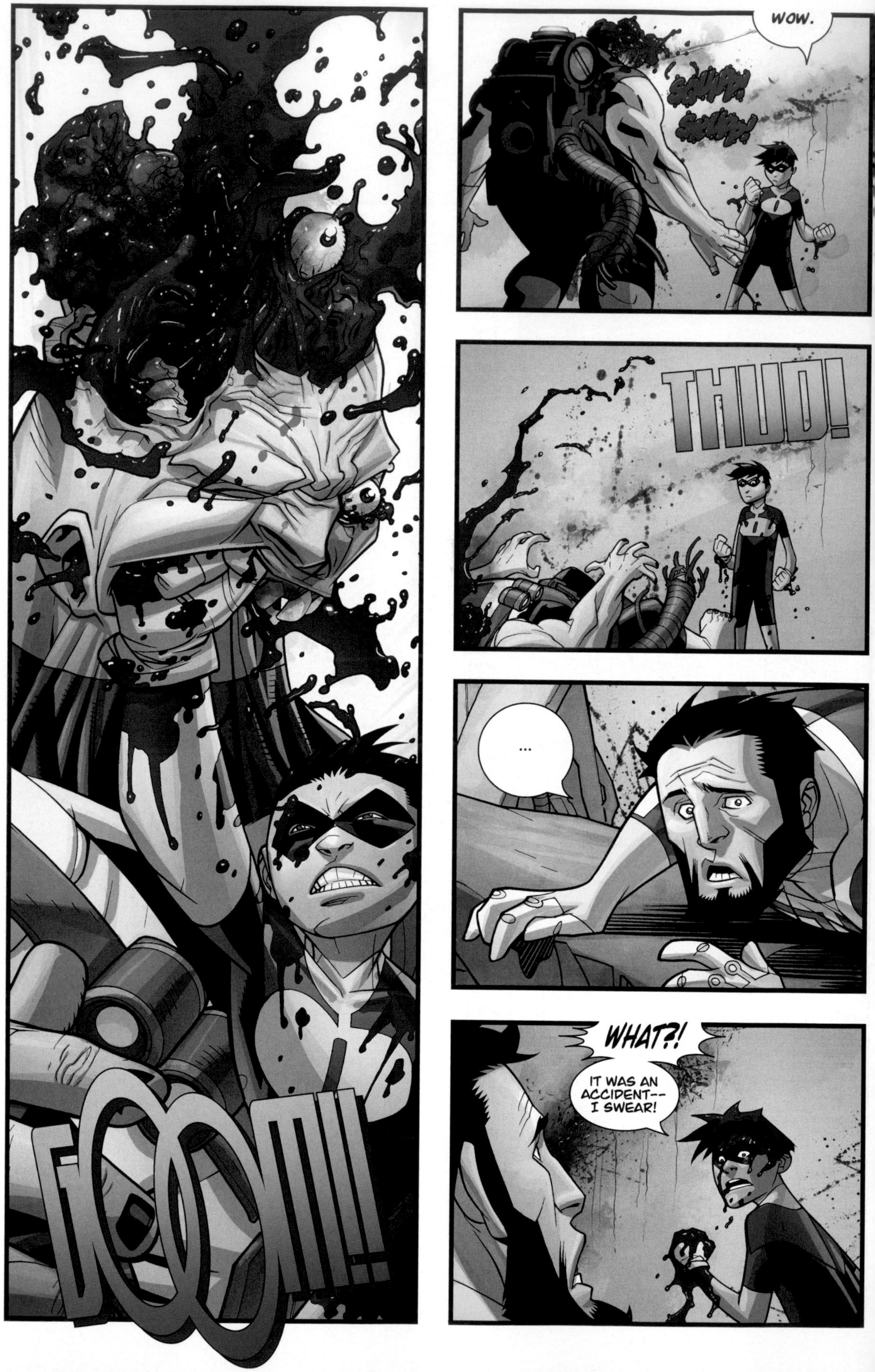
BOOM!!
WOW.
THUD!
...
WHAT?!
IT WAS AN ACCIDENT-- I SWEAR!

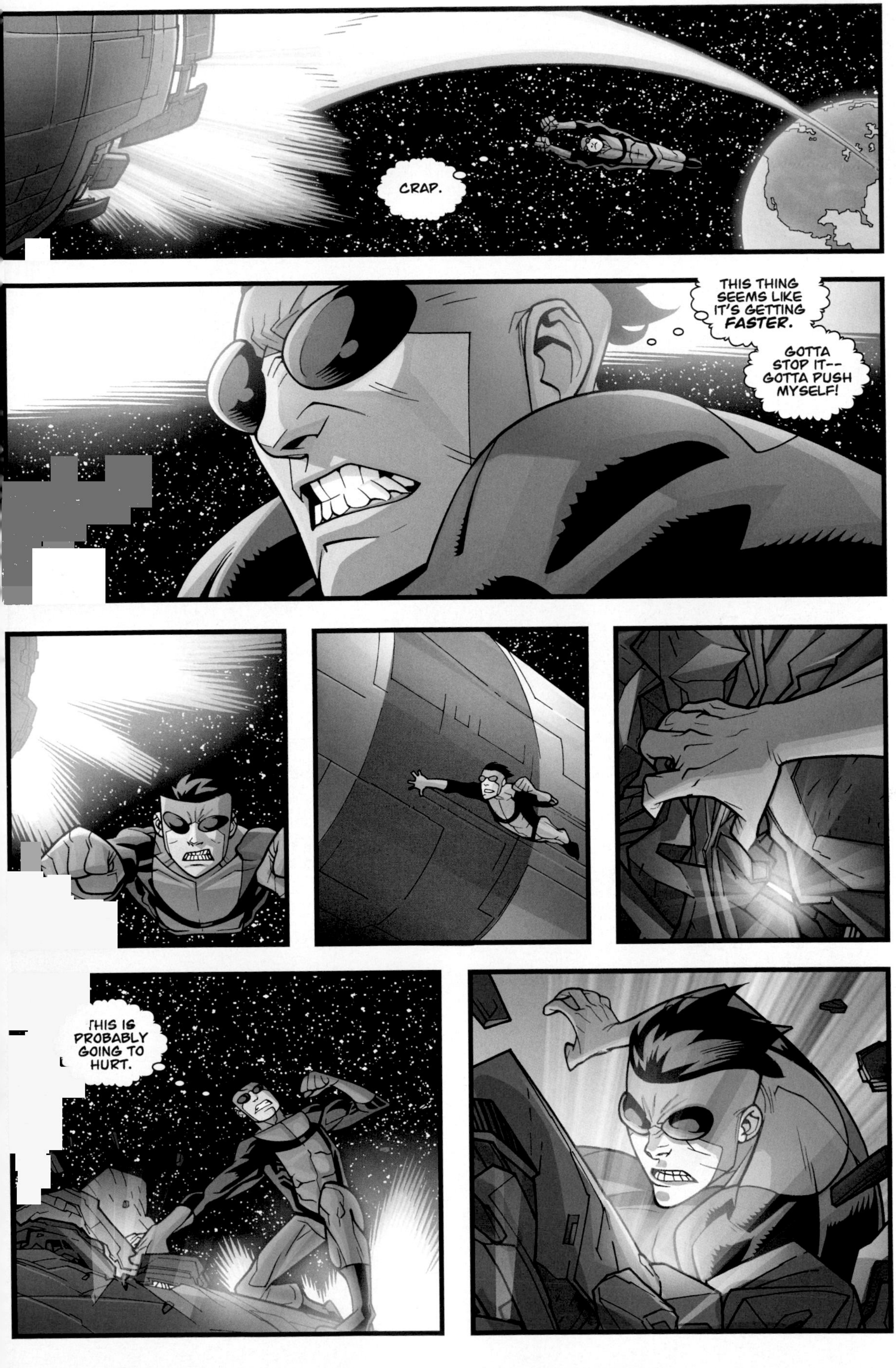
CRAP.
THIS THING SEEMS LIKE IT'S GETTING FASTER.
GOTTA STOP IT-- GOTTA PUSH MYSELF!
THIS IS PROBABLY GOING TO HURT.

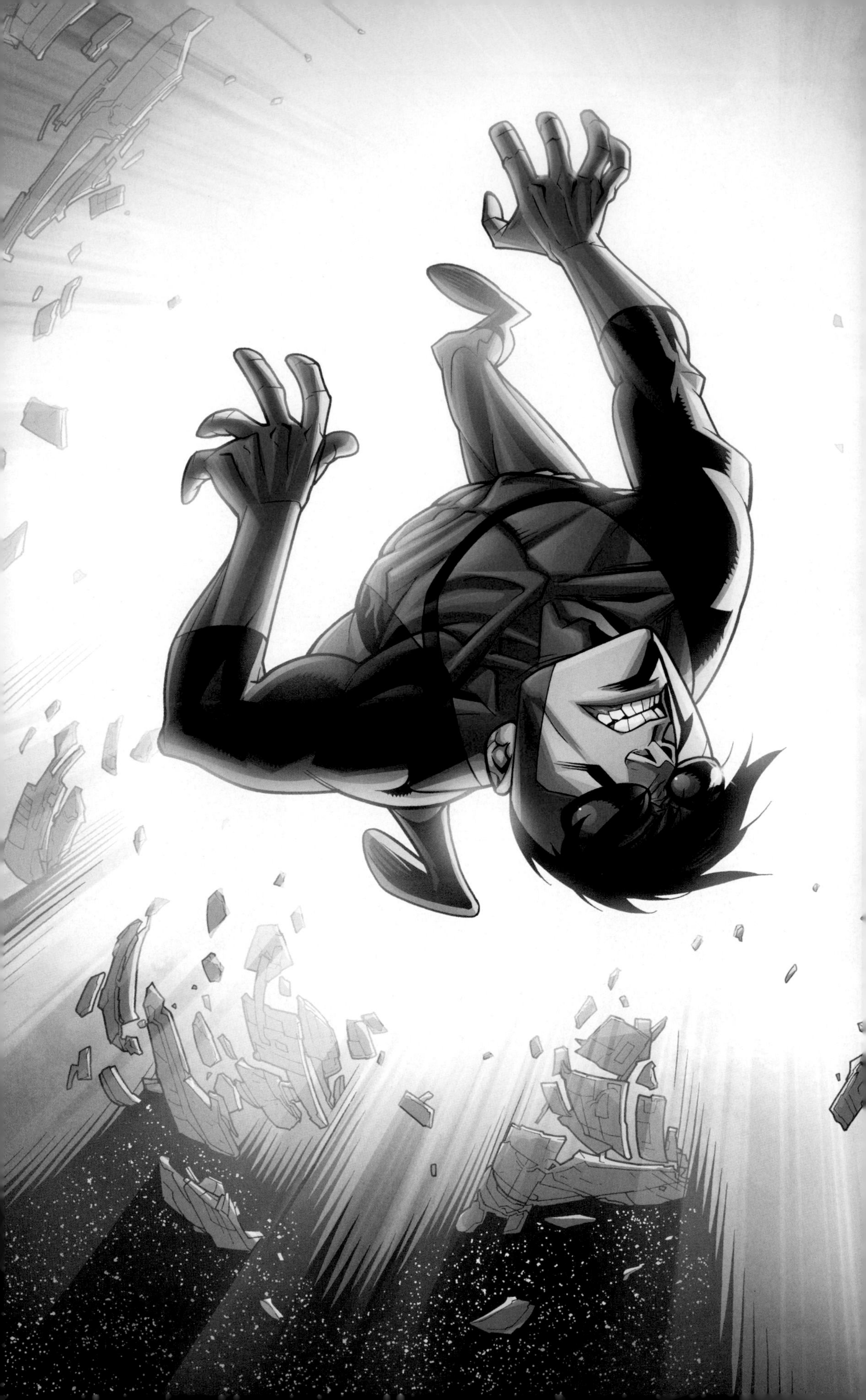

WOW.

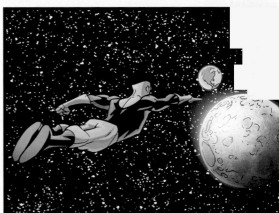

WHAT ARE YOU DOING?

WAS THAT INVINCIBLE?

I'M CALLING IT IN. HE WANTED TO BE NOTIFIED **PERSONALLY** OF ANY ACTIVITY INVOLVING INVINCIBLE.

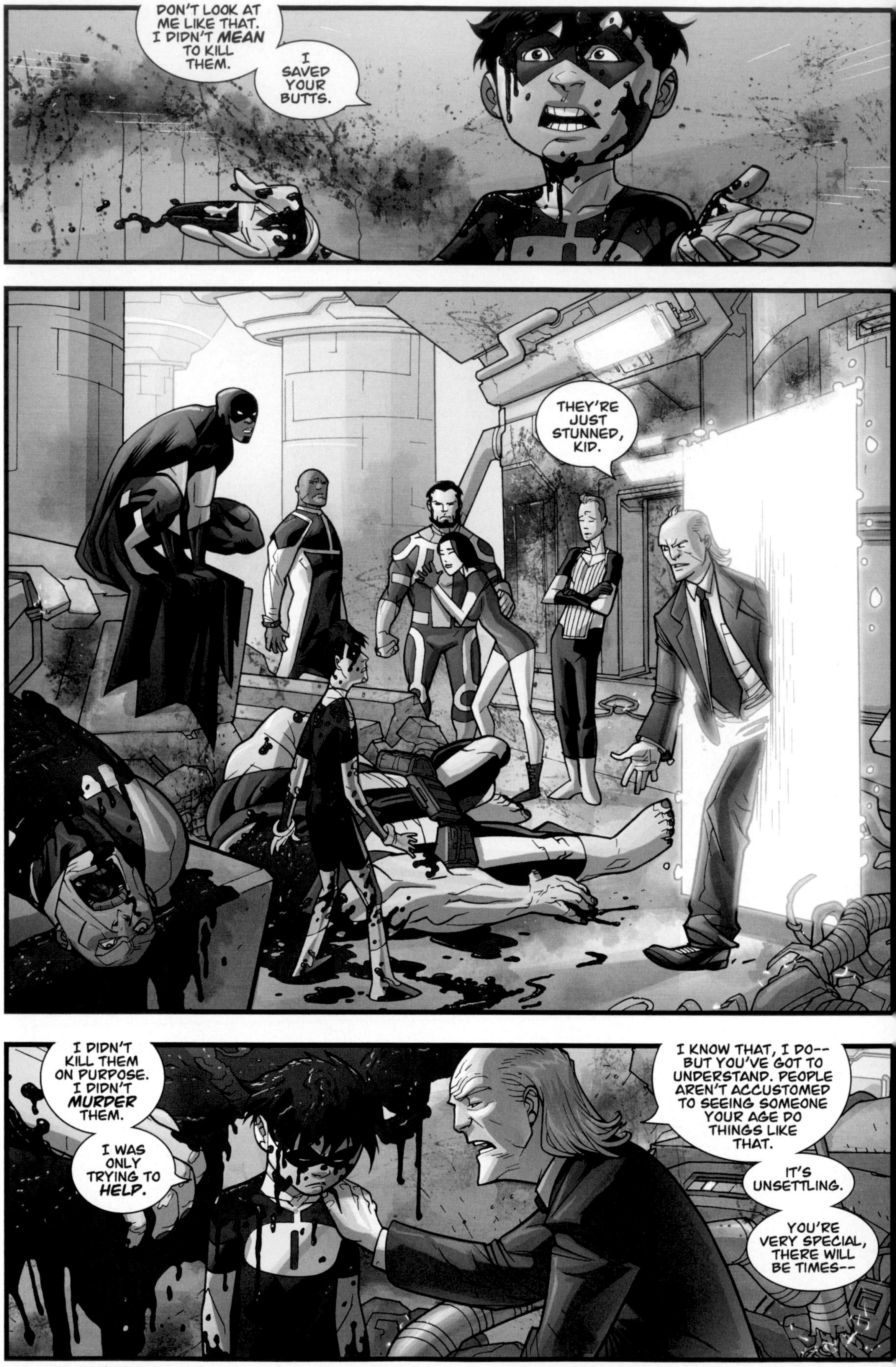
DON'T LOOK AT ME LIKE THAT. I DIDN'T MEAN TO KILL THEM.
I SAVED YOUR BUTTS.
THEY'RE JUST STUNNED, KID.
I DIDN'T KILL THEM ON PURPOSE. I DIDN'T MURDER THEM.
I WAS ONLY TRYING TO HELP.
I KNOW THAT, I DO-- BUT YOU'VE GOT TO UNDERSTAND. PEOPLE AREN'T ACCUSTOMED TO SEEING SOMEONE YOUR AGE DO THINGS LIKE THAT.
IT'S UNSETTLING.
YOU'RE VERY SPECIAL, THERE WILL BE TIMES--

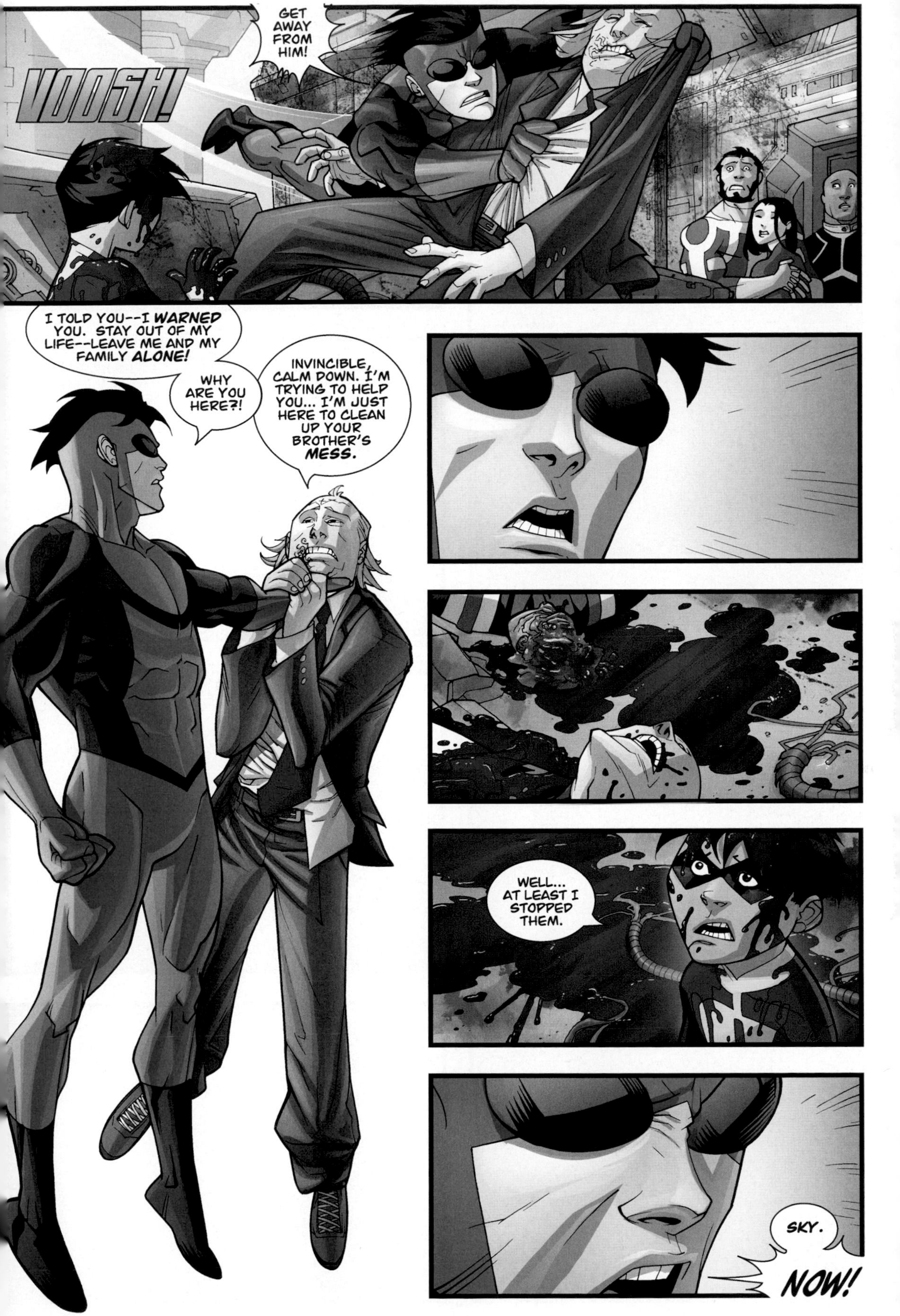
GET AWAY FROM HIM!
VOOSH!
I TOLD YOU--I WARNED YOU. STAY OUT OF MY LIFE--LEAVE ME AND MY FAMILY ALONE!
WHY ARE YOU HERE?!
INVINCIBLE, CALM DOWN. I'M TRYING TO HELP YOU... I'M JUST HERE TO CLEAN UP YOUR BROTHER'S MESS.
WELL... AT LEAST I STOPPED THEM.
SKY.
NOW!

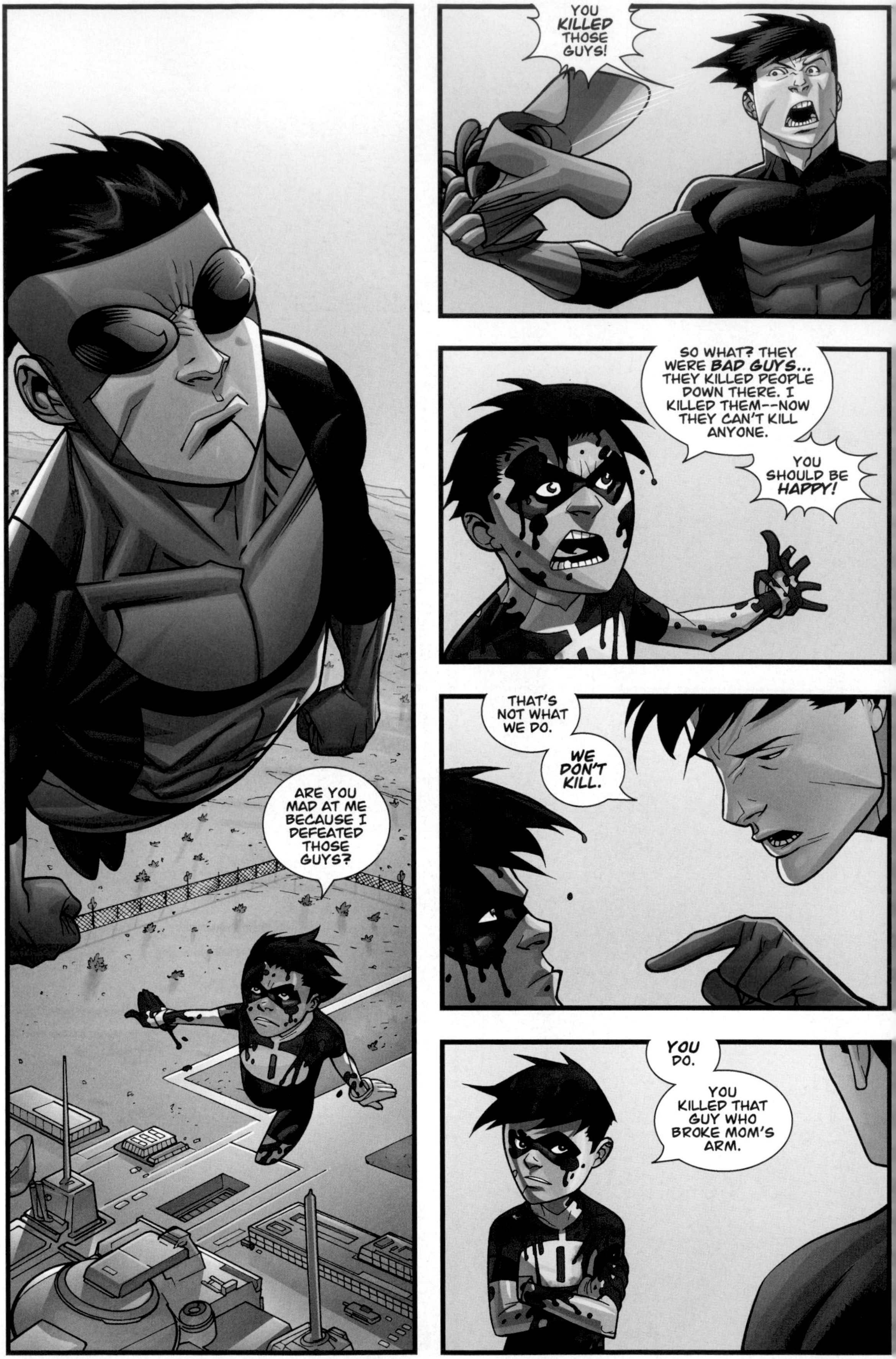

ARE YOU MAD AT ME BECAUSE I DEFEATED THOSE GUYS?
YOU KILLED THOSE GUYS!
SO WHAT? THEY WERE BAD GUYS... THEY KILLED PEOPLE DOWN THERE. I KILLED THEM--NOW THEY CAN'T KILL ANYONE.
YOU SHOULD BE HAPPY!
THAT'S NOT WHAT WE DO.
WE DON'T KILL.
YOU DO.
YOU KILLED THAT GUY WHO BROKE MOM'S ARM.

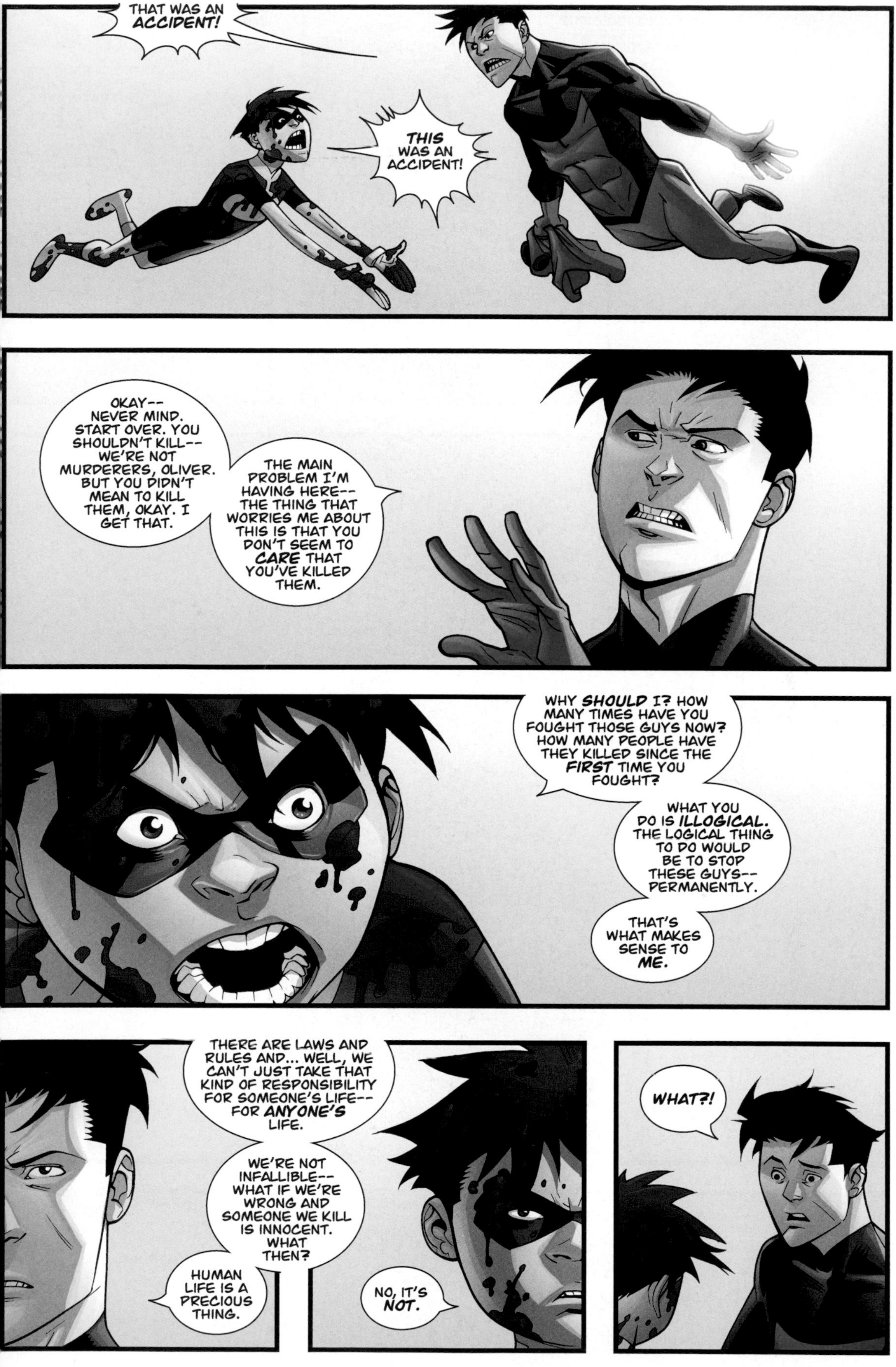
THAT WAS AN ACCIDENT!
THIS WAS AN ACCIDENT!
OKAY-- NEVER MIND. START OVER. YOU SHOULDN'T KILL-- WE'RE NOT MURDERERS, OLIVER. BUT YOU DIDN'T MEAN TO KILL THEM, OKAY. I GET THAT.
THE MAIN PROBLEM I'M HAVING HERE-- THE THING THAT WORRIES ME ABOUT THIS IS THAT YOU DON'T SEEM TO CARE THAT YOU'VE KILLED THEM.
WHY SHOULD I? HOW MANY TIMES HAVE YOU FOUGHT THOSE GUYS NOW? HOW MANY PEOPLE HAVE THEY KILLED SINCE THE FIRST TIME YOU FOUGHT?
WHAT YOU DO IS ILLOGICAL. THE LOGICAL THING TO DO WOULD BE TO STOP THESE GUYS-- PERMANENTLY.
THAT'S WHAT MAKES SENSE TO ME.
THERE ARE LAWS AND RULES AND... WELL, WE CAN'T JUST TAKE THAT KIND OF RESPONSIBILITY FOR SOMEONE'S LIFE-- FOR ANYONE'S LIFE.
WE'RE NOT INFALLIBLE-- WHAT IF WE'RE WRONG AND SOMEONE WE KILL IS INNOCENT. WHAT THEN?
HUMAN LIFE IS A PRECIOUS THING.
NO, IT'S NOT.
WHAT?!

PRECIOUS. HUMAN LIFE ISN'T PRECIOUS. NOT IN GENERAL-- NOT EVERYONE.

PEOPLE RISK THEIR LIVES EVERY DAY. THEY KILL EACH OTHER. IF THEY DON'T THINK THEIR LIVES ARE IMPORTANT, WHY SHOULD I?

MOST OF THEM ARE UTTERLY *INSIGNIFICANT*.

YOU SOUND LIKE *DAD*.

SO? WHY IS THAT BAD? WAS HE SO WRONG? DID NOTHING HE SAID MAKE SENSE TO YOU--EVEN ON A SMALL LEVEL?

HAVE YOU EVER THOUGHT THAT MAYBE OU FATHER WAS *RIGHT*?

...

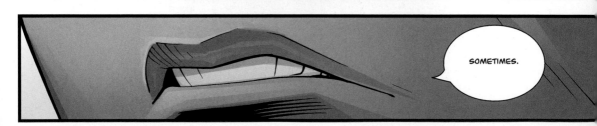

SOMETIMES.

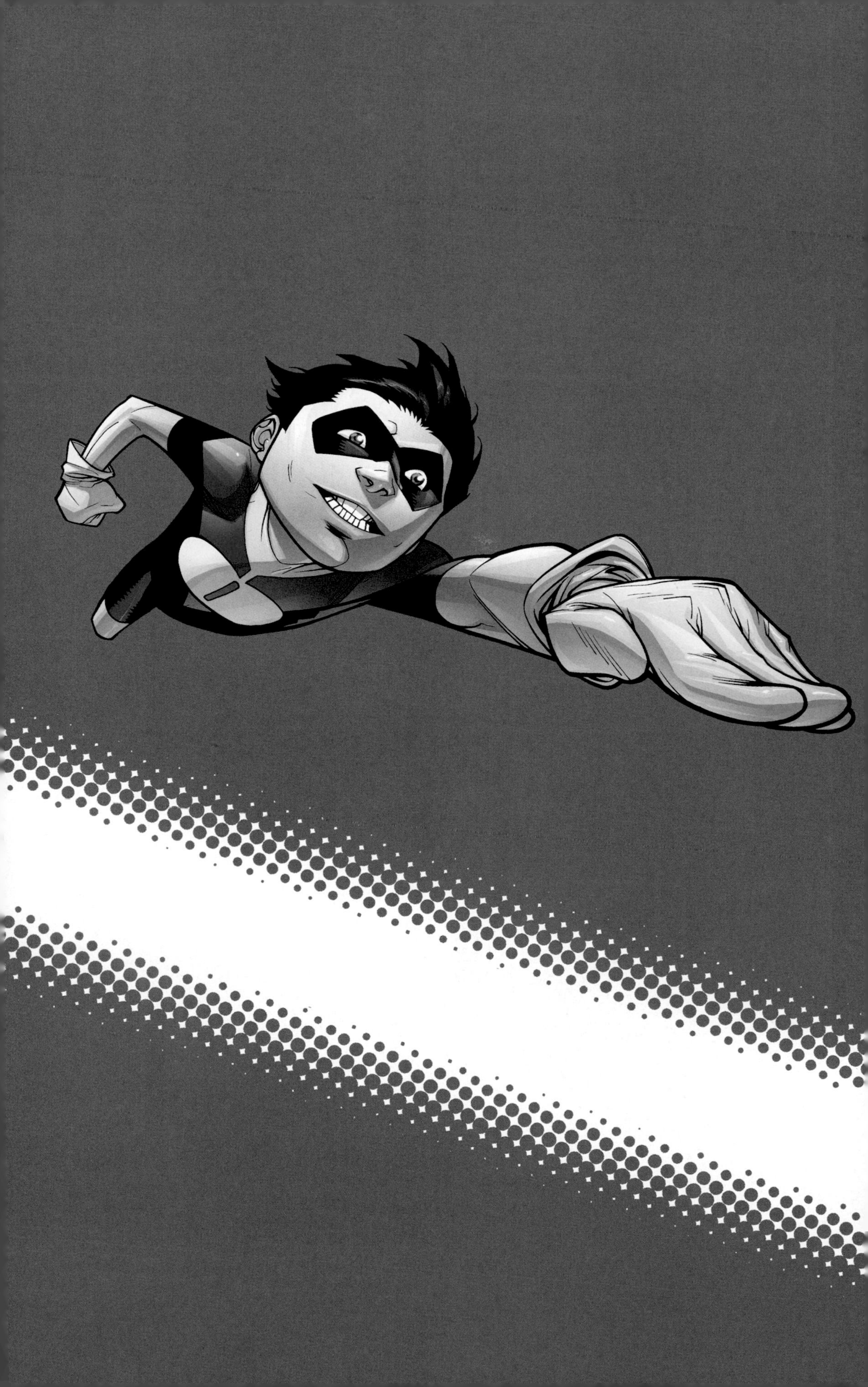

CHAPTER SIX

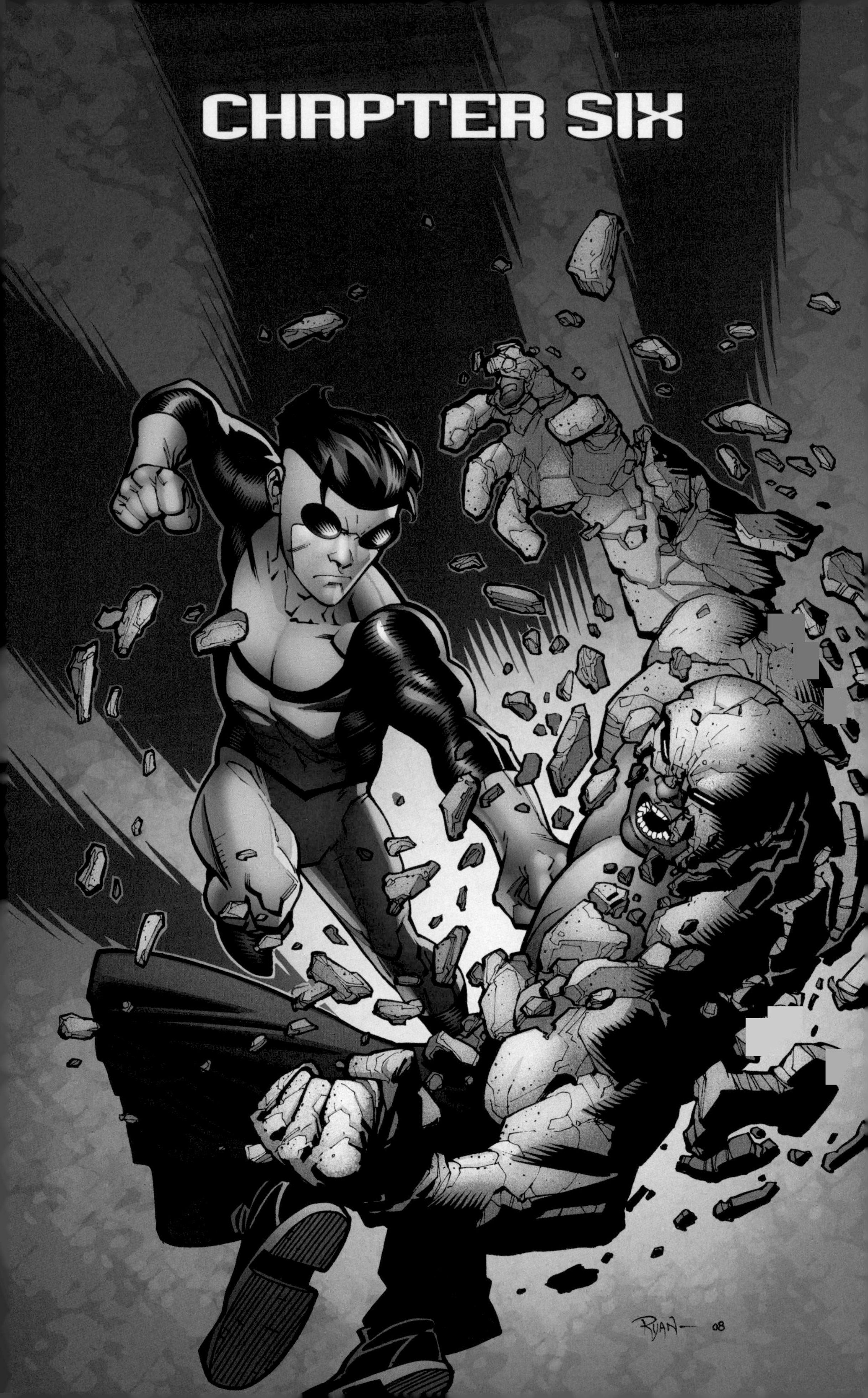
RYAN 08

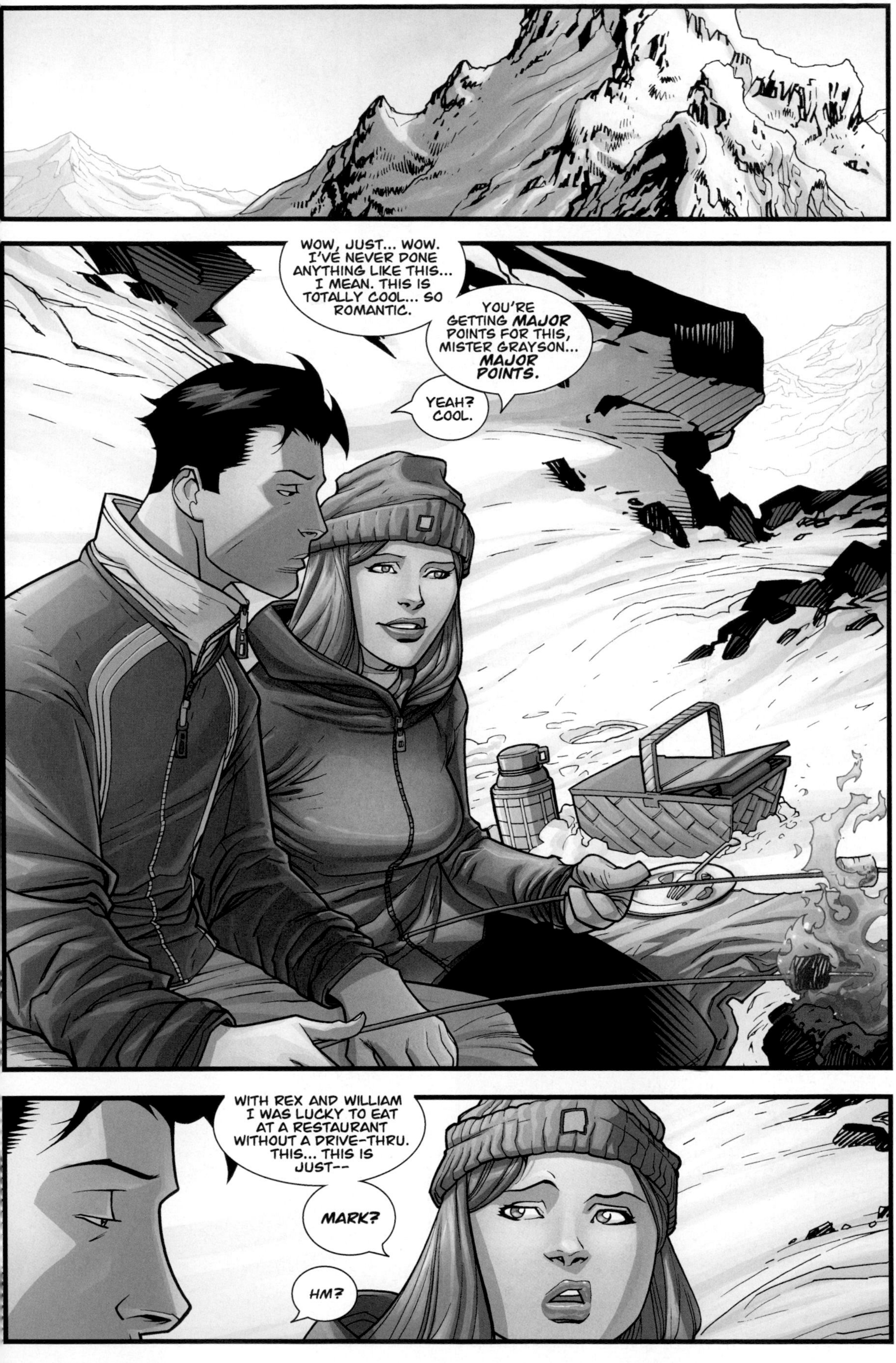
WOW, JUST... WOW. I'VE NEVER DONE ANYTHING LIKE THIS... I MEAN. THIS IS TOTALLY COOL... SO ROMANTIC.
YOU'RE GETTING MAJOR POINTS FOR THIS, MISTER GRAYSON... MAJOR POINTS.
YEAH? COOL.
WITH REX AND WILLIAM I WAS LUCKY TO EAT AT A RESTAURANT WITHOUT A DRIVE-THRU. THIS... THIS IS JUST--
MARK?
HM?

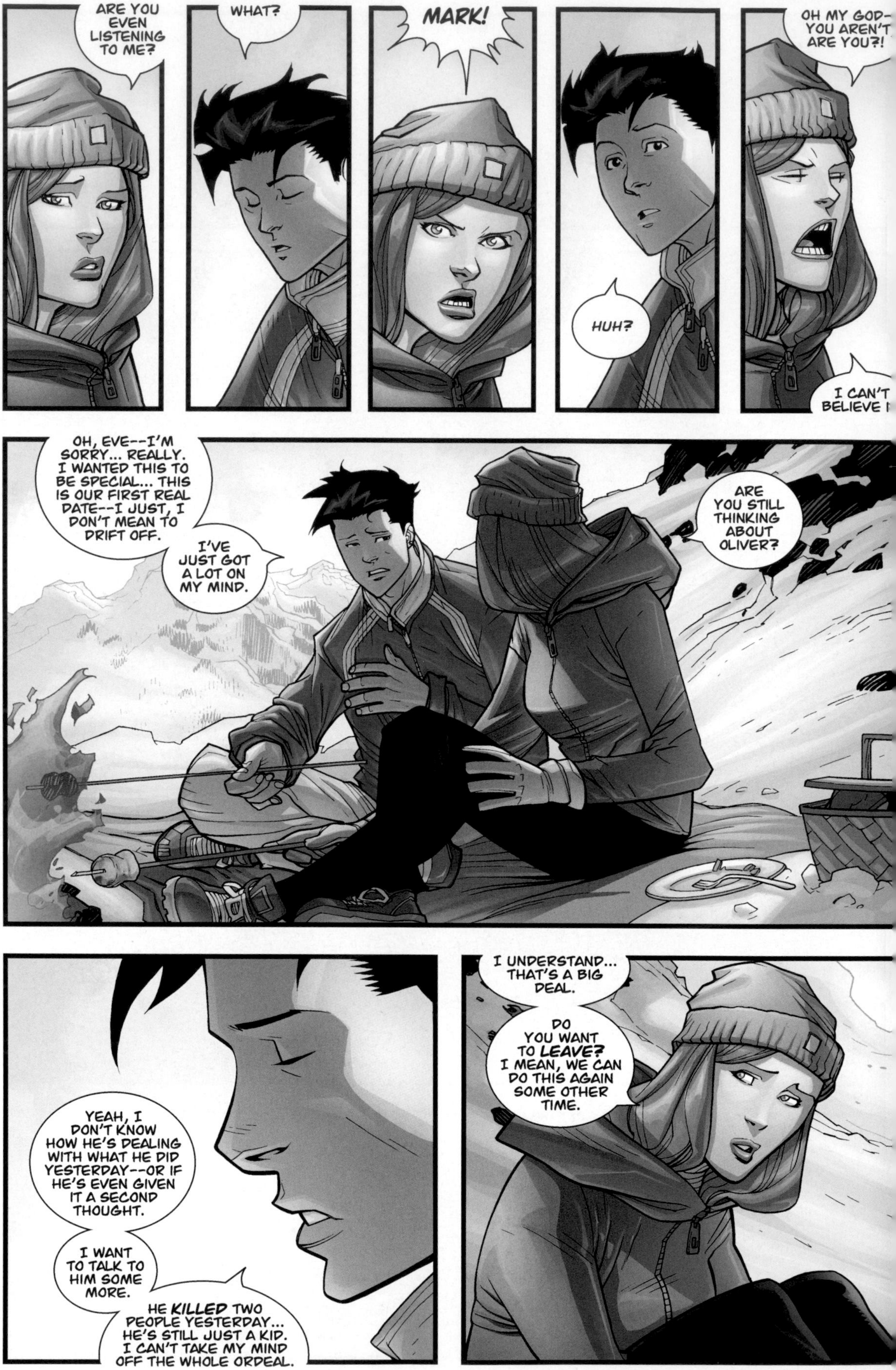
ARE YOU EVEN LISTENING TO ME?
WHAT?
MARK!
HUH?
OH MY GOD-YOU AREN'T ARE YOU?!
I CAN'T BELIEVE
OH, EVE--I'M SORRY... REALLY. I WANTED THIS TO BE SPECIAL... THIS IS OUR FIRST REAL DATE--I JUST, I DON'T MEAN TO DRIFT OFF.
I'VE JUST GOT A LOT ON MY MIND.
ARE YOU STILL THINKING ABOUT OLIVER?
YEAH, I DON'T KNOW HOW HE'S DEALING WITH WHAT HE DID YESTERDAY--OR IF HE'S EVEN GIVEN IT A SECOND THOUGHT.
I WANT TO TALK TO HIM SOME MORE.
HE KILLED TWO PEOPLE YESTERDAY... HE'S STILL JUST A KID. I CAN'T TAKE MY MIND OFF THE WHOLE ORDEAL.
I UNDERSTAND... THAT'S A BIG DEAL.
DO YOU WANT TO LEAVE? I MEAN, WE CAN DO THIS AGAIN SOME OTHER TIME.

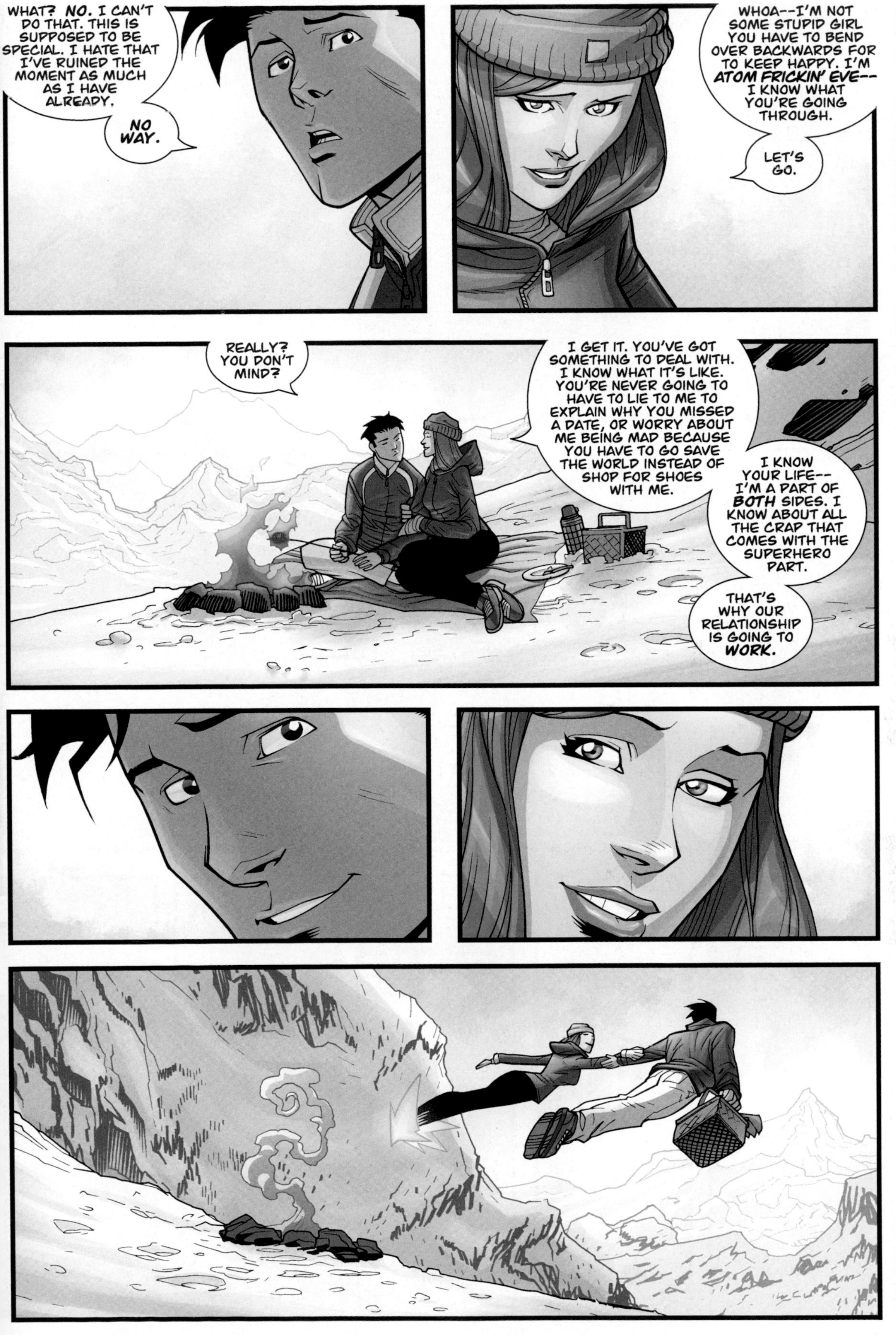
WHAT? NO. I CAN'T DO THAT. THIS IS SUPPOSED TO BE SPECIAL. I HATE THAT I'VE RUINED THE MOMENT AS MUCH AS I HAVE ALREADY.
NO WAY.
WHOA--I'M NOT SOME STUPID GIRL YOU HAVE TO BEND OVER BACKWARDS FOR TO KEEP HAPPY. I'M ATOM FRICKIN' EVE-- I KNOW WHAT YOU'RE GOING THROUGH.
LET'S GO.
REALLY? YOU DON'T MIND?
I GET IT. YOU'VE GOT SOMETHING TO DEAL WITH. I KNOW WHAT IT'S LIKE. YOU'RE NEVER GOING TO HAVE TO LIE TO ME TO EXPLAIN WHY YOU MISSED A DATE, OR WORRY ABOUT ME BEING MAD BECAUSE YOU HAVE TO GO SAVE THE WORLD INSTEAD OF SHOP FOR SHOES WITH ME.
I KNOW YOUR LIFE-- I'M A PART OF BOTH SIDES. I KNOW ABOUT ALL THE CRAP THAT COMES WITH THE SUPERHERO PART.
THAT'S WHY OUR RELATIONSHIP IS GOING TO WORK.

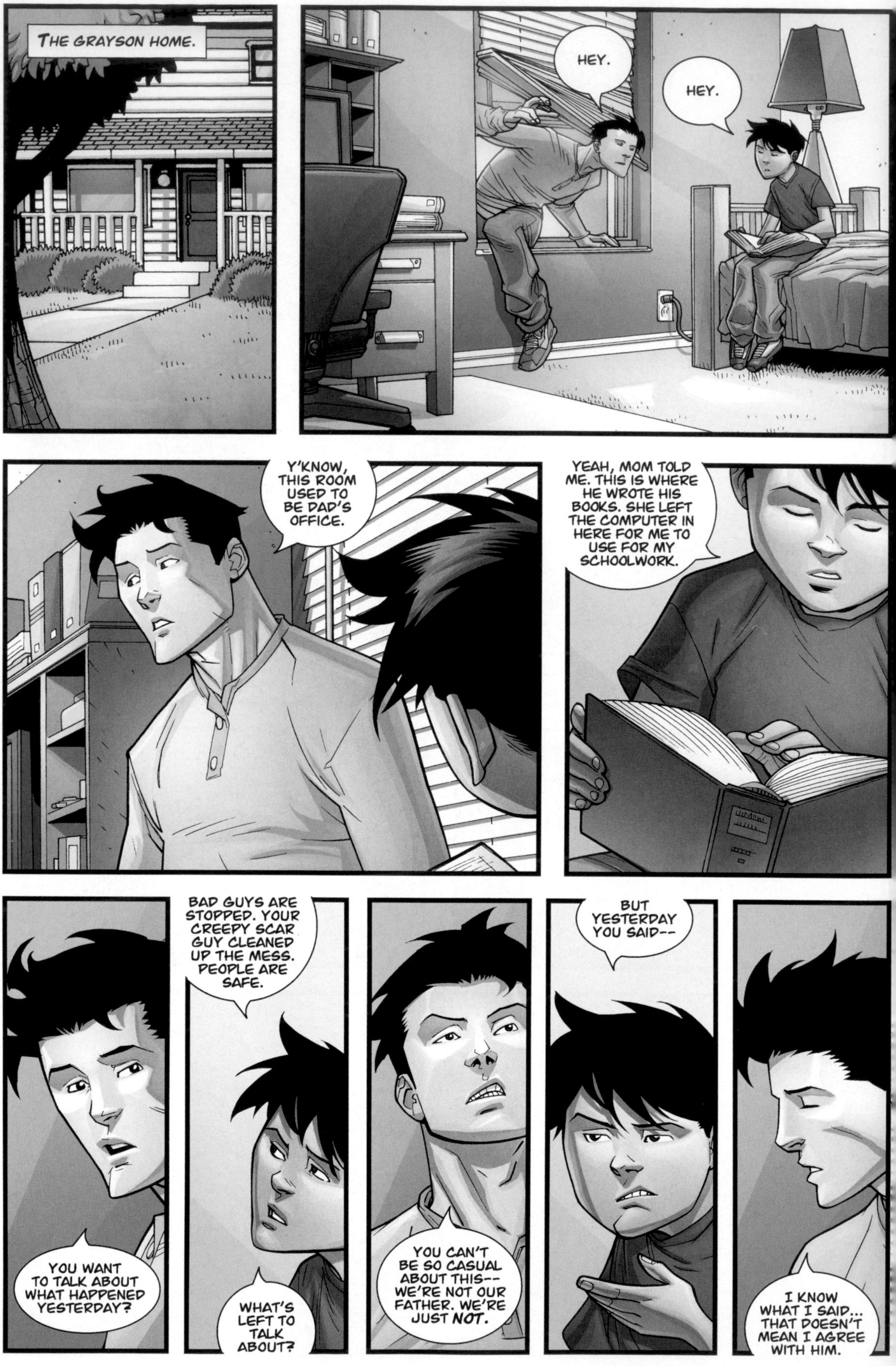
THE GRAYSON HOME.
HEY.
HEY.
Y'KNOW, THIS ROOM USED TO BE DAD'S OFFICE.
YEAH, MOM TOLD ME. THIS IS WHERE HE WROTE HIS BOOKS. SHE LEFT THE COMPUTER IN HERE FOR ME TO USE FOR MY SCHOOLWORK.
YOU WANT TO TALK ABOUT WHAT HAPPENED YESTERDAY?
BAD GUYS ARE STOPPED. YOUR CREEPY SCAR GUY CLEANED UP THE MESS. PEOPLE ARE SAFE.
WHAT'S LEFT TO TALK ABOUT?
YOU CAN'T BE SO CASUAL ABOUT THIS-- WE'RE NOT OUR FATHER. WE'RE JUST **NOT**.
BUT YESTERDAY YOU SAID--
I KNOW WHAT I SAID... THAT DOESN'T MEAN I AGREE WITH HIM.

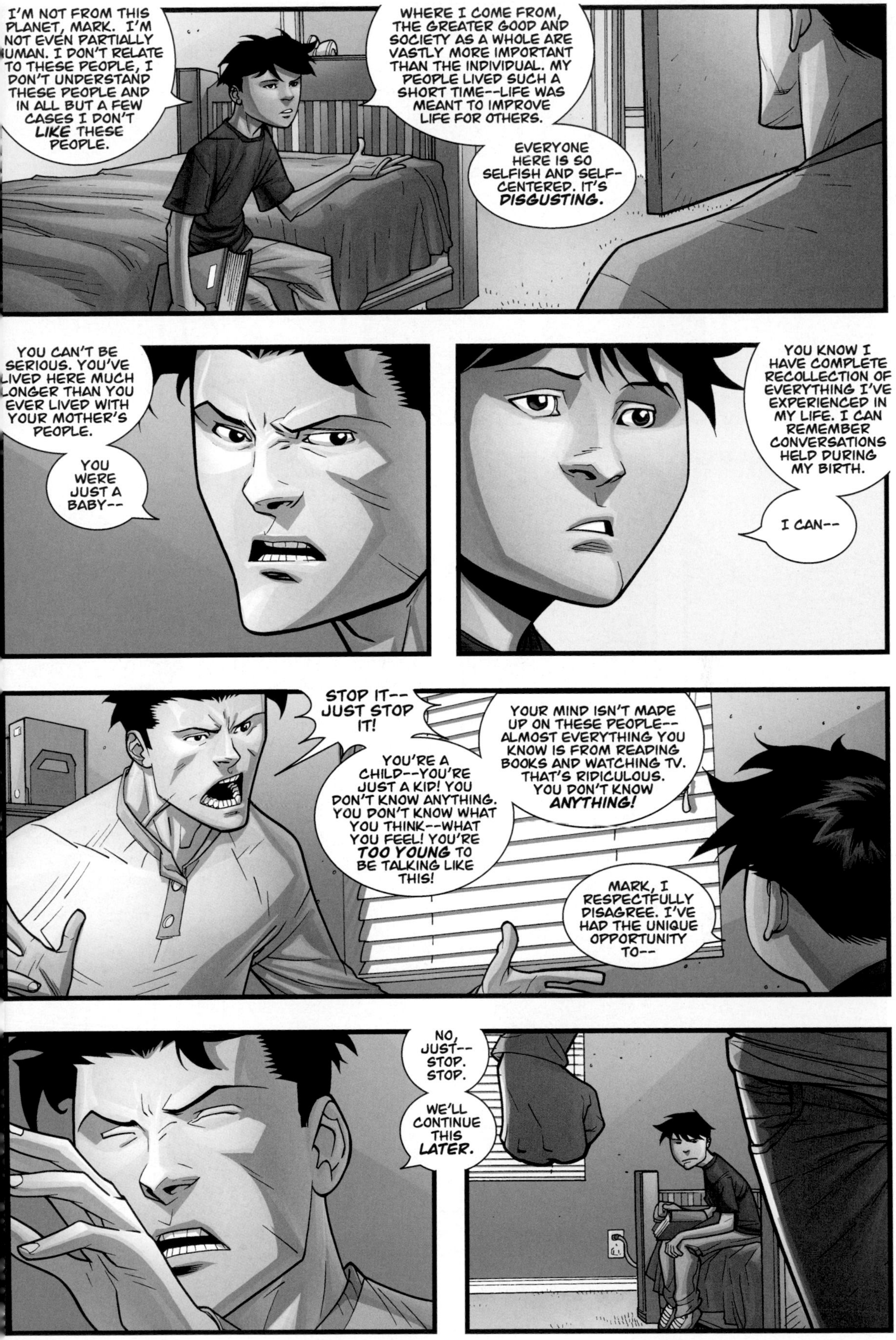

I'M NOT FROM THIS PLANET, MARK. I'M NOT EVEN PARTIALLY UMAN. I DON'T RELATE TO THESE PEOPLE, I DON'T UNDERSTAND THESE PEOPLE AND IN ALL BUT A FEW CASES I DON'T LIKE THESE PEOPLE.
WHERE I COME FROM, THE GREATER GOOD AND SOCIETY AS A WHOLE ARE VASTLY MORE IMPORTANT THAN THE INDIVIDUAL. MY PEOPLE LIVED SUCH A SHORT TIME--LIFE WAS MEANT TO IMPROVE LIFE FOR OTHERS.
EVERYONE HERE IS SO SELFISH AND SELF-CENTERED. IT'S DISGUSTING.
YOU CAN'T BE SERIOUS. YOU'VE IVED HERE MUCH ONGER THAN YOU EVER LIVED WITH YOUR MOTHER'S PEOPLE.
YOU WERE JUST A BABY--
YOU KNOW I HAVE COMPLETE RECOLLECTION OF EVERYTHING I'VE EXPERIENCED IN MY LIFE. I CAN REMEMBER CONVERSATIONS HELD DURING MY BIRTH.
I CAN--
STOP IT--JUST STOP IT!
YOU'RE A CHILD--YOU'RE JUST A KID! YOU DON'T KNOW ANYTHING. YOU DON'T KNOW WHAT YOU THINK--WHAT YOU FEEL! YOU'RE TOO YOUNG TO BE TALKING LIKE THIS!
YOUR MIND ISN'T MADE UP ON THESE PEOPLE--ALMOST EVERYTHING YOU KNOW IS FROM READING BOOKS AND WATCHING TV. THAT'S RIDICULOUS. YOU DON'T KNOW ANYTHING!
MARK, I RESPECTFULLY DISAGREE. I'VE HAD THE UNIQUE OPPORTUNITY TO--
NO, JUST--STOP. STOP.
WE'LL CONTINUE THIS LATER.

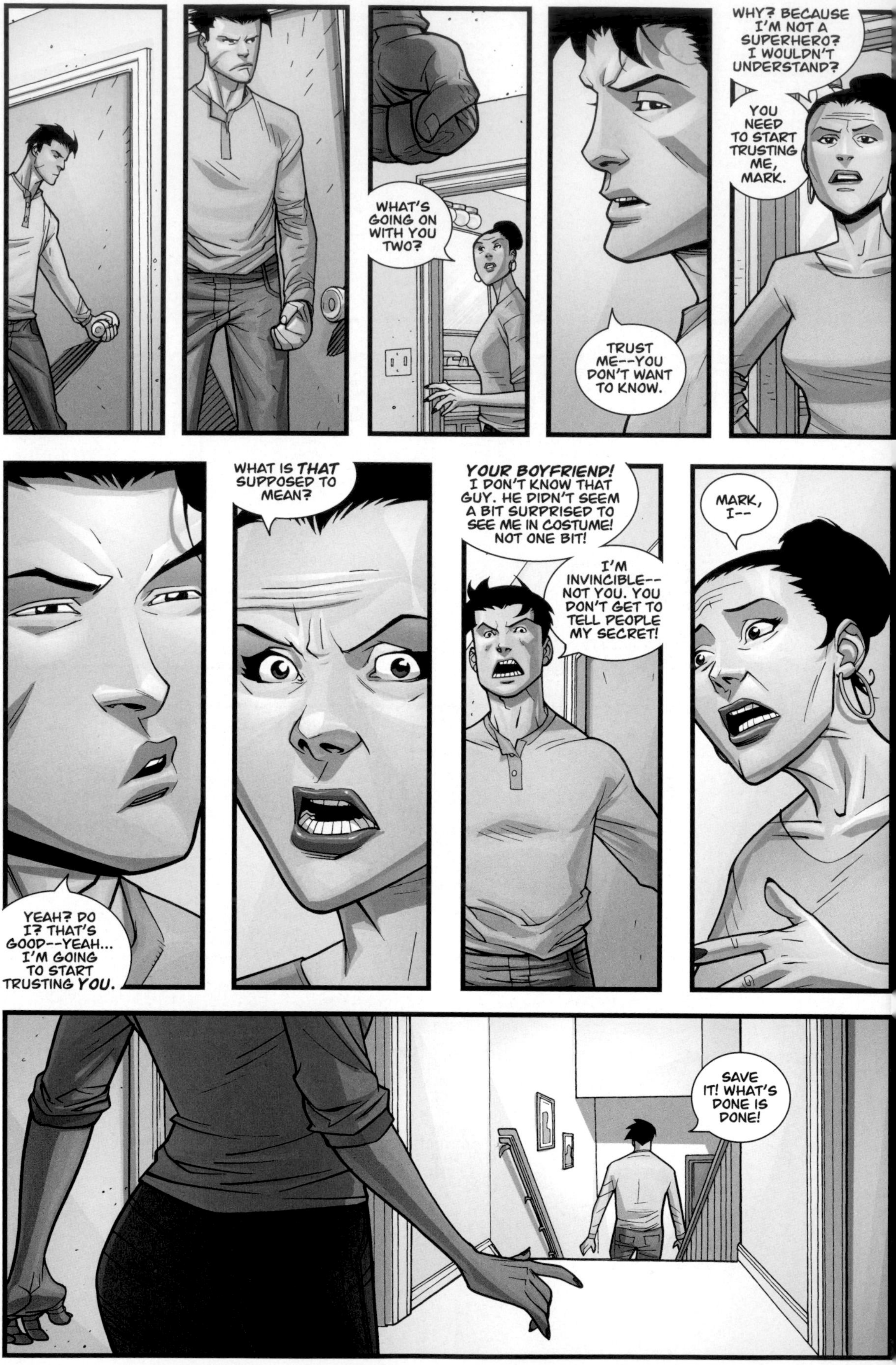
WHAT'S GOING ON WITH YOU TWO?
TRUST ME--YOU DON'T WANT TO KNOW.
WHY? BECAUSE I'M NOT A SUPERHERO? I WOULDN'T UNDERSTAND?
YOU NEED TO START TRUSTING ME, MARK.
YEAH? DO I? THAT'S GOOD--YEAH... I'M GOING TO START TRUSTING YOU.
WHAT IS THAT SUPPOSED TO MEAN?
YOUR BOYFRIEND! I DON'T KNOW THAT GUY. HE DIDN'T SEEM A BIT SURPRISED TO SEE ME IN COSTUME! NOT ONE BIT!
I'M INVINCIBLE--NOT YOU. YOU DON'T GET TO TELL PEOPLE MY SECRET!
MARK, I--
SAVE IT! WHAT'S DONE IS DONE!

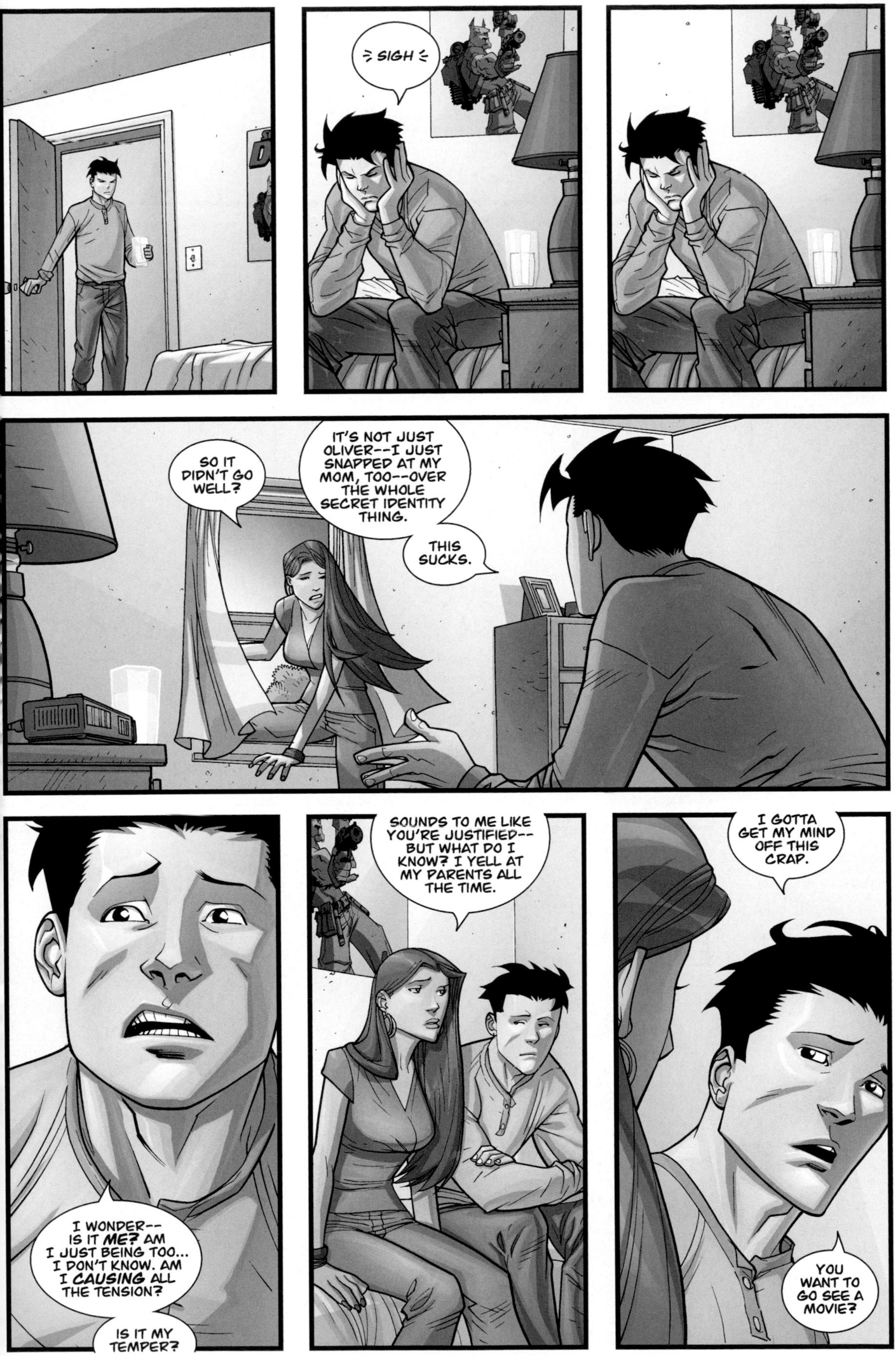
SIGH
SO IT DIDN'T GO WELL?
IT'S NOT JUST OLIVER--I JUST SNAPPED AT MY MOM, TOO--OVER THE WHOLE SECRET IDENTITY THING.
THIS SUCKS.
I WONDER-- IS IT ME? AM I JUST BEING TOO... I DON'T KNOW. AM I CAUSING ALL THE TENSION?
IS IT MY TEMPER?
SOUNDS TO ME LIKE YOU'RE JUSTIFIED-- BUT WHAT DO I KNOW? I YELL AT MY PARENTS ALL THE TIME.
I GOTTA GET MY MIND OFF THIS CRAP.
YOU WANT TO GO SEE A MOVIE?

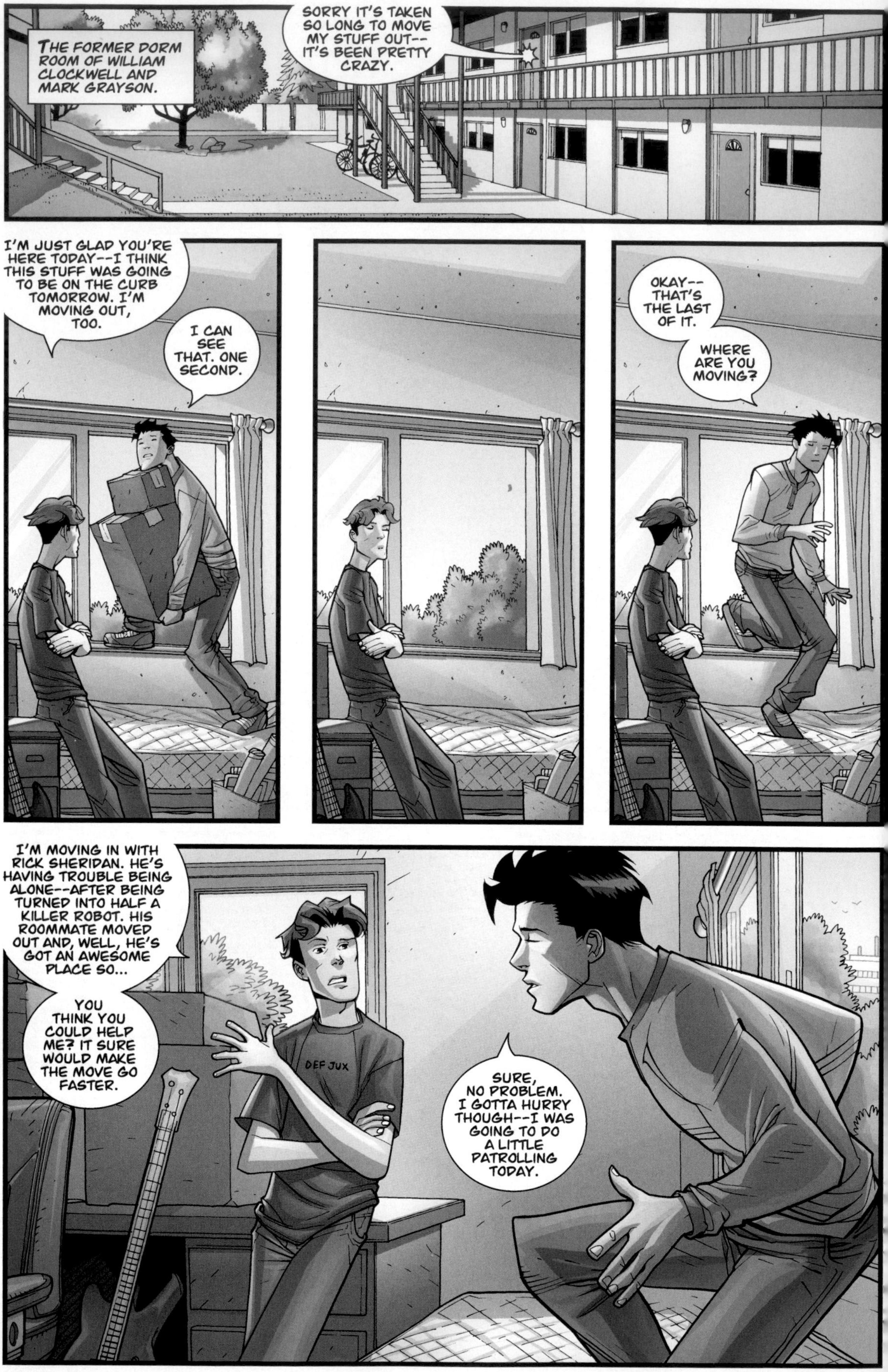

THE FORMER DORM ROOM OF WILLIAM CLOCKWELL AND MARK GRAYSON.
SORRY IT'S TAKEN SO LONG TO MOVE MY STUFF OUT-- IT'S BEEN PRETTY CRAZY.
I'M JUST GLAD YOU'RE HERE TODAY--I THINK THIS STUFF WAS GOING TO BE ON THE CURB TOMORROW. I'M MOVING OUT, TOO.
I CAN SEE THAT. ONE SECOND.
OKAY-- THAT'S THE LAST OF IT.
WHERE ARE YOU MOVING?
I'M MOVING IN WITH RICK SHERIDAN. HE'S HAVING TROUBLE BEING ALONE--AFTER BEING TURNED INTO HALF A KILLER ROBOT. HIS ROOMMATE MOVED OUT AND, WELL, HE'S GOT AN AWESOME PLACE SO...
YOU THINK YOU COULD HELP ME? IT SURE WOULD MAKE THE MOVE GO FASTER.
DEF JUX
SURE, NO PROBLEM. I GOTTA HURRY THOUGH--I WAS GOING TO DO A LITTLE PATROLLING TODAY.

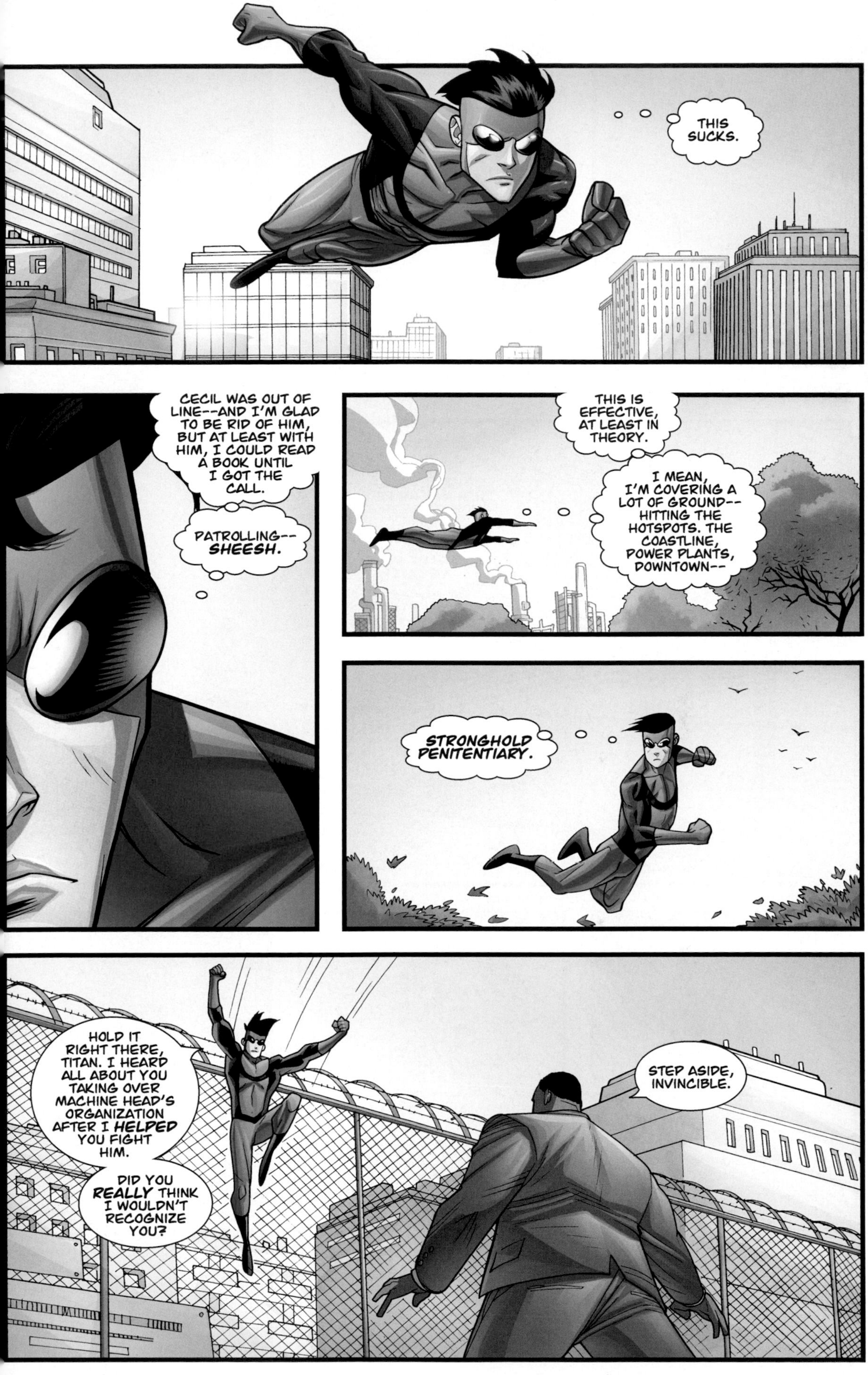
THIS SUCKS.
CECIL WAS OUT OF LINE--AND I'M GLAD TO BE RID OF HIM, BUT AT LEAST WITH HIM, I COULD READ A BOOK UNTIL I GOT THE CALL.
PATROLLING--SHEESH.
THIS IS EFFECTIVE, AT LEAST IN THEORY.
I MEAN, I'M COVERING A LOT OF GROUND--HITTING THE HOTSPOTS. THE COASTLINE, POWER PLANTS, DOWNTOWN--
STRONGHOLD PENITENTIARY.
HOLD IT RIGHT THERE, TITAN. I HEARD ALL ABOUT YOU TAKING OVER MACHINE HEAD'S ORGANIZATION AFTER I HELPED YOU FIGHT HIM.
DID YOU REALLY THINK I WOULDN'T RECOGNIZE YOU?
STEP ASIDE, INVINCIBLE.

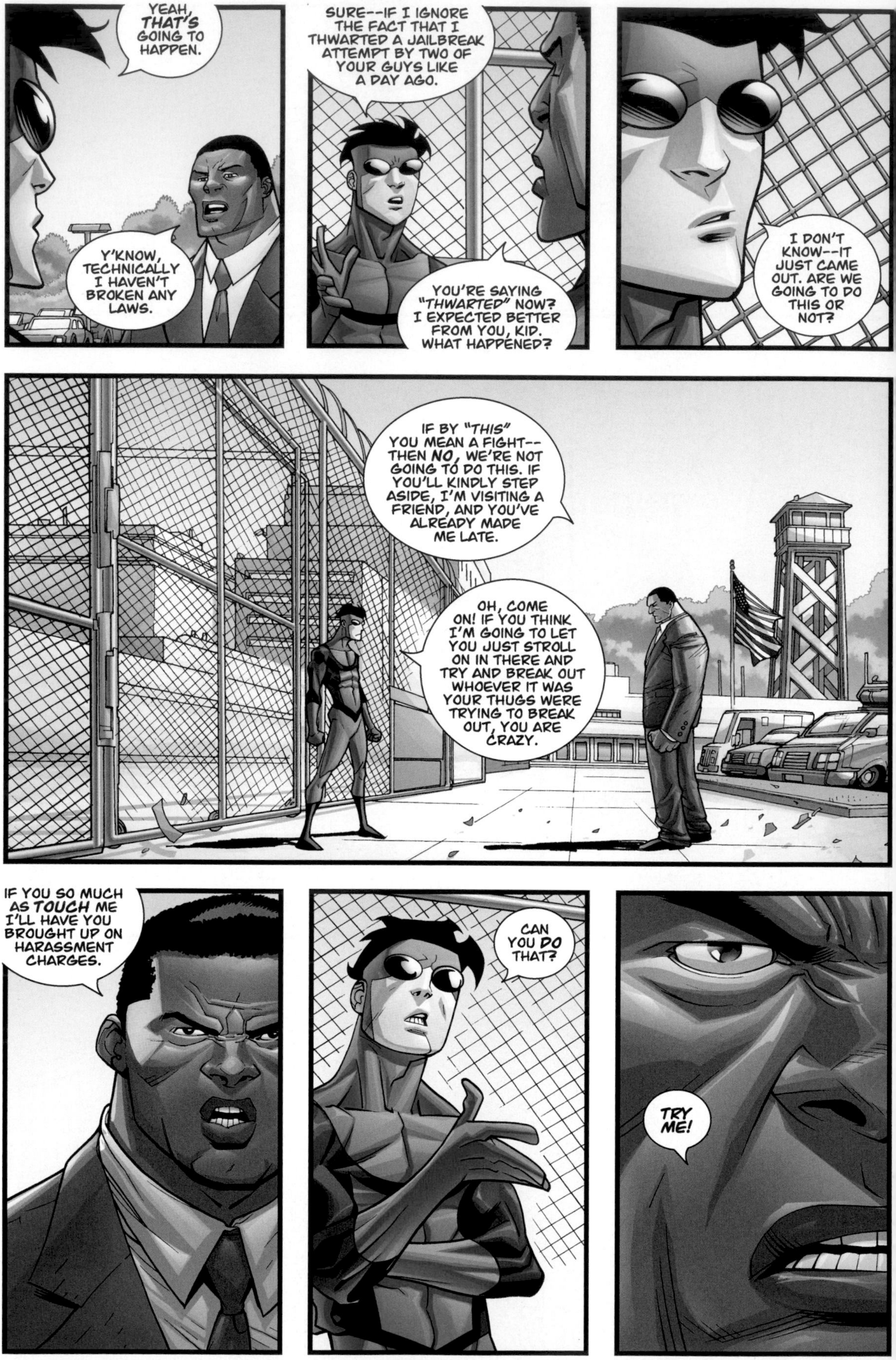
YEAH, THAT'S GOING TO HAPPEN.
Y'KNOW, TECHNICALLY I HAVEN'T BROKEN ANY LAWS.
SURE--IF I IGNORE THE FACT THAT I THWARTED A JAILBREAK ATTEMPT BY TWO OF YOUR GUYS LIKE A DAY AGO.
YOU'RE SAYING "THWARTED" NOW? I EXPECTED BETTER FROM YOU, KID. WHAT HAPPENED?
I DON'T KNOW--IT JUST CAME OUT. ARE WE GOING TO DO THIS OR NOT?
IF BY "THIS" YOU MEAN A FIGHT-- THEN NO, WE'RE NOT GOING TO DO THIS. IF YOU'LL KINDLY STEP ASIDE, I'M VISITING A FRIEND, AND YOU'VE ALREADY MADE ME LATE.
OH, COME ON! IF YOU THINK I'M GOING TO LET YOU JUST STROLL ON IN THERE AND TRY AND BREAK OUT WHOEVER IT WAS YOUR THUGS WERE TRYING TO BREAK OUT, YOU ARE CRAZY.
IF YOU SO MUCH AS TOUCH ME I'LL HAVE YOU BROUGHT UP ON HARASSMENT CHARGES.
CAN YOU DO THAT?
TRY ME!

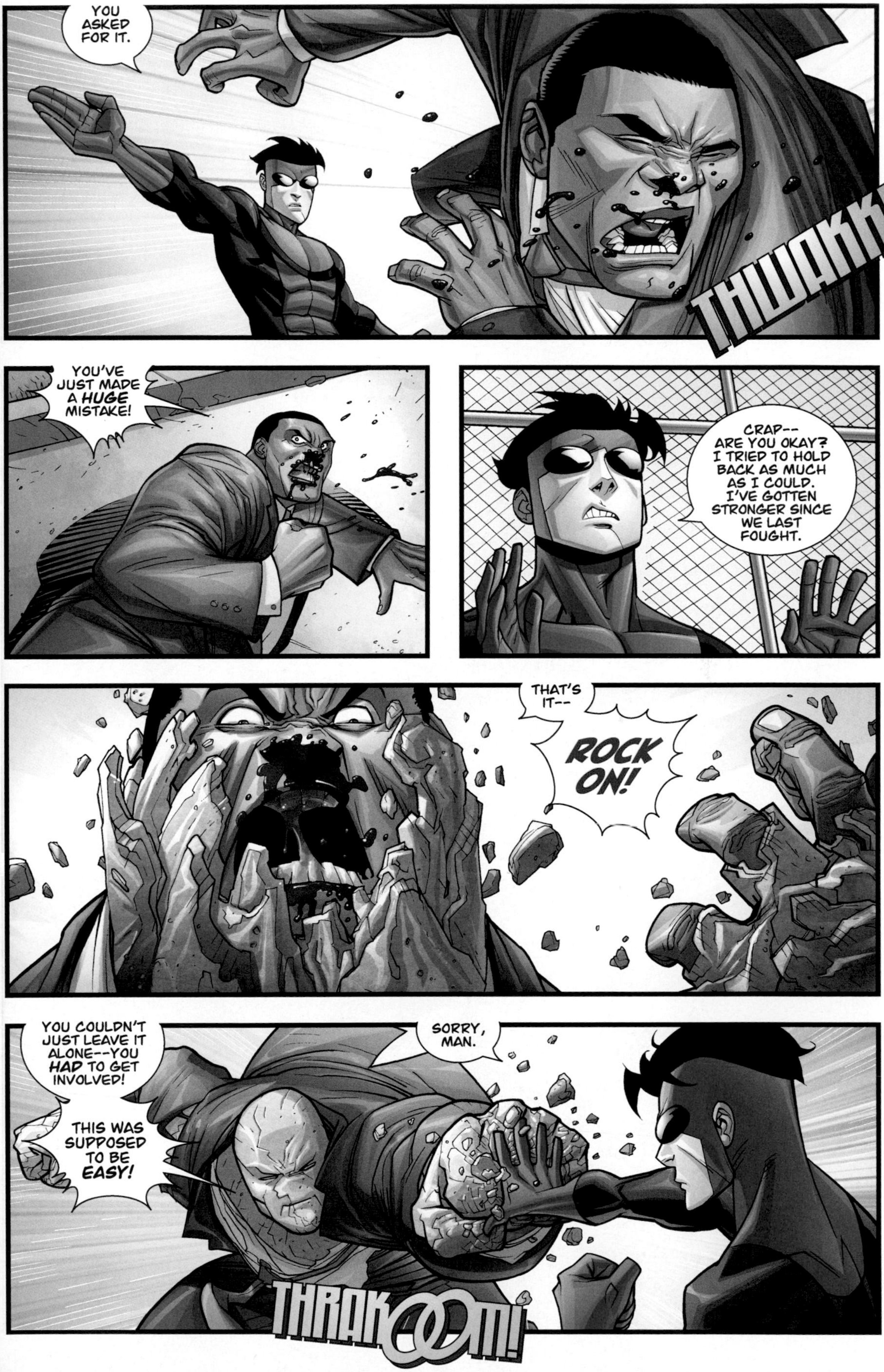
YOU ASKED FOR IT.
THWAKK!
YOU'VE JUST MADE A HUGE MISTAKE!
CRAP-- ARE YOU OKAY? I TRIED TO HOLD BACK AS MUCH AS I COULD. I'VE GOTTEN STRONGER SINCE WE LAST FOUGHT.
THAT'S IT--
ROCK ON!
YOU COULDN'T JUST LEAVE IT ALONE--YOU HAD TO GET INVOLVED!
THIS WAS SUPPOSED TO BE EASY!
SORRY, MAN.
THRAKOOM!

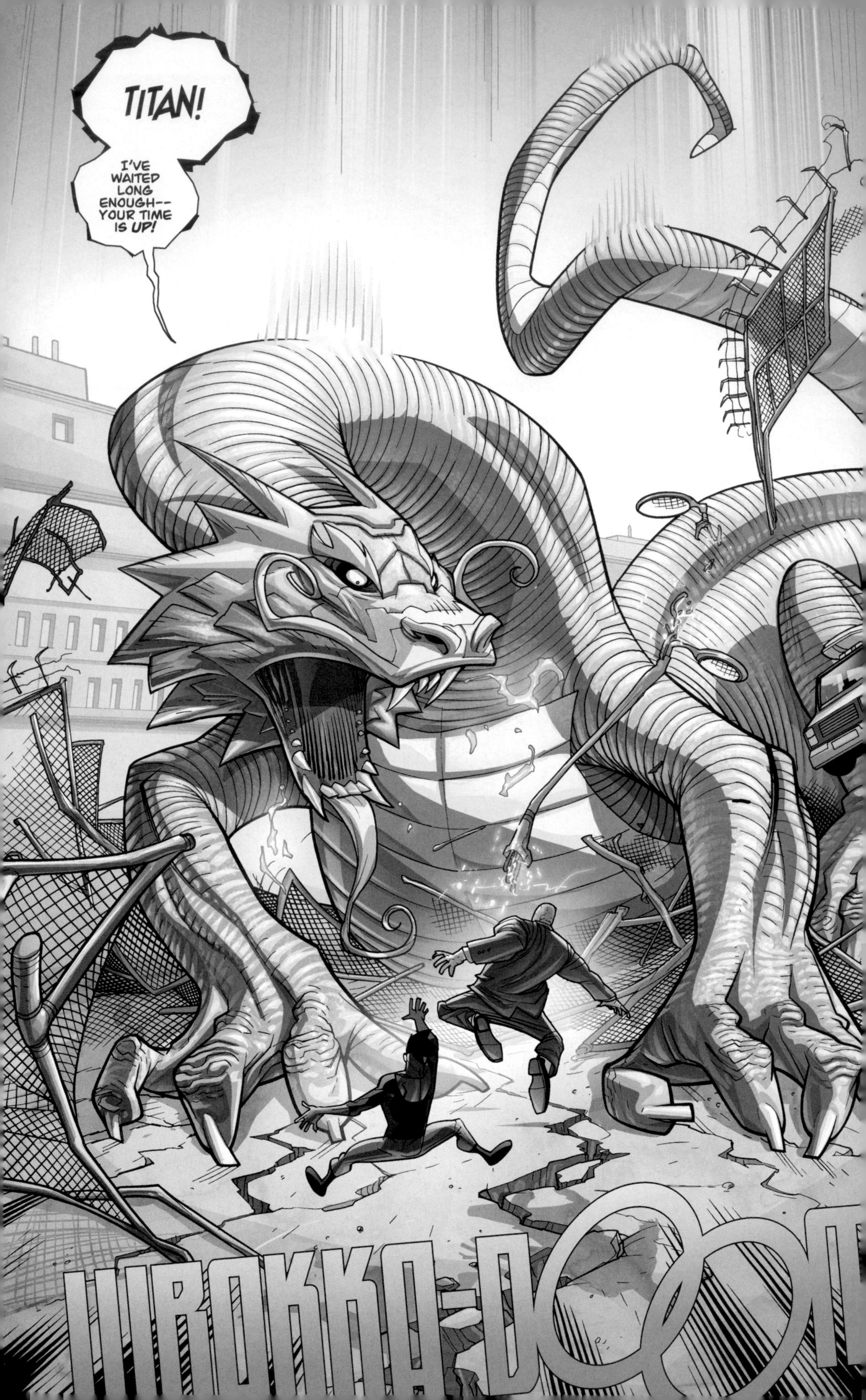
TITAN!
I'VE WAITED LONG ENOUGH-- YOUR TIME IS UP!
VROKKA-DOOM

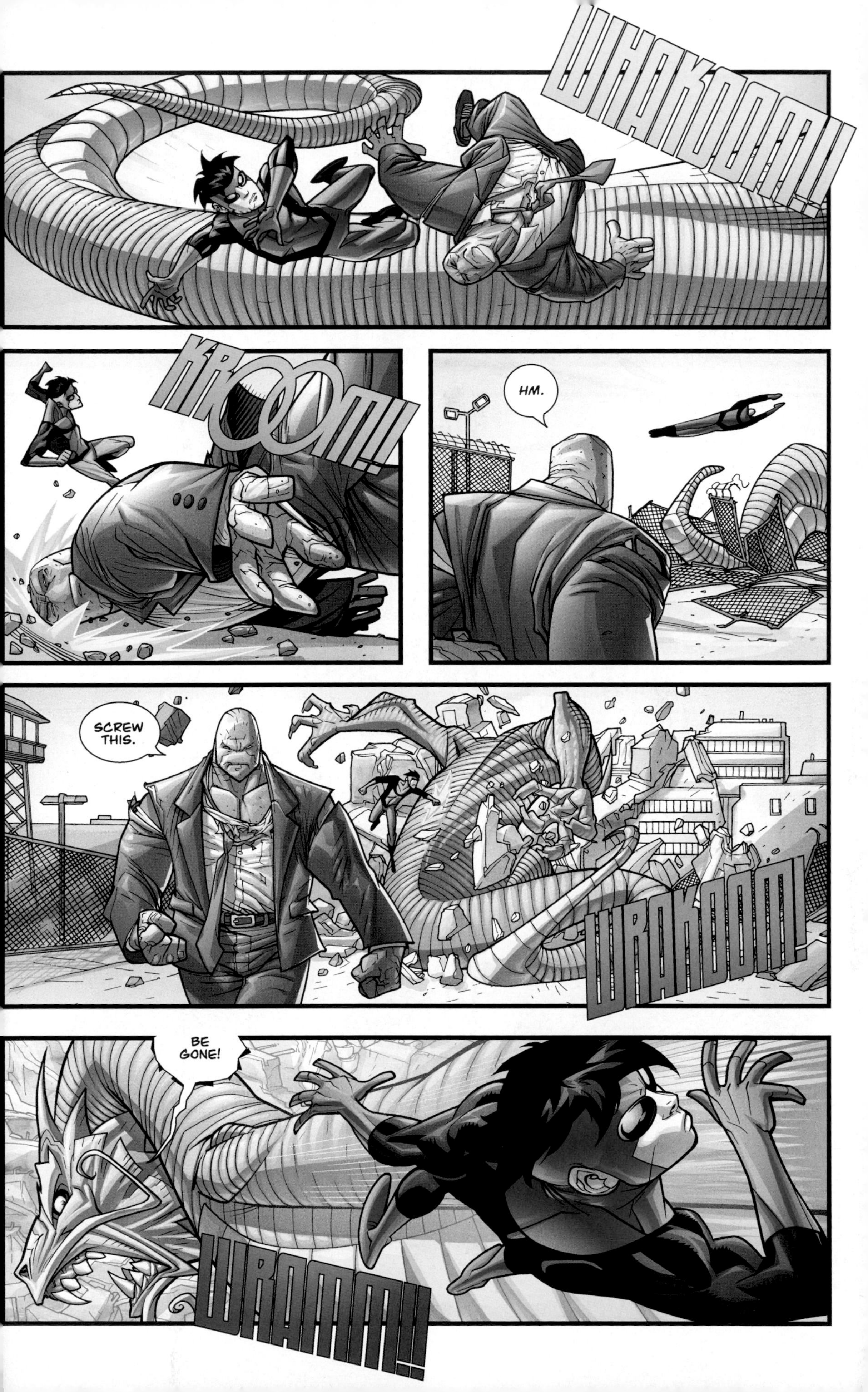
WHAKOOM!!
KROOOM!!
HM.
SCREW THIS.
WRAKOOM!
BE GONE!
WRAMM!!

EXCELLENT TIMING.

PLEASE ACCEPT MY APOLOGY FOR MY RECKLESSNESS, MASTER.

WE WILL DISCUSS THIS LATER.

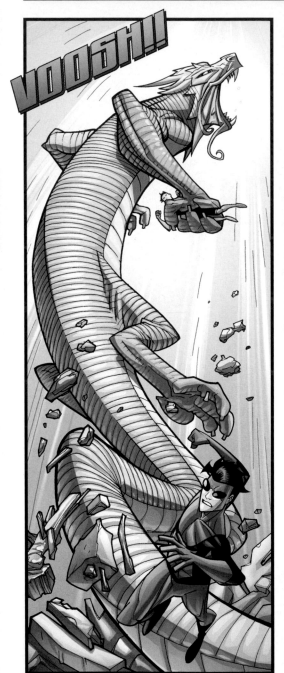

DANG.

HM?

GET BACK INSIDE!

IS SORRY!

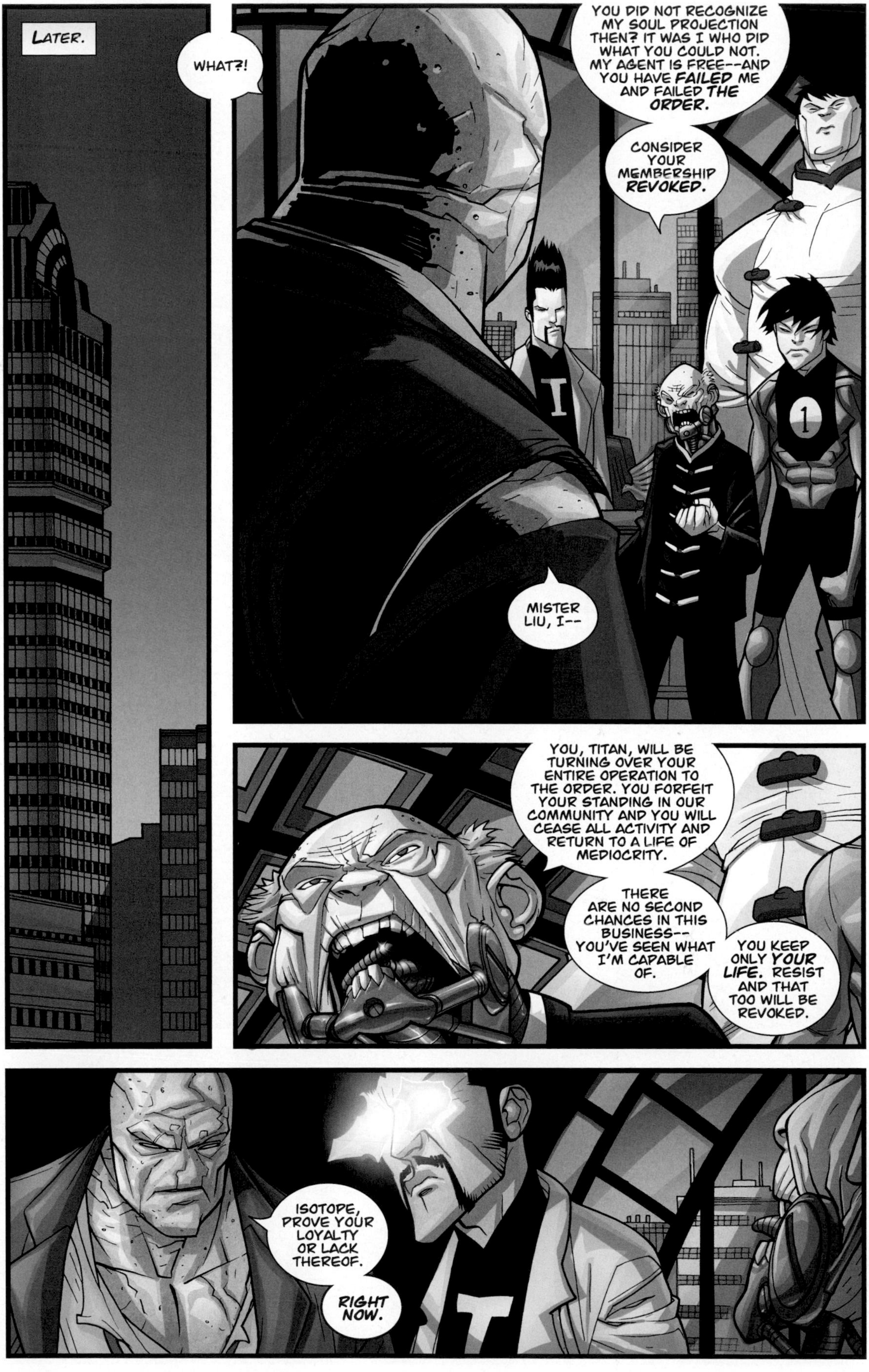
LATER.
WHAT?!
YOU DID NOT RECOGNIZE MY SOUL PROJECTION THEN? IT WAS I WHO DID WHAT YOU COULD NOT. MY AGENT IS FREE--AND YOU HAVE FAILED ME AND FAILED THE ORDER.
CONSIDER YOUR MEMBERSHIP REVOKED.
MISTER LIU, I--
YOU, TITAN, WILL BE TURNING OVER YOUR ENTIRE OPERATION TO THE ORDER. YOU FORFEIT YOUR STANDING IN OUR COMMUNITY AND YOU WILL CEASE ALL ACTIVITY AND RETURN TO A LIFE OF MEDIOCRITY.
THERE ARE NO SECOND CHANCES IN THIS BUSINESS-- YOU'VE SEEN WHAT I'M CAPABLE OF.
YOU KEEP ONLY YOUR LIFE. RESIST AND THAT TOO WILL BE REVOKED.
ISOTOPE, PROVE YOUR LOYALTY OR LACK THEREOF.
RIGHT NOW.

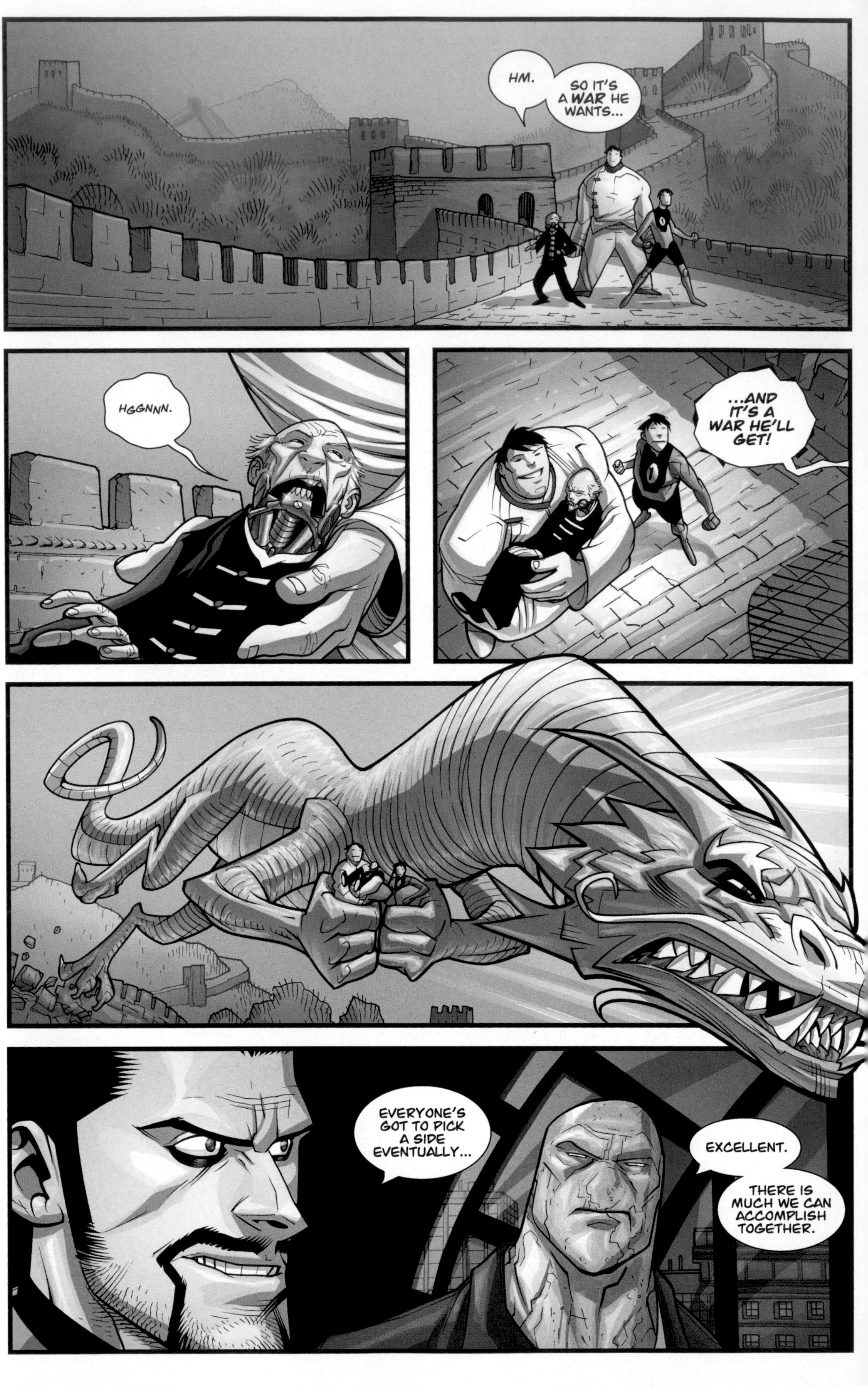
HM.
SO IT'S A WAR HE WANTS...
HGGNNN.
...AND IT'S A WAR HE'LL GET!
EVERYONE'S GOT TO PICK A SIDE EVENTUALLY...
EXCELLENT.
THERE IS MUCH WE CAN ACCOMPLISH TOGETHER.

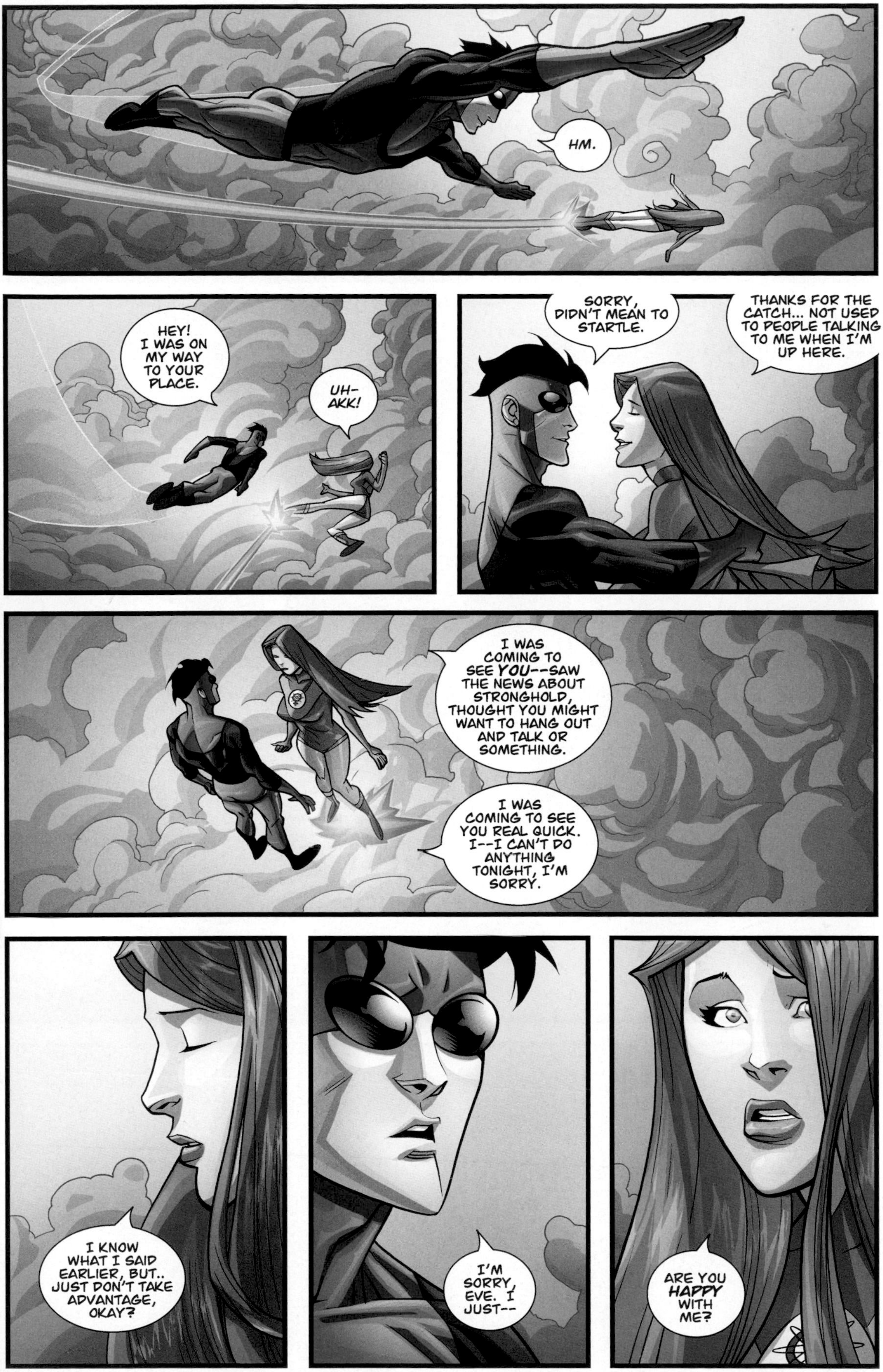
HM.
HEY! I WAS ON MY WAY TO YOUR PLACE.
UH-AKK!
SORRY, DIDN'T MEAN TO STARTLE.
THANKS FOR THE CATCH... NOT USED TO PEOPLE TALKING TO ME WHEN I'M UP HERE.
I WAS COMING TO SEE YOU--SAW THE NEWS ABOUT STRONGHOLD, THOUGHT YOU MIGHT WANT TO HANG OUT AND TALK OR SOMETHING.
I WAS COMING TO SEE YOU REAL QUICK. I--I CAN'T DO ANYTHING TONIGHT, I'M SORRY.
I KNOW WHAT I SAID EARLIER, BUT.. JUST DON'T TAKE ADVANTAGE, OKAY?
I'M SORRY, EVE. I JUST--
ARE YOU HAPPY WITH ME?

ARE YOU *KIDDING?* OF *COURSE* I'M HAPPY WITH YOU. JEEZ--C'MON! I-- I'M *TOTALLY* HAPPY WITH YOU.

YOU CAN'T TELL? REALLY? I DON'T KNOW WHAT TO SAY.

STOP-- STOP RIGHT THERE.

I'VE BEEN DISTRACTED, YES-- MY BROTHER *KILLED* A COUPLE GUYS, IT'S SOMETHING I'VE GOT TO DEAL WITH, I--

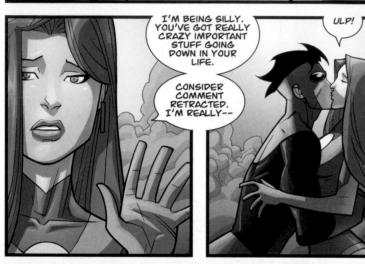

I'M BEING SILLY. YOU'VE GOT REALLY CRAZY IMPORTANT STUFF GOING DOWN IN YOUR LIFE.

CONSIDER COMMENT RETRACTED. I'M REALLY--

ULP!

REALLY, EVE-- YOU'RE *THE BEST.*

OKAY--*TOMORROW*, YOU AND ME, A REAL DATÉ. THE WORKS, DINNER, SKIING, HIKING, FLYING, WE CAN GO TO THE MOON IF YOU WANT--WHATEVER. JUST YOU AND ME, NO INTERRUPTIONS.

CECIL'S NOT GOING TO BE CALLING ME AWAY-- I CAN ACTUALLY PROMISE THIS. A DATE, A REAL DATE, FROM START TO FINISH-- WITHOUT A GIANT MONSTER INTERRUPTING.

I'LL MAKE IT SPECIAL. JUST GIVE ME TONIGHT TO CLEAR THIS MESS UP.

OKAY?

OKAY.

GREAT! I'LL BE AT YOUR PLACE AT FIVE. SEE YOU THEN!

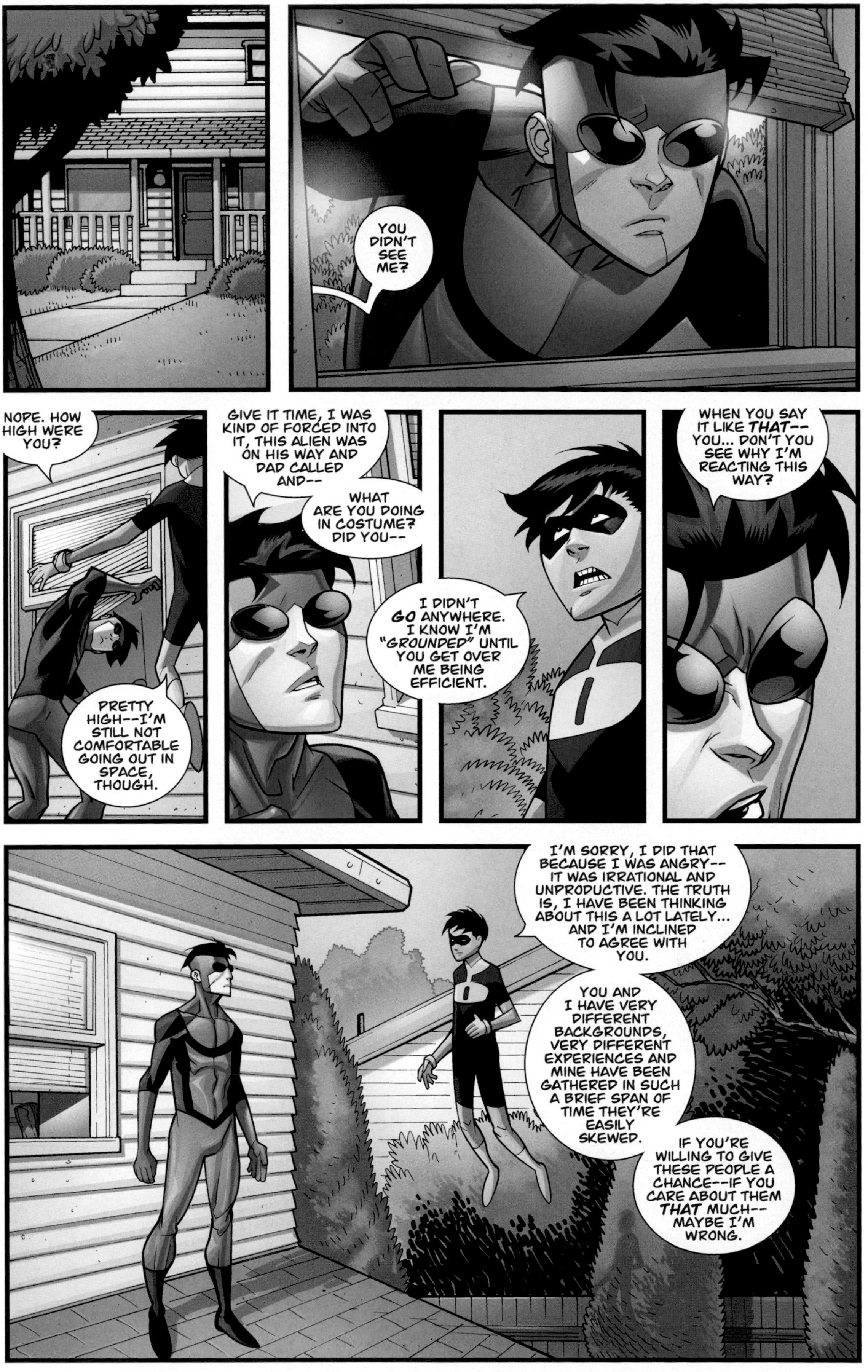
YOU DIDN'T SEE ME?
NOPE. HOW HIGH WERE YOU?
PRETTY HIGH--I'M STILL NOT COMFORTABLE GOING OUT IN SPACE, THOUGH.
GIVE IT TIME, I WAS KIND OF FORCED INTO IT, THIS ALIEN WAS ON HIS WAY AND DAD CALLED AND--
WHAT ARE YOU DOING IN COSTUME? DID YOU--
I DIDN'T GO ANYWHERE. I KNOW I'M "GROUNDED" UNTIL YOU GET OVER ME BEING EFFICIENT.
WHEN YOU SAY IT LIKE THAT--YOU... DON'T YOU SEE WHY I'M REACTING THIS WAY?
I'M SORRY, I DID THAT BECAUSE I WAS ANGRY--IT WAS IRRATIONAL AND UNPRODUCTIVE. THE TRUTH IS, I HAVE BEEN THINKING ABOUT THIS A LOT LATELY... AND I'M INCLINED TO AGREE WITH YOU.
YOU AND I HAVE VERY DIFFERENT BACKGROUNDS, VERY DIFFERENT EXPERIENCES AND MINE HAVE BEEN GATHERED IN SUCH A BRIEF SPAN OF TIME THEY'RE EASILY SKEWED.
IF YOU'RE WILLING TO GIVE THESE PEOPLE A CHANCE--IF YOU CARE ABOUT THEM THAT MUCH--MAYBE I'M WRONG.

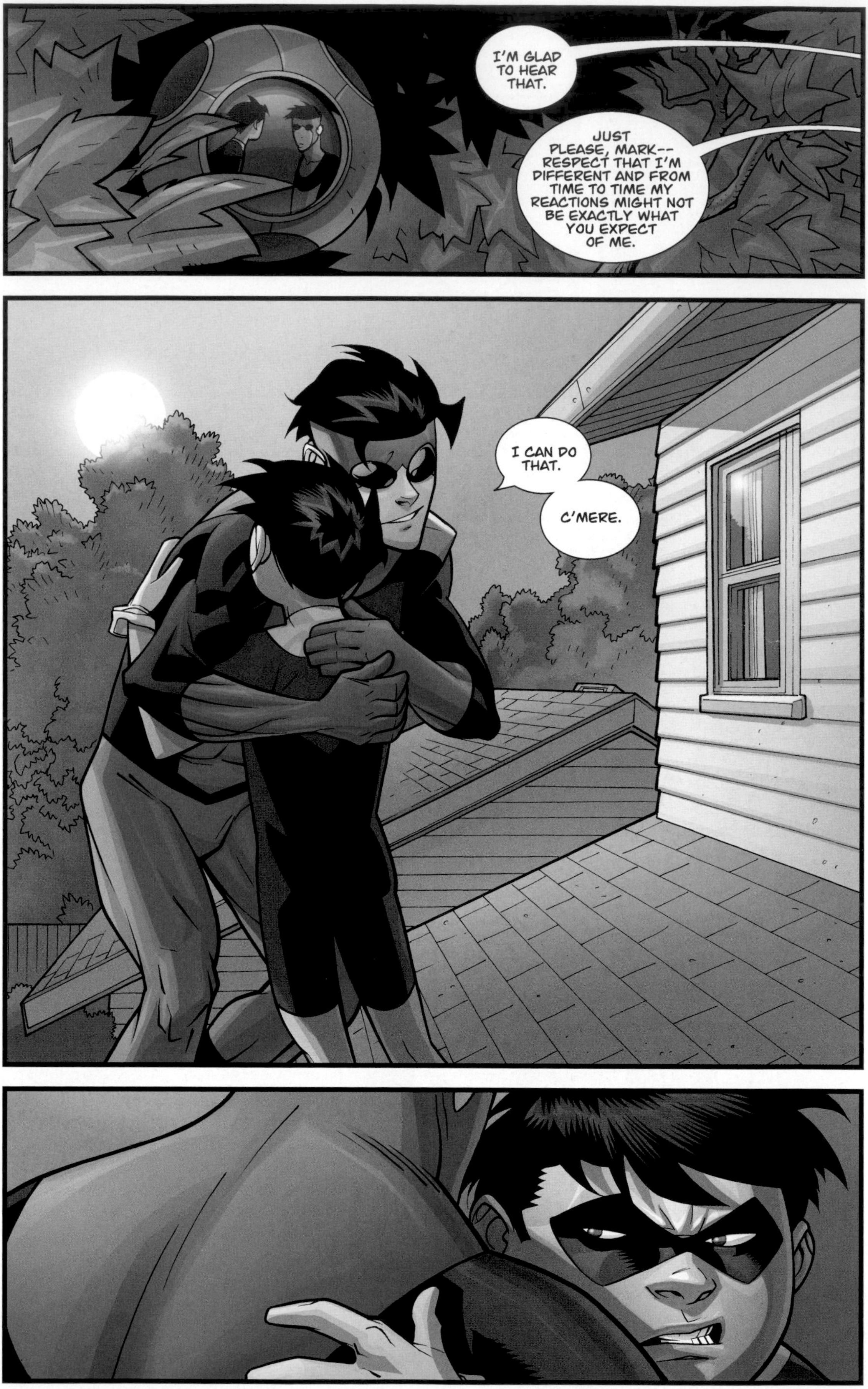
I'M GLAD TO HEAR THAT.
JUST PLEASE, MARK-- RESPECT THAT I'M DIFFERENT AND FROM TIME TO TIME MY REACTIONS MIGHT NOT BE EXACTLY WHAT YOU EXPECT OF ME.
I CAN DO THAT.
C'MERE.

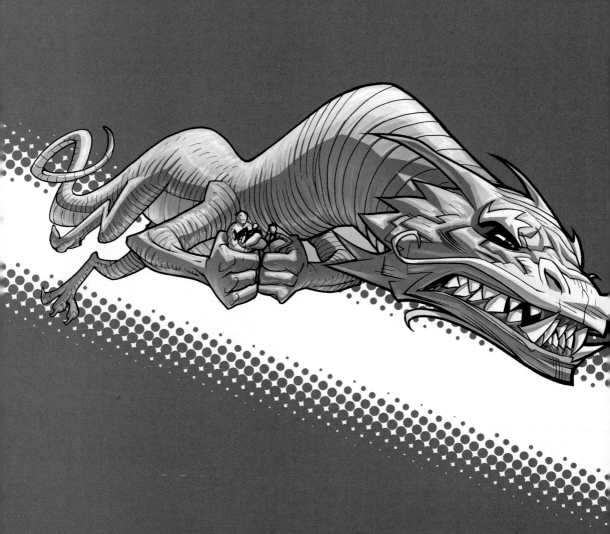

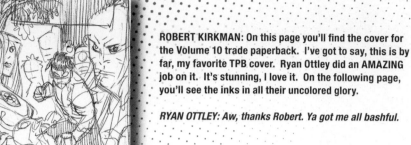

ROBERT KIRKMAN: On this page you'll find the cover for the Volume 10 trade paperback. I've got to say, this is by far, my favorite TPB cover. Ryan Ottley did an AMAZING job on it. It's stunning, I love it. On the following page, you'll see the inks in all their uncolored glory.

RYAN OTTLEY: Aw, thanks Robert. Ya got me all bashful.

SKETCHBOOK

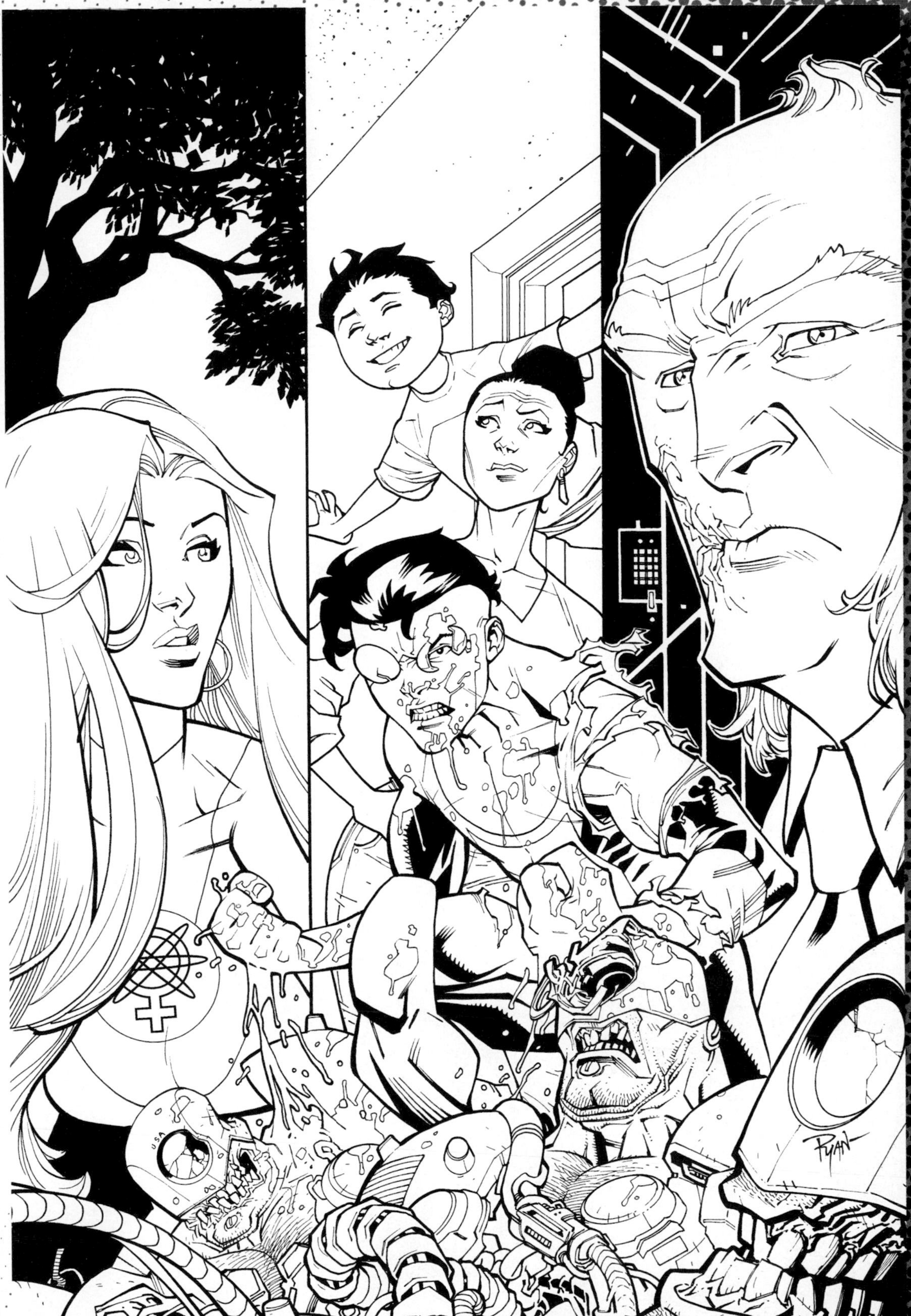

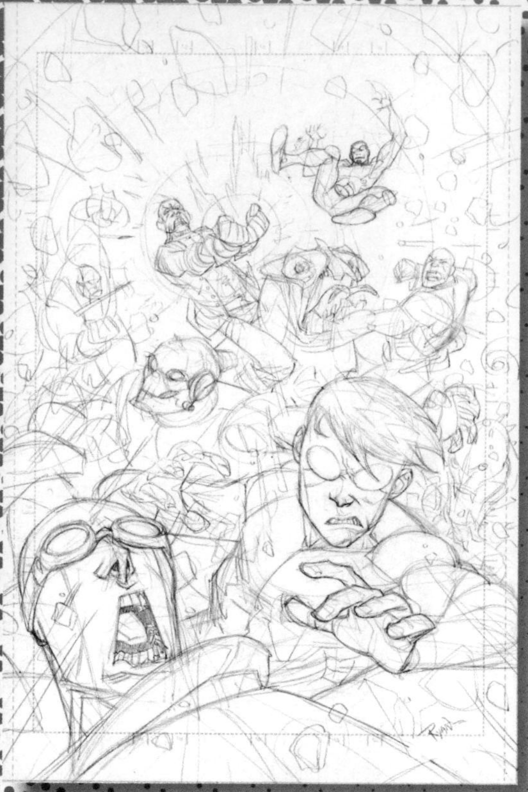

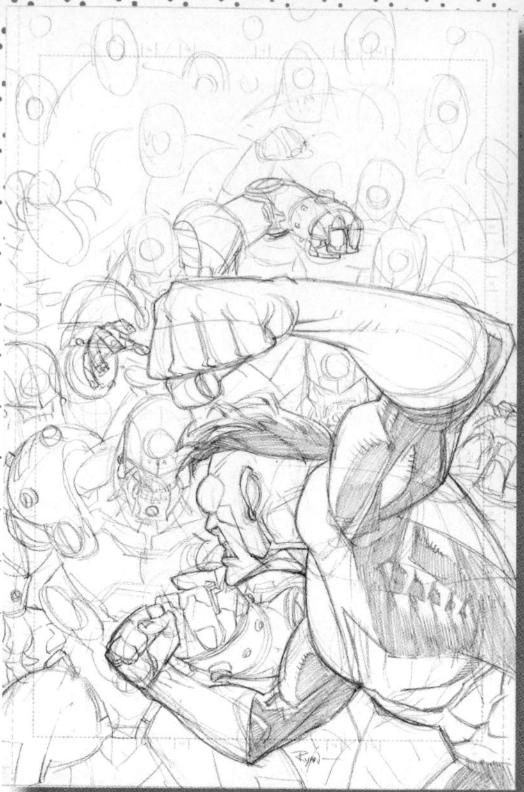

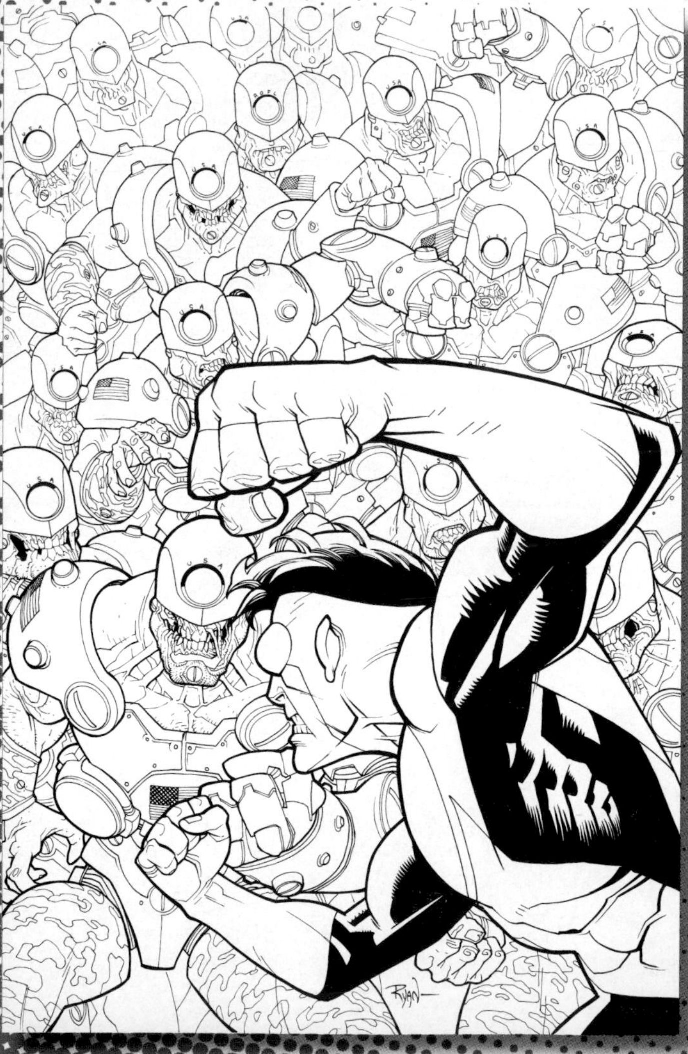

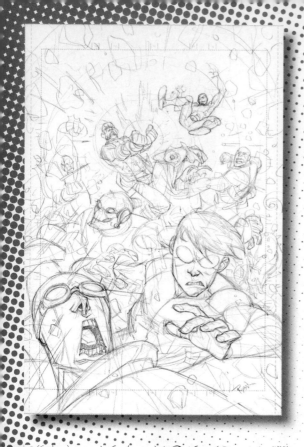

KIRKMAN: Here's some prelim work for the covers to 48 and 49. Fun fact, the covers to 48, 49 and 50 were colored by my pal Val Staples. He did a bang up, job, too--I'm very fond of these three covers.

OTTLEY: I love these covers too, especially 49. Val gave it a lot of depth doing that fade thing. Thanks Val!

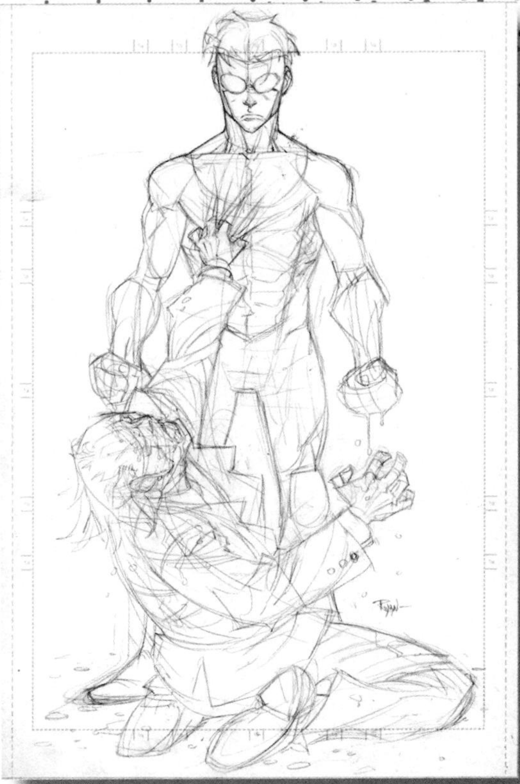

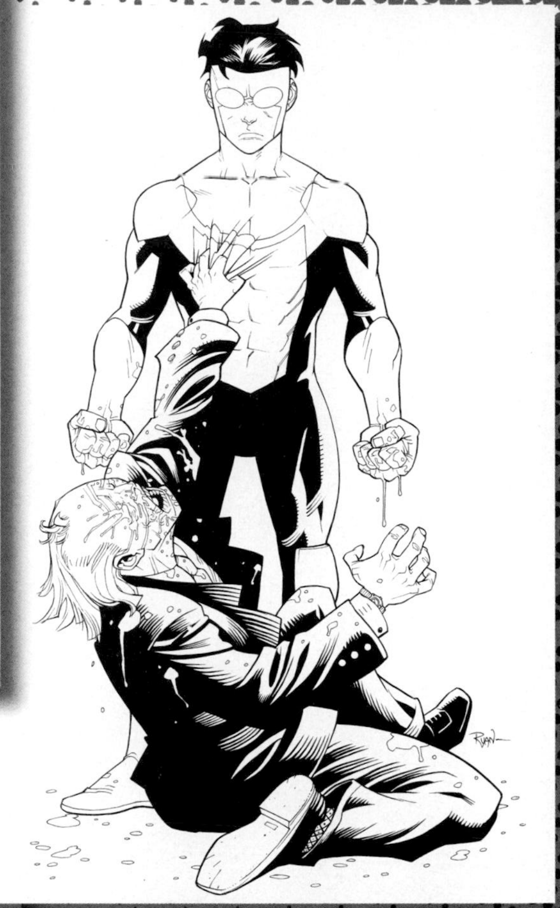

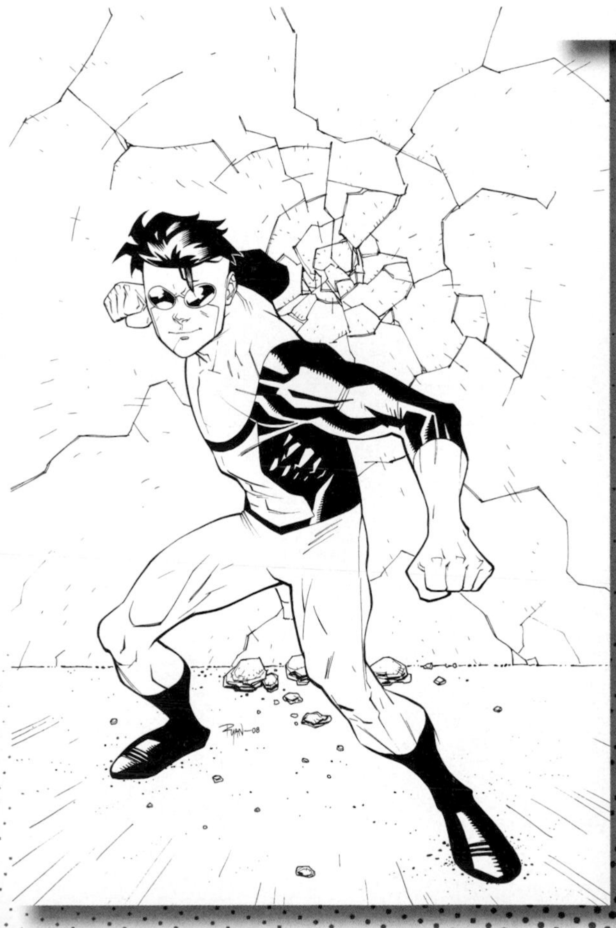

KIRKMAN: When Ryan originally did the pencils for the cover to issue 50, he had Cecil sitting on both his feet. I thought it looked like Cecil had knelt before Invincible--so I had him move the leg. FUN!

OTTLEY: The leg change helped it I think. He looks like he collapsed much harder and off balance. Good idea Robert, you should really sign these covers with me when you give good advice like this. HAHAHAHA! ahem.

KIRKMAN: Groan! When issue 51 sold out so quickly, we immediately went back to press with a second printing. It was a blast seeing Ryan redraw Cory Walker's cover for issue one, with the new costume. I don't remember whose idea it was, but I'm pretty sure it wasn't mine. On the next page, you can see it in full color.

*OTTLEY: It was most definitely your idea. Robert called me up and was telling me we need a variant cover, he didn't know what I should draw but he knew he wanted me to "make it look cool". When he doesn't have ideas this is usually his suggestion. And then BAM it hit him and he started talking super fast with excitement and this is usually the time when his Kentucky accent really gets kicked up a notch! He said "I know, I know, re-draw Cory's first cover exactly but with the blue costume! Yeehaw!" And so I did. I thought it was a great idea, Robert has a lot of those. *hug**

KIRKMAN: YEEHAW!

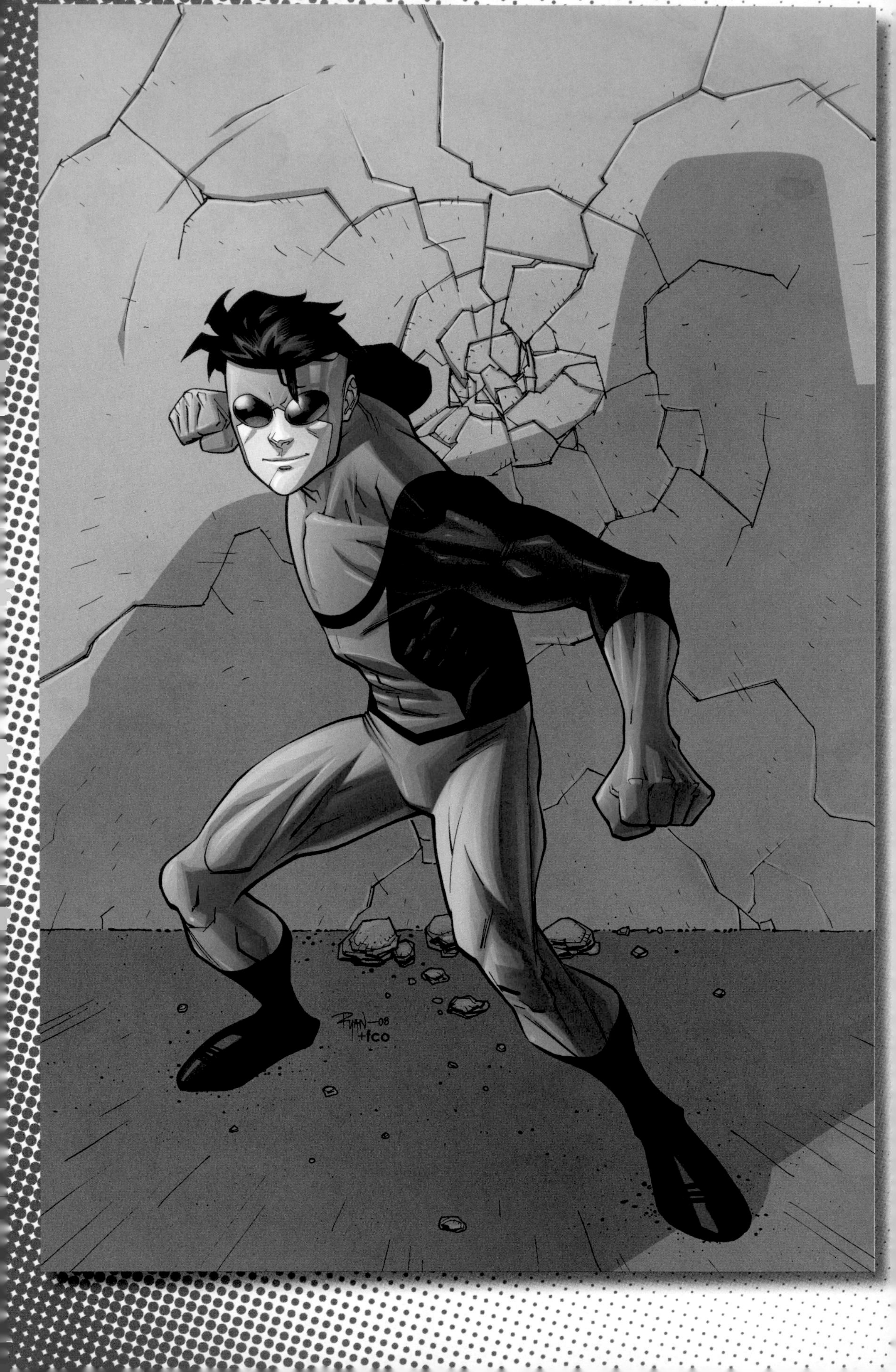
RYAN—08
+fco

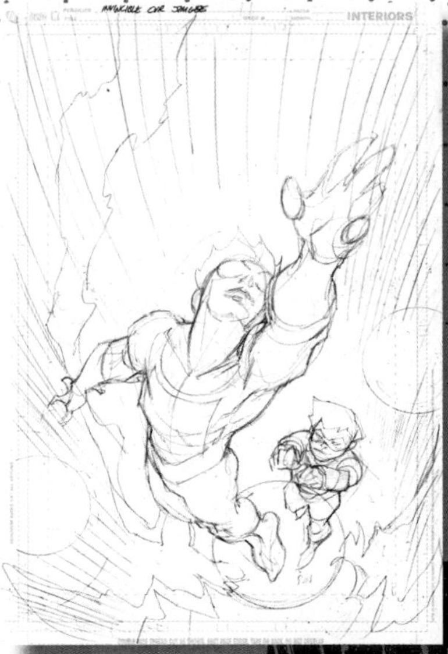
INTERIORS

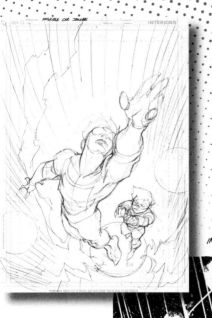

KIRKMAN: HOLY CRAP Jim Lee did a cover for us. I can't express how excited I was when he said yes. Jim is a totally cool dude. I owe him a ton for doing this for us and then he up and mailed me the original art when he was done! I couldn't believe it. If you see my writing a book for Wildstorm someday... that's why.

OTTLEY: Yeah this was nice, ya gotta love Jim Lee. I love that he did this for us. I didn't get any free art though, unless you count the interior pages which I drew. In that sense I made out like a bandit!

KIRKMAN: He asked me if you wanted it and I said no.

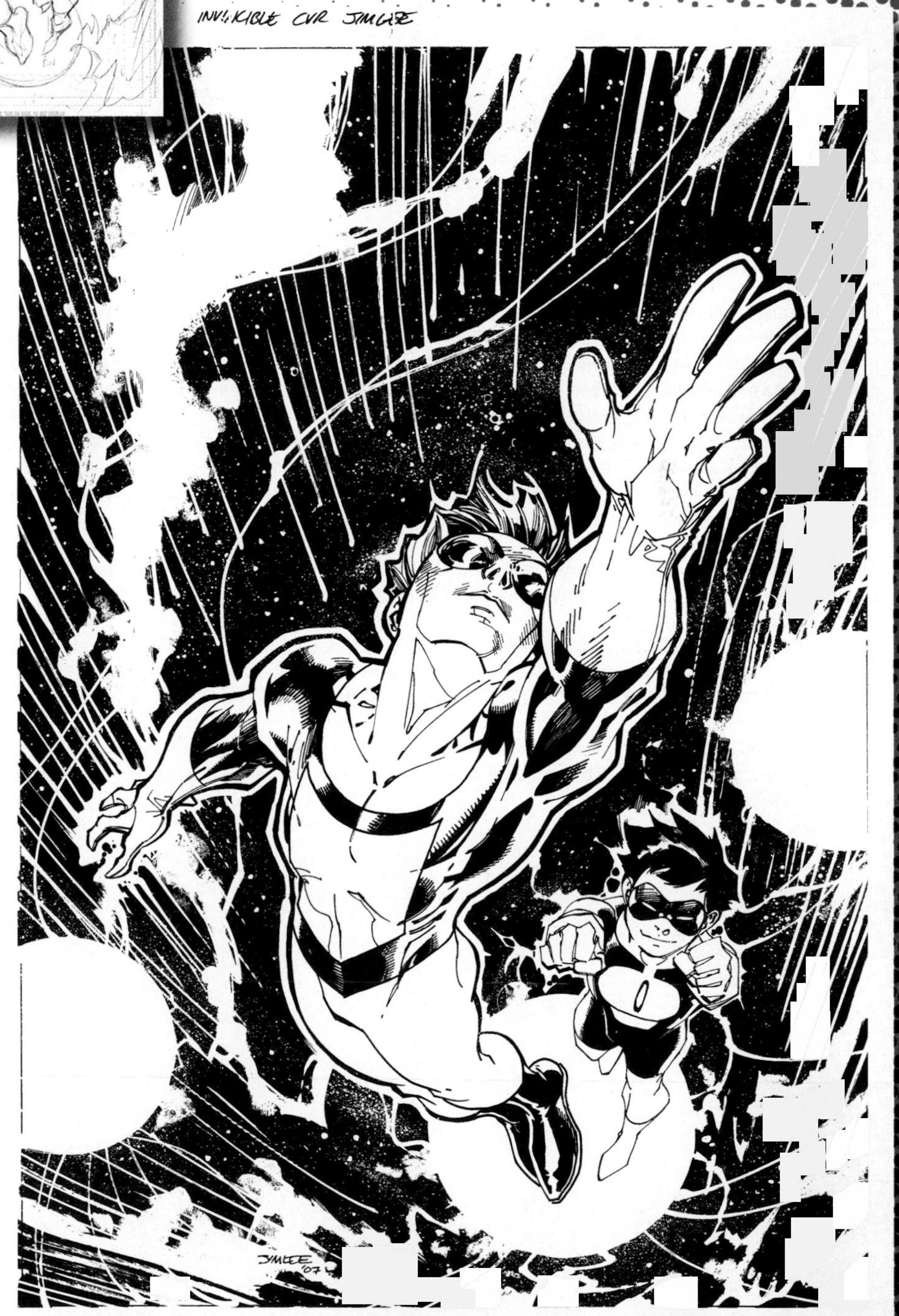

KIRKMAN: Holy crud, the cover to Invincible 52 was the cover that just wouldn't die! Ryan did the original version, of Oliver and Mark fighting in the clouds, and he hated it... right Ryan?

OTTLEY: HA! Hated it. Loathed it. I even gave it away for free. It's the only cover I've ever done that with. I was just having some artist block, it happens from time to time. But this cover was the worst. I remember I was extremely tired but I just had to finish the cover that day even though I wasn't feeling it. It seems you need energy to draw something energetic, I started with the figures and when I was done I almost tore it up. But instead I had the brilliant idea to try and "save" it by adding crappy clouds or smoke to cover up part of the figures. I was done and fine with it so I scanned it and sent it off to Robert. The next morning I looked at it and couldn't believe I drew that. I called Robert up super quick and said "Robert, I HATE that cover, please please please don't ever show that to anybody, I refuse to let that go as a cover, I don't even want it in the sketchbook section of the Trades or Hardcovers!" He said it looked fine to him but he agreed to my wishes. Aaaaaaaaaaaaand then the issue comes out, and somebody screwed up and had that black and white crappy cover as the pin-up in this issue. Not only that but there was a retailer variant cover that Image wanted for this issue and asked Robert for another image. He gave them this crappy cover, so it was the cover AND the pin-up and NOW it's in the sketchbook section. I don't know if Robert is trying to get back at me for something, but that's all I can come up with.

KIRKMAN: Oh, sorry about that. I forgot you said you didn't want anyone to see it. So anyway, then you went and did the cover where you swiped that McFarlane cover of Spider-Man fighting the Hulk... what were you thinking?!

OTTLEY: I don't know. Something is wrong with me maybe. The comic I was homaging was the first comic I ever read, Amazing Spider-Man 328, a McFarlane cover. So since that comic always really meant something to me I thought I'd do it for my first ever homage. Seems like during an artists block ya get pretty desperate to do something good but everything turns out lame.

KIRKMAN: I would have used it, it's a great drawing, but we were so early in our new costume stage, I didn't want to do an homage cover... Invincible looked pretty dopey on this cover... and I wanted him to look cool, to help sell the new costume... so on to version three!

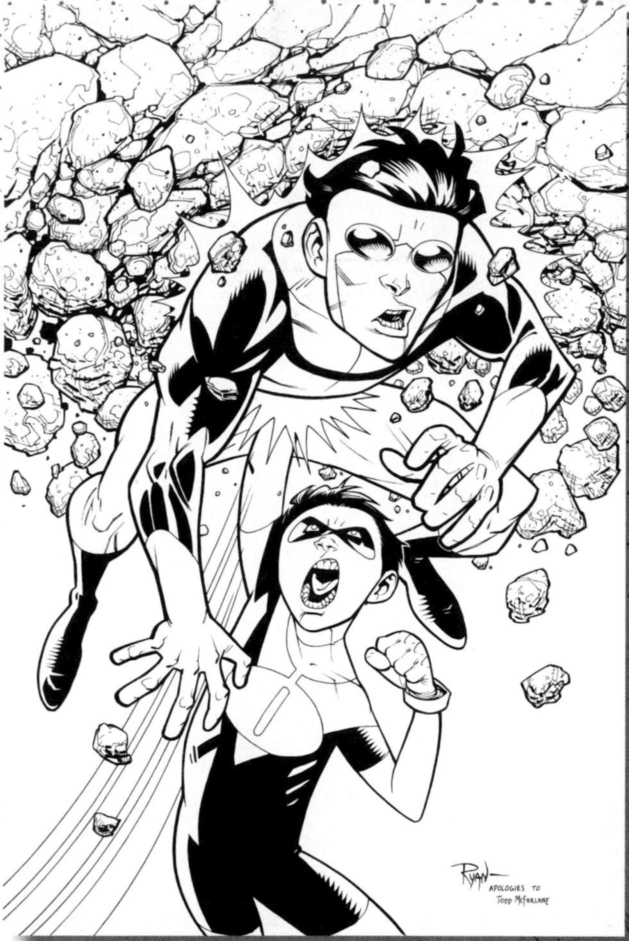
RYAN
APOLOGIES TO
TODD McFARLANE

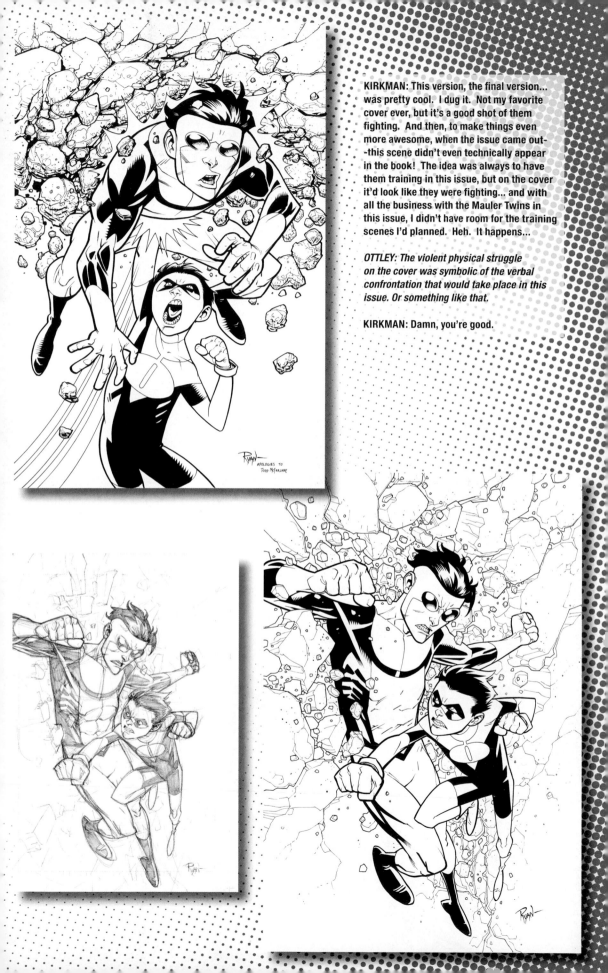

KIRKMAN: This version, the final version... was pretty cool. I dug it. Not my favorite cover ever, but it's a good shot of them fighting. And then, to make things even more awesome, when the issue came out--this scene didn't even technically appear in the book! The idea was always to have them training in this issue, but on the cover it'd look like they were fighting... and with all the business with the Mauler Twins in this issue, I didn't have room for the training scenes I'd planned. Heh. It happens...

OTTLEY: The violent physical struggle on the cover was symbolic of the verbal confrontation that would take place in this issue. Or something like that.

KIRKMAN: Damn, you're good.

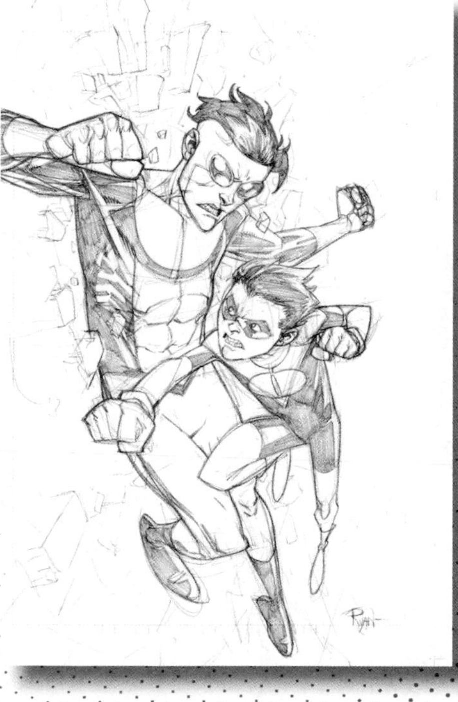

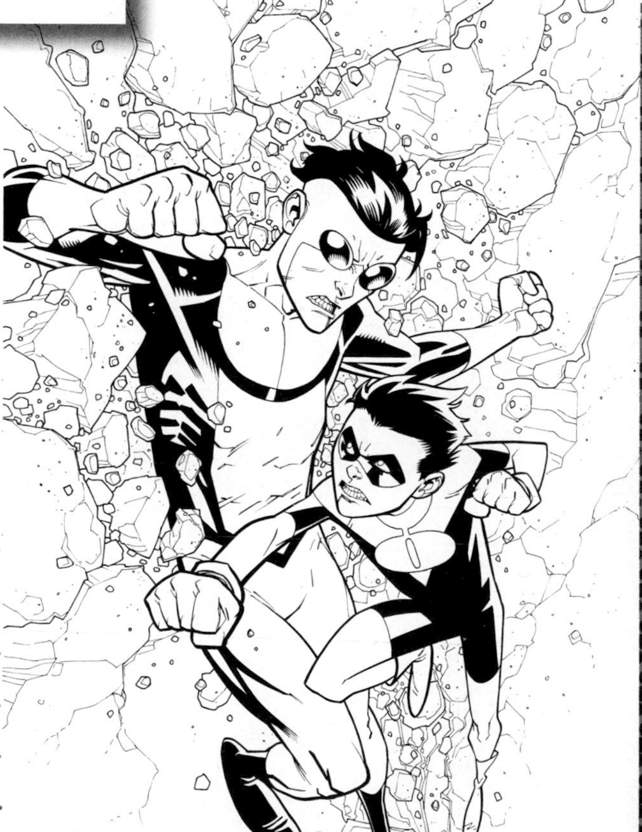

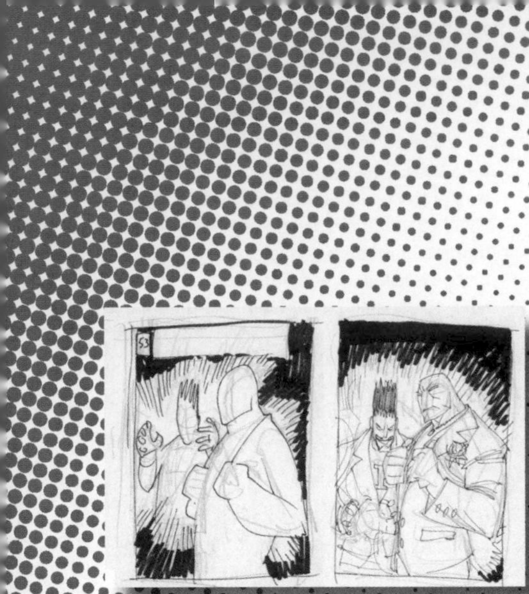

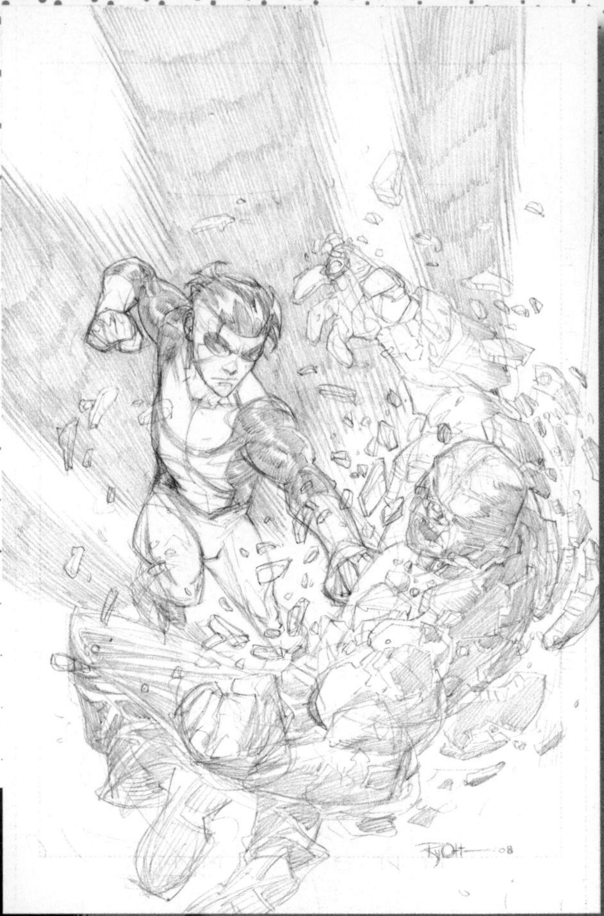

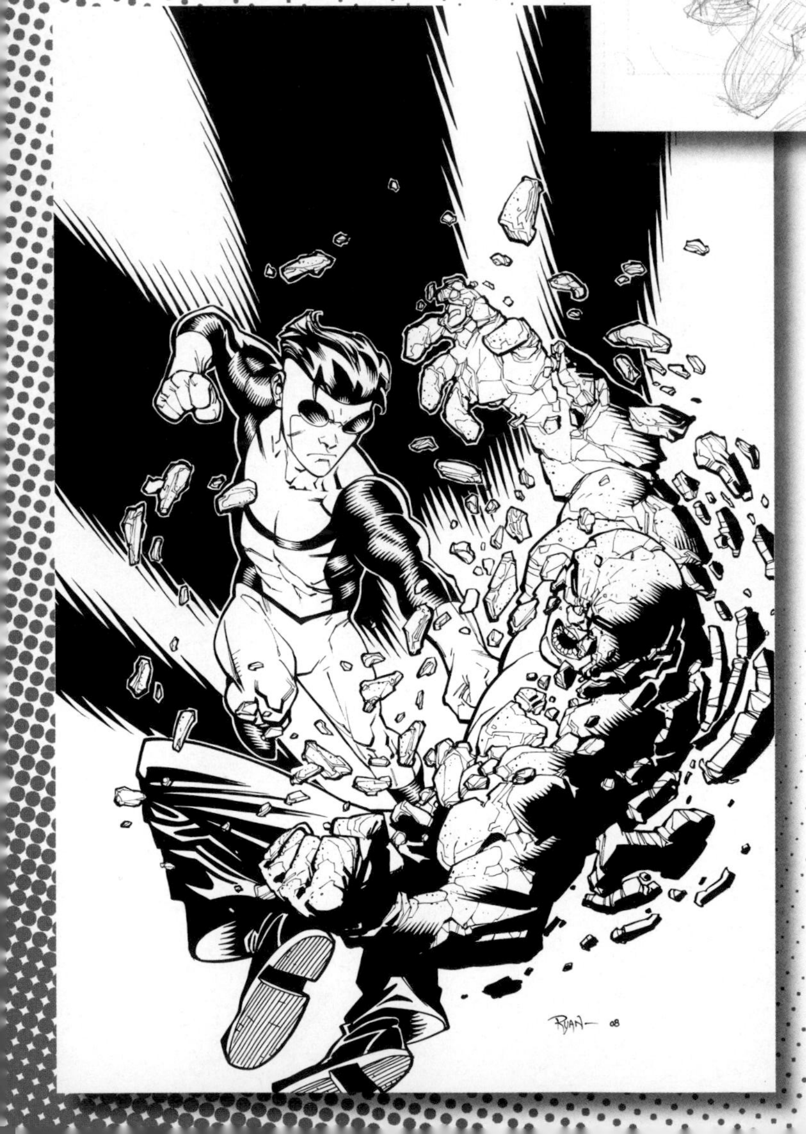

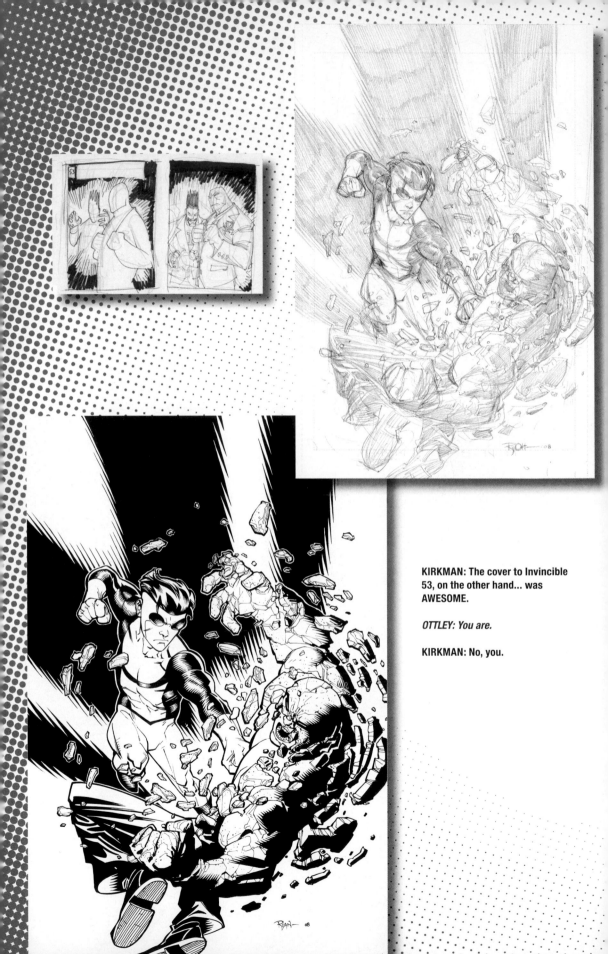

KIRKMAN: The cover to Invincible 53, on the other hand... was AWESOME.

OTTLEY: You are.

KIRKMAN: No, you.

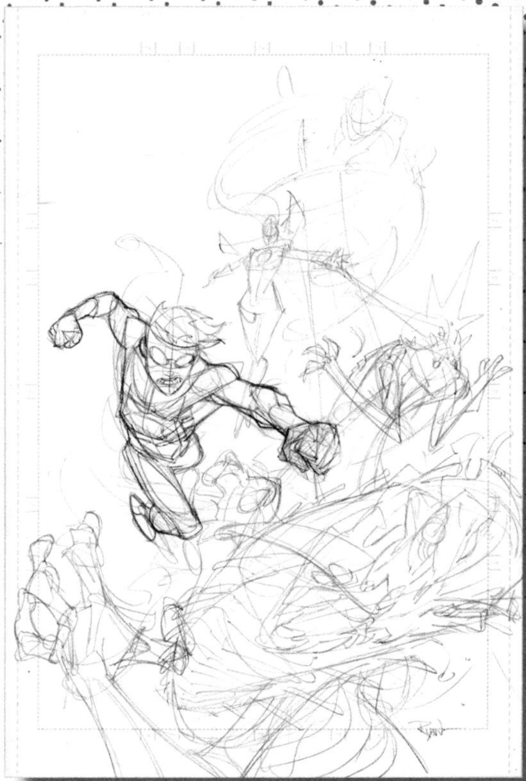

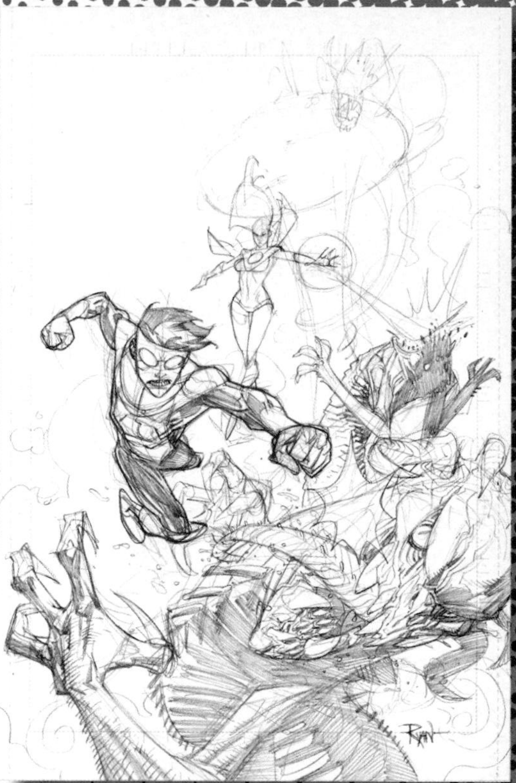

KIRKMAN: This is Ryan's cover for the EMERALD CITY COMIC-CON program book. If you ever want to take a trip to Seattle, come to this con--it's awesome!

OTTLEY: YES! I love Emerald City Con, I can't wait to go again. I was pretty happy when Jim Demonakos asked me to draw the cover for his program book, it really was an honor.

KIRKMAN: We plugged his convention, does he really need a name drop?

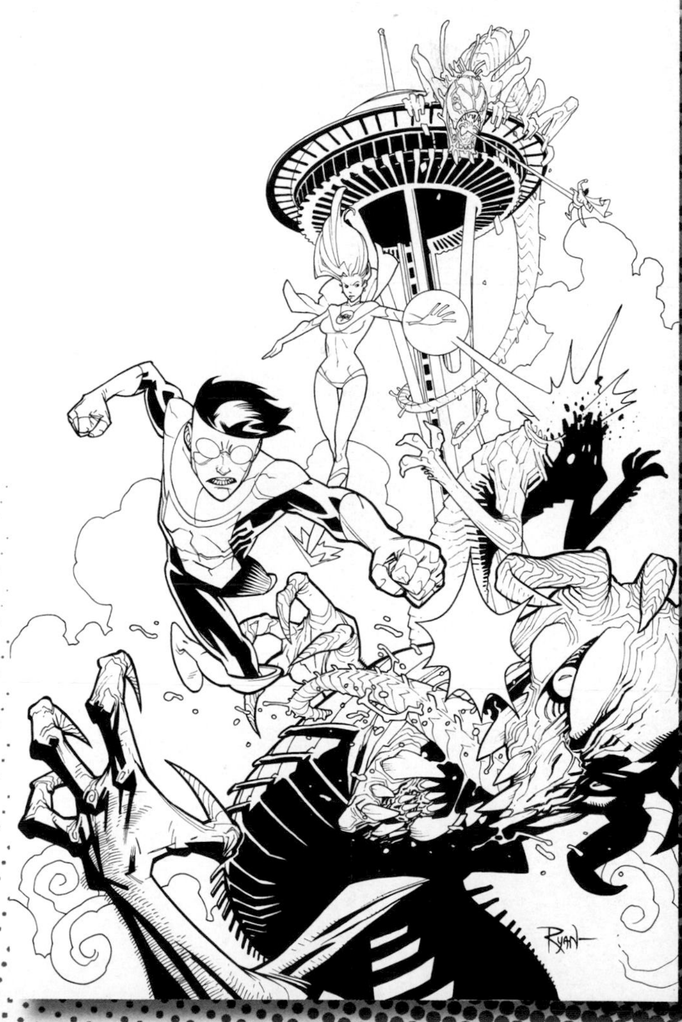
RYAN

KIRKMAN: Okay... the new costume. I knew that starting with issue 51, I wanted to change Invincible's costume--at least temporarily. I figured, hey--we've made it to issue 50, let's change the costume, that's always fun! So I told co-creator Cory Walker to start thinking about what we could change the costume to. He started with these, no-mask versions... I dig it, but I thought it was too much of a departure.

OTTLEY: Exactly, everyone would've known it was Mark Grayson, former Burger Mart employee.

KIRKMAN: Another round of costume changes from Cory. I like all of these, really, but I didn't think they were enough of a change. I wanted something more drastic, like the change from Spider-Man's original costume to the black costume.

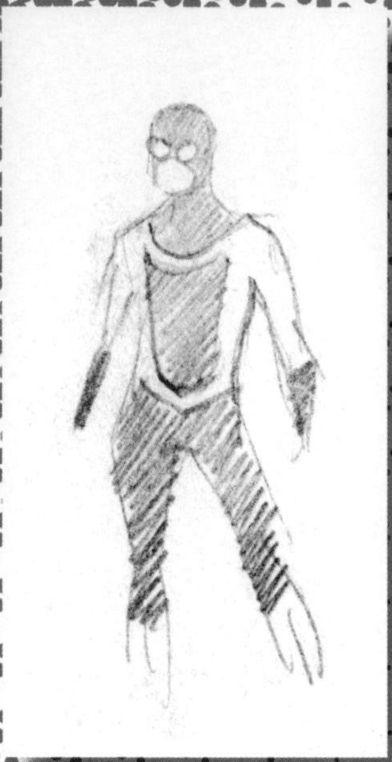

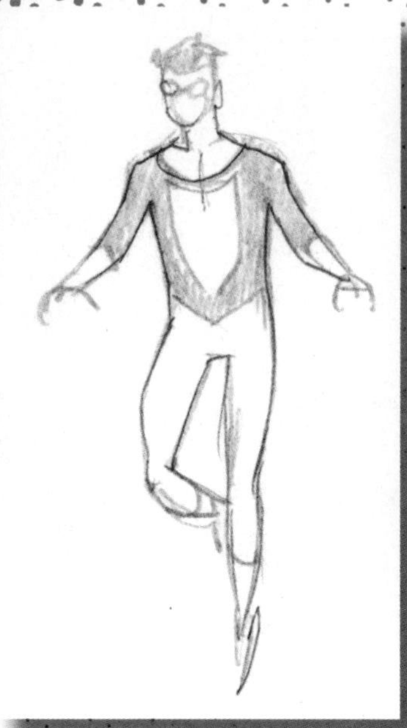

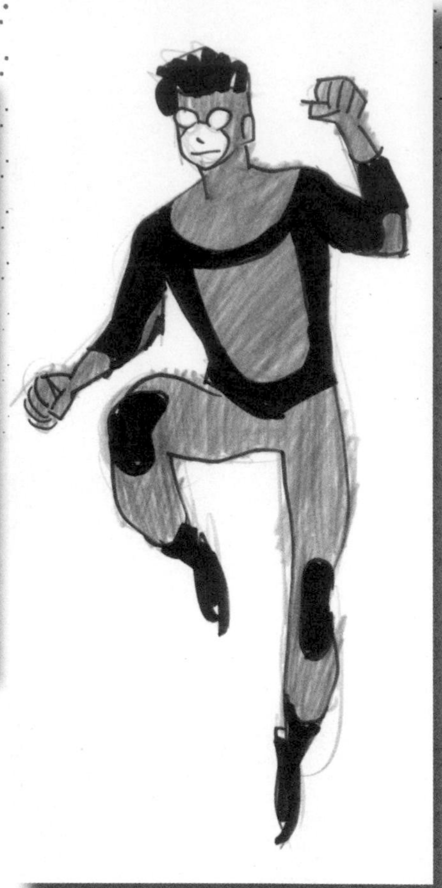

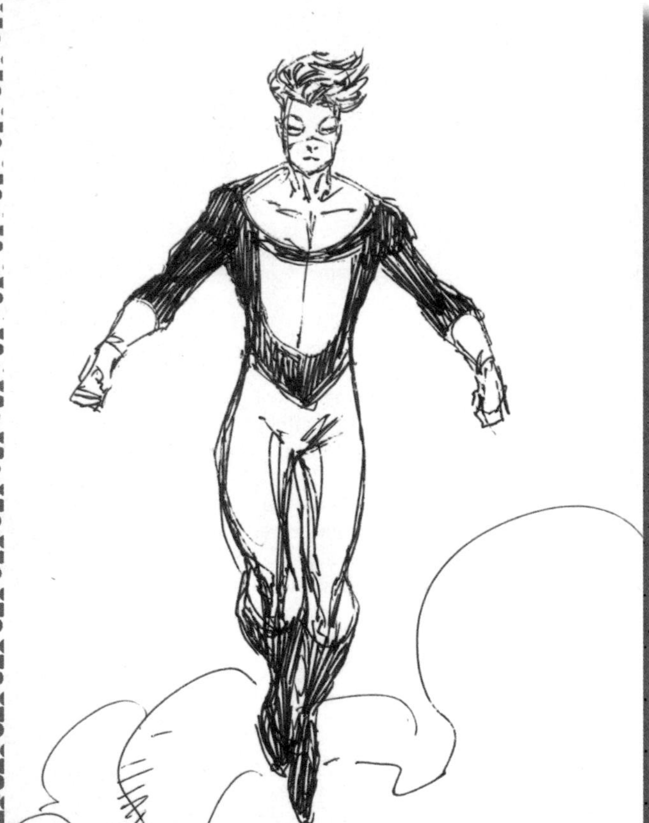

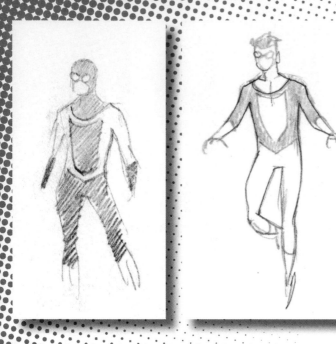

KIRKMAN: And that led to Comic-Con 2007, where the plan was for Ryan, Cory and I to sit down in a hotel room and figure out exactly what to do with the costume. Only, Ryan... God love him, was tired and went to bed at 10pm (I'm not even kidding). So what happened was Cory and I sat in the room and worked it all out. The results of which are seen on this page. As you can see, the costume originally had black knee pads, which, in hindsight, we probably should have kept--but y'know, I just didn't like them at the time. So there you have it, that's how we came up with the new costume you all love so much.

FUN FACT: Rob Liefeld stopped by the room later on after Cory left, and when I showed him the design Cory had done, he did a little sketch of his own on the same piece of paper. Neat!

OTTLEY:*Yeah I was tired. I get that way from time to time. Mostly at night. I should talk to my Doctor. No, but seriously at cons I do SO many sketches it kills me, I really wanted to go over with you guys and when you called it was 11pm and I was pretty out of it and felt horrible. I promise next time you change the costume I'll be there.*

KIRKMAN: Later on, Ryan did this design sheet we see here so that Jim Lee would have reference to do his cover.

OTTLEY: So why didn't we show Jim the sketches that Cory did instead of me re-drawing it? I forget.

KIRKMAN: Uh... I think Cory's sketch was too loose? Also, you wanted to add the points to the bottom of the "I" on his chest. I don't know. As an added bonus, Cory did a sketch much later (after the costume appeared in print) of what we SHOULD have done (man, I like this costume better) and we ended up using this as one of the Evil Invincible's in issue 60.

OTTLEY: Yeah this is one cool design, I can't wait to show some of my design rejects in the sketchbook section of the next trade paperback. I'm glad Cory helped out with a few good designs.

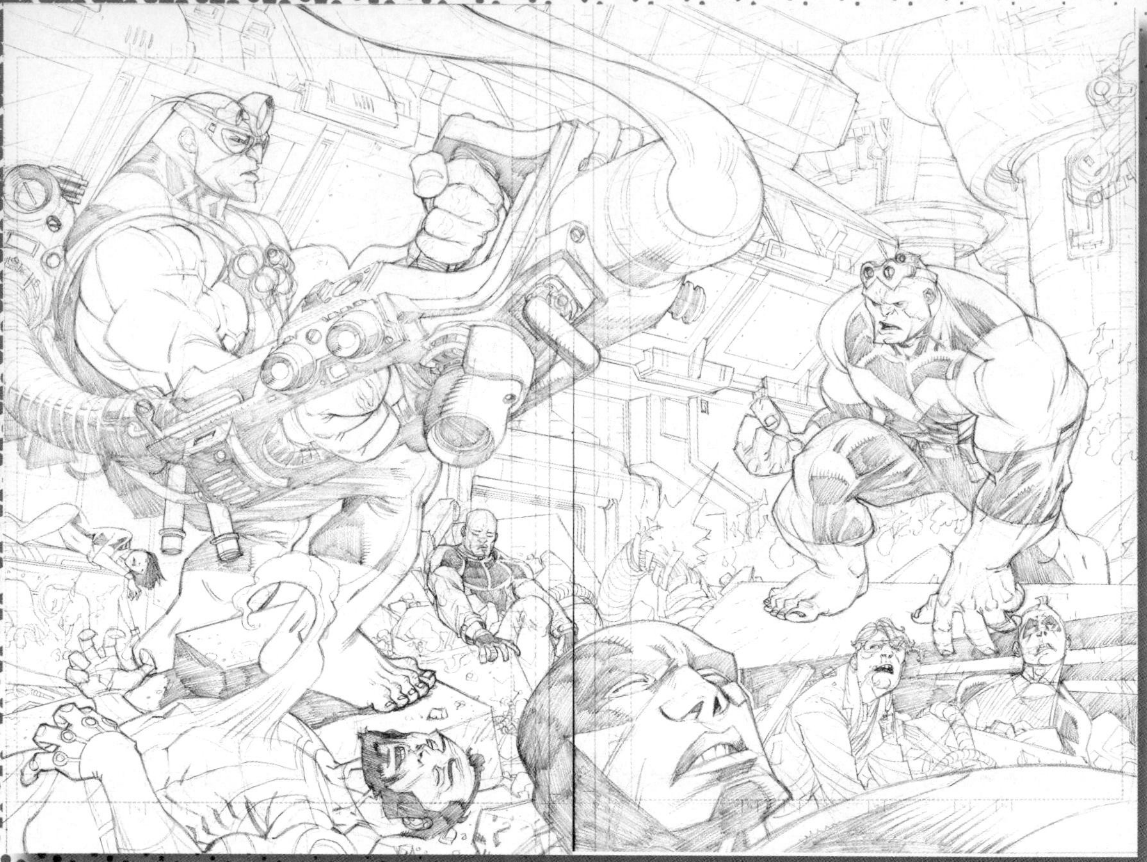

KIRKMAN: Awesome spread from Invincible 52 of the Mauler Twins... this page actually appeared in the New York Times. Swank!

OTTLEY: What?!? It did? Where and when? Why don't you ever tell me these things? That would be perfect to show all those non-comic reading adults that sneer when I tell them I draw comicbooks, they'd think I was doing something legit with my life. Seriously tell me what this is in, or send me your copy and I'll forgive you for not telling me about this AND for running that crappy cover in issue 52.

KIRKMAN: It was in the issue that announced I was a partner at Image... my mom has a few extra copies... I'll hook you up. Call me later.

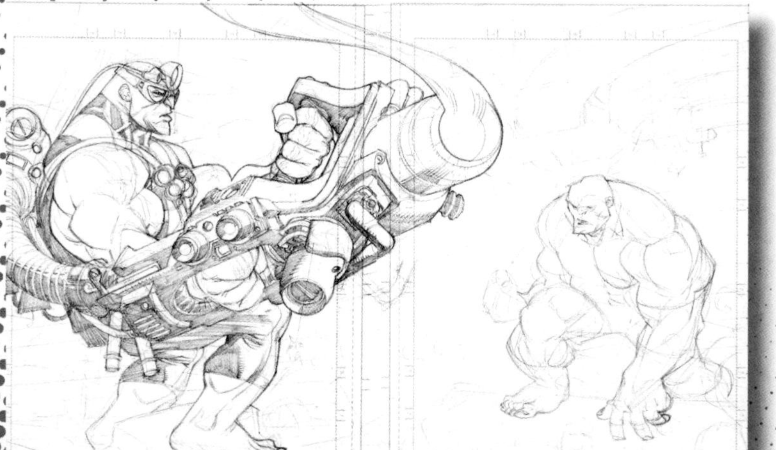

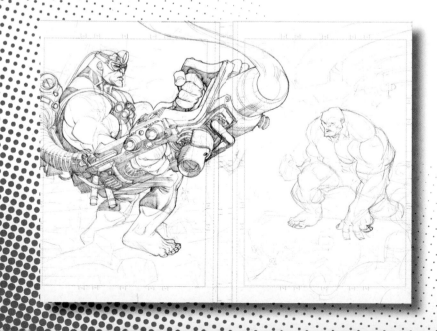

KIRKMAN: Oliver flies through a Mauler Twin. Y'know, some people claim to hate Oliver. I just don't get it. Also, the pencils for the splash page return of the dragon Omni-Man fights on TV in issue one of this series. See kids... nothing goes to waste in this series!! NOTHING!

OTTLEY: Yeah, people say I draw violence too violently. We should get Aubrey Sitterson, our Editor in on this part of our little sketchbook section conversation. So Aubrey used to work at Marvel as an Editor and I'm curious if they would say yes or no to something like this. I mean I don't recall seeing too much gore in comics from Marvel but I could be mistaken as maybe I just didn't buy any books with too much in it. Aubrey? Is there a line that one can't cross or is this kind of thing allowed?

SITTERSON: In my experience at Marvel, most content issues were taken on a case-by-case basis depending on the rating, the characters involved, the context of the violence, and about three dozen other variables. But, one of the general no-no's we had was showing exit wounds - so it was ok if someone got shot in the head, just as long as you didn't see the bullet come out the other side. Crazy, right? I don't ever remember having to deal with a preteen as a projectile, but I doubt it would fly (wakka wakka). If the stars were aligned though and we were able to get it printed, we'd have to remove the actual organs as well as tone down the red of the blood. In my infinite editorial wisdom, I probably would have suggested that the Mauler twins be given blue blood, which would have gone a long way to making the scene more Marvel-acceptable.

KIRKMAN: Zzzzzzzzzzz.

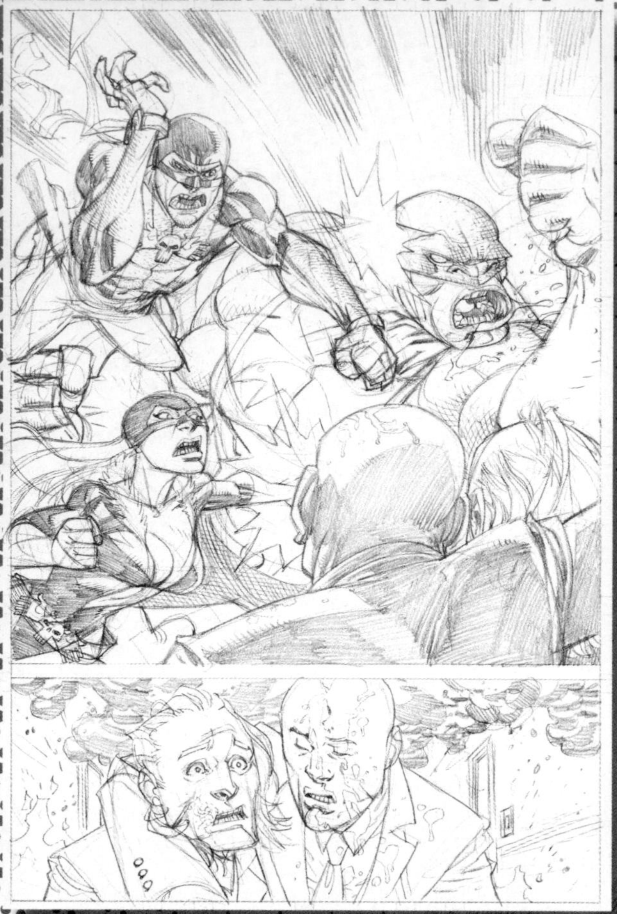

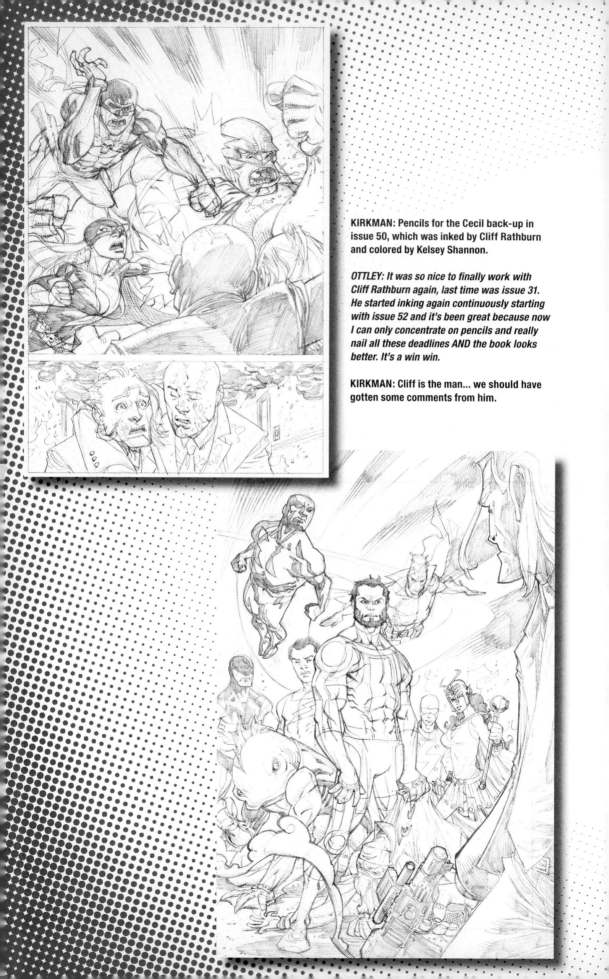

KIRKMAN: Pencils for the Cecil back-up in issue 50, which was inked by Cliff Rathburn and colored by Kelsey Shannon.

OTTLEY: It was so nice to finally work with Cliff Rathburn again, last time was issue 31. He started inking again continuously starting with issue 52 and it's been great because now I can only concentrate on pencils and really nail all these deadlines AND the book looks better. It's a win win.

KIRKMAN: Cliff is the man... we should have gotten some comments from him.

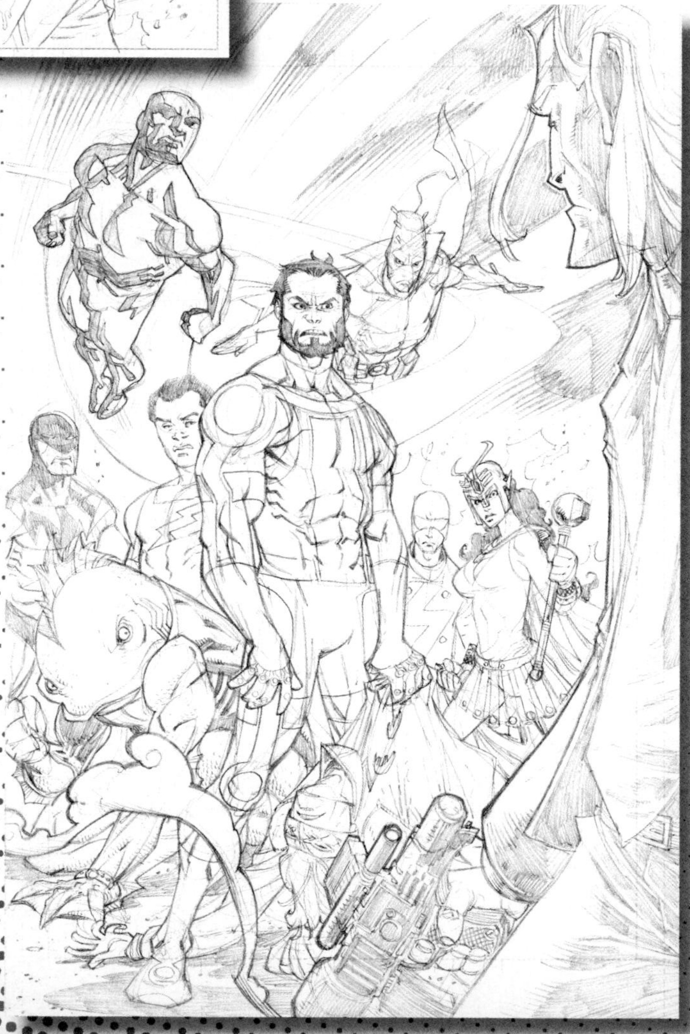

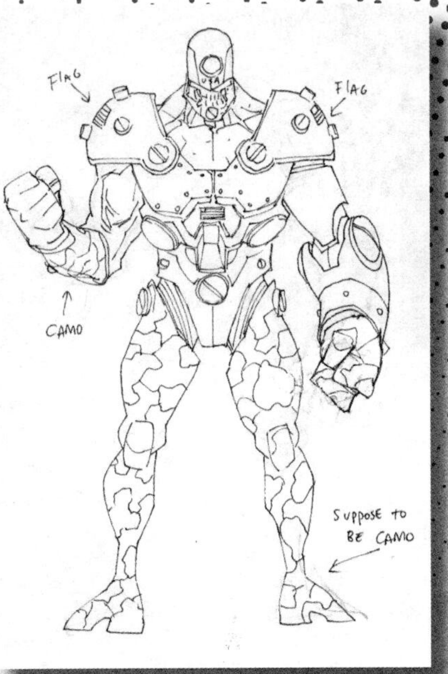
FLAG
FLAG
CAMO
SUPPOSE TO BE CAMO

KIRKMAN: Man, I swear I've never even SEEN this redesign of the Reanimen... weird. And Ryan's redesign of Angstrom Levy... I really wanted him to look more like a super-villain upon his return. Ryan did a great job of that.

OTTLEY: Yeah, I need to work on my design of mechanical things. I'm not too happy with the robots, Cory's original versions were much better. I'm happy with how Angstrom turned out, though.

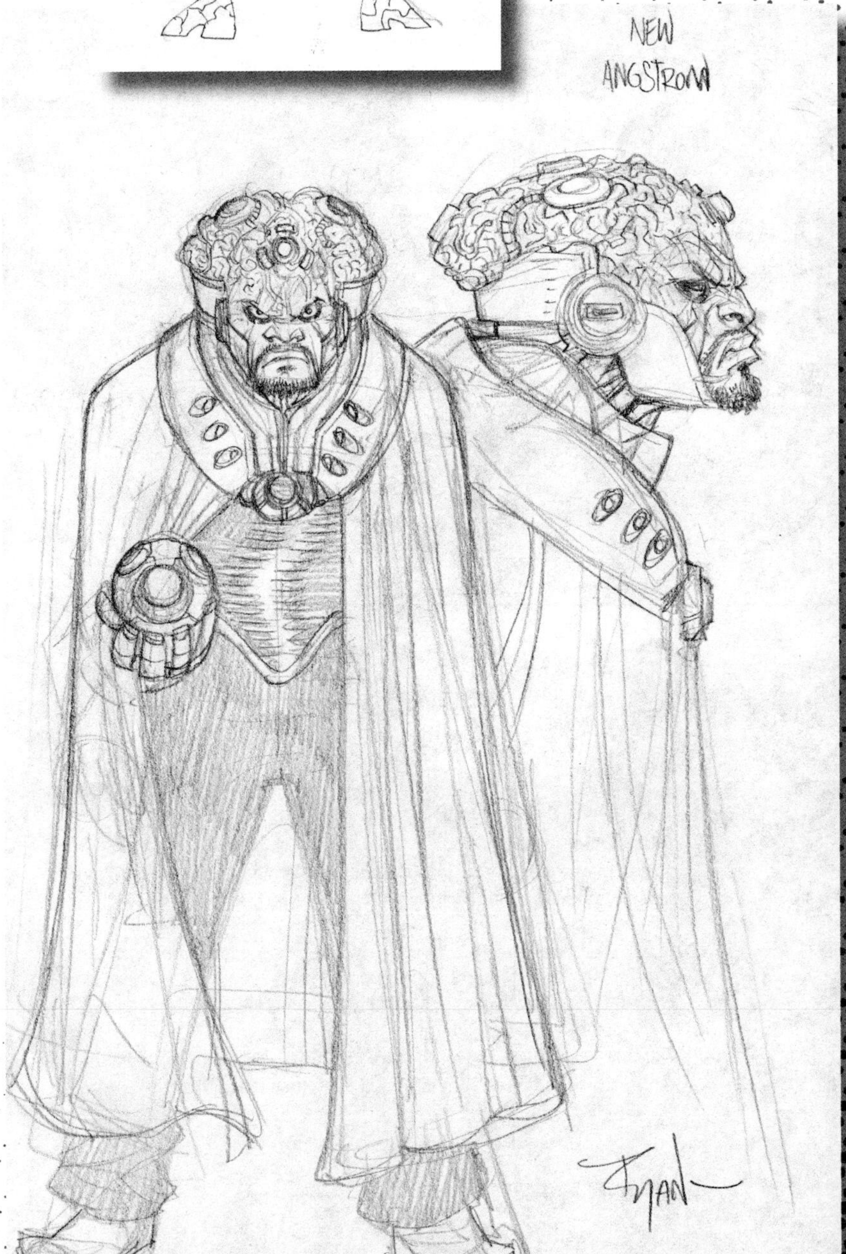
NEW ANGSTROM
Ryan

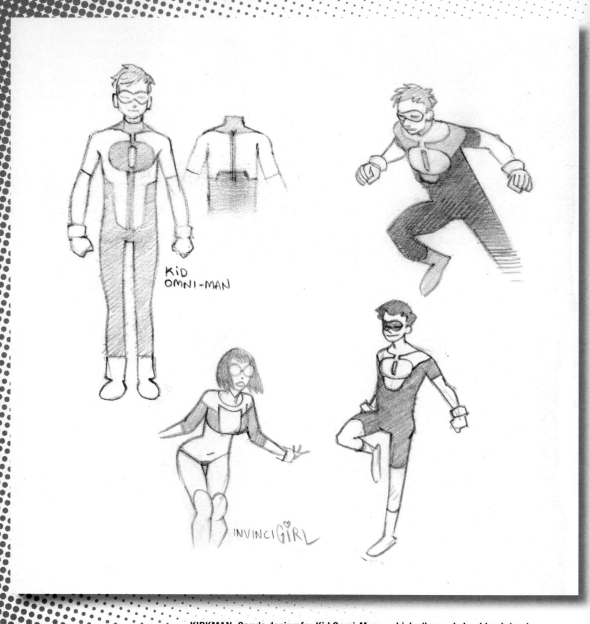

KID OMNI-MAN

INVINCIGIRL

KIRKMAN: Cory's design for Kid Omni-Man... which y'know, I should point out I originally wanted to call him, the uninspired name... OMNI-BOY. I'm glad Cory suggested Kid Omni-Man... I like that name much better.

OTTLEY: I laughed when you told me what Cory suggested, not only can he design awesome stuff but he can come up with some killer names. I think Atom Eve, Dupli-Kate, and Multi-Paul were all his right? Too awesome!

KIRKMAN: Atom-Eve and Robot were his. Dupli-Kate and Multi-Paul are extra stupid... those are mine. PowerPlex, Rex Splode... see, there's a pattern.

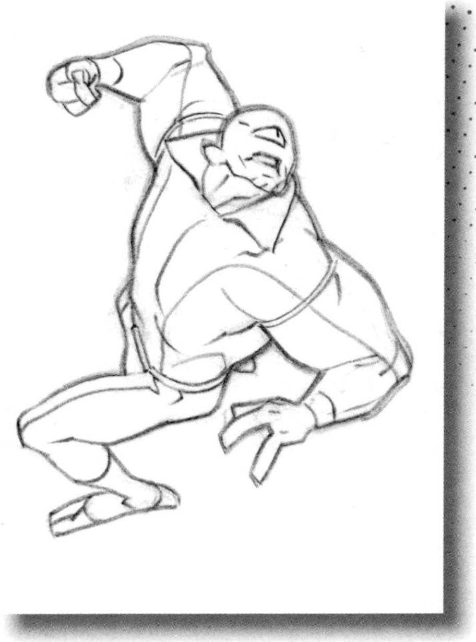

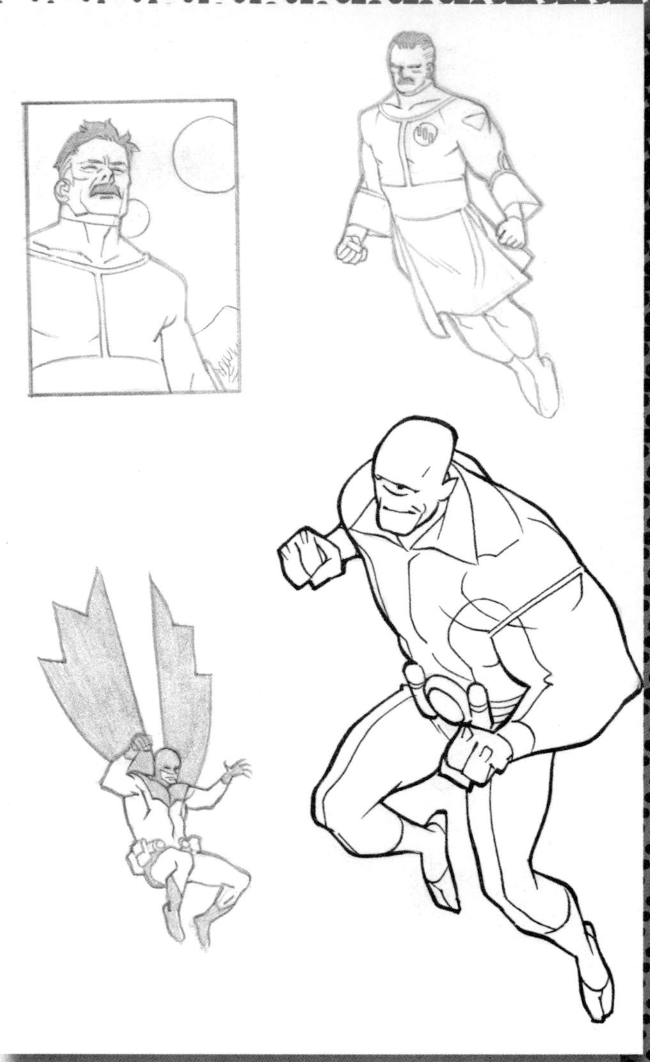

KIRKMAN: I'll leave you with some sweet Cory Walker sketches. He did this stuff for his daily sketchblog, which you can all find at corenthal. blogspot.com

OTTLEY: All I gotta say is RAD!

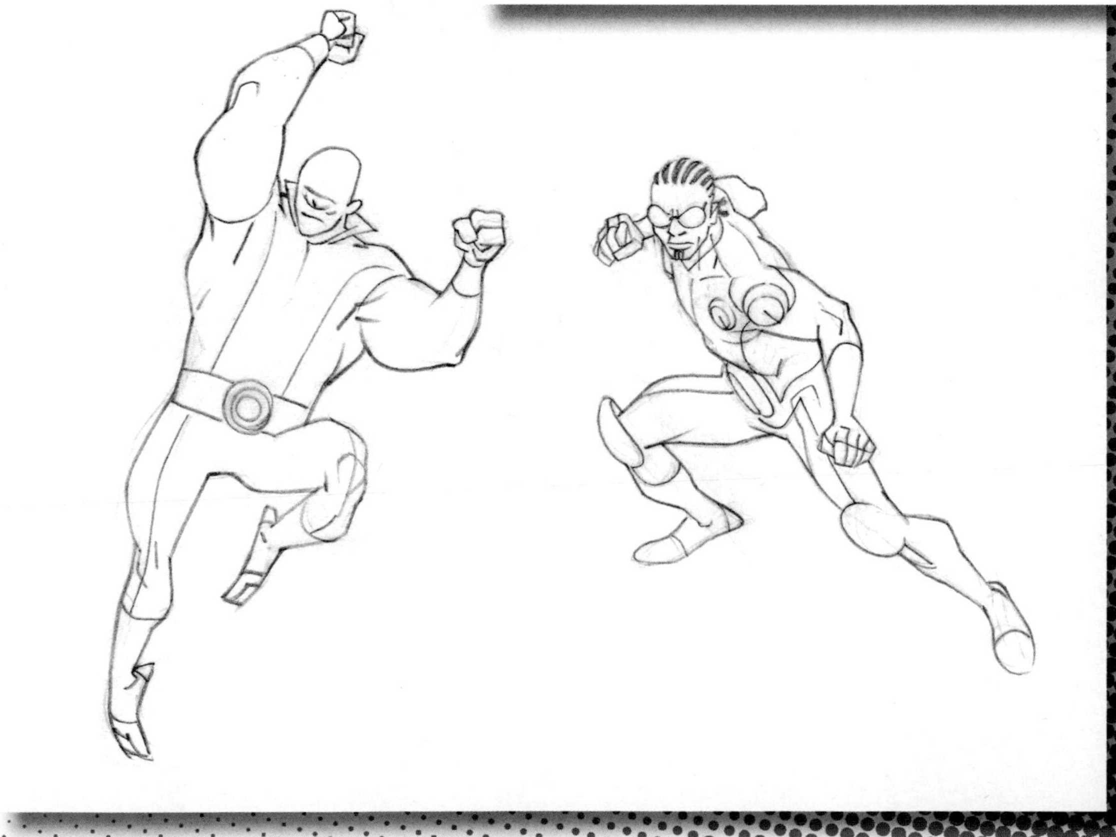

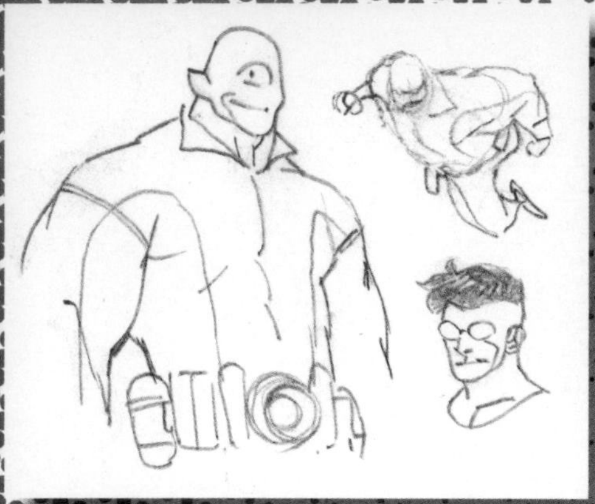

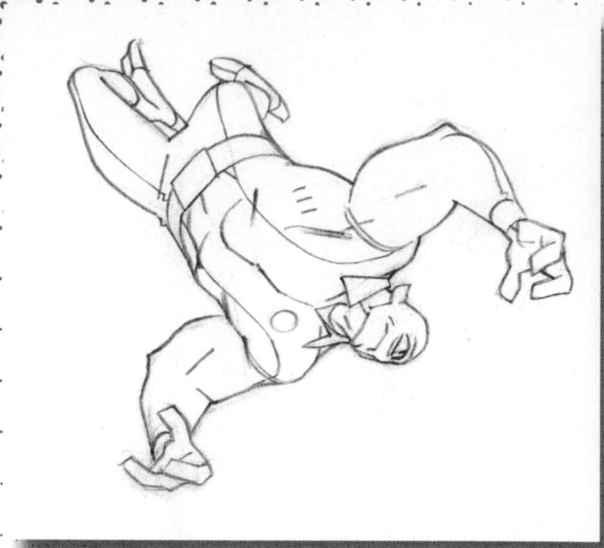

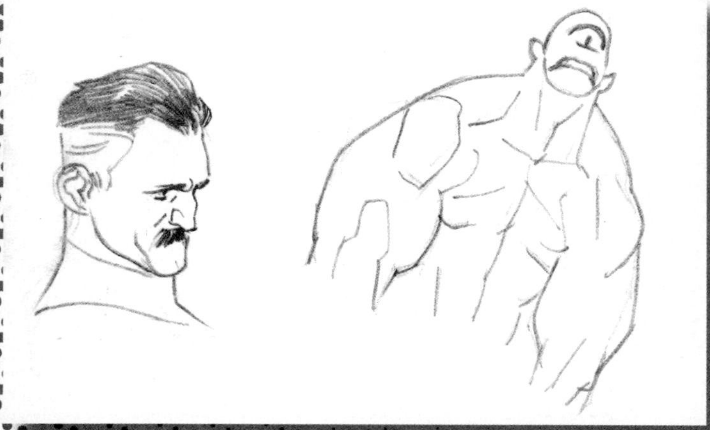

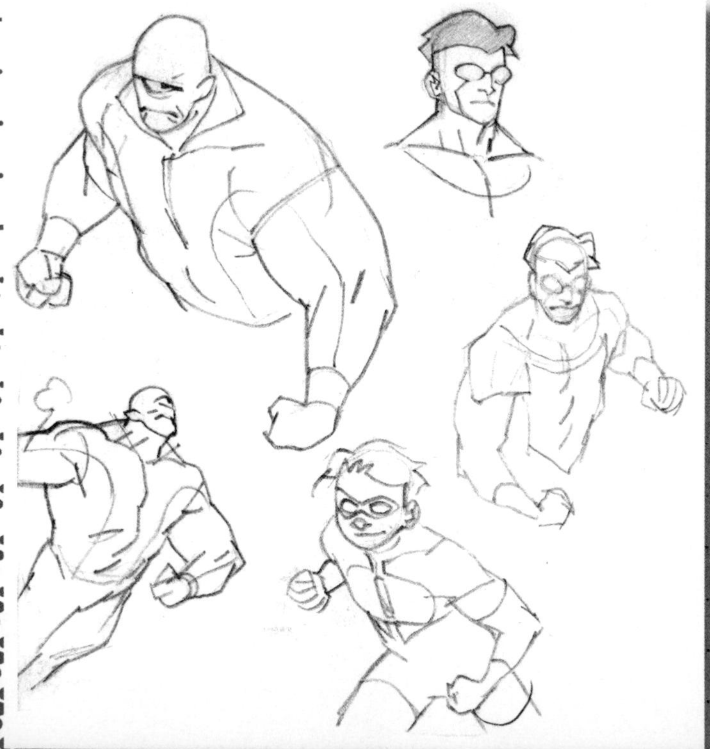

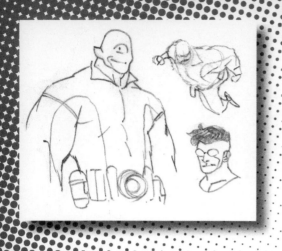

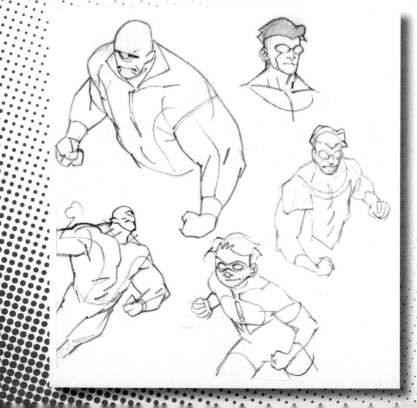

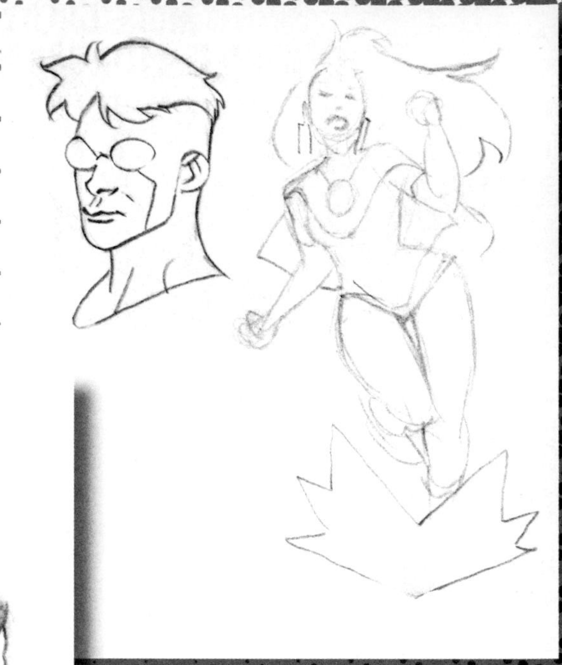

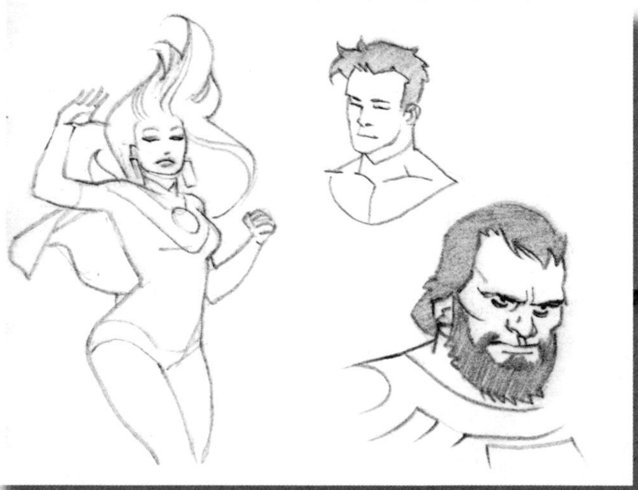

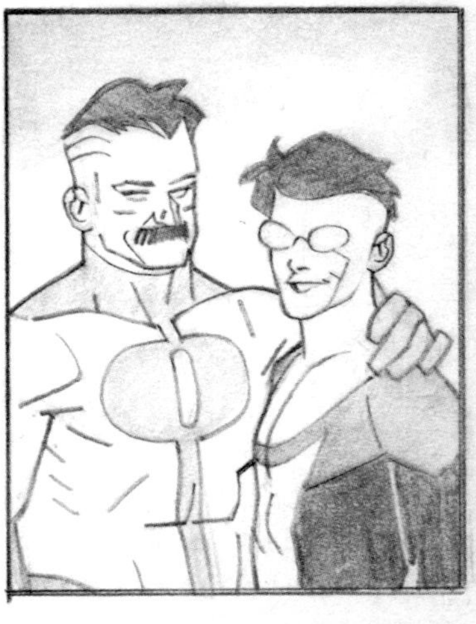

KIRKMAN: Hey, Cory drew Anissa, sweet! When are we going to see her again? Soon, I hope. Anyway, that's it for this sketchbook section. I hope you enjoyed it. I'll see you all back here for Volume 11, right? RIGHT?!

OTTLEY: See you soon!

SITTERSON: Peace in the Middle East!

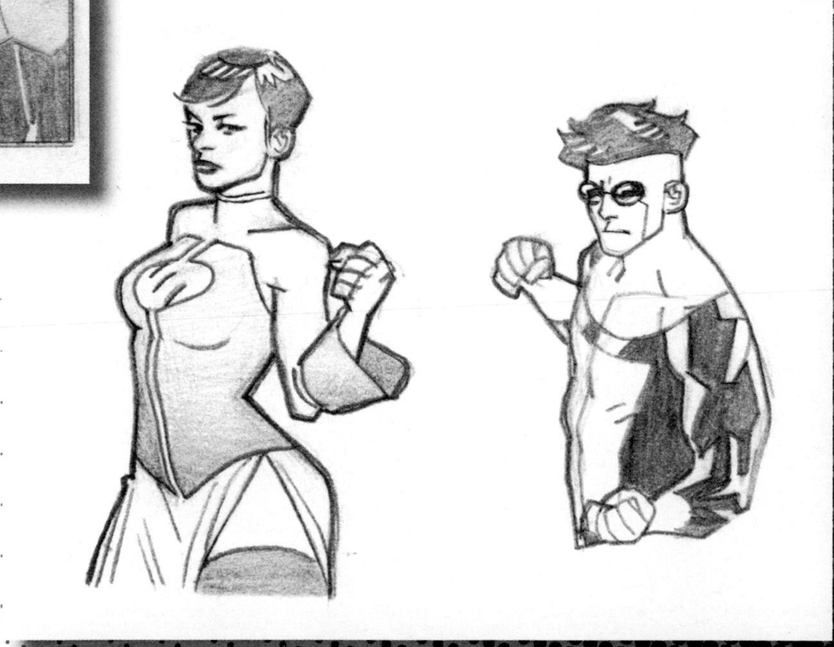

MORE GREAT BOOKS FROM
ROBERT KIRKMAN & IMAGE COMICS!

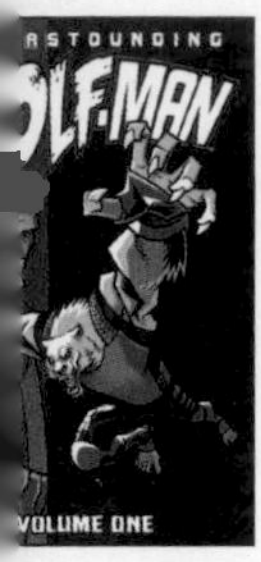
ASTOUNDING
OLF-MAN
VOLUME ONE
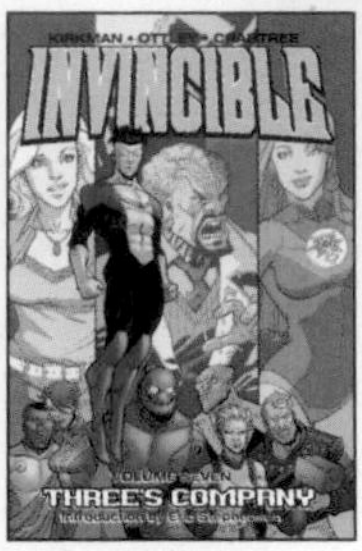
INVINCIBLE
THREE'S COMPANY
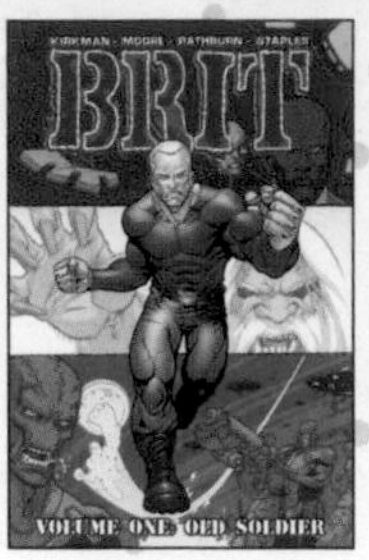
BRIT
VOLUME ONE: OLD SOLDIER
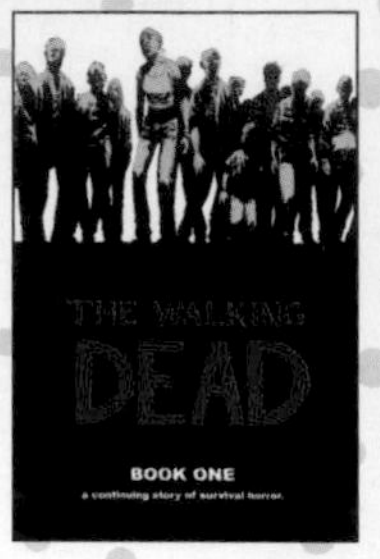
THE WALKING DEAD
BOOK ONE
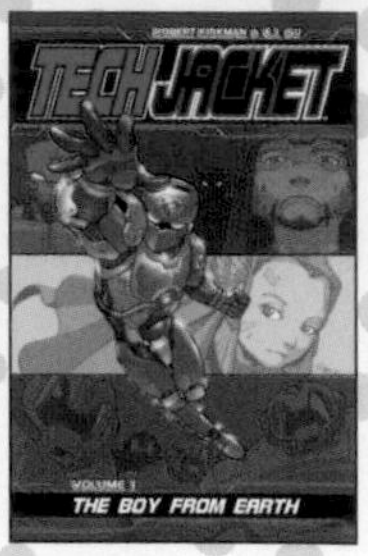
TECH JACKET
THE BOY FROM EARTH
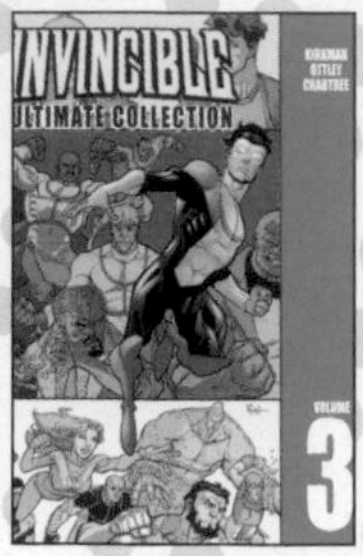
INVINCIBLE
ULTIMATE COLLECTION
3
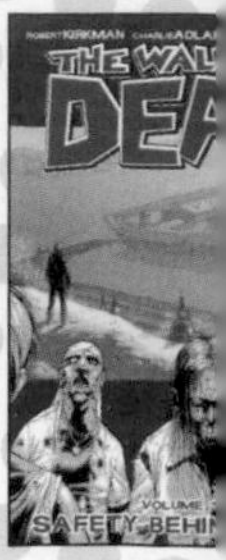

THE ASTOUNDING WOLF-MAN

VOL. 1 TP
ISBN: 978-1-58240-656-5
$14.99

BATTLE POPE

VOL. 1: GENESIS TP
ISBN: 978-1-58240-572-8
$12.95

VOL. 2: MAYHEM TP
ISBN: 978-1-58240-529-2
$12.99

VOL. 3: PILLOW TALK TP
ISBN: 978-1-58240-677-0
$12.99

VOL. 4: WRATH OF GOD TP
ISBN: 978-1-58240-751-7
$9.99

BRIT

VOL. 1: OLD SOLDIER TP
ISBN: 978-1-58240-656-5
$14.99

VOL. 2: AWOL
ISBN: 978-1-58240-656-5
$14.99

CAPES

VOL. 1: PUNCHING THE CLOCK TP
ISBN: 978-1-58240-656-5
$17.99

CLOUDFALL

GRAPHIC NOVEL
$6.95

INVINCIBLE

VOL. 1: FAMILY MATTERS TP
ISBN: 978-1-58240-711-1
$12.99

VOL. 2: EIGHT IS ENOUGH TP
ISBN: 978-1-58240-347-2
$12.99

VOL. 3: PERFECT STRANGERS TP
ISBN: 978-1-58240-915-5
$12.95

VOL. 4: HEAD OF THE CLASS TP
ISBN: 978-1-58240-440-2
$14.95

VOL. 5: THE FACTS OF LIFE TP
ISBN: 978-1-58240-554-4
$14.99

VOL. 6: A DIFFERENT WORLD TP
ISBN: 978-1-58240-579-7
$14.99

VOL. 7: THREE'S COMPANY TP
ISBN: 978-1-58240-656-5
$14.99

VOL. 8: MY FAVORITE MARTIAN TP
ISBN: 978-1-58240-656-5
$14.99

VOL. 9: OUT OF THIS WORLD TP
ISBN: 978-1-58240-827-9
$14.99

VOL. 10: WHO'S THE BOSS TP
ISBN: 978-1-60706-013-0
$16.99

ULTIMATE COLLECTION, VOL. 1 HC
ISBN 978-1-58240-500-1
$34.95

ULTIMATE COLLECTION, VOL. 2 HC
ISBN: 978-1-58240-594-0
$34.99

ULTIMATE COLLECTION, VOL. 3 HC
ISBN: 978-1-58240-763-0
$34.99

ULTIMATE COLLECTION, VOL. 4 HC
ISBN: 978-1-58240-989-4
$34.99

THE OFFICIAL HANDBOOK OF THE INVINCIBLE UNIVERSE TP
ISBN: 978-1-58240-831-6
$12.99

REAPER

GRAPHIC NOVEL
$6.95

TECH JACKET

VOL. 1: THE BOY FROM EARTH TP
ISBN: 978-1-58240-771-5
$14.99

TALES OF THE REALM

HARDCOVER
ISBN: 978-1-58240-426-0
$34.95

TRADE PAPERBACK
ISBN: 978-1-58240-394-6
$14.95

THE WALKING DEAD

VOL. 1: DAYS GONE BYE TP
ISBN: 978-1-58240-672-8
$9.99

VOL. 2: MILES BEHIND US TP
ISBN: 978-1-58240-413-4
$12.95

VOL. 3: SAFETY BEHIND BARS TP
ISBN: 978-1-58240-487-5
$12.95

VOL. 4: THE HEART'S DESIRE TP
ISBN: 978-1-58240-530-8
$12.99

VOL. 5: THE BEST DEFENSE TP
ISBN: 978-1-58240-612-1
$12.99

VOL. 6: THIS SORROWFUL LIFE TP
ISBN: 978-1-58240-684-8
$12.99

VOL. 7: THE CALM BEFORE TP
ISBN: 978-1-58240-828-6
$12.99

VOL.8: MADE TO SUFFER TP
ISBN: 978-1-58240-828-6
$14.99

VOL.9: HERE WE REMAIN TP
ISBN: 978-1-60706-022-2
$14.99

BOOK ONE HC
ISBN: 978-1-58240-619-0
$29.99

BOOK TWO HC
ISBN: 978-1-58240-759-3
$29.99

BOOK THREE HC
ISBN: 978-1-58240-825-5
$29.99

BOOK FOUR HC
ISBN: 978-1-60706-000-0
$29.99

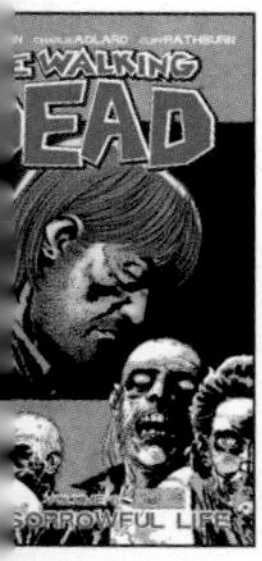
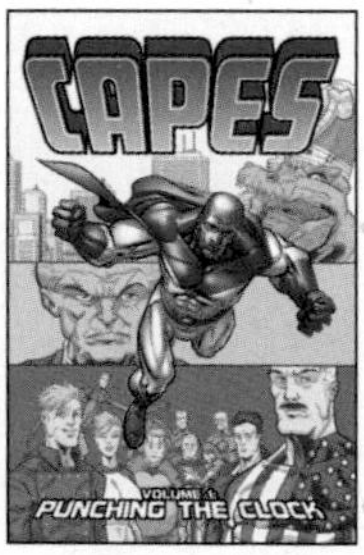
CAPES
PUNCHING THE CLOCK
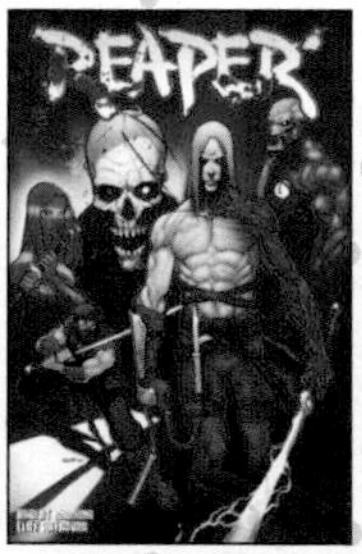
REAPER
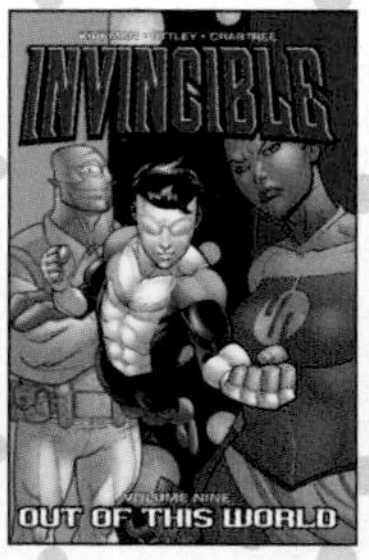
INVINCIBLE
OUT OF THIS WORLD
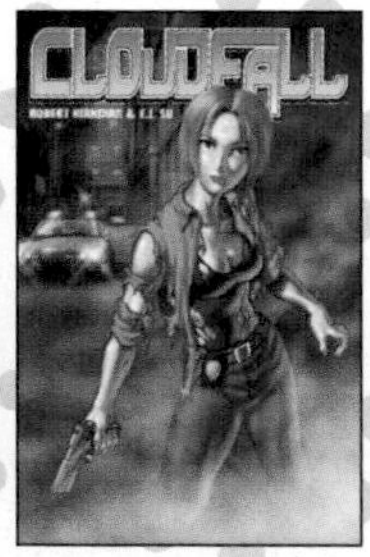
CLOUDFALL
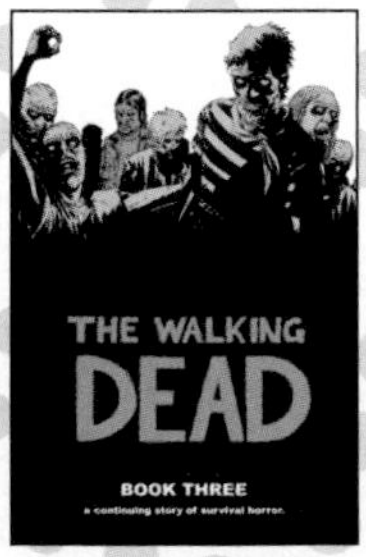
THE WALKING DEAD
BOOK THREE
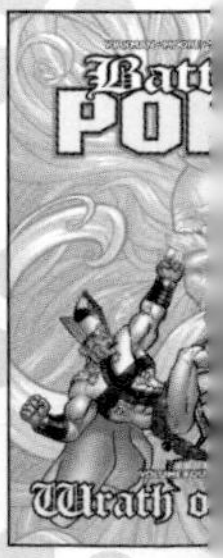

TO FIND YOUR NEAREST COMIC BOOK STORE, CALL:
1-888-COMIC-BOOK